PENGUIN BOOKS

A MIXTURE OF FRAILTIES

Robertson Davies has had three successive careers: first as an actor with the Old Vic Company in England; then as publisher of the *Petersborough Ontario Examiner*, and most recently as a university professor and first master of Massey College at the University of Toronto, from which he retired in 1981. He has over thirty books to his credit, among them several volumes of plays, as well as collections of essays, speeches, and *belles lettres*. As a novelist he has gained fame especially for his Deptford trilogy—*Fifth Business, The Manticore,* and *World of Wonders*—for the Salterton trilogy—*Tempest-Tost, Leaven of Malice,* and *A Mixture of Frailties*—and for the Cornish Trilogy—*The Rebel Angels, What's Bred in the Bone,* and *The Lyre of Orpheus.* His most recent novel, *Murther & Walking Spirits*, is published by Viking. He was the first Canadian to become an honorary member of the American Academy and Institute of Arts and Letters. He is a companion of the order of Canada and honorary fellow of Balliol, and he has received an honorary degree from Oxford. He and his wife now divide their time between homes in Toronto and in Caledon, Ontario.

Nothing softeneth the Arrogance of our Nature like a Mixture of some Frailties. It is by them that we are best told, that we must not strike too hard upon others because we ourselves do so often deserve blows. They pull our Rage by the sleeve and whisper Gentleness to us in our censures. HALIFAX

ROBERTSON DAVIES

A·MIXTURE·OF·FRAILTIES

Penguin Books

PENGUIN BOOKS
Published by the Penguin Group
Penguin Books USA Inc.,
375 Hudson Street, New York, New York 10014, U.S.A.
Penguin Books Ltd, 27 Wrights Lane,
London W8 5TZ, England
Penguin Books Australia Ltd, Ringwood,
Victoria, Australia
Penguin Books Canada Ltd, 10 Alcorn Avenue,
Toronto, Ontario, Canada M4V 3B2
Penguin Books (N.Z.) Ltd, 182–190 Wairau Road,
Auckland 10, New Zealand

Penguin Books Ltd, Registered Offices:
Harmondsworth, Middlesex, England

First published in Canada by The Macmillan Company of Canada Limited 1958
First published in the United States of America by Charles Scribner's Sons 1958
First published in Penguin Books in the United States by arrangement with
Everest House, Publishers in 1980

11 13 15 14 12

ISBN: 0 14 01.6791 9

Printed in the United States of America

One

IT WAS APPROPRIATE that Mrs. Bridgetower's funeral fell on a Thursday, for that had always been her At Home day. As she had dominated her drawing-room, so she dominated St. Nicholas' Cathedral on this frosty 23rd of December. She had planned her funeral, as she had planned all her social duties and observances, with care.

Of course the Prayer Book sets the form of an Anglican funeral, and Mrs. Bridgetower had no quarrel with that. Every social occasion has its framework; it is in enriching that framework with detail that the exceptional hostess rises above the mediocrity. Not two hours after her physician had pronounced her dead, her lawyer, Mr. Matthew Snelgrove, had put a fat letter in the hands of her son Solomon, on the envelope of which was written in her firm, large hand, *Directions for My Funeral*.

Poor Solly, thought her daughter-in-law Veronica, what a time he has had! The most difficult job of all had been getting, at short notice, a coffin which was as nearly as possible a mate to that in which the late Professor Bridgetower had been buried sixteen years before. Mrs. Bridgetower had supplied the number and specifications of that model, but styles in coffins change, so it was only by great exertions that a similar one had been found in time. And as Mrs. Bridgetower had said that she did not wish to lie in a vault, and as the frost was already in the ground, arrangements had to be made to dig her grave with the aid of blow-torches and pneumatic drills. There had been no difficulty in persuading her oldest friend, Miss Laura Pottinger, to arrange the flowers in the church—"dear Puss has always had unexceptionable taste in such matters"—but Miss Pottinger had been so swollen with grief and self-importance that she had quarrelled with everyone and struck at an undertaker's assistant with her walking-stick. Luckily Veronica had been able to spare Solly most of the dealings with Miss Puss. And Veronica had addressed the two hundred cards of invitation herself, for Mrs. Bridgetower, while insisting on a private funeral, had left a long list of those whom she wished to be present at it. She had also specified the gown in which she was to be buried, and as it would no longer go over her great bulk at the time of her death, Veronica had personally altered it and put it on the corpse—a task which she had not relished. Veronica also had dressed Mrs. Bridgetower's hair and delicately painted her face, for the *Directions* had said that this should be done, but were firm that no male undertaker should do it; Miss Puss had stood at her elbow during that macabre hour, offering advice and fretful comment. Veronica had done everything possible to spare her husband, who now sat beside her, pale and worried, not with grief but with fear that something might yet go wrong.

It was not the service which was troubling him. That was under way and out of his hands. It was the funeral tea which was to follow the return from the graveyard which was on his mind. That was certain to be an ordeal, for all the funeral guests were bidden, and most of them were certain to come. He had attempted, that morning, to remove his mother's accustomed chair from the drawing-room, fearing that the sight of it might distress some of her old friends. But the oldest of these, Miss Puss Pottinger, had caught him in the act, and berated him for heartlessness. Louisa's chair, she said through angry tears, must stay where it had always been; she, Miss Puss, would not permit this relic of a great and fragrant spirit to be banished to an upstairs room on the very day of the funeral. And to make sure that no one committed unwitting sacrilege by sitting in it, she would herself lay one of the funeral wreaths—the cushion of white roses from the Imperial Order, Daughters of the Empire—on the seat. So the chair remained, a shrine and, for Solly, a portent of the ordeal which was yet to come.

The service was running according to schedule. A full choir had been specified in the *Directions*, and as full a choir as could be mustered on a weekday was present. Because the schools had closed for the Christmas holidays, eighteen of the Cathedral's twenty boys had been secured; eight of the singing-men had been able to come. Forty dollars for the men and thirty-six for the boys; well, Mother had wanted it. They had sung Samuel Sebastian Wesley's *Man That Is Born* and had followed it with Purcell's *Thou Knowest, Lord*. Luckily in these two selections Mother's taste had agreed with that of the Cathedral organist, Humphrey Cobbler. The hazard was yet to come.

This hazard was Mrs. Bridgetower's personal contribution to the funeral service. She had attended many funerals in her time, and had been unfavourably impressed by the fact that what the Prayer Book had to say about death seemed to apply chiefly to men. A feminist of a dignified sort all her life, she felt that the funeral service lacked the feminine touch, and she had arranged for this to be supplied at her own burial. She had specified that a certain piece of music be sung, and that it be sung by a female voice. She admired, she said in her last letter to her son, the fine choir of men and boys which Mr. Cobbler had made so great an adornment of St. Nicholas', but at her funeral she wanted a woman to sing *My Task*, E. L. Ashford's lovely setting of Maude Louise Ray's dear and inspiring poem.

The Dean had not liked the idea, but he did not go so far as to forbid it. He knew that he would have to brave Miss Puss if he did so. But Humphrey Cobbler had hooted. Cobbler was a personal friend of Solly's and he had spoken with great freedom. "Music is like wine, Bridgetower," he had said; "the less people know about it, the sweeter they like it. You can't have that sickening musical bonbon at your Mum's funeral. It'll disgrace us all." But after prolonged argument he had succumbed. He had even undertaken to find a woman to sing.

She was about to sing now. The Dean, rather sneakily in Solly's opinion, was uttering a disclaimer.

"At this point," he said, "there will be sung some verses which were dear to our deceased sister, and which she specifically requested should be given utterance at this service." Then he seated himself in his stall, looking as much as possible as if he were someone else, somewhere else, and deaf.

It's not really the poem that's biting him, thought Solly, angrily. It's the idea of the poem applied to Mother. Well, she wanted it, and here it is. To hell with them all.

The singer was by the organ console, with Cobbler, and thus could not be seen by the mourners in the nave. Pure, sweet and clear, her voice made itself heard.

> To love someone more dearly ev'ry day;
> To help a wand'ring child to find his way;
> To ponder o'er a noble thought, and pray;
> And smile when ev'ning falls—
>   This is my task.

That was how she thought of herself, mused Veronica. Probably it didn't seem as sticky to her as it does to us. And Oh, that last six months! Was that what she called smiling when evening falls? But I tried; I really did try. I slaved for her as I never slaved for my own mother. I did all I could to make her feel our marriage was a good thing for Solly. Did I ever pierce through to her heart? I hope so. I pray so. I want to think kindly of her.

A very little wintry sun struck through one of the Cathedral windows. The calm, silvery voice, somewhat hollow and echoing under the dome, continued.

To follow truth as blind men long for light—Veronica cast a sidelong glance at her husband. Silently, he was weeping. He truly loved his mother, in spite of everything, she thought. How I wish I thought that his mother had loved him.

(2)

THE FUNERAL TEA was even more of an ordeal than Solly had foreseen. Such a function is not easily managed, and his mother's two old servants had been quick to declare that they were unable to attempt it. They were too broken up, they said. They were not so broken up, however, that they were incapable of giving a lot of trouble to the caterer who had been engaged for the work. They thought poorly of his suggestion that three kinds of sandwiches and three kinds of little cakes, supplemented by fruitcake, would be enough. The relatives from Montreal, the Hansens, would expect cold meat, they said; and as it was so near Christmas ordinary fruitcake would not suffice; Christmas cake would be looked for. Madam had never been one to skimp. When old Ethel, the cook, remembered that Thursday had always been Madam's At Home day, she had a fresh bout of grief, and declared that she would, after all, prepare the funeral tea herself, if it killed her. Solly had been unable to meet this situation and it was Veronica who, at last, made an uneasy peace between Ethel the cook, Doris the housemaid, and the caterer.

The caterer had his own, highly professional attitude toward funeral teas. What about drinks? he said. Sherry would be wanted for the women who never drank anything except at funerals, and there were always a few Old Country people who expected port—especially if there was cold meat. But most of the mourners would want hard liquor, and they would want it as soon as they got into the house. These winter funerals were murder; everybody was half perished by the time they got back from the graveyard. Solly would have to get the liquor himself; the caterer's banquet license did not cover funerals. He would, of course, supply all the glasses and mixings. He advised Solly to get a good friend to act as barman; it wouldn't do to have a professional barman at such an affair. Looked too calculated. Similarly, the icing which said Merry Christmas would have to be removed from the tops of the fruitcakes. Looked too cheerful.

Obediently, Solly procured and hauled a hundred and fifty dollars' worth of assorted liquors from the Government purveyor on the day before the funeral. But his acquaintance among skilled mixers of drinks was small, and in the end he had to ask the Cathedral organist, Humphrey Cobbler, to help him.

Was Solly grieving for his mother, when he wept during the singing of *My Task*? Yes, he was. But he was also grieving because Veronica had had such a rotten time of it during the past three days. He was worrying that there would not be enough to eat at the funeral tea. He was worrying for fear there would be too much to eat, and that the funeral baked-meats would coldly furnish forth his own table for days to come. He was worrying that Cobbler, triumphant behind the drinks-table, would fail to behave himself. He was worrying for fear the Hansen relatives would hang around all evening, discussing family affairs, as is the custom of families at funerals, instead of decently taking the seven o'clock train back to Montreal. He was hoping that he could live through the next few hours, get one decent drink for himself, and go to bed.

(3)

SOLLY AND VERONICA rode to the graveyard in an undertaker's limousine with Uncle George Hansen, Mrs. Bridgetower's brother, and Uncle George's American wife. But as soon as the burial was over they hurried to where Solly had left their small car earlier in the day, and rushed with irreverent haste back to the house, to be on hand to greet the mourners when they came ravening for liquor, food and warm fires.

"Do you think they'll all come?" said Veronica, as they rounded the graveyard gate.

"Very likely. Did you ever see such a mob? I didn't think more than a hundred would go to the cemetery, but it looks as if they all went. Have we got enough stuff, do you suppose?"

"I can't tell. I've never had anything to do with one of these things before."

"Nor have I. Ronny, in case I go out of my head before this tea thing is over, I want to tell you now that you've been wonderful about it all. In a week or so we'll go for a holiday, and forget about it."

(4)

WHEN THEY ENTERED the house it looked cheerful, even festive. Fires burned in the drawing-room, dining-room and in the library, where Cobbler stood ready behind an improvised bar. There was some giggling and scurrying as Solly and his wife came in, and Ethel and Doris were seen making for the kitchen.

"Just been putting the girls right with a strong sherry-and-gin," said Cobbler. "They're badly shaken up. Needed bracing. Now, what can I give you?"

"Small ryes," said Solly. "And for heaven's sake use discretion, Humphrey."

"You know me," said Cobbler, slopping out the rye with a generous hand.

"I do," said Solly. "That's why I'm worried. Don't play the fool for the next couple of hours. That's all I ask."

"You wound me," said the organist, and made an attempt to look dignified. But his blue suit was too small, his collar was frayed, and his tie was working toward his left ear. His curly black hair stood out from his head in a mop, and his black eyes gleamed unnervingly. "You suggest that I lack a sense of propriety. I make no protest; I desire only to be left to My Task." He winked raffishly at Veronica.

He's our oldest friend as a married couple, thought she, and a heart of gold. If only he were not so utterly impossible! She smiled at him.

"Please, Humphrey," said she.

He winked again, tossed a lump of sugar in the air and caught it in his mouth. "Trust me," he said.

What else can we do? thought Veronica.

The mourners had begun to arrive, and Solly went to greet them. There was congestion at the door, for most of the guests paused to take off their overshoes and rubbers, and those who had none were scraping the graveyard clay from their feet. It was half an hour before the last had climbed the stairs, left wraps, taken a turn at the water-closet, descended the stairs and received a drink from Cobbler.

They had the air, festive but subdued, which is common to funeral teas. The grim business at the graveside done, they were prepared to make new, tentative contact with life. They greeted Solly with half-smiles, inviting him to smile in return. Beyond his orbit conversation buzzed, and there was a little subdued laughter. They had all, in some measure, admired or even liked his mother, but her death at seventy-one had surprised nobody, and such grief as they felt for her had already been satisfied at the funeral. Dean Jevon Knapp, of St. Nicholas', bustled up to Solly; he had left his cassock and surplice upstairs, and had put on the warm dry shoes which Mrs. Knapp always took to funerals for him, in a special bag; he had his gaiters on, and was holding a large Scotch and soda.

"I have always thought this one of the loveliest rooms in Salterton," said he.

But Solly was not allowed to answer. Miss Puss Pottinger, great friend and unappeased mourner of the deceased, popped up beside him.

"It is as dear Louisa would have wished it to be," she said, in an aggressive but unsteady voice. "Thursday was always her At Home day, you know, Mr. Dean."

"First Thursdays, I thought," said the Dean; "this is a third Thursday."

"Be it what it may," said Miss Puss, losing control of face and voice, "I shall think of this as dear Louisa's—last—At Home."

"I'm very sorry," said the Dean. "I had not meant to distress y u. Will you accept a sip—?" He held out his glass.

Miss Pottinger wrestled with herself, and spoke in a whisper. "No," said she. "Sherry. I think I could take a little sherry."

The Dean bore her away, and she was shortly seen sipping a glass of dark brown sherry in which Cobbler, unseen, had put a generous dollop of brandy.

Solly was at once engaged in conversation by his Uncle George Hansen and Uncle George's wife. This lady was an American, and as she had lived in Canada a mere thirty-five years, still found the local customs curious, and never failed to say so.

"This seems to me more like England than at home," she said now.

"Mother was very conservative," said Solly.

"The whole of Salterton is very conservative," said Uncle George; "I just met old Puss Pottinger mumbling about At Homes; thought she was dead years ago. This must be one of the last places in the British Empire where anybody has an At Home day."

"Mother was certainly one of the last in Salterton to have one," said Solly.

"Aha? Well, this is a nice old house. You and your wife going to keep it up?"

"I haven't had time to think about that yet."

"No, I suppose not. But of course you'll be pretty well fixed, now?"

"I really don't know, sir."

"Sure to be. Your mother was a rich woman. You'll get everything. She certainly won't leave anything to me; I know that. Ha ha! She was a wonder with money, even as a girl. 'Louie, you're tighter than the bark to a tree,' I used to say to her. Did your father leave much?"

"He died very suddenly, you know, sir. His will was an old

one, made before I was born. Everything went to mother, of course."

"Aha? Well, it all comes to the same thing now, eh?"

"Solly, do you realize I'd never met your wife until this afternoon?" said Uncle George's wife. "Louisa never breathed a word about your marriage until she wrote to us weeks afterward. The girl was a Catholic, wasn't she?"

"No, Aunt Gussie. Her mother was a Catholic, but Veronica was brought up a freethinker by her father. Mother and her father had never agreed, and I'm afraid my marriage was rather a shock to her. I'll get Veronica now."

"Why do you keep calling her Veronica?" said Uncle George. "Louie wrote that her name was Pearl."

"It still is," said Solly. "But it is also Veronica, and that is what she likes me to call her. Her father is Professor Vambrace, you know."

"Oh God, that old bastard," said Uncle George, and was kicked on the ankle by his wife. "Gussie, what are you kicking me for?"

At this moment a Hansen cousin, leaning on a stick, approached and interrupted.

"Let's see, George, now Louisa's gone you're the oldest Hansen stock, aren't you?"

"I'm sixty-nine," said Uncle George; "you're older than that, surely, Jim?"

"Sixty-eight," said Jim, with a smirk.

"You look older," said Uncle George, unpleasantly.

"You would, too, if you'd been where I was on the Somme," said Cousin Jim, with the conscious virtue of one who has earned the right to be nasty on the field of battle.

"You people certainly like it hot in Canada," said Aunt Gussie. And she was justified, for the steam heat and three open fires had made the crowded rooms oppressive.

"I'll see what I can do," said Solly and crept away. He ran upstairs and sought refuge in the one place he could think of which might be inviolable by his mother's relatives. As he entered his bathroom from his dressingroom his wife slipped furtively in from the bedroom. They locked both doors and sat down to rest on the edge of the tub.

"They're beginning to fight about who's the oldest stock," said Solly.

"I've met rather too many people who've hinted that our marriage killed your mother," said Veronica. "I thought a breather would do me good."

"Mother must have written fifty letters about that."

"Don't worry about it now, Solly."

"How is Humphrey doing?"

"I haven't heard any complaints. Do people always soak like this at funerals?"

"How should I know? I've never given a funeral tea before."

(5)

WHEN SOLLY AND his wife went downstairs again they found that most of the guests had turned their attention from drink to food, save for a half-dozen diehards who hung around the bar. The mourners were, in the main, elderly people who were un-accustomed to fresh air in the afternoon, and the visit to the cemetery had given them an appetite. The caterer directed operations from the kitchen, and his four waitresses hurried to and fro with laden platters. Ethel and Doris, ranking as mourn-ers, pretended to be passing food, but were in reality engaged in long and regretful conversations with family friends, one or two of whom were unethically sounding them out about the chances of their changing employment, now that Mrs. Bridgetower was gone. (After all, what would a young man with an able-bodied wife want with two servants?) Miss Puss had been expected to pour the tea, a position of special honour, but she gave it up after over-filling three cups in succession, and seemed to be utterly unnerved; little Mrs. Knapp took on this demanding job, and was relieved after a hundred cups or so by Mrs. Swithin Shillito. The fake beams of the dining-room ceiling seemed lower and more oppressive than ever as the mourners crowded themselves into the room, consuming ham, turkey, sandwiches, cheese, Christmas cake and tartlets with increasing gusto. Those who were wedged near the table obligingly passed plates of food over the heads of the crowd to others who could not get near the supplies. The respectful hush had completely vanished, laughter and even guffaws were heard, and if it had not been a funeral tea the party would have been called a rousing success.

The mourners had returned from the graveyard at four o'clock, and it was six before any of them thought of going home. It was the general stirring of the Montreal Hansens, who had a train to catch, which finally broke up the party.

"Good-bye, Solly, and a Merry Christmas!" roared Uncle George, who had returned to the bar immediately after finishing a hearty tea. His wife kicked him on the ankle again, and he straightened his face. "Well, as merry as possible under the circumstances," he added, and plunged into the scramble for rubbers which was going on in the hall. Cousin Jim was sitting on the stairs, while a small, patient wife struggled to put on and zip up his overshoes. "Take care of my bad leg," he said, in a testy voice, to anyone who came near. It was some time before all the Hansens had gone. Several of them trailed back into the drawing-room, in full outdoor kit, to wring Solly's hand, or to kiss him on the cheek. But at last they went, and the Saltertonians began to struggle for coats and overshoes.

Mr. Matthew Snelgrove, solicitor and long-time friend of Mrs. Bridgetower, approached Solly conspiratorially. He was a tall old man, stiff and crane-like, with beetling brows.

"Will tomorrow, at three o'clock, suit you?" he said.

"For what, Mr. Snelgrove?"

"The will," said Mr. Snelgrove. "We must read and discuss the will."

"But is that necessary? I thought nobody read wills now. Can't we meet at your office some day next week and discuss it?"

"I think that your Mother would have wished her will to be read in the presence of all her executors."

"All her executors? Are there others? I thought that probably you and myself—"

"There are two executors beside yourself, and it is not a simple will. Not simple at all. I think you should know its contents as soon as possible."

"Well—if you say so."

"I think it would be best. I shall inform the others. Here, then, at three?"

"As you please."

Solly had no time to reflect on this arrangement, for several people were waiting to say good-bye. Dean Knapp and his wife approached last, each holding an arm of Miss Puss Pottinger, who wore the rumpled appearance of one who has been put into her outside clothes by hands other than her own. One foot was not completely down into her overshoe, and she lurched as she walked.

"We shall see Miss Pottinger home," said the Dean, smiling but keeping a jailor's grip on Auntie Puss.

"Solly, dear boy," cried that lady, and breaking free from the Dean she flung herself upon Solly's bosom, weeping and scrabbling at his coat. It became clear that she wanted to kiss him. He stooped and suffered this, damp and rheumy as it was; then, taking her by the shoulders, he passed her back to Mrs. Knapp. With a loud hiccup Auntie Puss collapsed, and almost bore the Dean's wife to the floor. When she had been picked up, she was led away, sobbing and murmuring, "Poor Louisa's last At Home —shall never forget—" They were the last to go.

"Well, well, well," said Cobbler, strolling in from the hall, when he had helped the Dean to drag Auntie Puss down a rather icy walk, and boost her into a car; "quite overcome with grief. Sad."

"She was drunk," said Solly. "What on earth did you give her?"

"The poor old soul was badly in need of bracing," said Cobbler. "I gave her a sherry with a touch of brandy in it, and it did the trick. But would she let well alone? She would not. She kept coming back. Was I to refuse her? I tried her once without the brandy, but she passed back her glass and said, 'This isn't the same'. Well—she had seven. I couldn't put her on the Indian List; she'd have made a scene. Whatever she feels like tomorrow, I am pure as the driven snow. Never say No to a woman; my lifelong principle."

He was helping Veronica to clear up the mess. Paper napkins were everywhere. Dirty plates covered the top of the piano. Cake had been ground into the carpet. The pillow of white roses in Mrs. Bridgetower's chair had been pushed under it by the callous Cousin Jim, who wanted to sit down and had no feeling for symbolism.

"For heaven's sake leave that," said Solly. "Let Ethel and Doris cope with it."

" 'Fraid the girls are a bit overcome," said Cobbler. "They told me they were good for nothing but bed. Odd phrase, considering everything."

"Humphrey, what *did* you do?" said Veronica.

"Me? Not a thing. Just my duty, as I saw it. People kept asking for drinks and I obliged them. Really, Solly, those Hansen relatives of yours are something special. Hollow legs, every one of them."

"Was there enough?"

"Just managed. Do you know that there were two hundred and forty-seven souls here, and not one of them was a teetotaller? I always count; it's automatic with me. I count the house at every Cathedral service; the Dean likes to know how he's pulling. I consider that the affair was a credit to your late Mum, but we nearly ran out of swipes. It was a close thing."

He sat down at the grand piano, and sang with great expression, to the tune of the popular ballad *Homing*—

> *All things get drunk at eventide;*
> *The birds go pickled to their snoozing;*
> *Heaven's creatures share a mighty thirst—*
> *Boozing—Bo-o-o-zing.*

"Humphrey, stop it!" said Veronica. "If you must do something, will you get me a drink? I'm completely done up."

Cobbler got them all drinks, and while Solly and Veronica sat by the fire, trying to forget the trials and miseries of the past few days, he played Bach choral preludes on the old piano, to heal their wounded spirits.

(6)

MR. SNELGROVE COMPLETED the reading of Mrs. Bridgetower's will the following afternoon, just as the library clock struck four. He had enjoyed himself. Modern custom did not often require him to read a will and he felt that there was something splendidly professional and lawyer-like about doing so. When a testator is dead he is in the hands of God; certainly this was the belief of Mr. Snelgrove who was, among other dignified things, chancellor of the diocese of which St. Nicholas' was the Cathedral; but the testator's affairs on earth remain in the hands of his lawyer. There is drama in such a position, and Mr. Snelgrove greatly relished it. He blew his nose and removed his pince-nez in order to rub his old eyes.

The setting in which Mrs. Bridgetower's will had been read was everything that the legal ham Mr. Snelgrove could have wished. Outside the windows a light snow was falling from a leaden, darkening sky. Inside the library a wood fire burned, its light being reflected in the leaded glass of the old-fashioned book-jails which lined the walls. The room was comfortable, dark, stuffy and rather depressing. It was Christmas Eve.

His listeners looked suitably grave and impressed. Dean Knapp, sunk in a leather armchair, stroked his brow reflectively, like a man who cannot believe that he has heard aright. Miss Puss Pottinger sat bolt upright on an armless chair, refusing to yield to the splitting headache which seemed to possess her whole small being; from time to time her gorge rose sourly and searingly within her, but she was a soldier's daughter, and she forcibly gulped it down again. The fumes from Solly's pipe were a great trial to her. He was perched on the arm of a large chair in which Veronica was sitting. It was Solly who was first to speak.

"I think I've got the drift of the will, but I'm not quite sure," said he. "Could you let us have the meaning of it in simple language?"

Mr. Snelgrove was happy to do so. Interpreting legal scripture to laymen was the part of his profession which he liked best.

"Shorn of technicality," said he, "the meaning of the will is this: all of your late mother's estate is left in trust to her executors—you, her son, Solomon Bridgetower—you, Laura Pottinger, spinster—you, Jevon Knapp, as Dean of St. Nicholas' Cathedral. That estate, as outlined here, consists of this house and its contents and considerable holdings in investments. You, Solomon Bridgetower, are to continue to occupy the house, which has always been your home, but it is the property of the trust, and you may not dispose of it. But the income from the estate is to be devoted to the educational project which your late mother has outlined."

"You mean, I don't get any money?" said Solly.

"You get a legacy of one hundred dollars," said the lawyer.

"Yes, but I mean—the investments, and the money that brought in my Mother's own income, and all that—I don't quite follow—?"

"That money is all to be devoted to the education, or training, of some young woman resident in this city of Salterton, who is desirous of following a career in the arts. The young woman is to be chosen by you, the trustees. She must be not more than twenty-one at the time she is chosen, and you are to be responsible for her maintenance and training, in the best circumstances you can devise, until she reaches the age of twenty-five. She is to be maintained abroad in order, as your mother says, that she may bring back to Canada some of the intangible treasures of European tradition. That phrase, of course, rules out any possibility of her being trained in the States. And when she is twenty-five, you are to choose another beneficiary of the trust. And so on, unless the conditions under which the trust exists are terminated."

"And I get nothing except a hundred dollars and the right to live in the house?"

"You get nothing, unless the condition is fulfilled which brings the trust to an end. If, and when, that condition is fulfilled and you are still living in this house, you receive a life interest in your mother's estate. Bequests are made to the two servants, Ethel Colman and Doris Black, which will be payable when the condition is fulfilled. Laura Pottinger receives a bequest of the testator's collection of Rockingham china. The Cathedral Church of St. Nicholas will receive all of the testator's holdings in certain telephone and transportation stocks."

"There is a condition attaching to this latter bequest. Until the Cathedral gets the telephone stock, the Dean is to preach, every St. Nicholas' Day, a special sermon on some matter relating to education, and these sermons are to be known as the Louisa Hansen Bridgetower Memorial Sermons. If there is any failure in this respect, the bequest is forfeit."

Solly still looked puzzled. "And all of this hangs—?"

"It all hangs on your having a son, Mr. Bridgetower. When, and if, you and your wife, Pearl Veronica, née Vambrace, produce male issue, who is duly christened Solomon Hansen Bridgetower, he becomes heir of all his grandmother's estate save for the bequests I have mentioned. But you are to have a life interest in the estate, so that he will not actually come into possession of his inheritance until after your death."

"And if we have a child and it is a girl?"

"The trust will remain."

"But it's fantastic."

"Somewhat unusual, certainly."

"When was this will made?"

"I read you the date. Your mother made this will less than three months ago."

"It puts my wife and me in a pretty position, doesn't it?"

"It does not put anyone in an enviable position, Solomon," said Mr. Snelgrove. "Did you not notice what it does to me? I am not an executor, though as an old and, I believed, valued friend of your Mother's, I might have expected that confidence; I am named solely as solicitor to the executors—a paid position. And the condition is made that if I have not settled all your Mother's affairs within one year from the day of her death, the estate is to be taken out of my hands and confided to Gordon Balmer—a solicitor for whom your Mother knew that I had a strong disapproval. You did not perhaps notice her comment that she thought that my 'natural cupidity' would make me hurry the business through. 'Natural cupidity' is a legal expression which she picked up from me and has turned against me. Your Mother has given us all a flick of her whip."

"These memorial sermons," said the Dean; "they are to be preached until the Cathedral inherits? But what if the Cathedral never inherits? What if there is no son? I know many families—large families—which consist solely of daughters."

"It will be many years before anything can be done to meet that situation, Mr. Dean," said Snelgrove. "Meanwhile the sermons must be delivered, in hope and expectation. Any failure could cost the Cathedral a considerable sum."

The Dean wrestled within himself for a moment before he spoke. "Could you give me any idea how much?" he said at last.

"It would run between seven and ten thousand a year, I think," said Snelgrove. All the executors opened their eyes at the mention of this sum.

"Then Mother was very rich?" asked Solly. "I never knew, you know; she never spoke of such things. I had understood she was just getting by."

"There are degrees in wealth," said Mr. Snelgrove. "Your Mother would not seem wealthy in some circles. But she was

comfortable—very comfortable. She inherited substantially from
her own family, you know, and there was rather more in your
father's estate than might have been expected from a professor
of geology. He had very good mining contacts, at a time when
mines were doing well. And your mother was a lifelong, shrewd
investor."

"She was?" said Solly. "I never knew anything about it."

"Oh yes," said Snelgrove. "I don't suppose there was anyone
in Salterton who followed the Montreal and Toronto markets so
closely, or so long, or so successfully, as your mother. A remarkable woman."

"Remarkable indeed," said the Dean. He was thinking about
those sermons, and balancing another curate and new carpets
against them.

Veronica had not spoken until now. "Shall we have tea?" said
she.

They had it from a remarkably beautiful Rockingham service.
Miss Puss, who said nothing all afternoon, eyed it speculatively.
Veronica noticed that she did so.

"Yours, Miss Puss," said she, smiling.

"Mine," said Puss Pottinger, softly and without a smile, "if
and when."

(7)

"IT WAS CHRISTMAS Day in the workhouse," declaimed Humphrey
Cobbler, pushing himself back from the late Mrs. Bridgetower's
dining-table. Christmas dinner with Solly and Veronica had
made him expansive.

"Shut up, Humphrey," said Molly, his wife. She was a large,
beautiful, untidy woman, always calm and at ease. She threw a
grape at her husband to silence him, but it missed his head and
set an epergne jingling on the built-in sideboard.

"No offence meant," said Cobbler, "and none taken, I'm sure.

I merely wished to convey to our young friends here, who have been studiedly avoiding the subject of Mum's Will all through this excellent dinner, that we are privy to their dread secret, and sympathize with them in their fallen state. I was about to do so through the agency of divine poesy, thereby showing a delicacy which I could hardly expect you, my thick-witted consort, to appreciate."

Raising his glass, he declaimed again:

> It was Christmas Day in the Workhouse;
>   The maddest, merriest day;
> And all the paupers had gathered then
>   To make high holiday.
>
> Then in strode the Workhouse Master
>   As they cringed by the grimy walls;
> 'I wish you a Merry Christmas,' said he;
>   The paupers answered—

"What have you been hearing?" said Solly. "You aren't going to tell me that people are chattering about it already?"

"Not precisely chattering," said Cobbler; "more a kind of awed whispering. Rumours reached me this morning, just before we celebrated the birthday of the Prince of Peace with a first-rate choral service, that your Mum's Will was in the nature of a grisly practical joke, and that you are left without a nickel."

"I thought it wouldn't take long to get around," said Solly. "Who was talking? There are only three people who know; they might have had the decency to keep quiet for a few days, at least. Who was it?"

"Calm yourself, my dear fellow," said Cobbler. "You are—let's see, what is it—twenty-seven. You really ought to have more worldly wisdom than to say that only three people know about your Mum's Will. You and Veronica know, and the Dean and unquestionably the Dean's wife; Puss Pottinger knows, and she is a mighty hinter; Snelgrove knows, and certainly his wife, and his partner Ronny Fitzalan, and probably at least **two** girls in his office who made copies of the will for the executors. Your excellent Ethel and Doris, who have hopes of legacies, have undoubtedly picked up a few things by listening at doors or hiding under your bed. That's twelve people already. What I know I was told this morning by one of my tenors whom you don't know, but who knows you. He heard it last night when he was carol-singing at the hospital. Your late Mum was notoriously a rich woman; everybody wants to know who gets the lolly."

"I certainly didn't know she was a rich woman," said Solly.

"That sounds silly, but I believe it," said Cobbler. "One never thinks of one's parents with any realism. She was always pretty tight with money when you wanted it; probably she told you she hadn't much, and you believed her, like a good boy. She came the penniless widow. You didn't use your eyes. You didn't look at this big house, full of hideous but expensive stuff; you didn't reflect that your Mum lived in considerable state, with two servants, in an age when most people have none; you didn't think that she had all this without doing any work for it. You didn't think that it costs a lot of money to continue the habits of the Edwardian era into the middle of the twentieth century. Nothing is so expensive as living in the past. No; you believed what you were told. You accepted all this as a normal, poverty-ridden hovel. But everybody else in Salterton knew that your Mum was a very warm proposition, and they were all crazy to know how she would cut up when she was gone."

"What business was it of theirs?"

"Don't be stupid; people who mind their own business die of boredom at thirty. Don't you suppose the hospitals hoped for a chunk? Your father was a professor at Waverley University for years; do you think Waverley didn't have its hand out? The Cathedral wanted a slice, too. But nothing doing. And they say you don't get a red cent. Where is it all going? I don't mean to pry, you understand. I'm just aching to know."

"All you have heard is that none of the places that expected a legacy got anything, and that I am not the heir?"

"Precisely. Are you going to give us the real story, or do you want Molly and me to feel that we aren't trusted, now that you are poor like us?"

"I suppose it'll all come out in a few days. You might as well know."

And so Solly told the Cobblers the conditions of his mother's will. They opened their eyes very wide, and Cobbler gave a long whistle, but it was his wife who spoke.

"That's what you can really call laying the Dead Hand on the living, isn't it," said Molly. "I suppose it's something to be proud of, in a way; not many people have the guts to make a really revengeful will. They're too anxious to leave a fragrant memory, and few things are so fragrant as a million dollars. I suppose its well over a million?"

"Haven't any idea," said Solly. "But I'm sure you're wrong about revenge. I mean, Mother was capricious, and very strong-minded, but revenge—it doesn't seem like her."

"Seems very much like what I knew of her," said Cobbler. "You really must grow up, you know. Your Mum told you that she loved you, and you believed her. She made your life a hell of dependency, and you put up with it because she played the invalid, and tyrannized over you with her weak heart. She beat off any girls you liked, until you got up enough gumption to marry Veronica—or Veronica got enough gumption to marry you; I never quite knew which it was. That was only a bit more than a year ago. What peace have you known since? She made you come here and live with her, and like a couple of chumps you did it. She let it be known as widely as possible that your marriage grieved her."

"Look here, you're talking about my Mother, who was buried the day before yesterday. I don't expect you to behave like other people, but you must show some decency. I know better than anybody how difficult she was, but she had very good reasons for everything she did. Of course they're not easily understandable, from an outsider's viewpoint. I've read and re-read her will to-day; it's very full, and very personal. She says that she has left the money away from me to prove me—to test what I can do absolutely on my own. She says she knows it will be hard, and advises me to take my father as an example. I know—it sounds very odd by modern notions of such things, but it is quite obvious that she meant it kindly."

This was greeted with a studied silence by the others.

"Well, look at it from her point of view," said Solly, when the silence had begun to wear on him. "She always knew I was rather a feeble chap; it was her last try to put some backbone into me."

"You're not a bit feeble," said his wife, laying her hand on his.

"Yes; yes, I am. I don't pretend that this will isn't a shock, and I won't pretend to think it's really fair. But I see what she meant by it. And your suggestion that it was because of our marriage is sheer nasty spite, Humphrey. I won't say Mother liked Veronica, but I know she respected her. And certainly Ronny was as good as any daughter could have been to her during the past six months. You didn't marry me for money, did you?" said he, smiling at his wife.

"I don't think that is what Humphrey meant," said Veronica.

"Well, what else is there?"

"Darling, if you haven't thought of it, I won't find it very easy to explain. Your mother leaves you her money—or the income from it, which is the same thing—if we have a son. Well? Must we set to work, cold-bloodedly, to beget a child, hoping it will be a son? If it is a daughter—try, try again. You know what people are. They'll be ready to make the worst of it, whatever happens. They'll have a splendid, prurient snigger at us for years. Don't you see?"

"Oh I'm sure Mother never meant anything like that," said Solly.

"Then why did she make such a will?" said Molly. "You've got to consider the generation your mother belonged to. She wasn't a big friend of sex, you know. She undoubtedly thought it would dry up the organs of increase in you both. Very pretty. Sweetly maternal."

"I wish you people would get it into your heads that you are talking about my Mother," said Solly, with some anger.

"Now look, Solly," said Cobbler, "talk sense. Ever since I first met you your main topic whenever you were depressed is what a hell of a time your mother was giving you. I've heard you talk about her in a way which surprised even me—and I specialize in speaking the unspeakable. You can't make a saint of her now simply because she is dead."

"Shut up," said his wife. "Solly needs time to get used to the fact that his mother is dead. You know how you carried on when your mother died. Roared like a bull for days, though you rarely gave her a civil word the last few times you met."

"Those were quarrels about music," said Cobbler. "We disagreed on artistic principles. Just showed how really compatible we were that we could talk about them at all. I bet Solly never talked to his mother about such things."

"The terms of her will showed that she cared a great deal about artistic principles. Or about education, anyhow," said Solly.

"I have not forgotten that she requested that *My Task* be sung at her funeral," said Cobbler. "The bill for that caper is outstanding, by the way. I only got a girl to do it at the last moment."

"She sang it very nicely," said Veronica.

"Good voice. A girl called Monica Gall. And it will be ten dollars."

"Include it in the bill you send to Snelgrove," said Solly, "along with the charges for the choir, and yourself."

"I played gratis."

"Well, don't. Send Snelgrove a bill. I don't wish to think that my Mother was obliged to you for anything."

"Oh, for God's sake don't turn nasty, just because I spoke my mind. If you want friends who echo everything you say and defer to all your pinhead notions, count me out."

"Shut up, both of you," said Molly. "You're carrying on like a couple of children. But listen to me, Solly. You and Veronica may have some hard days ahead of you, and you've got to make up your minds now to stick together, or this idiotic will can make trouble between you. And the fact that you have no money will make it all the easier."

"We have just as muoh money as we ever had," said Solly. "I still have my job, you know."

"A junior lecturer, and quite good for your age. A miserable salary, considering that you are expected to live the life of a man of education and some position on it. Still, Humphrey and I are living very happily on less. But if I understand the conditions of the will, you have to live in this house, and keep it up, and keep Ethel and Doris on that money, and go on having children until you have a son. They say that clever men tend to have daughters, Solly, and I suppose you qualify as a clever man, in spite of the way you are behaving at present." Molly's affectionate tone took the sting out of her words. "But I think you should recognize that your mother has laid the Dead Hand on you and Veronica in the biggest possible way, and the sooner you see that the better you will be able to deal with it."

"And you'd better not begin by holding a grudge against me," said Cobbler. "You are going to want all your friends, now that you have joined the ranks of the struggling poor. You are going to feel some very sharp pangs, you know, when you see all that lovely money, which might have been yours, going to support dear little Miss God-knows-who, while she studies flower arrangement in the Japanese Imperial Greenhouses, at the expense of your Mum's estate. So stop snapping me up on every word. I had nothing personal against your Mum. It is just that she symbolized all the forces that have been standing on my neck ever since I was old enough to have a mind of my own. And to prove my goodwill, I give you a toast to her memory."

Amity was restored, and they drank the toast. Perhaps only Molly and Veronica heard Cobbler murmur, as he raised his glass, "Toujours gai, le diable est mort".

TWO

MRS. BRIDGETOWER'S WILL would not, under ordinary circumstances, have become a matter of public interest until the probate was completed but, as Cobbler pointed out, there were institutions in Salterton which hoped for a legacy. Chief among these was Waverley University, and the rumour that it was to have nothing aroused some waspishness in the Bursar's office. Universities are, in a high-minded way, unceasingly avaricious. The thought that the wealthy widow of a former professor—a member of the family, so to speak—had not remembered the Alma Mater in her will (particularly when her son and presumed heir was also of the faculty) was unbearable. The rumour was that a trust had been set up, and morever a trust with an educational purpose; if this were true, it was a slap in the face for Waverley. But was it true?

It is not a university's function to pry into private affairs. That is the job of a newspaper. Thus it was that, acting on a discreet tip from the Bursar's office, the Salterton *Evening Bellman* sought information from the three executors in turn. From Miss Puss it received the sharpest of rebuffs; the Dean temporized, and said that he was not free to speak until he had consulted the others; it was Solly who said that a trust was to be established, and that details should be sought from Mr. Snelgrove. The lawyer, who loved secrecy, called the executors together to urge them to say nothing to anyone; nobody had any right to know anything about

Mrs. Bridgetower's estate until after probate. It was Solly who pointed out that this was impossible.

A detailed knowledge of law and ordinary common sense are not always found together, and it was Solly who had to explain the situation to Mr. Snelgrove, as tactfully as possible. According to the will, the girl who was to benefit from Mrs. Bridgetower's money must be chosen and launched on her course of study within a year of her benefactress' death: Mr. Snelgrove was also to have the probate completed by that time, or else suffer the humiliation of seeing this juicy plum pass into the hands of another lawyer. Therefore, whether the trust was legally in existence before the probate or not, the girl must be chosen within a year, and that could not be done unless some knowledge of the impending trust were available to at least a few people. It took a surprisingly long time to get this through Mr. Snelgrove's head, though he had drawn Mrs. Bridgetower's will and ought to have foreseen it. His was the perplexity of the man who understands his situation intellectually but has not comprehended it emotionally, and he continued to say "Yes" and "I see" when it was amply clear that he did not see at all.

Though Solly was willing that something should be known of the trust, he was not willing that it should be publicly known that his mother had used him shabbily. His state of mind was by no means an uncommon one: his mother had been the bane of his life, but after her death he was determined that no one should think ill of her. So, after consultation with Veronica, he paid a visit to Mr. Gloster Ridley, the editor of *The Bellman*, explained the situation to him, and asked for his help in putting the best face on the matter. This stroke of diplomacy, undertaken without the knowledge of the other executors or of Snelgrove, had excellent result. *The Bellman* published a reasonable amount of information about the trust and its purpose, made it clear that nothing would happen for some time, said kind things about the late Mrs. Bridgetower's lifelong enthusiasm for the education of women, and gave no hint that the lady's son had been left a mere token bequest, or that there were any curious conditions attaching to the trust. Thus an agreeable version of the truth was made public, and the murmurs at Waverley were, for the moment, stilled.

Mr. Snelgrove and Miss Puss were displeased, however. They both possessed that type of mind which gets deep satisfaction out of withholding information. If Miss Puss could have bought shoes without confiding her size to the salesman, she would have done it. So another meeting was called, and Solly was raked over the coals for talking to the press. Already he was learning useful lessons from his experience as an executor, and he let Snelgrove and Miss Puss talk until they were tired. Then he covered all his previous arguments once again, and pointed out that the effect of the newspaper article had been good, and that it had substituted a body of carefully chosen fact for spiteful rumour. He received unexpected support from Dean Knapp. It would be too much to say that Miss Puss and the lawyer were mollified, but they were temporarily subdued. Solly had a pleasant feeling that he was becoming the guiding spirit of the executors.

It was his idea, for instance, that the executors should always meet in the Bridgetower house. Snelgrove had read the will there, to satisfy his sense of drama; Solly contrived that the executors should meet there, arguing that, as the house was the property of the trust, the trustees should make use of it for their official deliberations. This gave him a certain advantage, for while it was true that the house was part of the trust, it was also his dwelling, and he played the role of host there. Miss Puss was first to recognize the implications of this, and she took her revenge at that second meeting, when she and Snelgrove were angry with Solly about the newspaper account of Mrs. Bridgetower's will.

Veronica had met her at the door, and welcomed her. "I think, dear, that it would be better if you were not present at the trustees' meetings," said Miss Puss.

"Oh, I wouldn't dream of coming into the meeting," said Veronica; "I just wanted to help you with your coat."

"I am sure you mean everything that is kind, dear," said Miss Puss, "but we must avoid any appearance of impropriety. I say this both as an executor and a friend. I am sure you hear everything in good time, as it is." Veronica retired to another room with a red face, and a sense that she had been presumptuous in a house which was now, apparently, even less her home than when her mother-in-law had been alive.

Solly had overheard this exchange, and he was angry. He had not much spirit when it came to fighting for himself, but he was ready to fight anyone for Veronica. Therefore he took it out of Miss Puss rather more than was necessary, in a quiet way, and stored up a considerable quantity of resentment against her, to be worked off at his future convenience. If his mother had truly meant her will to make a man of him, it was working rapidly to make him a hard and bitter man. Laura Pottinger was his mother's oldest friend, and as such she had domineered over him from boyhood. But he was strongly conscious of the fact that as he had grown up, she had grown old, and he meant to put her in her place over and over again, if that should be necessary, until she learned what her place was.

It was clear to him also that Mr. Matthew Snelgrove would have to be dealt with, for the lawyer took the line that the three executors needed guidance, and he was their obvious guide. When he had at last been made to realize that he could not in any way call in the information which *The Bellman* had given out, he warned the executors strictly against revealing any further terms of the will.

"I must tell you," said Solly, "that Veronica and I have already had a talk with Ethel Colman and Doris Black. They have both been with the family a long time, and had a right to expect legacies. You know that there are legacies for them—when I have a son. We thought it right that they should know."

"But that is exceedingly irregular," said Snelgrove. "I am

charged with the very difficult task of settling this large estate in a year; how am I to do so if my prerogatives are taken from me and information revealed and expectations raised before I have even had time to settle to the work?"

"The whole thing is irregular," said Solly, "and Veronica and I feel that Ethel and Doris deserve any consideration we can give them. They have a right to know where they stand. We can't possibly keep them both, or even one of them, on my salary. They must be free to take other jobs. And you might as well know that I offered to raise the money for their legacies myself, so that they could have them now. Otherwise we don't know how long they may have to wait."

"But if you have told them the conditions of the will, they are certain to talk," said Snelgrove. "You know how things get around—even when nobody runs to the newspapers."

"I know that you read my mother's will on Christmas Eve to the four of us and that on Christmas Day quite a few people knew that I had been cut out of it," said Solly. To his astonishment, and triumph, the other three all blushed in their various ways. "Certainly I didn't tell anyone in that time."

"If irresponsible talk is permitted, your Mother's reputation may suffer," said Miss Puss. "That ought to mean a great deal to you."

"And so it does," said Solly, "but I think that you will agree that my Mother has made it somewhat difficult to prevent hard things being said. People at Waverley have not stuck at saying she tricked them—led them to think they were to get a substantial sum, and then didn't come through with it. You ought to know, Auntie Puss, that she didn't care what anybody said, when she wanted things her own way."

Miss Puss changed her tack. "I suppose it is inevitable, but I wish that you did not involve Veronica so much in these affairs. I suppose she sympathized with the servants without any regard for the reflection on dear Louisa."

"Veronica is my wife, Miss Puss," said Solly. "Mother often

seemed to forget that, but there is no reason why anyone else should do so. She is in this as much as I am. I'll tell her whatever I think proper—and that is everything."

A fight seemed imminent, and Snelgrove intervened, choosing his point of pressure badly. "You have offered to pay Ethel and Doris legacies; what will you do for money? Have you insurance? Or savings?" He knew very well that Solly had neither.

"I have talked to my bank," said Solly, with a smile. "They are very friendly, and are ready to lend me money on my expectations."

"Be careful of borrowing on that security," said Snelgrove. "You may involve yourself irretrievably. What if you never inherit?"

"You'll excuse me if I am more optimistic about that than an older man might be," said Solly. "I offered to get the banker a doctor's certificate that I am—in good health; he very decently said I needn't bother. I have a young and healthy wife. I assure you, Miss Puss and gentlemen, that I mean to inherit just as fast as I can."

"Of course; of course," said the Dean, and then blushed, realizing that his encouragement might be misinterpreted. He was extremely uncomfortable.

"My chief concern is that a proper regard be shown for dear Louisa's wishes," said Miss Puss, who had an ill-understood but powerful feeling that Solly was outraging his mother's memory with indecent talk.

"Apparently she wished for a grandson," said Solly, "and I am going to do everything in my power to gratify her."

It was in this uncomfortable strain that the executors' meetings continued. Solly called them whenever he thought it necessary. He summoned the Dean, Miss Puss and Snelgrove to tell them that Doris Black had decided to leave his employ, and that Ethel Colman meant to continue to live in the house as cook, on a reduced salary. She was already in receipt of the Old Age pension and meant to retire in another two or three years anyhow. She did not want to take another position at her time of life. Both the women had accepted his offer of a cash settlement of their legacies, and both were ready to sign a paper waiving any future claim on the estate. Snelgrove, groaning and protesting, was instructed to prepare such a paper and see it properly signed.

As he gained the commanding position among the executors, Solly developed quite a taste for meetings and schemes. He urged that they should lose no time in seeking out the beneficiary of Mrs. Bridgetower's trust. He overrode the objections of Snelgrove and Miss Puss, pointing out that the choice might be a difficult and time-taking one. After one meeting, which filled three and a half rancorous hours, he insisted that a vote be taken, giving vast offence to Snelgrove, who had a tongue but no vote. The Dean voted with Solly, and within a week a discreet notice appeared in the *Bellman* explaining what the trust would be empowered to do, and asking those who were interested to make application in writing to Matthew Snelgrove, solicitor to the Bridgetower Trust.

It was a major victory, but it was not achieved quickly. Three months of the precious year of grace had elapsed, and it was the beginning of April when the advertisement appeared.

(2)

CONSIDERING THE CARE which the executors took in wording their advertisement, it was misinterpreted in a remarkable number of ways. It was clearly stated that the recipient of Mrs. Bridgetower's bounty must be female, not over twenty-one or under that age in December of the current year, and a resident of the city of Salterton. Nevertheless four young men proposed themselves; thirty-two applicants were over-age, one of them confessing to forty-six; they hailed from everywhere within the range of *The Bellman's* circulation. It was made plain that the beneficiary must be a student of the fine arts, and these were defined as painting, sculpture, music, literature and architecture, and reasonable branches thereof. The applicants, who reached a total of eighty-seven, interpreted the word "reasonable" in a large and generous sense.

There were potters who wanted to study in England, and weavers who wanted to study in Sweden. There was a jeweller who did not want to be a goldsmith or a silversmith, but said she was "very hot on design". The nearest thing to a sculptor was a young man who had done some interesting things in soap and saw no reason to go beyond this convenient medium. There were some genuine painters, and one real etcher. There were a few musicians, but all were over-age. The writers supplied depressing, ill-spelled and dirty manuscripts of their work, all of which seemed to be intended for poetry. There was one girl who wanted to be a recreation director and felt that a few years among the folk-schools of Europe would be good both for her and Europe. There were five girls who, representing themselves as writers, were in fact scholars who wanted to use the money for projects of research. There were dancers, one of them specializing in what she called "modern ballroom and tap". There was a girl who wanted to perfect herself in the use of the piano-accordion and the electric guitar. All expressed themselves in terms of inordinate ambition unfettered by modesty, and promised great achievement if they should be chosen.

It took the executors three weeks' work to reduce the applications to a short list. Solly could have done it in a night, but the others disapproved of his frivolous way of howling with delight or despair as he read the letters. They insisted that, in fairness to everybody and in keeping with the solemnity of their position, each letter should be read aloud and seriously discussed. This gave Miss Puss great opportunities to reflect on the quality of the young people of today, and to compare them, much to their disfavour, with the young people she had known at the turn of the century. Mr. Snelgrove also felt it necessary to say his say on this congenial theme; although he complained tirelessly about the amount of time the proceeding took, he could not keep away from it. Solly explained to him that, as he was not an executor, it was not necessary for him to attend all of these sorting meetings, but the lawyer did not choose to understand the hint. It was clear that he loved it, for it fed his sense of importance. It began to appear, also, that he was proving to the ghost of Mrs. Bridgetower that as she had chosen to oppress him, he could suffer with the best of them. He was also ticking up the legal expenses involved in settling her will.

When at last the short list was agreed upon, it was very short indeed. It contained only two names—Nicole John, who wanted to be an architect, and Birgitta Hetmansen, who was a painter.

Miss John exploded within a week. In reply to Snelgrove's letter, asking her to meet the executors for a preliminary talk, there came a reply from her father saying that his daughter's health would make the acceptance of any such benefaction entirely out of the question; he expressed huffy surprise that the executors had not thought of consulting him before entering into a plan to take his daughter from her home. Nothing further was seen or heard of Miss John.

Miss Hetmansen was a different matter. She appeared with a large portfolio of her work, and photographs of pictures which she had sold. She had some newspaper clippings in which her drawings and paintings were given favourable criticism. She had a very good letter from her teacher. She was a dark, personable, quiet girl and she pleased Miss Puss by comporting herself like a lady—not a lady of Miss Puss's own era, but the nearest thing that could be expected in these dark days.

She knew what she wanted. Her desire was to go to Paris, and she could name the teachers with whom she wanted to study, and knew where they were to be found. In all, the executors had three meetings with Miss Hetmansen, and at the last of these her teacher appeared, and spoke of her in high terms. The executors were delighted. It looked as though they had found their swan.

But one day Solly was called to the telephone to speak to Miss Puss. "We must have a meeting at once," said she; "I have terrible news." When the executors had gathered a few nights later, she brought out this news with a great show of reluctance. She had it on good authority that Miss Hetmansen was not a virgin.

"Does it matter?" said Solly.

"Let us never forget that the Louisa Hansen Bridgetower Trust is the creation and memorial of a woman who stood for everything that was finest in Canadian life," said Miss Puss. "We are certainly not going to spend one cent of her money on a hussy."

"She's not a hussy," said Solly. "She's very nice. You said so yourself."

"Any girl of whom it is possible to say what I have just said, when she is a mere twenty years old, is a hussy," said Miss Puss. She then fixed the Dean with a bloodshot green eye, and continued, with menace. "And if this is brought to a vote, don't suppose that you men can overrule me. I'll take it to the courts for a decision, if need be. Perhaps you care nothing for these things, but I knew Louisa's mind as none of you ever did." She was ready for war. "If you are afraid to tell this girl that she is not acceptable, and why, I am quite ready to take that duty on myself."

But it was agreed that this would be unnecessary. Miss Hetmansen's letters and pictures were returned to her by mail, with a note saying that if she heard nothing further from the executors within seven days, it would mean that her application had been unsuccessful.

Miss Hetmansen was not a fool. She knew why she had been refused. She had succumbed to the importunities of her teacher coolly, and almost absent-mindedly, with a vague feeling that an affair might do something for her colour sense. Apparently all it had done was to lose her a lot of money, and make her teacher untrustworthy as a critic of her work. She did not really care. She had great faith in her talent and she would get to Paris anyway. She was not the gossipy sort, but she remarked to a few people that the Bridgetower Trust, as it had now begun to be called, was primarily a good conduct prize, and strictly for amateurs.

And thus the trustees were left without a candidate, and it was June.

(3)

A SUPERSTITIOUS BELIEF persists in Canada that nothing of import-ance can be done in the summer. The sun, which exacts the utter-most from Nature, seems to have a numbing effect upon the works of man. Thus Matthew Snelgrove, while assuring Solly that he was going ahead at full speed in settling Mrs. Bridge-tower's estate, went to his office later in the morning, and left it earlier in the afternoon, and was quite unavailable at night. Dur-ing the whole of August he went with his wife to visit her girl-hood home in Nova Scotia, where he gave himself up to disap-proving contemplation of the sadly unruly behaviour of the sea. Miss Puss Pottinger, according to her custom, went to Preston Springs for two weeks in June, to drink the waters and then, greatly refreshed, she went to a severely Anglican lakeside resort in Muskoka, and there hobnobbed with some Sisters of St. John who had a mission nearby. Solly and Veronica went on a leisurely, cheap motor trip, hoping that a change of air might hasten the conception which had, so far, eluded them. They needed a holiday from the obtrusive benevolence of their cook Ethel, who had stayed with them at a reduced salary, and never allowed them for a moment to forget it; they were learning that a faithful family retainer is a two-edged sword. The Dean went to his summer cottage, removed his clerical collar and settled himself to fish by day and read detective stories by night. They were all glad to forget about the Bridgetower Trust.

But early in September Solly woke up one morning with a painful sense that only three months remained in which to make a choice. "We must get to work at once," said he to Veronica.

"Is there really such a hurry?" said she. Their holiday had greatly improved her health, and she looked dark, beautiful and serious as she lay by him in the large, old-fashioned bed. "Would a few months make such a difference?"

"The will says, 'Within a calendar year of the date of my death'. Nobody would object if we stretched it a little, I suppose, but I am determined that it shall be carried out to the letter. Besides, I want to make old Snelgrove jump. He has a very poor opinion of me, and so has Puss. I'll show them. We'll send an accordion-player or a soap sculptor abroad to study, if need be, but we'll do it in the prescribed way and in the prescribed time."

"You've become very determined."

"I have indeed."

(4)

"IF YOU'RE ABSOLUTELY STUCK for somebody to squander your Mum's money on, why don't you have a look at Monny Gall?" said Cobbler to Solly. It would be wrong to say that Solly had confided the growing embarrassment of the Trustees to his friend; Cobbler had been insatiably curious about everything connected with the Bridgetower Trust since he heard of it on Christmas Day, and he wormed information out of Solly and Veronica at every opportunity. It fascinated him, he explained, to think of so much lovely money looking for somebody to spend it.

"Who's Monny Gall?"

"If you ever listened to your local radio station you would know. She is the soprano of the Heart and Hope Gospel Quartet, who broadcast on behalf of the Thirteenth Apostle Tabernacle five mornings of the week, from nine-thirty to nine forty-five. I breakfast a bit later than you proletarians, and I never miss the H. & H."

"Do you mean that it is good?"

"It is very good in its way. That's to say, it primes the pump of sweet self-pity, mingled with tremulous self-reproach and a strong sense of never having had a square deal from life, which passes for religion with a lot of people—housewives mostly. It is run by an unctuous gorilla who calls himself Pastor Sidney Beamis; he dishes out the Hope in a short, moderately disgusting prayer in which he tells God that we're all pretty awful but that the Thirteenth Apostles are having a bash at sainthood. The Heart is supplied by the Quartet, which is composed of his own family and Monny Gall. Pastor Beamis supplies a hollow, gutty bass; his son Wesley weighs in with a capon tenor—all head-voice and tremolo; Ma Beamis has a contralto tone like a cow mooing in a railway tunnel; and Monny Gall has a very nice soprano indeed—sweet, pure, and very naturally produced. You should hear them in *Eden Must Have Been Like Granny's Garden*, or *Ten Baby Fingers and Ten Baby Toes, That Was My Mother's Rosary.*"

"It sounds perfectly filthy."

"It is. It fills me with perverse glee. But Monny is worth re-deeming from this musical hell. She has positively the most promising voice I have ever heard in an untrained singer."

"Then what is she doing with the H. & H.?"

"Why shouldn't she be with it? Her Ma, who is an extremely formidable old party, is a pillar of the Thirteenth Apostle Taber-nacle. She tells Monny to sing for Beamis, and Monny sings. For nothing, what's more. For the greater glory of Beamis."

"But if she's musical, why does she sing *Granny's Toes*, and so forth?"

"I didn't say she was musical; I said she had a lovely voice. You make the common error of assuming that singers are necessarily musicians. There are people, my dear Bridgetower, who sing because God has made them singers; very often they have no taste at all; they will sing anything, so long as they can open their mouths and give. That's Monny. Caught young, and taught well, I don't know what she mightn't rise to."

"You appear to be greatly interested in her."

"I am."

"Is she pretty, as well as stupid?"

"Bridgetower, you wound me! She isn't pretty and she isn't plain; she's just a girl. But she has an unusual voice, which Beamis is wrecking. You ought to remember her; she's the girl who sang *My Task* at your Mum's funeral."

"I don't remember anything about her."

"I do," said Veronica, who usually kept silent while Solly and Cobbler carried on their long, wandering, often quarrelsome conversations. "I thought it was a lovely voice. Sweet and pure and rather remote."

"Exactly. Monny can take a lot of the sting out of *My Task*. It's sheer gift; she hasn't any ideas about it. But something in her voice suggests beauty, and calm, and even reason, when what she is singing is unalloyed boloney."

"She hasn't put in an application for the Trust."

"Don't suppose the notion ever occurred to her. She's no climber. Her Ma keeps her down."

"Are you suggesting that we should write her to consider it? Snelgrove would have a fit!"

"Yes, and if it were thought that I had brought her name up, old Puss would have a fit. She hates me with the one pure passion of her life; she's always trying to get my job away from me. I'm not her notion of a Cathedral organist. But I could get hold of Monny and ask her to put in a bid, if you like."

"We've got to find somebody, and I don't give a damn who it is."

"Oh come, Bridgetower; you are speaking of money; don't be bitter."

"Why shouldn't I be bitter? I'm not greedy, God knows, but I'm human. The income on more than a million dollars, that might have been mine, is to be spent on a stranger. If my mother had left no money at all, I wouldn't have cared. If she had left the bulk of it to a charity, I wouldn't have cared. But she left it as she did to hurt me, and to register a final protest against my marriage. God, you'd think Veronica was a leper, and not just the daughter of a man she and Father quarreled with twenty years ago. She has done everything that a will can do to humiliate and hurt me. I'm convinced she left me that hundred dollars simply to make the will hard to break. It would serve her right if her money did go to some wretched gospel-howler. If it outraged her cankered old soul in its smug Anglican heaven I'd be glad of it!"

"Oh Solly darling, you'll only make yourself ill," said Veronica.

"Let him have it out," said Cobbler. "Choking back hatred and hurt feelings causes ulcers, high blood-pressure and arthritis. Fact. All the medical books say so. Better get it out in words. It's the inarticulate people, who can't rail against fate, who get nasty diseases. Have a good rage, Bridgetower. Would you care to hit somebody? You may hit me one moderate blow if it would really help. Pretend I'm your late Mum."

"Don't joke about it," said Solly. "Don't you realize we've got to maintain this bloody great house on my cottage salary? That old Ethel hangs over us and pities us and bullies us because we're poor, and makes a favour of staying here when we'd a thousand times rather she went somewhere else. Just try to teach an extravagant old cook something about economy, if you want to break your heart! And people keep writing to us for money; they think this damned Bridgetower Trust is a grab-bag for every kind of good cause. If we say the Trust can't give, they ask us for something personally. What have we got to give? The estate pays the taxes on this house, but apparently the estate has no obligation to pay its running expenses without a special meeting of trustees. So last week I had to beg the Dean and old Puss for enough money to get the downstairs drain unplugged, and it took an hour and a half of humming and hawing, and suggestions about trying Draino, to get it. I face a future of that kind of thing. A happy prospect, isn't it?"

"As Molly said, it's the Dead Hand," said Cobbler.

"Dead Hand!" Solly thumped the table. "It's the live hand,

too. This house is part of a trust. During the summer Veronica put away some trinkets and odds and bobs that used to clutter up the mantelpieces. Last week old Puss came in, missed them at once, and insisted that they be put back. And when we boggled at it, she got Snelgrove to phone and say that, legally, we must maintain the house precisely as the Trust received it. Isn't that a sweet situation? She hinted that we ought to put away the Rockingham, but I'm going to use it every day, to spite her. I'll feed the cat off it; that's my right, and I'll do it."

"Your late Mum was really a corker," said Cobbler. "Most people want to ensure that everything they leave will remain untouched, but she has actually found a way to do it. Of course she was singularly fortunate in having an old poison-pot like Puss for a best friend."

"Well, you see how it is," said Solly. "I'm completely tied, and Veronica is put in a most humiliating position. What can we do? The only possible thing is to maintain what dignity we can, and insist that the terms of the will be kept as strictly for everyone else as they are for us. Therefore I insist that somebody be chosen and sent abroad by the Trust within the allotted time, and I do not give a damn who it is or what they are studying, or what rage, despair and misery comes of it. What Mother began, I shall finish, and nothing will come in my way."

"All right," said Cobbler; "I'll talk to Monny Gall."

(5)

IT WAS WELL into October before Monica Gall met the executors. She had, prompted by Cobbler, written a letter of application, in which she said simply that she liked singing, and wanted to learn more about it, and mentioned her connection with the Heart and Hope Quartet as evidence that she was serious, and had sung publicly. She gave the name of Pastor Sidney Beamis as a reference.

Miss Puss Pottinger was inclined to dismiss her application on the first reading. Miss Pottinger knew nothing of Pastor Beamis, and had never set foot in the Thirteenth Apostle Tabernacle, but she had a powerful contempt for what she called "back-street religion". This condemnation was superficially unjust, for the Tabernacle was in a disused shop on a business street. But it was to the back streets of the religious life that Miss Puss referred; in her Father's house were many mansions, but some of them were in better parts of the Holy City than others; the Thirteenth Apostle Tabernacle obviously belonged in the slums of the spirit.

The Very Reverend Jevon Knapp also disapproved of Monica's sponsorship, but he knew much more about it. He had an eighteenth century distaste for Enthusiasm in religion, which he was prepared to defend on theological and philosophical grounds. He disliked the untidy beliefs of the Thirteeners, as they were often called. This sect had been founded in the U.S.A. by one Myron Coffey, an advertising salesman who found himself, in 1919, forty-five years old and not doing well in the world. It was in that same year that Mr. Henry Ford, speaking in a witness box in Chicago, made his great declaration that "History is bunk." These apocalyptic words struck fire in Coffey. History was indeed bunk; the seeming division of history into years and eras was an illusion; the whole world of the senses was an illusion, obviously created by the Devil. All mankind of whom any record existed, were in fact coevals in the realm of the spirit, which was the only real realm. Christ, Moses, Jeremiah—they were all right here, living and breathing beside us, if we could just "make contact". That could be done by prayer, searching the Scriptures, and leading a good life; Coffey explained the good life in terms of what he believed his mother's life to have been—unstinting service to others, simple piety, mistrust of pleasure, and no truck with thought or education beyond what was necessary to read the Good Book. All these wonders came to Coffey in a single week, culminating in a revelation that he was the Thirteenth Apostle, destined to spread the good news to mankind. And that

news was that the New Jerusalem was right here, if only enough
poor souls could "make contact". God was here: Christ was now.
He fought down any last feeling that perhaps it was Mr. Ford
who was really the Thirteenth Apostle, and set to work. Thirty-
odd years later, in two or three hundred cities in the U.S.A. and
Canada, a few thousand Thirteeners continued his mission.

Dean Knapp knew all this, and thought poorly of it. He also
had a poor opinion of the Thirteeners' local shepherd, Pastor
Beamis. The Dean had met him, and thought him an ignoramus,
and possibly a rogue, as well. He was professionally obliged to
think as well of everybody as possible, but he confided to Mrs.
Knapp that Scripture came to his aid in the matter of Beamis;
did not *Leviticus* xxi 18 expressly forbid the priesthood to "he
that hath a flat nose"? And had not Beamis the flat, bun-like,
many times broken nose of the ex-pugilist? Mrs. Knapp warned
him not to speak such frivolities in the hearing of those who
might not understand; the Dean's passion for Biblical jokes had
put him in hot water many times. But she knew very well what
her husband meant; there was about Beamis a hairiness, a clumsiness, a physically unseemly quality which sat ill upon a spiritual leader. The Jews of the Old Testament had done wisely to
forbid the priesthood to grotesques.

It gave Solly much satisfaction to override Miss Puss and the
Dean. Monica Gall should not be passed over because she belonged to a sect for which they felt a Pharisaical distaste, said he,
and thereby gave offence to the Dean, who was not accustomed
to be called a Pharisee by young men of twenty-seven. He had to
swallow it, and after a good deal of haggling it was decided that
Monica should be interviewed.

But should they not have some expert advice, asked the Dean.
They had sought counsel outside their own group about Miss
Hetmansen's work; could they judge a singer unaided? By a
little juggling Solly was able to lead the Dean into proposing
Humphrey Cobbler as advisor to the Trustees in matters of
music; Miss Puss did not like it, but she did not oppose the Dean

as she would have opposed Solly in such a suggestion. She contented herself with saying that Cobbler was probably a capable musician, though a detestable man.

Thus it was that on a Thursday night in mid-October the executors and their solicitor gathered in the drawing-room of the Bridgetower house, and there received Mr. and Mrs. Alfred Gall, their daughter, Monica, and Pastor Sidney Beamis.

Pastor Beamis had not been invited, but he was the first to stride into the room.

"Well, well, good evening Reverend Knapp," he cried, seizing the Dean's hand in his clammy, pulpy paws; "this is certainly a wonderful thing you fine folks are proposing to do for our little girl. Yes, and considering you're all Church of England people it shows a degree of inter-faith fellowship which is more than warming—more than warming. Now I know you weren't expecting me, and I'm not going to butt in, but because I have watched Monny grow, so to speak, from a gawky kid into a lovely girl, and because I think I may say that it has been my privilege, under God, to humbly have coaxed along her talent, I just couldn't stay away. I just had to be here." He dropped his voice, and whispered to Knapp in a priest-to-priest tone—"Family aren't much in the way of talkers; thought I might be able to steer 'em a little." He gave the Dean an understanding leer, and patted him on the back. The Dean reclaimed his hand and wiped it on his handkerchief.

Pastor Beamis was so striking a figure that he temporarily obscured the Galls. He wore the full regimentals of a Thirteener shaman. His suit was of gray flannel, much in need of pressing; he had on a wing collar, and a clergyman's stock, which was of a shrill paddy green; the ensemble was completed by a pair of scuffed sports shoes in brown and white, above which could be seen socks in Argyll design. Inside these garments was a body which had won him the name of Chimp during his days in the ring; his face was large, baggy and bore blatant signals of hope, cheer and unremitting forgiveness.

The Galls, thought Solly, might have posed for a picture of Mr. and Mrs. Jack Sprat. Alfred Gall was thin to the point of being cadaverous, stooped, pale and insignificant. His wife was covered with that loose, liquid fat which seems to sway and slither beneath the skin, and she, because she wore too tight a corset, wheezed whenever she made the slightest effort. She had a look of nervous good-nature, and every few minutes she eased her false teeth, which seemed to pain her; indeed, as the evening wore on she began to suck air audibly, as though her dentures were hot.

Monica, as Cobbler had said, was neither pretty nor plain, though she was of a trim figure. She was plainly dressed, as became a Thirteener, and it was apparent to the X-ray eye of Miss Puss that the disqualification which had brought about the fall of Birgitta Hetmansen did not apply here.

Conversation proceeded uneasily. It was necessary, first of all, to make it clear to Pastor Beamis that Monica had not been summoned to receive a large sum of money. This task fell to Snelgrove, who found it congenial. It was then explained to the Galls how the Trust was expected to work.

"If your daughter should become the beneficiary, it would give her a most unusual opportunity to pursue her musical studies," said the Dean.

"Yeah, I see," said Mrs. Gall, and fidgeted with the handle of her purse, sucking air painfully. "It'd take her away from home, though." She had chosen to sit on a low sofa, and appeared to be suffering discomfort from her corset, which had visibly ridden upward.

"Never had much of a chance m'self," said Alfred Gall. "Workin' since I was sixteen. Never known much else but work, I guess." He laughed a short hollow laugh, like a man making light of an incurable disease.

Pastor Beamis was right; the Galls were not great talkers. Nor, it was soon clear, were they among those who eagerly embrace good fortune. They thought it might be nice if their daughter had a chance to study music abroad, but in the depths of their hearts it was a matter of indifference to them. The Pastor supplied all the enthusiasm. He talked a great deal about the opportunities a singer enjoyed to do the Lord's work, by uplifting people and turning their minds to the finer things of life; in his own work he had been able to observe the splendid harvest of souls which could be reaped through the Ministry of Music. He pleaded eloquently with the Galls not to deny their daughter the chance that was being offered to her to be a force for good in the world. It was at this point that Solly thought it necessary to correct the balance of power.

"We haven't made up our minds about Miss Gall, you know," said he. "We have considered her application carefully, and this interview is merely to find out more about her. None of us has heard her sing; she may not be the person we are looking for at all."

"You haven't heard her on the Heart and Hope?" said Beamis. He was very merry about this. "You folks must be late risers. Certainly is nice to be some people! Our little program enjoys a very high rating locally, you know. And of course we tape it and broadcast it from seven other stations, beside the local one. It's by far the biggest religious independent in the province—barring metropolitan city broadcasts, of course. Monny's voice is known— and loved, as I can show letters to prove—by close to twenty thousand daily listeners."

"What is she paid for that work?" asked Miss Puss.

"The Heart and Hope is not a paid quartet. We merely announce that we are unpaid on the air, and freewill offerings come in by every mail. Silver coins—O, it would touch your heart, some of them—and dollar bills and quite a few fives and tens. The law forbids us to ask for money on the air, but it comes, all the same. And every cent goes into the Tabernacle treasury."

"You are the treasurer?" said the Dean, who could not resist it.

"I take care of the financial end, and of course the books are open to inspection by any of our members, any time they choose to see them." Pastor Beamis fixed the Dean with a grimace in which brotherly love, transparent honesty and sorrow were mingled.

"You have some other work, then?" said Solly to Monica.

"She's a clerk at the plant where her Dad works," said Beamis. "In the Costing Department. Monny did very well in Commercial at High. But you're wrong when you say you haven't heard Monny; she sang at your dear Mother's funeral. A lovely little Classic—*My Task*—sweet thing. And did you realize that Monny had never seen or heard of it until eighteen hours before she went on the air—sorry, before the sad occasion? Mr. Cobbler brought it to her the night before; she ran through it a coupla times with him; sang it perfectly at three the next afternoon. Monny's quite a little trouper. Get up anything at short notice and turn in a fine performance. Not many singers can do that. You've heard her, and you didn't even notice!" Pastor Beamis laughed chidingly.

"Our attention was elsewhere," said Miss Puss, and the Pastor's rubber face immediately assumed an expression of understanding and condolence; but he was not abashed, which was what she had hoped for.

"I think we should hear Miss Gall now," said Solly. "I'll ask Mr. Cobbler to come in."

(6)

"WELL?" SAID SOLLY to the executors, when at last Beamis had herded his charges out of the house and disappeared, still talking, down the walk. "What did you think of her?"

"There is no question in my mind that she is a very nice girl," said the Dean. "It seemed to me that she handled herself modestly and with dignity in a difficult situation. But whether she is the girl we are looking for is very much an open question. I'm not impressed by her parents, or by that man, who seems to be a dominating influence in her life—if I may make such a remark without being accused of Phariseeism," he added, cocking an eye at Solly.

"I suppose it's ability, rather than character, that we're looking for," said Solly, avoiding the glance and looking at Snelgrove.

"Are they ever found apart?" said the lawyer.

"Very often, in the arts, I believe. Are we going to hold it against the girl that her parents are stupid and dominated by a quack evangelist? I thought she seemed intelligent and pleasant. If she can really profit by the kind of training we are able to give her—I should say, that we can pay for—isn't that the main thing?"

"Unless you believe that the girl is a genius, and so beyond the usual rules of probability, you must certainly take these other things into account," said the Dean. "You can educate her beyond her parents, and make her into something that they might not recognize, but you will not really raise her very far. You can polish and mount a pebble, but it remains a pebble. I do not blame the girl, of whom I know no more than the rest of you, but it is plain that she is being exploited by that creature Beamis; she sings in his quartet, which consists otherwise of his own family, and which I happen to know coins money. If she were a person of real character—more character than her parents, for instance —would she put up with that?"

"She's only twenty, Mr. Dean," said Solly, "and, saving your reverence, it is not easy for a very young person to rebel against a clergyman who has full parental support. It seems to me that her voice is the real clue to the problem. What did you think of it?"

"I really can't say," said the Dean. "I was so embarrassed by the things she sang. I don't pretend to a deeply informed taste in music, but really—!"

"I can't quite agree," said Miss Puss, who had sat in uncharacteristic silence since the Galls left. "I was greatly moved by her singing of Tosti's *Good-Bye!*—a song I have not heard in many,

many years. I suppose I am the only person here who recalls that it was the favourite ballad of Queen Victoria. Unfashionable now, possibly, but truly touching. Once, many years ago, I heard Melba sing it. And, do you know, this girl reminded me uncannily of Melba? Did you feel that?"

She had turned to Snelgrove. He had never heard Melba, but he knew she had been intensely patriotic during the First Great War, and was therefore an artist of the highest rank, so he frowned in a critical fashion and replied, "Not quite Melba, perhaps, but I felt there was a smack of Clara Butt."

This remark set Miss Puss and the lawyer off in a competition of recalling all the great singers they had heard, and as neither had wide experience this quickly became all the great singers they had heard of, whose names they brought up with apparent casualness; they did not say they had heard these queens of song, but they were not unwilling that others should think so; in charity it may be assumed that they had heard them on the gramophone. The names of Emma Eames, Amelita Galli-Curci, Geraldine Farrar, Louise Homer, Luisa Tetrazzini and Ernestine Schumann-Heink were used very freely, and startling comparisons drawn, without much regard for whether these ladies had been sopranos or contraltos. This cultivated pow-wow did much to raise the spirits of Miss Puss and Mr. Snelgrove, and to give them, for the first time, a sense that they were patrons of art and fountains of culture. When the lawyer had scored heavily by dragging in "our great Canadian diva, Madame Albani, whom I was once lucky enough to hear in Montreal" Solly thought that this had gone far enough.

"Perhaps we should return to the present day and hear what the one expert among us thinks of Monica Gall's voice," said he. Cobbler, who had remained at the piano, dug vigorously into his hair with his fingers, until it stood on end like the wool of a Hottentot. Then he fixed the executors with his bright black eyes.

"Nice voice," said he. "Nice tone; well-placed, really, considering that she's had no training at all. But that's the trouble, you see: maybe we've heard all there is. Maybe nothing further would come, however much you trained it. Oh, that's not quite fair; it would be bound to develop a little bit, but who can say how much? Promising, probably. But how can you tell? We didn't really hear enough."

"Then why did you not ask to hear more?" said Snelgrove. He liked an expert to behave like an expert, and not temporize.

"We could have listened to her for another hour without learning anything more than we did. Her music was terrible. I knew how things stood as soon as she opened her portfolio; it was jam-packed with that awful cheap music printed on gray paper. All tripe. *Good-Bye!* was her star piece; I suppose Beamis thinks it's a classic. So it is, in the musical hell he and the Heart and Hope Quartet inhabit. To find out what her voice is really like, you'd have to work with her for a few months—increase her range, give her something to sing that would show what she could do, and generally explore the possibilities."

"That's not very helpful," said Miss Puss.

"I'm afraid it isn't. But it's honest. There's one thing to be said in the girl's favour. She's stood out against some very bad musical influences; her only teacher, I understand, is an aunt who plays the piano a little. And the Beamis association is abominable; couldn't imagine anything more calculated to wreck a voice and debauch a singer's taste. Yet, the fact is that the girl sings with a good deal of taste and a nice feeling for the words, considering the stuff she's singing. It must be native to her, though where she gets it I can't imagine. You're dead right, Miss Pottinger; she really did tear off old *Good-Bye!* with quite a sense of style, and it's not the easiest song in the world. There may be something there, if you want to dig for it."

"We haven't any time for digging," said Solly. "We're desperate; the income on something like a million dollars has to be spent on somebody, beginning not later than next December 23. Can't we get some clearer opinion than what you've said?"

"Not from me," said Cobbler. "I can't square a flat Yes or No with my professional honesty; if I say she's no good I may be wronging you and the girl, and if I say she's a wonder the odds are just as strong that I am wrong. Certainly, if it were a question of some lessons with me, I'd say go ahead. I'd be happy to get such a pupil. But you are going to spend such a lot of money; you've got to show big results or look silly. If you want another opinion, I know where you can get one."

"Yes?"

"Next month Sir Benedict Domdaniel is conducting two concerts in Toronto, on his way back from Australia and the States. He'll be there for ten days or so, rehearsing. If you like, I'll write to his agent and ask if he'll hear the girl, and give you his word on her."

The effect of this was an even greater tonic to Miss Puss and Snelgrove than the mention of Melba had been. This was culture indeed—to enlist the opinion of one of the greatest conductors in the world who was also—this weighed heavily—a British knight! Why were they trifling with a cathedral organist when such distinction lay within their grasp? Condescendingly, as people used to hob-nobbing with gifted knights, they asked Cobbler to make the necessary arrangements, and of course to enquire, tactfully, what Sir Benedict's fee would be for such an interview.

It had not occurred to them to offer Cobbler any fee whatever.

(7)

THE PATTERN UPON WHICH the Bridgetower Trust was to operate had already established itself before the Trust was officially in being—for Snelgrove made it very clear that until the probate of Mrs. Bridgetower's will the Trust had no funds, and a trust without funds was a mockery. The pattern was a simple one: nothing could be done without prolonged discussion, in which Miss Puss and Solly were certain to be opposed, with the Dean trying to keep peace and advocate common sense, and Snelgrove making all the trouble possible to an expert who has great influence but no vote. The seemingly simple matter of getting Monica Gall away to Toronto for an interview with Sir Benedict Domdaniel became, in their hands, an elaborate and vexatious manoeuvre.

The Dean thought that the Trust should pay her fare on the train, but need not necessarily pay for her meals while she was absent. Snelgrove said that as the Trust had no funds, it could not pay for anything. Solly pointed out that the Trust had already spent money, which Snelgrove's firm had advanced, on repairing drains in the Bridgetower house. Snelgrove countered by saying that he could justify such an expenditure before a court, but he could not justify spending any money on a candidate for the Trust's bounty who might prove, in the end, to be unsuccessful. Miss Puss felt that it was undesirable to encourage Monica to hope for success by paying her fare, but that the Trust ought to pay the fare of an older woman who would accompany her to Toronto, as a chaperone. The Trust would be in a very bad position, she pointed out, if any harm befell Monica while she was on a journey to a large city, undertaken at the request of the Trust. She was herself prepared to go with the girl, and to remain with her during her interview with the great man; Monica had shown herself to be a poor talker, and somebody who was not awed by greatness should certainly be on hand to see that her chances were not spoiled by sheer social ineptitude. Solly, out of spite, agreed, but said that if anybody went with Monica it should certainly be an accompanist, and recommended Cobbler for that task; his wife, Veronica, would be prepared to drive the two of them to Toronto in their car, and serve as moral watchdog; the Trust could defray the expenses of the motor trip and still be money ahead. It took an evening of wrangling to reach a deadlock on this question.

Another evening was consumed in haggling about Sir Benedict Domdaniel's fee. His agent had written to Cobbler saying that the great man could see Miss Gall, and would send a written opinion to the Trust, and that his charge for an audition would be two hundred and fifty dollars. Miss Puss was outraged, and spoke to Cobbler as though he himself had demanded this shocking sum; he replied, with spirit, that men like Domdaniel asked big fees for auditions simply in order that they should not be plagued by people who were not serious; he added some ill-considered words about amateurs, which gave deep offense. Snelgrove refused utterly to advance money for such a purpose. And so, after a very long and heated argument, it was decided that if Monica Gall herself could raise Domdaniel's fee, and her own journey-money, she could risk it on her chances. The Trust asked Cobbler to put this proposal to her, and he refused flatly to do it, adding with heat that if the Trust meant to be cheap, he was not going to be the goat for them. In the end, Snelgrove was instructed to offer her this unique opportunity to invest in her own future, by letter.

The Trust was somewhat astonished to receive a reply, by return of post, in which Monica said that she would be glad to pay her own expenses, and thanked them for the chance. It was a very good letter, typed and expressed in the dry language of business, and it made Solly and the Dean, at least, feel that Monica had not revealed the best side of herself at the earlier interview.

(8)

THE DATE OF Monica's meeting with Sir Benedict Domdaniel was set for November the first. On the fifth of the month Cobbler received the following letter, which he read aloud that evening to the assembled Trust.

Dear Humphrey Cobbler:
It was good to hear from you again. I recall with pleasure working with you during the Three Choirs Festival of 1937, and I hope that all goes well with you here.
Now, about your protégée, Miss Monica Gall. I had meant

to give her an hour, at most, but as she has probably told you, we worked for nearly three. It took quite a time to get at her, for somebody—I believe she said one of the lady members of your Trust—had filled her full of nonsense about how to behave herself with me. She began by singing the two Handel songs you had hastily primed her with, but they told very little, as you can imagine. Then she sang Tosti's *Good-Bye!* which I had honestly never expected to hear sung seriously again on this earth, and did quite well with it. I asked her if she knew *The Lost Chord*, meaning to be facetious, and she shamed me by pulling a tattered copy out of her satchel and singing it quite seriously and nicely. Then she sang a lot of trash which is apparently in her wireless repertoire.

After this we had a talk, and I was strongly impressed by her sincerity, and absolute simplicity: She tells me she sings because she always has done so, and likes it, but it had never occurred to her to make a career of it. We were quite matey by this time, and she told me a good deal about her home, and her work, and then I took off my coat and she took off her shoes, which were much too tight, and we did some scales and exercises, and I found that with a bit of encouragement she has roughly twice the voice she has been using, with lots more to come.

What surprised me most was that she plays the piano well—facility and quite nice natural taste—but terrible stuff. It seems an aunt taught her. She played what she called *Dance, Micawber*, and instead of being a Dickensian medley by some lesser Percy Granger it was Saint-Saens' *Danse Macabre*. When I mentioned Bach she looked prim, and I gather there is some queer religion behind her, for whom the classics of church music spell Popery or Pride. I think this is the clue to the girl; a real natural talent has been overlaid by a stultifying home atmosphere and cultural malnutrition.

In my opinion she is well worth any encouragement your Trust or whatever it is can give her. The voice is good—quite good enough to be worth proper training—though as you know it takes a year or eighteen months of work before the real nature of a voice emerges, and any serious predictions about a career can be made. But if this girl is not a singer of exceptional quality, she is certainly a musician; she has done a great deal under what appear to be extremely unfavourable conditions. I repeat, the great thing that seems to be wrong with her, considered as a possible artist, is that she has lived for twenty years in circumstances which are not discouraging to art—we see plenty of that—but in which art in any of its forms is not even guessed at. I discount, you understand, all this pseudo-religious twaddle she has been exposed to—music in the service of cant. She seems to have come through that so far without any irreparable harm. But she really doesn't know a damned thing.

If you can get her three or four years of training, or anything approaching it, do so by all means. If she is coming to England send her to me; I will be glad to give any advice or supervision I can.

You finally *did* marry that beautiful mezzo from Presteigne, did you not? Molly Ellis? I have the warmest recollections of her in *Gerontius*. Give her my best wishes.

Yours very sincerely,
BENEDICT DOMDANIEL

"Thank God," said Solly when the letter was finished; "that seems to settle that. We've found our phoenix."

Three

MONICA PUT OFF inviting George Medwall to her farewell party until the day before it was to take place. In this, as in so many other things in life, she was trying to eat her cake and have it too. To eat it, by inviting the young man whom she liked best among those she knew: to have it, by pretending that she might, after all, not ask him, thus being fully loyal to Ma and the Thirteeners. No wonder, then, that the cake stuck in her throat and that when she came at last to invite him she did so in an off-hand and almost cold fashion.

George did not seem to mind. He was a realist, and he knew that a party dominated by Ma Gall and composed chiefly of young Thirteeners would have nothing to attract him but Monny herself. Monny attracted him powerfully. They were both employed by Consolidated Adhesives and Abrasives, the biggest industry in Salterton, and still called, by those who remembered its humble nineteenth century beginnings, the Glue Works. George was a foreman with a department of his own, and Monica was a clerk in the costing department; they worked in separate buildings, a quarter of a mile apart, but he contrived to catch sight of her, if not actually to speak to her, every day. If Monica was to leave Salterton for several years, George meant to see her whenever he could, under whatever circumstances.

She approached him in the cafeteria, when they had both finished lunch.

"Sure I'll be there," said George. "We've still got fifteen minutes before one. Let's go for a walk."

Bundled up against the sharp December weather, and under an iron sky, they walked up and down beside the blank wall of a large building in which the boiling-vats were housed. It was not precisely a lovers' lane, but they were together.

"I'm sorry to give you such short notice," said Monica, who was ashamed of the way in which her invitation had been phrased.

"That's okay," said George. "I guess it wasn't very easy for you to ask me at all."

"Well—you know how it is."

"Sure. Don't think it worries me. But I'm certainly glad you're getting away from all that, Monny."

"What do you mean by 'all that'?"

"You know. Beamis, and the Heart and Hope. All that stuff."

"They've been very good to me. I wouldn't have had this chance if I'd never been heard on that program."

"I know. But you're moving up into a bigger league, now. And about time. You've got a chance for some first-class training. It'll make a big difference."

"It's not going to turn me against people who have been good to me, if that's what you mean."

"Nothing would do that, Monny. You're not that kind. But you see what I mean, don't you? You'll be a long way off, and on your own. Not such a strong home influence; not so much religion. A bigger world altogether."

"Oh, is that it? My home influence doesn't quite come up to your standards, is that it?"

"Now, Monny, don't take me up wrong. I never said a word against your home. But you know—it'll be different."

"You'd better not say anything against my home."

"No, no; I was just trying to be realistic about what's happened."

"Oh, realistic! You always want to be realistic; it's your favourite word."

"I guess so; I've tried to be realistic about my own life. It only makes sense."

"I know. And it's made you the youngest foreman in the plant. But not the best liked, if you care to know."

"I can't help that."

"You could if you wanted to. But you hadn't been a foreman six weeks before you came down like a ton of bricks on senior men that were here long before anybody'd ever heard of you. Talked to them in a way they'll never forget or forgive. I suppose that was realistic."

"As it so happens, it was. But let's forget that; I don't want to talk about those old dead-beats now."

"They weren't dead-beats."

"Now Monny; it was before you ever came to the plant. How do you know?"

"Some of them were Dad's friends. That's how I know."

"Be reasonable. Can I run my department by letting fellows get away with murder, on the chance that they're friends of somebody in another department, who may have a daughter that I'll get to know some day? Why, I didn't even know your Dad then. And I won't pretend it would have made any difference, if I had."

"Oh? My Dad's an old dead-beat, too, I suppose?"

"Say, what are we fighting about, anyway?"

"We're not fighting. But I just can't stand the way you brush aside everybody that hasn't got ahead as fast as you have. They're human, too, you know. I know them, and Dad's one of them. They haven't all had your chances. Dad's been working since he was sixteen; work's all he's ever known—"

"Sure. He's told me about it."

"And just what do you mean by that?"

"That's your Dad's favourite routine. Work at sixteen. Work ever since. Never known anything but work. Excuses everything, I suppose."

"Excuses what, may I ask?"

"Oh, nothing. Forget it."

"No, I won't forget it. Come on, George. What does it excuse? You can't hint like that about my Dad and then just brush it off. —What are you laughing at?"

"I'm laughing at you, Monny. You know, you ought to make a fine singer. You've got the temperament."

"Meaning what?"

"You're what's called a romantic. You see everything in full Technicolor all the time. Feelings before facts, that's you. But it's time somebody knocked some sense into your head."

"Go on."

"You swallow all that stuff about your Dad. Fine. Every kid believes what his father tells him, and so he should, but there's got to be a day when he makes his own judgement. Your dad's okay, I guess; I don't know him very well. But the reason he's still pushing a broom here in the plant is simply because he can't do anything better. There's no disgrace in it. But let's not say it's because he's had a raw deal, eh? He's had the best deal he could get from life. Lots of fellows started even with him. One of them was Thurston, the plant manager—"

"Who climbed and clawed and lickspittled and backstabbed his way to the top. Your hero, I suppose. A realist."

"Now Monny, don't go in for that stuff about everybody who's a success being a bastard. That's for failures of sixty; not for kids of twenty."

"My Dad, George Medwall, is not a failure."

"Monny, you're crazy. I wasn't talking about your Dad. But I will, as you seem to have him on the brain. If your Dad and your Mother are your ideals in life, don't take this money they're offering you to go away and study; stay right where you are. You've got all you want in life; stick with it."

"You leave my family out of this! You talk like that awful old Miss Pottinger; you'd think she found me frozen to the bottom of a garbage can after a long winter. I'm proud of my family. Proud!"

"Sure; sure."

"And don't treat me like a fool. Don't take that soothing tone. You make me sick, with your superior ways. What have you got to be superior about?"

"Monny, this doesn't make any sense."

"Yes it does. Now let me tell you something, and don't ever forget it, George, because I mean every word. If there's one thing I hate in this world, it's ingratitude and disloyalty. And nothing, absolutely nothing, is going to make me disloyal and ungrateful. This sudden good luck isn't going to make a fool of me."

"Nothing could make a fool of you, Monny. But don't call it luck. People only get chances if they're ready for them. It's not luck. It's character."

"Loyalty's character, and so is decency. So don't talk realism to me if it just means being sniffy about my family and friends. I know them a lot better than you do. What makes you think you have a right to talk to me like this?"

Here was George's golden opening, but his realism did not extend far enough to reveal it to him. So he took it as a rebuke, and they walked the length of the boiler building in uneasy silence. George did not know what he should do, but he decided that it might help if he ate a small—a very small—portion of crow.

"I guess I've said too much. If you want to disinvite me to your party, Monny, go ahead."

"If my family gives you such a pain, perhaps that would be best," said Monica, hoping furiously that he would urge her to relent. But George had a terrible trick of believing that people always meant what they said. And at this unlucky moment, the one o'clock whistle blew.

"I guess I'd better say good-bye, then," said George; "since I'm not to see you tomorrow night."

"Good-bye, George," said Monica, giving him her hand; "and lots of luck."

And thus she parted from the only man whom she had ever been disposed to consider as a suitor. Though George was grieved, he did his afternoon's work with his accustomed thoroughness, but Monica spoiled several important sheets of figures, and if she had not been leaving anyway her boss would have spoken sharply to her.

(2)

At supper that night, Mrs. Gall asked Monica, "bolt outright" as she herself would have described it, whether George Medwall was to be expected at the farewell party. When Monica said that he would not be there, and let it be thought that she had decided not to ask him, Ma Gall expressed great satisfaction.

"Glad you come to your senses at last about that fella," said she. "Now you're going away is a good time to break off with him. I never had any time for him myself, and your Dad'll back me up on that."

"Foreman at twenty-eight," said Mr. Gall. "Gone up like the rocket; he'll come down like the stick."

They continued their discussion of George for some time, congratulating their daughter on her astuteness in having seen through him—a fellow who set himself up to give lip to men old enough to be his father, and one who, by accepting a foreman's job, had automatically removed himself from the jurisdiction of the union. Mr. Gall was a great partisan of the union, which was a very quiet and conservative affair at the C.A.&A., but which he liked to think of as a bulwark against unimaginable tyrannies. George, being outside the union, was certainly not to be trusted; he had lined himself up with the bosses. Mr. Gall knew all of these bosses personally, and was known by them, and on the human level, so to speak, he got on well with them and even liked them: but in another compartment of his mind they figured as faceless, bowelless, jackbooted tyrants, and he was pledged to thwart them in every possible way. George was on the wrong side of the fence.

For Mrs. Gall, George summed up what she most feared in a young man who might become a son-in-law. He was not a Thirteener; he was not even a church-goer and felt no shame about saying so. He did not drink, he saved his money, and he was civil; she gave him all that. But there was in him a quality of ambition which disquieted her; it prevented him from being what she called likable. Furthermore, it had been clear during his two or three brief visits to the house that he thought of her only as Monica's mother, and Mrs. Gall thought of herself very much as a Character, with a capital letter. It was as a Character that she liked to meet the world, and young people especially.

Monica had heard all that she could bear about George's shortcomings by the time supper was over, so she quickly washed the dishes—it was her night—and got out of the house, saying that she was going to Aunt Ellen's for a while. All the way there she reproached herself for having managed her talk with George so badly, and thought of clever defences of his character which she could have opposed to her parents' criticism—if she had dared. But it is never easy for children to defend their friends against disapproving parents.

Why had she flown out at George, turning everything he said to bitterness? It was not a lovers' quarrel, for she and George were certainly not lovers. He had never even kissed her, though once or twice it had been a near thing. If she had known it, George's realism was of the sort which says that a fellow does not kiss a girl unless he is serious about her; seriousness means an engagement, and he would not be engaged until he had enough money saved to marry; to kiss a girl to whom he could not offer marriage would be to trifle with her, not merely emotionally, but economically, and George's whole moral system was rooted in his conception of economics. But George and Monica worked upon each other as only lovers are supposed to do; she had more than once detected beneath his words a criticism of her family, and that she would not tolerate.

It was her old problem of wanting to have her cake and eat it.

She felt, and despised herself for feeling, critical of her father and mother, of her older sister Alice, of Pastor and Mrs. Beamis and their son, Wesley, of the whole Thirteener connection, for everything about them ran contrary to her great dream of life. While it had remained a dream, impossible of realization, she had been able to keep that criticism in its place. She had prayed for strength against it, and now and then her prayer seemed to be answered. But this Bridgetower Trust business had upset her whole life. It had suddenly brought the dream out of the realm of the utterly impossible into the realm of the remotely possible. That afternoon with Sir Benedict Domdaniel had been at once the most elevating and releasing experience of her life, and at the same time ruinous to the balance which she had established between dream and reality. Since then criticism of her family and her circumstances had raged within her, and when George had hinted at what was so tumultuously present in her mind she had been unable to keep her head. It was as though he had read her intolerable, inadmissable thoughts, and dared to share them.

She would get advice from Aunt Ellen. After all, Aunt Ellen was responsible for much that was wrong with her.

Aunt Ellen was not at home, and she let herself into the little stucco cottage with the key which Aunt Ellen had given her years ago, when she was twelve. The tiny living-room was as neat as such a cluttered room could be. Monica switched on the lamp with the shade of pleated rose silk, and went at once to the bookshelves, from which she took a large, worn volume, and settled herself on the sofa with it.

Aunt Ellen's house, to anyone less accustomed to it than Monica, spoke all that could be known about Miss Ellen Gall. She was Mr. Gall's older sister, and in her younger days had been considered a "high-flyer" by many who knew her. She had been a milliner, during the last era in which such work was done in individual shops, at Ogilvie's, which in those remote days had been an important "ladies' ready-to-wear" in Salterton. She still sold hats there, though she no longer made them; indeed, for many years she had been forelady of Ogilvie's hat department. From a pretty girl she had grown into a pretty woman, and latterly into a woman almost old, but still soft and pleasing, and very ready to smile. Her house, with all its odds and ends, was the house of a pretty woman.

But Ellen Gall had had a soul above hats, devoted to them as she was. She had played the piano with facility, and as the Galls had been Baptists before Mr. Gall and his wife took up with the Thirteeners, Ellen had found herself organist and leader of the choir at the smallest and least important of Salterton's Baptist churches. She had never fully mastered the instrument, and she still used the pedals sparingly and tentatively, but she had played the organ, almost every Sunday, for more than twenty-five years. What she played was the piano music which she thought suitable to solemn occasions, and with an occasional gentle kick at the tonic or the dominant in the pedals she managed to the complete satisfaction of the church, which did not, by the way, pay her anything for this service. She had, at various times, given lessons in playing the piano, at fifty cents for a half-hour. But of late, when people had taken up the fad of Conservatory examinations and did not care for the sweetly pretty drawing-room music she liked, she had had no new pupils.

There are great musicians in the world who do not live in rooms which speak so decisively of a life given to music as the living-room of Miss Ellen Gall. There was no picture which was not musical in theme. Over the piano hung a collotype of an extremely artistic girl with a birdsnest of dark hair, playing the 'cello to a rapt old man with a white beard; it was called *Träumerei*. Over the bookcase was a picture of Beethoven, much handsomer than life, conducting the Rasumovsky quartet with great spirit. A little plaster bust with a broken nose, said to be Mendelssohn, sat on top of the rosewood upright piano. And everywhere on the walls were little pictures of opera singers, cut out of magazines and framed.

There was only one picture without musical significance in the room, and that was of a middle-aged man, somewhat bald, wearing rimless pince-nez. He had been Miss Ellen's fiancé, a high school teacher, and a man of great cultivation, for he had once had a poem printed in *Saturday Night*. They had been engaged for many years, waiting for his mother to die; it was agreed between them that their marriage would be too great a blow for the old lady to sustain, and they had considerately spared her. But when, at last, she did die, the high school teacher took a chill a few weeks later, and himself died of consumption the following spring. He had made Miss Ellen his heir, and she had moved his books and all his furniture into her house. But he had made her a legacy of something much greater; he had left her with the consciousness of having been loved deeply and gratefully (if not very adventurously), and this romance had sweetened Miss Ellen's life as many a marriage has failed to do. In her crowded, fusty little house she lived with her own kind of music, and with memories which made up even for the obvious decline of Ogilvie's.

The book which Monica took down was *The Victor Book of the Opera*, which the gramophone company had produced in 1917 to demonstrate the wonders of opera to a public which knew little of that art form—and also to let it be known what recordings of opera were available. Most of the singers whose pictures appeared in it, with elaborate coiffures, or richly whiskered, were dead; the costumes in which they were represented might appear, to a modern taste, to be funny and unbecoming. But to Monica, as to Aunt Ellen, it was still the bible of a great art with which they had no direct connection, and at which they dimly guessed. They listened to the Saturday afternoon broadcasts from the Metropolitan, of course, but in the theatre of their minds it was these dead ones of the past who appeared—Nordica, Emma Eames, Scotti, Caruso, and the brothers de Reske; from the fruity voice which served as guide to the broadcasts they heard of new singers, and new costumes and settings, but these never had the reality of the pictures in the book. This was the key to a great, glorious, foreign world; but it was a key which unlocked, not the door, but a spy-hole in it. And now, breathtakingly, the Bridgetower Trust seemed to have opened the door itself.

It was very like—well, rather like—another book in Aunt Ellen's library, which she and Monica had both read with deep enjoyment more than once. This was *The First Violin*, by Jessie Fothergill; in it, a humble English girl with a lovely voice was engaged as companion to a wealthy old lady who took her to Germany to study; and there she had learned to sing from the magnetic—but daemonic and sardonic—von Francius, and had engaged in a long and sweetly agonizing romance with one Courvoisier, who was first violin in the orchestra, a man of mystery, and, in the end (for this was an English novel and such a dénouement was inevitable) had proved to be a German nobleman, disguised as a musician for reasons highly creditable to himself and shaming to everybody else. It all took place in the real Germany, of course, the Germany before the end of the century, when Germans were terribly musical and cultured and even more romantic than the French. Domdaniel would do very well as von Francius, though he was rather too affable for a genuinely daemonic genius, and showed quite ordinary braces when he took off his coat. And who was to be the First Violin; who was to be Courvoisier?

It was awful to admit the thought, but how would it be possible to bring Courvoisier home to meet Ma? In the book he seemed to be a Catholic; wasn't there some mention of a chapel in his ancestral Schloss? No Protestant would want a church right in the house. Ma would simply fly right off the handle at the thought of a Catholic; she might even greet Courvoisier by singing one of those Orange songs she remembered from her childhood—

Up the long ladder
And down the short rope;
Hurrah for King Billy,
To Aitch with the Pope!

Ma always sang "To Aitch," with an arch look, for a Thirteener would not use the word itself; but somehow that only made it worse. Ma and Pa were wonderful, of course. They had given her everything, except music. That had come entirely from Aunt Ellen. The Galls had never been able to afford a piano, though they had somehow afforded a succession of second-hand cars. But as Ellen had a piano, and obviously didn't need a car, what was the odds? If Monny wanted a piano, she could go to Ellen's. She owed everything to Ma and Pa, and if only the Bridgetower Trust had not suddenly disorganized her life she need never have faced the problem of confronting them with Courvoisier, and Courvoisier with them. But now this problem, and everything that went with it, possessed her, and made her quarrel with George, who was the only thing even remotely like Courvoisier on the horizon.

Girls in novels never seemed to have parents except when they were of some use in the plot, and then they were either picturesque or funny. The Galls, were neither; they were oppressively real and many-faceted. The girl in *The First Violin* was a vicar's daughter, which was considered very humble by the other people in the book, but was not nearly so humble as being the daughter of one of the maintenance staff at the Glue Works. The only creature remotely like a vicar whom Monica had met was Dean Knapp, to whom she had taken an unreasonable dislike—not because of anything he had done or said, but because Miss Pottinger had hissed at her that she must address him as "Mr. Dean" and not, as she had supposed proper, as "Reverend Knapp". A vicar's daughter would have known that. And the vicar and his wife in the novel had had the good sense to keep out of the story.

Pondering on *The First Violin*, Monica hunted up the book, which she had not read for two or three years. What a *very* musical book it was! The chapters were headed, not with bits of poetry as in Francis Marion Crawford, many of whose works she had read in the set which had belonged to the dead high school teacher, but with quotations of music. She had played them all, but they were so short that they did not really mean much. One was called *Träumerei*, like the picture over the piano. She picked out the theme again, and it remained unrevealing as ever. She put the book aside and began to play. Turn to music when you are unhappy, dear; that was the frequent counsel of Aunt Ellen.

She played *Danse Macabre*, for it reminded her of Domdaniel, and was besides a nice gloomy piece, suiting with her mood of romantic turmoil. She brought out very strongly the motif which her aunt had assured her was the rattling of dead men's bones. It cheered her greatly, so she followed it with that sweet *Flower Song* by Gustave Lange, which was one of Aunt's favourites. As she played, Miss Gall returned.

It was always easy to talk to Aunt Ellen. She didn't have to have things explained to her so much as Ma always did, and when she disagreed she never jeered, which was Ma's way. Besides, Aunt Ellen was a specialist in romance and dreams, and she never seemed to think that anything was really impossible. When the wonderful news had come about the Bridgetower Trust, Aunt Ellen had not waited for Monica to suggest that this might be the pathway to the wonderful world of opera; she had been first to say it; she had led the way in marvellous speculation. There was no dream that had to be shielded from her, for fear that she might mock; she was eager for dreams, and provided cup after cup of the sweet, milky tea which she and Monica found so helpful in the dreaming game. But about family—well, even Aunt Ellen might not see what Monica was driving at there. And so Monica took what seemed to her to be a safe tack.

"That boy I've sometimes spoken about, Auntie, George Medwall, said something to me today which made me as mad as hops." And she gave a version of George's few words which would have surprised him very much if he could have heard it. Monica had no intention of being untruthful; she merely told Aunt Ellen what George's words had conveyed to her at the time, with certain accretions which had developed since.

"Of course everything will be changed for you now, dear," said Miss Gall, "and I dare say you will get into quite a different sort of life. But you were very right not to hear a word against your family. The Fifth Commandment is sacred; honour thy father and mother. As we grow older we see it more that way. Your parents have been very good to you." As she spoke, Miss Gall cast about in her mind for concrete instances of this goodness, but could find nothing sufficiently impressive to bring out. "We never fully know what our parents have done for us," she said, vaguely, and then added, finding safer ground, "I know my father and mother were very, very good to me, and I don't suppose a day passes that I don't remember them and feel their love for me, and my love for them, all over again." She smiled; she had turned a difficult corner very neatly.

"Yes, I know, Auntie, but they don't really seem to like the idea that I'm going away to study music. Music isn't real to them, the way it is to you and me. Ma never mentions it, except to make fun."

"Oh, you musn't mind your mother's fun," said Miss Gall. "She's always been like that. So gay when she was a girl, and it's grown with the years. That's really wonderful, you know, dear. So many people get gloomy as they grow older. We always supposed that was what drew Alfred to her."

"Were they very much in love?" said Monica.

"Well, dear, I really couldn't say. I suppose they must have been. Alfred was very set on marrying her."

"Was Dad very ambitious, as a young man?"

"Oh yes, I should certainly say he was. That was why he left school so young, you know. He wanted to be independent; he wanted to buy a car."

"Didn't he have to leave school?"

"Gracious, no; father pleaded with him to stay at school. There was no need for him to leave; father was doing quite well, you know. But Alfred would have his way. And then he would have his way about marrying. And so it went, you see."

"You mean his parents didn't want him to marry Ma?"

"They never discussed it with me, dear, but of course I couldn't help picking up a little of what was going on. It all seemed to be hasty, and there were quarrels, and your Mother's family—"

"Yes? Go on, aunt, what about them?"

"Nothing dear, really. Just that they were rather strange people, and didn't want your mother to marry anyone."

"They thought Dad wasn't good enough? Was that it?"

"No; if there was anything of that sort, it was on the Gall side. And of course my parents were disturbed that your Mother was quite a bit older than Alfred. But your Mother's family were— oh, I guess you've said it all when you say they were odd."

"And Grandpa Gall didn't want him to marry into such an odd family?"

"Well, dear, parents often don't see things as young people do. And it's worked out very happily, so there's no good in talking any more about it, is there? No good ever comes of criticising people, or guessing what might have happened if they'd done something they didn't do. We have to take care that we always do the right thing ourselves, don't we? And what a job it is!"

"But don't you think George Medwall was terrible? I mean, hinting that home influence would hold me back, and all that. I think that's a terrible thing to say to a person, don't you?"

"I suppose he doesn't really understand. Of course, there will be changes in your life, and probably in the way you look at a lot of things. But I'm sure there'll be nothing that your Father and Mother wouldn't approve of. You know, dear—we've talked about it over and over again—a life given to music is such a wonderful thing. Living for a great art, and meeting wonderful, cultured people, and being all the time in contact with lovely things—it's bound to change you. You'll soar far above us I dare say."

"Oh, I won't," said Monica. "I'd hate to be like that. And I'd never feel I was above you, Aunt, never if I got to be the top soprano at the Metropolitan. It just wouldn't be possible for me. You've taught me all I know about music; how to read and play the piano, and harmony and theory, and accompany myself, and everything. If it hadn't been for you there just wouldn't have been any music for me. I owe my chance to you! This Bridge-tower Trust is really yours; you must know that. I couldn't ever repay you, not if I lived to be a thousand and got to be the great-est singer in the world!"

"You can repay me by being a great artist, dear. And a great artist is always a lovely person, remember that. The really great ones were always simple and fine, and loved everything that was sweet in life. Keep yourself sweet, Monny, and remember that any gifts you have really belong to God. If you do that, you won't have to worry about me. I'll be so proud of you, I'll just be full of it all day and every day. And don't worry about your parents. They'll be proud, too. They're just too shy to say how proud they are of you. And I know you'll always be what they want you to be."

Miss Gall was capable of talking in this strain at length, and so was Monica, so their conversation was long, repetitious and vastly comforting. When Monica went home at last she was per-suaded that, when the time came, Courvoisier and Ma could be very happily reconciled to one another. It was just a job of keep-ing your aims clear and your ideals high.

(3)

FOR SEVERAL DAYS it had been clear to Monica and her sister Alice that the farewell party was going to be one of Ma's "nights". Mrs. Gall was a woman whose normal lethargy and low spirits were relieved, from time to time, by brief bouts of extreme gaiety. For weeks she would declare that she couldn't be both-ered with people—had no use for them at all, and didn't want the house cluttered up with them; at these times she was morose,

untidy and rather dirty in her dress, never took her hair out of
curlers, wore her teeth only at meals and—the girls knew this but
did not speak of it even to each other—did not wash very often.
Then, suddenly, the cloud would lift, the hair would be released,
the teeth brought out of the sweater pocket where they had lain
unseen but not always unheard, and Mrs. Gall would "doll up",
to use her own expression, and ask the girls, jeeringly, why they
never brought anybody into the house? Did they want to send
her crazy for lack of company? Then the baking would begin,
and in a few days there would be a party, consisting chiefly of a
Gargantuan feed, with Mrs. Gall the heart and soul of it. For a
day or two afterward she would exult, breaking into sudden
laughter as she recalled the rare old time she had had. Then, in
an hour or two, she would fall into a pit of gloom from which
even Pastor Beamis, toiling manfully, could not lift her.

She was conscious of this pattern in her life, and attributed it
to her indifferent health. Everything she ate, she declared, ran to
fat. She was a burden to herself; her breath was short, and she
suspected the worst of her heart. From time to time she made attempts to get her fat down, picking at her food for a few days
until she was so low in spirits that she would have a fit of weeping, and take a medicinal slice of pie. A doctor had once told
her that sugar was a stimulant, and indeed it was to her; she resorted to it as a wealthier and more sophisticated invalid might
have taken to a costly drug.

Perhaps the most extraordinary manifestation of her depression
was that while it lasted she refused to go to the services and
prayer-meetings of the Thirteeners. Her faith was as strong as
ever, she protested, but she couldn't face the people; she simply
wasn't up to it. She could endure no one but her family, and
toward them she was morose, demanding—in Alice's word
"cussed". Pastor Beamis paid more sick-visits to her than to any
other member of his flock.

The quantity and elaboration of the baking that had gone on
before the farewell party made it clear that Mrs. Gall was going

on the razzle as never before. It had been estimated that there would be, at the outside, twenty guests, and she had made ten large jellies, four layer-cakes, a fruit-cake, six dozen tarts and unnumbered cookies; in addition she had baked a ham and a turkey, made a mountain of potato salad, and had rifled her preserve cupboard to produce mustard pickles, chili sauce, pickled beetroot, pickled watermelon rind, pickled crabapples, pickled corn and pickled onions. A vast coffee urn had been borrowed from the Thirteeners' church, and in addition there was to be a punch, made of cold tea, grape juice and ginger ale, with extra sugar to make it fizz.

"I don't want nobody goin' home sayin' they didn't get their bellyful," she said, as she surveyed these provisions on the afternoon before the great event. Out of the corner of her eye she saw Monica wince, and Ma Gall was gratified. Although she could never have formulated such a theory, she had a deep conviction that there was something salty, honest and salutary about bad grammar; it checked a tendency in the girls to get stuck-up notions. She could speak as fancy as anybody when she chose, but she didn't choose to indulge her daughters in this way. She deeply believed—though again this belief never jelled into anything so clear as a theory—that everybody, in their inmost thoughts, was ungrammatical, and that they translated those thoughts into fancy talk when they spoke, as a form of affectation. But they didn't impose on her. No siree, Bob!

"What are they going to do—besides eat themselves out of shape?" asked her daughter Alice.

"Oh, they'll find plenty to do. Somebody'll know some games, or somethin'," said Mrs. Gall. "Why don't you plan it, instead of leavin' the whole thing to me?"

"What can we do that anybody wants to do that Mrs. Beamis won't pull a long face at?" said Alice.

"Alex and Kevin'll have lotsa things planned, you'll see," said Mrs. Gall. "They're regular corkers, those two fellas. Laugh!— Say, will you ever forget the time they sneaked upstairs and got into a lot of your clothes and came down again like a couple of girls?" Mrs. Gall laughed till she wheezed, turned a dirty red, and coughed deeply and ventriloquially, like a bull bellowing in a distant field.

"Yes, and they burst two of my dresses under the arms," said Alice, sourly. "Big sissies. It was a thrill for them to get into a girl's stuff and mess around with it."

"Aw, they're a great coupla boys," said Mrs. Gall. "They got some life in 'em, and that's what I like. Not always pilin' on the agony till they're so stiff-rumped they can't have any fun." Again her eye wandered to Monica, who, as the supposed guest of honour, was showing little zeal for the party which lay ahead.

Night came, and with it the guests. Monica and Alice dressed in the small room which they had always shared, contriving somehow to make quite elaborate preparations in the two-foot gangway which was all the space left in the room between the double bed, the chest of drawers and the single chair. Alice depressed Monica by her unceasing gloomy predictions about the party. The elder of the two, Alice was the rebel; she was sick of the Thirteeners, and she was pretty sick of Ma. She was also sick of Monica, and the Bridgetower Trust had deepened her disgust with her sister's pretensions to culture. Alice was noisily anti-intellectual, though she had no clear notion of what it was that she was opposing. She was convinced that music and all that stuff was a lot of bull, and that was all there was to the matter. She worked in a bank, and had plans to better herself. The first step in these plans, Chuck Proby by name, was coming to the party. He worked in the bank, too.

"Chuck says all this religion is a lot of crap," said Alice, putting as much colour on her mouth as she thought Ma would endure without noisy rebuke.

"If Ma heard you use a word like that she'd wash your mouth out with soap," said Monica, who was rubbing Italian Balm into her hands.

"Ma's no one to talk about the words anybody else uses. Did

you hear what she said when she finished laying the table to-night? 'There; let 'em eat till they're pukin' sick', that's what she said. But the other day when I lost the heel off my shoe and said Damn she yelped about it for half an hour. No swearing—oh my, no!—but she'll talk as common as she likes. But anyhow, Chuck says all this religion is a lot of crap. He says he's a Probyite. He means by that he believes in himself. That's what makes me so crazy about him. He'll do something in the world. Not like Pa."

"Pa's never had a real chance, Alice. He started to work at sixteen—" Monica's voice died away, for she was remembering what her aunt had told her, what George had said—all the disturbing things which gnawed at Pa's meagre personal legend. Alice was laughing.

"Crap," said she, "crapola!"

(4)

By NINE O'CLOCK the party was beginning to warm up. It had started badly, for the earliest guests to arrive were twelve young Thirteeners, the others in the sept of thirteen with which Monica, at puberty, had been received into the Beamis flock. They were evenly divided as to sex, and there were three couples among them who were supposed to be romantically interested in each other. But vitality did not seem to be a characteristic of young Thirteeners, and they were quiet, almost furtive, in their approach to merry-making. They hung about the walls, and said "Yes, thanks," and "No, thanks," when addressed, and showed a distressing tendency to whisper among themselves. Miss Ellen Gall had come early, but she was not one to make a party "go", and thus the whole burden fell on Mrs. Gall. She pumped up gusto enough for everybody, pressing the sweet punch and cookies on them as soon as they arrived, toiling round and round the room, sucking air through her false teeth, and shouting "Havin' a good time? That's right; enjoy yourselves!" in a way

which made it clear that no lack of enjoyment would be toler-
ated. But the young Thirteeners were leavened after ten minutes
by the arrival of Chuck Proby, who had a very wordly air, and
then by Mrs. Gall's favourites, Alex Graham and Kevin Boyle.

Alex and Kevin were close friends. They shared a boarding-
house and, frequently, they shared a bed. They were happy
together, giving each other advice about clothes, and helping
each other in the demanding task of setting their hair in becoming waves. Mrs. Gall, it need hardly be said, knew nothing of
these intimacies and failed to understand Alice's broad hints; to
her they were just a pair of vivacious boys who were always
ready for fun, never spoke ill of anybody, and paid her flattering
attentions. They were not Thirteeners, but they were pleasantly
solemn about religion, and occasionally ventured philosophical
reflections to the effect that there were a lot of things in the Uni-
verse that we didn't understand yet, and that it stood to reason
that there was Something at the back of the wonderful world
which we saw all around us. In the circle in which the Galls
moved, the subdivision of humankind to which Alex and Kevin
belonged was not understood—and indeed, if its existence were
recognized at all it was thought to appear only among people
whom wealth or an unwholesome preoccupation with the arts
had corrupted; true, they seemed a little girlish, but in Mrs.
Gall's view there was nothing wrong with them that a couple of
good wives couldn't put right, and she was always on the lookout for suitable girls for them; she would have been well pleased
if her own two daughters had fallen in with this plan. They were
great ones to "josh" with her, and Mrs. Gall could forgive anything in a josher. They made their entrance joshing.

"Madame," said Alex, seizing her hand and kissing it amor-
ously, "the Count and I are too much honoured by the invitation
to your soirée."

Kevin produced a bouquet of paper flowers from behind his
back and presented it to his hostess. "Mine heart, she ees too
full," said he.

Mrs. Gall laughed, wheezed, and roared in her chest. "There you go!" she said, when she could speak; "I knew you two would be up to somethin'. Come on and have somep'n t'eat, and cut it out, now! Remember my heart."

"As if we could forget it," said Kevin. "Biggest heart in Salterton, and mine—all mine!" He feigned romantic ecstasy.

The young Thirteeners giggled nervously, anxious to show appreciation yet fearful of attracting attention lest they should be involved in the joshing, for which they knew they had no talent. Alex and Kevin greeted them all, still in their characters as foreign noblemen, but when they came to Monica they fell on their knees like Moslems, and bumped their heads on the floor.

"Proper deference toward a great talent," they whispered. Then Mrs. Gall led them off to be plied with sugar, in solid and liquid form.

Chuck Proby was alone in his failure to respond to this joke. He wore, without disguise, the look of a young man with a future who feels superior to his company.

The ascendency of Alex and Kevin was not to last long. Very soon after their arrival Pastor Beamis came in, accompanied by Mrs. Beamis, who looked as though she had been carved out of teak (though not by pagans) and their son Wesley, who was small, thin, pimply and had a bad breath, but strove to offset these handicaps by great high spirits, within Thirteener limits. But the crown was put on the party by the great man whom they brought with them. It was none other than Gus Hoole, the radio announcer and director of the Heart and Hope program.

The international world of entertainment had not heard of Gus Hoole, and might possibly never do so. But for a few thousand people in Salterton and its environs, he was emperor of a world of mirth, and at the centre of all the stirring, bustling things that came into their lives. He was head announcer at the local radio and television station, and there was no appeal for a good cause, no interview with a visiting celebrity, no civic function on a large scale, in which he did not have a part. He was a

fountain of the newest repartee; he had a never-failing flow of
heart-warming rhetoric; he had a sure instinct for making things
go. He was, indeed, a truly kind and generous man who really
liked to make people happy, and to assist crippled children, the
aged, the blind, the tubercular, the cancerous, the amputees, the
mentally retarded and all the other afflicted persons whom the
streamlined benevolence of our day has taken to its great, de-
partmentalized heart. But he had so exposed his good instincts
to the air that they had become gross, ropy and inflamed. To have
Gus Hoole do good to you was not unlike a very rough rape. He
entered the crowded small house, and gave it precisely the same
treatment as if it were a vast drill-hall, filled with people who
must be persuaded to part with money in the name of charity or
patriotism. Not that he roared; television does not need roarers;
he merely boomed, in the heavy, pseudo-masculine, soggily sincere tones of a popular announcer.

"Wanted to come. Wouldn't be kept away," he said, in response
to Mrs. Gall's flustered, overwhelmed greeting. "Least I could do
for our Monny, whom we are so soon to lose to the B.B.C. Can't
stay long, I'm afraid. But wanted to come for as long as I could."

Whereupon he took charge of the party. He was a man of professional tact, and he knew that the Thirteeners belonged in that
category of religion which they themselves called "the moderate-
stricts". Therefore dancing was out, and there must be no jokes
mentioning drink or sex. Jokes about the excretory functions
would be acceptable, however, and he made two, which were
greeted with loud laughter topped by Mrs. Gall. He led singing,
for he was an adept in tongue-twister songs such as "One warm
worm wiggled up the walk, while another warm worm wiggled
down". He guided them through a song in which the boys had to
match themselves vocally against the girls, singing in falsetto.
He was rich in riddles and puns. He mustered enough hats for a
game which involved the very rapid putting on and taking off of
unsuitable hats, and in this Pastor Beamis showed himself to immense advantage. The party began to go swimmingly—so well,

in fact that Gus Hoole felt it was safe to make a joke about drink, and did so. No one laughed so loudly as Pastor Beamis.

"That's a hot one," said he, at last, wiping his eyes. "Though it's not really a joking matter, of course. You can see right here, Gus, that when a bunch of fine kids get together for a good time, they don't need that stuff at all. They're just naturally drunk on their own high spirits."

"But that doesn't mean you, Ma," said Kevin, nudging Mrs. Gall. "Don't think I don't know about that jug you've got hidden under your bed." She shrieked, and roared in her throat until it seemed almost that she might have a seizure. Kevin slapped her on the back and plied her with the sweet punch. "You're drunk on sugar, Ma, that's what's the matter with you," he said. She guffawed again, wildly, exaggeratedly, on a higher note, until Alice wondered if she might not actually throw up, right in the middle of the carpet.

There was no doubt about it, Gus Hoole made Monica's farewell party. Monica admitted it; she strove to enjoy it. Yet, somehow, real enjoyment would not come, coax it as she would with laughter. Aunt Ellen enjoyed it. She was not of the same world as Gus, but she was a simple woman, impressed by success, and she was quite prepared to admit that he was much her superior in matters of this kind. And there was no question but that Gus was giving his all.

He even had what he thought of, professionally, as a "running gag", for the occasion. He had to be at Salterton's largest hotel at half-past ten, to supervise the drawing of the winning tickets in a charity raffle. That was why he was wearing his dinner jacket. (He had comically begged to be excused for appearing "just in my working clothes".) And so, from time to time, he looked at his wrist-watch, murmuring audibly, "Mustn't be late; they pay me ten dollars a minute for this kind of thing downtown." This show of comic avarice on the part of Gus, the widely-known, the professional Big Heart, was uproariously funny to the party. Even the young Thirteeners loosened up, and sniggered and neighed their delight. Then, with one of his famous lightning changes of mood, Gus became serious.

"Gotta go, folks," said he, "and when you gotta go, you gotta go." (A whoop from Ma Gall, who found a lavatorial significance in this.) "But seriously, I wish I could stay here with you lovely folks and emcee this affair right through till dawn. But the Mater Dee will be looking for me at the Paraplegics' Ball in just fifteen minutes, and it's time to say Good-bye. Before I go, Syd"—here he turned with an affecting boyishness to Pastor Beamis—"would it be too much to ask to hear the Heart and Hope just once again?"

Pastor Beamis patted Gus on the shoulder like a man whose heart is too full for speech. Quickly he gathered Mrs. Beamis and Wesley to him, and then beckoned to Monica, who found herself reddening as she joined them in the familiar formation.

"Doh," whispered Beamis, and his wife emitted a low moo, upon which the others formed a chord. "Granny" murmured the leader, and slowly, with immense expression, the quartet sang *Eden Must Have Been Like Granny's Garden*, much the most popular thing in the semi-sacred department of their repertoire.

It would be cynical to suggest that during this rendition there was any competition for the limelight, but if such a thing had been possible, Gus Hoole was certainly the winner. He stood motionless during the four verses, and as the motionless actor on the stage always draws the eyes of the audience, so did Gus. When the Quartet had finished, a few callow Thirteeners thought to applaud, but Gus stilled this unseemliness with a quick gesture. Stepping forward, he kissed Monica lightly on the cheek, exercising the license which is allowed in the entertainment world, and then, in a carrying emotional whisper, he said, "So long, kid; come back some day," and went out, with head bent. It was a splendid exit.

Not everyone was sorry to see him go, strange as this may appear. Alex and Kevin resented his professional intrusion on their preserve as funnymen of the party. Mrs. Gall, though honoured by his presence, was debarred by it from playing her role as the Earth-Goddess, the Many-Breasted Mother, dispensing food and drink. And so, as soon as Gus had left the house, she called everyone to supper by shouting "Eats! Eats!" and bustling them into the back parlour, or dining room, where the table was laid. Mr. Gall was set to work carving the turkey; Pastor Beamis hacked somewhat inexpertly at the ham. The young Thirteeners, considering their general lack of vitality, ate astonishingly. Indeed, two of the young men had a merry contest as to which could eat most, and made a great thing of it, egged on by the Thirteener girls. Ham, turkey, salad, pickles—the party chewed its way through these in short order, and then set to work on the sweet things. Because Christmas was not far away, there were crackers, and funny paper hats; the only person who did not wear a paper hat was Chuck Proby who, when urged to do so by Mrs. Gall, said: "Well, in the banking business we got to be careful," and escaped with his dignity uncompromised.

When at last they had eaten—not everything, for that would have been impossible without some apparatus for forcible feeding, but as much as it seemed that flesh could bear—Mrs. Gall disappeared to the kitchen, and returned almost at once, with the crown of the feast. This was a huge tray of small mince pies. The recipe called for a teaspoonful of brandy to be poured over each of these before it was eaten, but as Mrs. Gall had no use for brandy she substituted—such is the genius of the born cook—the juice from two bottles of maraschino cherries.

"Come on, now," she cried. "Every one you eat means a happy month next year. Ain't that so, Pastor?"

And so the company, protesting that it could eat no more, ate a great deal more, and stowed away mincemeat soaked in maraschino cherry juice until the young men groaned and rubbed their stomachs histrionically, and the girls protested that they could touch their last swallow, that their back teeth were submerged in food, and all the other jolly things which people say to please so bounteous a hostess as Mrs. Gall. Pastor Beamis won the prize for eating most mince pies (nine) and when he un-wrapped it, it was a toy set of bagpipes. When he danced about the room playing his pipes, even Mr. Gall laughed a little, and said that the Pastor was a card. Then they all settled down to "top off" with shortbread and coffee.

It was at this time that Alex and Kevin crept away, to return in a few minutes wearing Derby hats, spats, and carrying canes; in their eyes they painfully gripped watch crystals, to simulate monocles. For the enjoyment of the sated guests—some of whom were already showing signs of that grim malady, a cake hang-over—they acted out a little dialogue of their own composition, in which they declared that they were from jolly old London, by Jove, and that they were waiting impatiently for the arrival of Miss Monica Gall, the Salterton nightingale, don't y'know, who was coming over to Blighty to show them a thing or two about singing, eh what? Their English accents were not very well as-sumed, their English slang was derived from hearing people who had read Wodehouse talk about him, and their little masque did not seem to have a beginning or an end or much perceptible point, but it was received with enthusiasm, and Mrs. Gall was in gales of mirth, just from looking at them being so funny.

"Yeah, that's the way she'll be talkin' when she gets back," said she, jerking her head toward Monica. "Just you be careful, my girl, not to pick up a lotta snottery when you're over there among all them dudes. You got to keep your feet on the ground, and not get so's we can't understand a word you say."

"Monny'll be right up with the bigwigs when she's having lessons from Sir Thingumyjig," said Wes Beamis.

"Well, for her sake I hope they're more open-handed in Eng-land than they've been here," said Mrs. Gall. "The idea—invitin' us over there to talk about Monny's future, and never so much as offered us a cuppa coffee!"

"But Monny's getting the interest on a lotta money," said Mr. Gall. "You have to remember that."

"A cuppa coffee wouldn't have hurt," said his wife. "But no, they just sat around that room like so many Stoughton bottles, and looked at us as if we was poison."

"Let the boys go on, Ma," said Monica.

The entertainment by Alex and Kevin did not so much come to an end, as it fell apart, and the evening took another sudden turn toward seriousness, as it had when Gus Hoole was taking his leave. Pastor Beamis spoke of the loss to the Thirteener Church which was caused by Monica's great good fortune. He referred feelingly to the blow that had been sustained by the Heart and Hope quartet. He and his wife and Wes wanted Monica to remember them, when she was far away, and to remember their repertoire, too, so that sometimes she might sing the Lord's songs in a strange land. And in order to keep them in her mind, he asked her to accept a gift.

Wesley Beamis produced it, from the entrance hall, and Monica unwrapped it as they all looked on. It was a dressing case, fitted with a mirror, brushes, bottles and hangers upon which clothes could be folded. Monica, who had a headache, was moved, and cried a little, but she pulled herself together and made a speech.

"I'll never be able to thank you enough," said she; "not just for this, though it's lovely, but for all the good times and all the kindness. Please don't talk as if I could ever forget you. I couldn't, and I wouldn't if I could. I'll always keep this with me, whatever happens, and no matter how long I'm away, or whatever happens to me—" She could say no more.

Pastor Beamis struck up *God Be With You Till We Meet Again*, and they all sang it, fervently and with a warmth which was, to Monica, agonizingly sweet and embracing. As she stood among them weeping, part of her feeling was of deepest shame that she could ever, for a moment, have felt stifled and cramped in this atmosphere, or have wished to get away from it. Miss Ellen Gall, in the back parlour among the ruins of the feast, wept too.

The guests went home, each with a kind word, and Wesley

Beamis, made bold by the example of Gus Hoole, pressed a maraschino-tainted kiss upon her cheek at parting. He had had hopes of Monica, but now they were gone.

When the Galls were alone, Ma was seen to be slumped in a chair, beet-red in the face, and utterly exhausted. But she roused herself, thrust a piece of fruitcake into her mouth and rose.

"Come on," said she; "let's get these dishes done before we go to bed. I don't want any slopdolly housekeeping here." She kicked off her shoes, removed her teeth, and went to the kitchen.

There she found that Alex and Kevin were well advanced on the first lap of the dish-washing. Good boys, thoughtful boys: make wonderful husbands.

Four

CHRISTMAS EVE. Unhappy and nauseated from the crown of her head to the soles of her feet, Monica lay in her berth aboard the *Duchess of Richmond*. Although she had several blankets and the steam heating hissed and muttered in the pipes, she was clammily cold. The boat—no, the doctor had said she must always call it the ship—toiled laboriously upward, seemingly determined to reach the sky, and hung poised for a few dreadful moments at the crest of the wave; the screws, lifted from the water, caused the whole vessel to shudder awesomely; then it plunged, writhing, into the depths again. Everything in the cabin jingled and shifted; the vomit-can, hooked ingeniously over the side of her berth, chattered metallically. Down the hallway, but clearly audible through the ventilation louvers in the door, somebody dropped a loaded tray.

The light in the middle of the cabin turned on with a snap, and Stewardess Rose Glebe was in the room, heavily rouged and bursting with well-being.

"Well, and how's the lonely girlie now?" she carolled. "Still a weeny bit sicky-pussy? Never mind, dear, you're not the only one. Only six at First Class dinner tonight."

Holding Monica firmly with one arm, Stewardess Glebe dealt the pillow several punishing blows. Monica retched powerfully but without result.

"Poor kiddie," said the angel of light, laying her back again and straightening the blankets. "Nothing to come, eh? That's no good; got to get something into your tummikins dear, or you'll wrench it loose with that there straining. Now look; I've brought you a lovely apple, all cut in pieces, and some ginger ale. You just get that down. No matter if you can't keep it. You've got to have something to raise, or you'll harm yourself. Doctor's orders. I'll come back before I go off duty, and help you down the hall, to the W, then I'll tidy your bed for the night. Now, now, you mustn't feel so sorry for yourself. Could be much worse, I tell you. Though it's a pity about Christmas Eve."

"Can it be worse than this?" asked Monica, faintly.

"Much worse on the voyage over," said Stewardess Glebe. "That was a crossing, if you like. The old North Atlantic's no millpond in winter."

With a smile of extreme cheer she vanished through the door.

Monica lay with her eyes closed for a few minutes, gathering courage. Then, with extreme caution, she took a sip of ginger ale and felt better at once. She nibbled a bit of apple, and became conscious that she was very hungry. Soon she was able to get up, bathe her face, and turn out the centre light; she switched on the reading-lamp in her berth and lay as quietly as the ship would allow, eating the apple lingeringly.

How noisy the ship was! All that creaking and groaning, night and day. And how empty! But then, as a fellow passenger had asked her, who would cross the North Atlantic in Christmas Week unless they had to? There were only twenty-two First Class passengers altogether, and of these seventeen were men— middle-aged, dull-looking men, obviously travelling on business. One of them, with whom she had had a brief conversation, was an apple man from British Columbia. Monica had anticipated the sea voyage as an exciting and perhaps even a romantic introduction to her new life. But when she found herself seated at a table in the dining saloon with a widow who was going to scatter her husband's ashes in his native Scotland, and a female Major in the Salvation Army, she had revised her opinion. Not that she had been allowed much time to explore the possibilities of the ship, for it had left St. John in heavy weather, and Monica had been in her berth since the second day; this was the fourth day and the storm—not that the doctor or Stewardess Glebe would admit that it was a storm—seemed to be growing worse.

She had not lost heart, in spite of her illness. She had been elated at the thought of travelling First Class, and she did not know that this had been the cause of hot debate among the Bridgetower Trustees. Miss Pottinger and the Dean had thought Tourist Class much more suitable, but Solly had once more been indiscreet in talking to the newspaper, and the *Bellman* had announced its intention of providing Monica with a large bouquet of flowers, with which she was to be photographed, at the dock. It had been considered wrong that a protégée of the late Louisa Hansen Bridgetower should be photographed in anything less than First Class accommodation, and so, with much grumbling from Mr. Snelgrove, that was what had been provided. The *Bellman's* flowers, firmly held in a cage which the ship provided for them, rustled and waved in a corner of her cabin.

Getting away had been a strain. None of the Galls were travellers, and the belief had grown up among them, unspoken yet plainly understood, that once Monica had gone they need never expect to look upon her face again. People did travel about the world, it was true, and return to their families even after many years of absence, but the Galls could not believe that this would be so with one of their own. The sea voyage would almost certainly end in shipwreck; the more Mrs. Gall thought of it, the surer she became. True, she did not say this to Monica in so many words, but she had a way of looking at her daughter, and melting into silent tears, which made speech unnecessary.

Mr. Gall's solicitude expressed itself differently. Although he had been apparently indifferent to Monica's fate since her childhood, he now took great pains to find out what kind of toothpaste she liked, and what her preference was in cold cream, and bought her large stores of these things to take away. He was apparently convinced that the ordinary necessities of life could not be bought in England, and he repeatedly made her promise that, when these things were exhausted, she would let him know, so that he could send more. He seemed to be provisioning her for a voyage to the Isle of the Dead.

Monica had borne herself bravely through the partings, and had pooh-poohed the notion that there was any danger at sea, but during the days of her illness she had been troubled by a duality of mind. Certainly it had seemed to her that no vessel built with human hands could do what the *Duchess of Richmond* was doing and stay afloat. She had prayed, but the Thirteener faith had not armed her against such misery as this; she had tried to believe the ship's doctor, when he had assured her that nobody ever died of it (ha ha), and that her best plan was to stop thinking about herself and get up on deck; she had submitted to the shameful ordeal of a soapy-water enema given by Stewardess Glebe, who insisted that this treatment was sovran for sea-sickness; she had, in the worst of her trouble, fallen into a sleep which was more like a swoon, and troubled by horrible dreams. But, although one half of her mind told her that she was about to die, the other half had continued to dwell on hopeful visions of what she would do when, at last, the ship reached port. Refreshed by the apple and the ginger ale, she gave herself up to such speculation now.

England was sure to be fun. She had never thought much about that country, or made any special study of anything connected with it, but when she knew she was going there everything she had ever heard about England—and quite a few things she had never been conscious of hearing—collected and formed a pattern in her mind and she became, so far as her circle was concerned, an authority on the subject. England would be very quaint, and the people—though not so go-ahead and modern as the Canadians—would be exceedingly polite, honest and quaint as well. The Cockneys would be especially quaint, because they were so quick-witted, and so full of independence and courage. Cockneys might be expected to wear suits with hundreds of pearl buttons on them, on Sundays, just as they did in the photographs sent out by the British travel agencies; there would be splendidly uniformed soldiers, as seen in whisky advertisements; people in official positions were very likely to wear little wigs; there would be innumerable quaint customs—beating the boundaries, flinging the pancake, chewing the gammon, and the like, as described by the British Information Service; children might be expected to talk like grown-ups; it would rain most of the time, and this would be borne with immense good-humour; coffee would be awful but tea would be drunk in bucketsful; and there would be a lot of culture and gracious living and characteristic English understatement in evidence everywhere.

This was the country which was to transform her. She was determined that in most things she would be transformed. The simple clerk at the Glue Works (for she saw, more clearly every day, how simple she had been) would, after experiences which would deepen and ripen her emotional nature, change into the internationally-known diva. She would never forget her family, of course, and she would certainly never be a loose-liver, as some internationally-known divas had so reprehensibly been, but she would no longer be bound by the chains of the Thirteeners or the social habits of Salterton. Monica Gall, the internationally-known diva. . . .

The name was not quite right. Indeed, the more often she repeated it, the less appropriate it sounded. Gall, in particular, would not do. An Irish name, Aunt Ellen had explained. Would it be better changed to Gallo, perhaps? Monique Gallo? Distinguished in appearance, with a spiritual beauty which seemed to shine from within, elegant yet simple in manner, living solely for her art and yet a familiar figure in the best society in Europe, Monique Gallo took shape in her mind. Monique Gallo, robed as Norma, acknowledging the applause of a vast audience before the curtains of a great opera house; Monique Gallo, in a black velvet gown relieved only by a few fine diamonds, graciously bowing at the end of a recital, while her accompanist wiped away his tears of pure artistic joy; Monique Gallo being drawn in torchlit triumph through the streets of Prague by a crowd of enthusiastic students, who had taken the horses out of her carriage. . . . Why horses; why a carriage? Oh, probably a temporary gasoline shortage. . . . Monique Gallo, who sang every kind of music with unmatchable understanding, concluding her recital with some simple, lovely ballad which left not a dry eye in the house. Monique Gallo telling stricken young men (not a bit like foremen at a Glue Works) that she must live for her art alone— an attitude which, while it broke their hearts, compelled them to love her all the more.

The apple and the ginger ale had been gone for perhaps half an hour before the picture began to darken. Not Monique Gallo now, but plain Monica Gall was musing on the plain words of Humphrey Cobbler when last she had seen him—"chances are about a hundred to one that your voice is any better than scores of others; only work will tell the tale; this Bridgetower thing is really pretty much a fluke." Well, it was a chance. She could always go back home and get a job.

The *Duchess of Richmond* climbed higher peaks, shivered more terribly, plunged in corkscrew fashion to even more abysmal depths. Monica turned very cold, broke into an icy sweat, and was noisily, searchingly sick into the rattling container . . . And again . . . And (Oh God, have mercy!) again.

(2)

"Miss Gall, from Canada? I'm from Jodrell and Stanhope. Here's my card—Frederick Boykin. I'll see to your luggage. Hope you had a pleasant voyage? Well, yes, I suppose it's bound to be a bit rough this time of year. Yes, it is a little foggy, but that's common in London, you know. Oh dear no, this isn't a *real* London fog; just a bit of a haze. Taxi! That's right, three cases and a trunk. Well, you can put two of the cases on the

roof, can't you? You get inside Miss Gall, and I'll see to this . . .
There; that's that. They hate trunks. Can't think why; they
charge enough for 'em. Now, my instructions are to take you to
Marylebone Road—Three Arts Club—ladies' club, very respectable, and you'll see Mr. Andrews tomorrow. Pity you can't see
more out of the window. I suppose you saw a good deal of England coming down on the boat-train? Raining all the way? But
you expected that, you say? Well I suppose it does seem queer to
you, coming from all your snow, and so forth. . . . The smell? I
can't really say that I'd noticed any smell. Bit smoky, perhaps,
but that's because of the haze—keeps the smoke down . . . Here
we are; you go right ahead, I'll attend to everything. They're expecting you."

Thus, within a quarter of an hour of her arrival in London,
Monica found herself in a very small room, with nothing whatever to do. She had liked Mr. Boykin, who was stout without being fat, and cheerful in what she supposed was the traditional
Cockney way, and knew what he was doing. She had not so
much liked the secretary of the Club, who was a very competent
lady with a brand of genteel, impersonal hospitality which was
new to Monica, and chilling. And what was she to do now?

She would read her book. Before leaving Canada she had laid
in intellectual provision in the form of *War and Peace*, in a
single large, heavy volume, complete with maps of Napoleon's
Russian campaign, and an informative introduction by a celebrated critic. Under normal circumstances she would never have
considered tackling such a cultural monster, but it seemed appropriate to the new life she was going to live. Aunt Ellen had
advised it, for her dead fiancé had often spoken of *War and
Peace* as the greatest of all novels. To read it would undoubtedly
result in permanent mental enrichment. Seasickness had come
between Monica and Tolstoy on the voyage, and she had read,
in all, four confusing pages. She would get down to serious work
on it now.

Many travellers have discovered that a book which seems

strikingly appropriate in one country is insupportably tedious in another; the Lost Property offices of the world's airports are heavily stocked with volumes which have not travelled well. In less than ten minutes Monica had decided that Anna Pavlovna Sherer's party was not precisely what she needed at the moment (though unquestionably cultural); she was in the greatest city in the world, and she did not want to waste time sitting in a little room, with a bad light and a funny smell, reading about people who did not seem certain what their own names were. She would go for a walk.

The genteel secretary caught her in the hall, and cautioned her not to go far, not to get herself lost, and to appeal to a policeman if she did so. This was dampening to Monica's spirits, as was also the smell of Marylebone Road, which was just like that of her bedroom, only more intense and wet.

It was a sour, heavy smell; a wet smell, of course, in which the smoke of soft coal played a large part. But it was not a constant smell. Sometimes the soft coal was so powerful that Monica choked a little; and then, in a few yards, it would have changed to a smell like damp mattresses; once, Monica was reminded of the time when a wool warehouse had burned down in Salterton. It was not an actively unpleasant smell; indeed, it had a caressing friendliness about it—almost a familiarity, as though she had known this smell at some earlier time in her life, and were encountering it again. But in spite of this delusive familiarity the smell was the queerest thing Monica met in the Marylebone Road, which seemed to her, in other respects, not greatly unlike Toronto.

Baker Street. Had she, at some time, heard something about Baker Street? Nothing came to mind, and yet there seemed to be some familiarity in the address. The street names were pleasant; Nottingham, Devonshire, Harley—wasn't there something about Harley Street? It was odd; being in London was like being in a dream, or in a life you had lived before, in which things seemed to have meaning but wouldn't be pinned down.

But she had been warned not to go too far, and the haze seemed to be increasing as the light failed. She found her way back to the Club without difficulty, listening as she walked to the unfamiliar voices—some of them very hoarse and almost incomprehensible. The secretary shot a meaningless, professional smile at her as she passed the office door.

The smell inside the Club had deepened, and was a little warmer than it had been before, and there was a heavy premonition of food in it now. Monica lay on her bed until the gong sounded for dinner, and thought about Monique Gallo, to whom London and all the capitals of the world would seem like home.

(3)

THE BASEMENT DINING ROOM of the Club was terrifying. It was not very large, but it was filled with alarmingly worldly girls who seemed to be perfectly at home. In the presence of these girls, with their loud, assured English voices—fully understandable and yet, for that very reason, so foreign and unaccustomed in tone and tune—Monica was, for the first time since she left home, afraid. But the efficient secretary came to her aid.

"Miss Stamper," she said to a girl who was sitting alone at a table for two, "this is Miss Gall from Canada. I'm sure you'll find a lot in common."

Monica's first impression of Miss Stamper was that she was dirty. Her hair was dull. Her face seemed to have grime under the surface of the skin. Her stubby fingers were dark. But her round face was cheerful.

"I wonder why she thinks we'll find anything in common," said she. "Are you new here, too?"

By the time they had eaten the watery soup and moved on to the fatty mutton, they were on excellent terms. Peggy Stamper was from Norwich, and she had come to London to learn sculpture. She had been doing a lot of clay modelling, which explained and almost excused the grime. She was not yet nineteen, which gave Monica a certain advantage in age, but Peggy was English, and was thus better equipped to meet the strongly national atmosphere of the Club. It was, she said, intended for girls who were engaged in the arts, or studying them, in London, but what it really worked out to be was a cheap residential place for girls whose artistic inclinations had lapsed, or had always been secondary to some other sort of job. She was there because an aunt, who was partly paying for her training, thought it a safe place for her to be, but she meant to get out as soon as possible.

As they ate a pudding unknown to Monica, which seemed to be called Spotted Dog, she told Peggy about herself. But she noticed, with surprise, as though outside herself, that there were things she did not tell: Peggy heard a good deal about Monica, but she heard nothing of the Glue Works—only of an office job; nothing was said of Pastor Beamis and the Thirteeners—only of some broadcasting experience; the Bridgetower Trust emerged as the sponsor of a far-reaching contest in search of gifted young women, with Sir Benedict Domdaniel as its dominating figure. Not a word did she say with intent to deceive, but in that room, within earshot of those very English voices, facts presented themselves, somehow, in a rather different guise.

Indeed, as Monica went to bed, she was astonished to recall how the facts which she had given to Peggy, without being in the least distorted had been, by some instinct of caution deep within her, edited. Was it Peggy's fault? No, she had been very friendly, though in a way which was new to Monica—a way which suggested that she was glad to hear anything which she was told, but was not really seeking information and was not, perhaps, deeply interested. Was it something about England, which made real truth and real revelation impossible? Had that dreadful week on the Atlantic really drawn such a broad line between herself and her past? She was uneasy and puzzled until she went to sleep.

(4)

Mr. Miles Peter Andrews was the most elegant young gentleman that Monica had ever encountered in the flesh, yet he was
not really what she would have called a snappy dresser—not as
Alex and Kevin were, certainly. Cheerful Frederick Boykin had
brought her from Marylebone Road by taxi to Fetter Lane, off
which, in Plough Court, were the offices of Jodrell and Stanhope.
She now sat in the private room of the junior partner, who
looked at her in a weary, lawyer-like fashion, which made Monica feel that he could see right through her.

As a matter of fact, Mr. Andrews knew next to nothing about
her, and was trying to get his bearings. This was the girl from
Canada, referred to his firm by—who was it—a Canadian firm
called Snelgrove, Martin and Fitzalan, of some place called Salterton. It would have astonished the members of the Bridgetower
Trust if they could have known how much in the dark Mr.
Andrews was about everything connected with their protégée.
Mr. Snelgrove, who had been entrusted with all the arrangements, had spoken importantly about "our opposite number in
London—fine old firm", as though Jodrell and Stanhope were in
almost daily contact with his own office. It may even have been
that Mr. Snelgrove believed this to be—in a large, general way—
the truth. But the fact was that on only one former occasion had
Jodrell and Stanhope ever done any business in London for
Snelgrove, Martin and Fitzalan of Salterton, and that had been
many years ago, when Miles Peter Andrews was at Marlborough.
He had been given Monica to look after because, as the junior,
he got all the odds and ends, and perhaps also because his wife
was musical in a well-bred, desultory way. Mr. Andrews caressed
his handsome moustache and blinked sorrowfully across his table
at Monica.

"Your first visit to London, Miss—ah—Miss Gall?"

"Yes, sir. I came down from Liverpool yesterday afternoon."

All things considered, it was unfortunate that Monica called him "sir", though she did so from the best of motives; she thought she should be polite, and Mr. Andrews was in roughly the same relationship to her as her former boss at the Glue Works—a man of power on the other side of a desk. But the word spoke volumes—volumes perhaps of untruth, but nevertheless, volumes—to Mr. Andrews' English ear. He allowed his fine eyes to fall to the file which Mr. Boykin had laid on his desk. There was not much in it, but a letter from somebody called Matthew Snelgrove made it clear that Miss Monica Gall was the beneficiary of a trust which was empowered to pay for her musical education. Mr. Snelgrove, for all his assumption of familiarity with Jodrell and Stanhope, had not thought it necessary to tell them that the yearly income from about a million Canadian dollars might be spent on this project. So Mr. Andrews drew his own conclusions from the fact that he had been called "sir", and also from Monica's style of dress, which he knew to be neither smart nor expensive. When he spoke again his tone was distant, though kindly.

"Well, Miss Gall," said he, "we must make you as comfortable as possible, mustn't we. Our Chief Clerk, Mr. Boykin, has arranged digs for you at a very good address—a Mrs. Merry in Courtfield Gardens. She knows that you are a music student, and I believe she has made some special arrangement about noise. Now, as to money: we are empowered to pay all your fees for instruction, and any large bills; they can be rendered here, without reference to you. But you'll need money for ordinary expenses. What do you think you'll need? By the month, let's say?"

"I—oh, I wouldn't have any idea," said Monica. "I don't know anything about what it costs to live here. I'm not very good at English money yet. What would you think?"

"I don't suppose it will be very long before you know other students, and music students aren't very flush of money, as a usual thing. You wouldn't want to be above or below the average. Would five pounds a week do it? Say twenty-five pounds a month? That's three hundred a year, you know; very handsome, really, and all your big bills paid."

Monica, who knew nothing about it, agreed that this was so, and Mr. Andrews thought so, too, for a girl of the sort who called him "sir".

"Now as to teaching," he continued, "I see that is all to be in the hands of Sir Benedict Domdaniel. He will tell you what to do, and we shall pay the bills. I see here that Boykin is writing to Sir Benedict today, to say that you have come, and you will undoubtedly be hearing from him very shortly. So there really isn't anything more to discuss, is there? Except, of course, that if you need any help, or anything like that, get in touch with us. I'm away rather a lot, so you'd better ask for Boykin."

Mr. Andrews rose to his impressive height, and turned out the very faint gleam of geniality which had illumined his large blue eyes. Monica was shown out into Plough Court by Mr. Boykin, who assured her that he would see that she was moved to Courtfield Gardens that very afternoon.

(5)

"YOU'LL BE WANTING A FEW STICKS, won't you?" said Mr. Boykin. He sat on Monica's trunk, which he and a disgruntled taxi-man had just dragged and boosted up three flights of stairs, getting his breath and surveying her new quarters.

"Semi-furnished was the wording of the advertisement," said Mrs. Merry. Her manner was not defensive, but there was a hint in her voice that, if hostility should arise, she was ready for it. "I naturally expected that the young lady would want to have her own things about her. It was never mentioned to me that the young lady was from the Dominions." Mrs. Merry contrived, in this statement, to make it clear that in her view being from the Dominions was the sort of thing which a tenant would conceal for as long as possible.

Unquestionably Monica would be wanting a few sticks. There

were no carpets on the floors and no curtains on the windows. The bedroom contained a single bed, a washstand upon which stood a very large jug in a basin, and a very small clothes-press in the Art Nouveau manner, with a bit of looking-glass let into the front of it. The sitting-room was furnished with one of those day-beds upon which it is uncomfortable to sit and even more uncomfortable to lie, a large discouraged pouffe covered with grubby cretonne, and a dirty, scarred little object which was probably once described as "a handy smoker's chairside table". There was nothing else.

The rooms were small and the distemper on the walls had been marked and scuffed by many tenants. Outside the windows, two feet from the glass, was the decorative balustrade which ran across the face of the house—a kind of fence with bulbous stone palings—so that it was easy to look out at the sky, but very hard to see down into the street.

"There are facilities for light housekeeping, as you see," said Mrs. Merry, opening the door of a small cupboard in which, indeed, there was a very old, scabby gas-ring and some shelving. She unveiled this wonder as though it clinched the desirability of her rooms.

"And when may we expect the piano?" said she.

"I'll have one sent round when Sir Benedict gives the word," said Mr. Boykin. Mrs. Merry thawed a little at the mention of a title.

"I shall have to hold you responsible for any damage done in moving the instrument upstairs," said she. Adding, to Monica, "You'll be able to make as much noise as you like up here; there's nobody on this floor in the daytime, and rarely anyone downstairs."

"That'll be great," said Monica, who was thoroughly unnerved by Mrs. Merry, and anxious to placate her. If Mrs. Merry wanted noise, she would promise noise.

"I'll be getting along," said Mr. Boykin. "Anything you want, give me a tinkle."

"Well—what about the sticks?" said Monica. "Shall I get them, and have the bill sent to you? Or what?"

Mr. Boykin had not foreseen this; he had assumed that Monica would buy her own sticks.

"I'll have to speak to Mr. Andrews about that," he said. "Don't do anything until you hear from me."

"And what about Sir Benedict?"

"We'll be getting on to him; you wait till you hear from us."

"Yes—and money? How do I get money to live?"

"Haven't you any on hand?"

"Very little." As a matter of fact, Monica had twenty pounds in five-pound notes which she did not mean to touch. That was insurance against anything going wrong with the Bridgetower Trust. She was young, but she was no fool about money.

"Well, I haven't had any instructions yet. But don't worry. I'll get everything straightened away just as soon as I've had a talk with Mr. Andrews. A Happy New Year, Miss Gall."

Mr. Boykin took his leave, reflecting that the law would be the most delightful profession in the world if only it didn't involve these odd little necessities to take care of people; they always wanted things which were, to the legal mind, superfluous and looked badly on itemized statements. Still, the girl had to have some furniture. And she was quite right not to buy it herself. That girl had her head screwed on right.

"What do I do about heat?" asked Monica when he had gone.

"The gas-fire and the hot-plate work from the meter above the door," said Mrs. Merry. "You will be wise always to keep a stock of shillings on hand; it is useless to apply to me, for I simply cannot undertake to make change for my tenants. It is a rule which I have been compelled to make," she said reproachfully, and left Monica alone in her splendour.

(6)

SPLENDOUR IT WAS, to Monica, for she had never had a place of her own before, nor had she lived in such a grand house. Mrs. Merry's establishment was in one of South Kensington's Italianate terraces, with an imposing entrance hall and a handsome, sweeping staircase. It was true that Monica's rooms were on the floor which had once sheltered the servants, and lacked the high ceilings and ornate plasterwork of the lower apartments: it was true, also, that the gas-fire was an inadequate, popping nuisance, and the inconveniently placed meter demanded shillings with tiresome frequency; and it was true that·quite a long journey had to be made to the bathroom on the lower floor, for the large jug and basin were apparently not intended for use. But it was her own place, not to be shared with Alice or anyone, and she had high hopes of it. She settled down to wait for news from Mr. Boykin.

During the first week of waiting she passed the time by exploring the part of London in which she found herself. She walked in Kensington Gardens and Hyde Park. The Albert Memorial, coming to her as a surprise, seemed a beautiful thing, and the Albert Hall, from the outside, splendid. She walked the Natural History Museum and the Victoria and Albert, and told herself that they were immensely educational. She found Cheyne Walk and the river. She became so well known in Harrods that the detectives began to watch her closely. While she was exploring it was not hard to keep her spirits up.

It was another matter when she was in her rooms in Courtfield Gardens. Mrs. Merry was no cheerful Cockney; indeed, she was like nothing of which Monica had ever heard. She seemed to be rather grand, for she spoke in a refined manner, making a diphthong of every vowel, and she wore a look of suffering bravely borne which was, in Monica's eyes, distinguished. If

Mrs. Merry had given her any encouragement, Monica would have confided in her and sought her advice, but Mrs. Merry kept her tenants in their place by an elaborate disdain, which she made particularly frosty for Monica's benefit. And so Monica spent her evenings alone, sitting on the day-bed as long as she could endure it, and going to bed when she could bear no more. During the first day or two she attempted to get on with *War and Peace,* but found it depressing, and as time wore on she suffered from that sense of unworthiness which attacks sensitive people who have been rebuffed by a classic. She read magazines and newspapers. There appeared to be an extraordinary amount of rape in London.

Meals were her greatest worry. Where could she eat? There were plenty of places which offered food, it was true, but she did not like any of them. There were horrible, dirty little holes-in-the-wall, which depended heavily on sausages and boiled cabbage for their bill of fare. And there were foreign restaurants which alarmed her because the food was all described in unknown tongues, and incomprehensible purple writing, and besides it was all too expensive to be enjoyed. In Chelsea she found coffee bars, but they seemed to be the exclusive property of oddly-dressed young men and women who made her feel awkward and unwelcome, and anyhow they did not offer much to eat. There were other Chelsea restaurants, kept by very refined ladies who, like Mrs. Merry, gave out an atmosphere of highbred grievance; they provided extremely quaint and individual surroundings, stressing Toby jugs and warming-pans, but gave surprisingly little food for what they charged. And none of the food agreed with her. After a few days her largest meal had become a bready, cakey tea at a Kardomah in Brompton Road.

She could cook nothing in her room, for she had no pots—not even a kettle. It was a new and disagreeable experience to Monica to have to go to a public place and choose every bite that she ate, and she quickly came to dread it. She tried to reach Peggy

Stamper at the Three Arts Club, but she had gone, leaving no address.

By the end of the second week she had a cold, and could barely repress panic about money. There had been no word from Mr. Boykin. Every day, after the tenth day, she had told herself that she would call him on the telephone, or go to Plough Court to find him, but she did not do so, and knew, in her heart, that she was afraid. After all, what assurance had she that Jodrell and Stanhope would really do anything for her? Perhaps there had been some change in the situation in Canada; perhaps the Bridgetower Trust had collapsed, or changed its mind; perhaps, owing to one of those muddles about dollar and sterling currency, of which she had vaguely heard, it had proved impossible to get any money to England to support her; perhaps—this was when the cold had taken a turn for the worse—they had forgotten about her, or decided that she would not do, and would disclaim any knowledge of her if she went to see them.

Meanwhile she had made quite a hole in her reserve fund of twenty pounds. Eating was horribly expensive, and she tried to economize by bringing things to her rooms in bags, and eating them there. But this diet of apples and buns brought her no comfort. The cold—feverish and wretched, now, in spite of innumerable shillings pushed into the maw of the gas-meter—the raw damp of a London winter, and the peculiar London smell were wearing her down. She began to have spells of crying at night. And then, as the third week wore on, she dared not cry, because letting down the barriers of her courage in any way brought such horrible speculations, and tumbled her into such abysses of loneliness, that she could not sleep, but lay in her bed for hours, trembling and staring into the darkness. The charm of having her own establishment had utterly worn off, and her two bare rooms echoed hollowly.

She did not pray, for as *War and Peace* seemed to have lost its magic in crossing the ocean, so did the religion of the Thirteeners. That blatant, narrow faith could not be hitched to anything in her present situation; never, in this strange land, did she hear anyone speak in a voice which suggested the aggressive certainty of Pastor Beamis.

Yet she continued to write home, once a week, saying nothing of her misery and her fears. She was, she told her family, waiting to begin her studies; meanwhile she was seeing something of London.

What was the good of complaining to them? What could they do? And would they not be likely to say that it was just what they expected? Had they not, right up until the last minute, expressed doubt about the whole venture, which only the thought of the easy money kept from bursting into outright contempt? She was outside the range of her religion, and outside the range of her family. Whatever was to come, she must meet it alone.

If nothing had happened by the end of the coming week, she would get a job. Probably it would have to be dish-washing, or something of that sort; so much an outcast did she now feel that she could not conceive of getting the sort of clerical work she had done at home. In time—perhaps in two or three years—she would be able to scrape up enough money to go home, if the disgrace were not too great. Monica Gall, who was taken in by that crooked Bridgetower crowd—who had the nerve to think she could sing!

By this time her cold was much worse, and she had an ugly sore on her upper lip.

But on the Tuesday of the fourth week, Mrs. Merry hooted refinedly up the stair-well that she was wanted on the telephone. It was Mr. Boykin.

"Well, Miss Gall, how is it going?" said he. "Hope you didn't think we'd forgotten all about you? Ha ha. Takes a little time to get an answer from Canada. But we now have the go-ahead on the extra furniture for you, and Mr. Andrews suggests that I go with you to one of the second-hand shops in King's Road and see what we can do. Would this afternoon be convenient? Sure you've nothing else on? Very well; perhaps you'll make a sort of tentative list of what you'll be wanting. Oh, and Sir Benedict is now back from Manchester, and he says we may as well have the piano sent around at once, as you'll be wanting one. And he can see you next Friday at three-thirty, if you've nothing else to do at that time. His house is in Dean's Yard, Westminster. I'd be very punctual, if I were you; he's put off someone else in order to fit you in. 'Til this afternoon then."

(7)

"WHY DO YOU WANT TO BE A SINGER?" said Sir Benedict.

Monica blushed, and held a handkerchief to the coldsore on her lip. "I'm sorry to waste your time like this," said she; "it's just that, I've such an awful cold I can hardly make a sound. I'm awfully sorry."

"Oh, I didn't mean that. Of course you're terribly roopy; I just wanted to remind myself of what you sound like. But what I meant was, what's behind all this? Here you are, and these people in Canada are prepared to spend a great deal of money on your teaching. Is there something special about you? Why do you want to sing?"

"I want to be an artist."

"Why?"

"Well—because it's a fine thing to be."

"Why?"

"Because—because it makes you a fine person, and you can help people."

"How?"

"You bring great music to them. You sort of—enrich their lives, and make them better."

"Why do you want to do that?"

"It's what we're here for, isn't it?"

"I really don't know. Is it?"

"Well that's what art is for, isn't it? To make people better? I mean, you give people art, and it raises them up, and they see things differently, and it—it sort of—"

"I don't want to put words into your mouth, but perhaps you are trying to say that it *refines* them."

"Well; yes, really."

"Has it refined and enriched you?"

"I don't know."

"You're not sure?"

"I'm not very good at it, yet."

"But you think you'll be good at it if you have instruction?"

"Yes. I mean—well, yes."

"Why?"

"I hope I have some talent."

"Don't you know?"

"It's not a thing you can very well say about yourself."

"Why?"

"Well—it sounds like blowing your own horn."

"And why shouldn't you blow your own horn?"

"You're not supposed to."

"You mean that you have travelled three thousand miles, at the expense of these people in your home town, to study singing under my guidance, and yet you think it indelicate to tell me, of all people, that you have talent."

"It's really for you to decide that, isn't it?"

"Partly. But you ought to know yourself."

"Well then, I think I have talent. And I want to sing more than anything else in the world."

"That's better. But I wonder if you'll think that when you're fifty. It's a dog's life, you know, even if you do well at it. But there; you see you've got me talking silly now. Every old hand tells every novice that a life in music is a dog's life. It's not really true. If you're a musician that's all there is to it; there's no real life for you apart from it. Now listen: I haven't been bullying you like this just for fun: I've been trying to find out what you're up to. All I know at present is that you have a pretty fair little voice

—good enough among several hundred others just as good. What training will do still remains to be seen. But unless you have some honest appraisal of yourself you haven't much chance. And all that appears now is that you think you have some talent, and are bashful about saying so: you want to sing, with some vague notion of benefitting mankind in general, and raising people a little above the mire of total depravity in which God has placed them. What do you want out of it for yourself?"

"I hadn't thought much about that."

"Little liar! Now, answer me honestly: haven't you had day-dreams in which you see yourself as a great singer, sought after and courted, popular and rich—probably with handsome men breaking their necks to get into your bed?"

Monica blushed deeply, and was silent. None of her day-dreams had ever included bed.

"You see! I was right. In your heart of hearts you think of singing as a form of power: and you've got more common sense in your heart of hearts than you have on that smarmy little tongue of yours. You're right; singing is a form of power—power of different kinds. Singing as a form of sexual allurement—there's nothing wrong with that. Very natural, indeed: every real man responds to the woman with the golden, squalling, cat-like note, and every real woman longs to hurl herself at the cock-a-doodling tenor or the bellowing bass. Part of Nature's Great Plan. But sex-shouting's a trap, too. At fifty, your golden squall becomes a bad joke. What then? Teaching? If you're not born to it—and few of the sex-shouters are—it's a dog's life; pupils are fatheads, most of 'em. Are you trying for—well, when you're trained—a possible twenty-five years of that kind of glory? Because it is glory, you know—real glory."

"I hadn't thought of it that way."

"Not refined enough? Well, there's another kind of singing. The technique is the same, but the end is different. It depends on what you have in your head and your imagination; it means being a kind of bard, who reveals the life that lies in great music and poetry. You use your voice to give delight. That's what music used to be for, you know—to capture the beauty and delight that people found in life. But then the Romantics came along and turned it all upside down; they made music a way of churning up emotions in people that they hadn't felt before. Music ceased to be a distilment of life and became, for a lot of people, a substitute for life—a substitute for a sea-voyage, or the ecstasies of sainthood, or being raped by a cannibal king, or even for an hour with a psychoanalyst or a good movement of the bowels. And a whole class of people arose who thought themselves music-lovers, but who were really sensation-lovers. Not that I'm a hundred per cent against the Romantics—just against the people who think that Romanticism is all there is of music. Well, there are the two kinds of singing. The sexual singer is, in pretty nearly all respects, the greater of the two, just as a mountain torrent is necessarily a greater force than the most beautiful of fountains: when she sings, she's a potent enchantress, and the music is merely the broomstick on which she flies. With the bardic singer, the music comes first, and self quite a long way second. Now: which sort of singing appeals to you?"

"Oh, the second, of course. The—bardic kind."

"If you really mean that, I think the less of you for it. Far better to set out aiming as high as you can, and killing yourself to be one of the big, adored, sexy squallers. It argues more real vitality and gumption in you. Still, I don't trust you to know what you want. You're too full of a desire to please—not to please me, but to please your family, or your schoolteachers, or those people—the What's It's Name Trust—who are paying the shot for you. Those people never want you to have great ambitions or strong, consuming passions. They want you to be refined—which means predictable, stable, controlled, always choosing the smallest cake on the plate, never breaking wind audibly, being a good loser—in a word, dead. I admit that the world couldn't function properly without its legions of nice, refined, passionless living dead, but there is no room for them in the arts.

So we'll see what you are after you've had a few months of work. At the moment you're just a nice girl with pots of money to spend on training. So let's get to work."

"You'll let me study with you, then?"

"Not for a while. Not till we find out what your politics are."

"Politics?"

"Haven't you any politics?"

"Well, Dad's a good union man, of course, so he always votes Conservative; he says the working man can get most out of them."

"Sorry. Just a bad joke of mine. Let me give you a short talk on politics, and then you'll have to go. There are, the world over, only two important political parties—the people who are for life, and the people who are against it. Most people are born one or the other, though there are a few here and there who change their coats. You know about Eros and Thanatos? No, I didn't really suppose you did. Well, I'm an Eros man myself, and most people who are any good for anything, in the arts or wherever, belong to the Eros party. But there are Thanatossers everywhere —the Permanent Opposition. The very worst Thanatossers are those who pretend to be Eros men; you can sometimes spot them because they blather about the purpose of art being to lift people up out of the mire, and refine them and make them use lace hankies—to castrate them, in fact. You've obviously been in contact with a lot of these crypto-Thanatossers—probably educated by them, insofar as you have been educated at all. But there's a chance that you may be on the Eros side; there's something about you now and then which suggests it."

Sir Benedict had risen, and was pushing papers into a briefcase. He rummaged on the top of his piano, and found a box containing some conductor's batons, and he put this in the case also.

"I'll get in touch with you from time to time to see how things are going and if your political colour has begun to show. Our first big problem is that you don't appear to know anything ex-

cept how to read music and play the piano. I'll arrange some
language lessons for you. And we must get your voice out from
under wraps. You're all buttoned up, vocally and spiritually. I'm
going to send you for a few months to the very best vocal coach
in London—old Murtagh. He's a real artist, by the way, so take
a good look at him. He'll unbutton you! He'll get a good healthy
yell out of you if anybody can! Yes, I'll start you next Monday
with Murtagh Molloy."

Five

"YOU'VE THE BAR'L OF A SINGER," said Mr. Molloy, giving Monica's waist a squeeze which was certainly intended to be professional, but which had a strong hint of larkiness about it, too. He had been feeling her diaphragm with his stubby, nicotine-stained fingers, blowing out sour clouds of cigarette smoke meanwhile. Suddenly he drew her arms about his waist. "Feel this," said he, and Monica felt his bulging, rubbery abdomen spring into embarrassing life under her hands. "That's the way to do it," said Murtagh Molloy, winking and lighting another cigarette.

This was going to take some getting used to, thought Monica. Sir Benedict had said that Molloy was the best singing coach in London, and she had expected someone comparable to himself; someone surprising, perhaps, but distinguished. Had not Domdaniel described him as an artist, an Eros-man? But here, on the second floor of a house in Coram Square, was a stumpy Irishman, bald and fifty if he was a day, who bade her feel his stomach, and talked about singing as if it were wrestling. Murtagh Molloy was a long way from the daemonic von Francius in *The First Violin*.

"Ben wants me to do what I can for you," said Mr. Molloy, "and I'll do't because he's an old friend. But I'll be frank; if you don't come across with the goods—out you'll go. I won't waste time on duds, and it's not everyone I can teach anyhow. You've got to be *simpatico*—d'you know *simpatico*? Means we've got to get along. I worked with a dozen teachers when I was young. I even had a few lessons with ffrangcon-Davies in his last years. You wouldn't know anything about him; a great, great artist. Why, I even worked for a while with William Shakespeare—ah, I thought that'd make your eyes bug—not the poet, of course, but the singing teacher—died, oh, it must be more than twenty years ago. But the greatest of them all was Harry Plunket Greene. You've heard of him? No? He was in Canada often. Worked with him off and on for years. Well, the point is, I was *simpatico* with 'em all, and that's why they could teach me, and that's why I could learn from them. If you're *simpatico* you can get down to business without a lot of palaver; hard words don't hurt, and praise doesn't puff y'up—makes you humble. Now, let's hear you sing something. What've you there?"

"I've got a terrible cold," said Monica, apologetically.

"You don't have to tell me that. But Plunket Greene used to say that all a singer needed was two teeth and a sigh. D'you get that? Something t'articulate with, and a wisp o'breath. What's that? Old Tosti's *Good-Bye!* That'll do fine."

Monica fought down her fears as well as she could, and sang. To her surprise, she sang rather well. Molloy accompanied her with a delicacy and helpfulness which she had not expected from the blunt, punching manner of his speech. But a greater surprise was to follow.

"Would you believe I once heard old Tosti play for Melba when she sang that?" said Molloy. "Long, long ago, but I recall it very well. I'll give you an idea."

He sang the song himself. It was unlike any singing Monica had ever heard, for although his voice was unremarkable in tone, and he sang without a hint of exaggeration or histrionics, it became as he sang the most compelling and revealing of sounds. The song invaded and possessed her as it had never done in all the time she had known it. Her own rendition, moulded by Aunt Ellen, was carefully phrased and built up emotionally until, she flattered herself, the final repetitions of "Good-bye" provided a fine and satisfying climax. But as Molloy sang the song there seemed to be no calculation of this kind, and the phrasing was hardly apparent. Yet the whole song was sung with a poignancy of regret which was the most powerful emotion that Monica had ever heard expressed in music. "It's unbearably sad when you really understand it," Aunt Ellen had said, thinking of her dead lover, and Monica had striven to re-create that sadness herself; sometimes she had succeeded, until the sob mounting in her throat brought on a prickling of the eyes, and then a fullness in the nose which ruined the singing. But that was real feeling, wasn't it? And that was what made great music, surely? Yet here was Murtagh Molloy, apparently as cool as a cucumber, giving rise to a sadness in her which swept far beyond anything she could associate with Aunt Ellen and the dead schoolteacher. This was the sadness of all the world's parting lovers, of all the autumns since the beginning of time, of death and the sweetness of death. Monica was moved, not to tears, but to a deep and solemn joy. This, then, was the bardic singing of which Dom-daniel had spoken.

"I surprised you, did I?" Molloy was looking intently at her. He winked, and picked up what was left of his cigarette from the end of the keyboard. "When you came in here you thought I couldn't sing because I didn't look like it. Well, it's a long study, girl, and while I was at it me beauty went on me. Now, how do you think my performance compared with yours?

—"Ah, now, don't blush; I shouldn't have asked you. But you see the difference, don't you? You were dipping your bucket into a shallow well and I was dipping mine into a deep one. No, no, not experience; I've had no more experience than most men. But I know what to do with mine, and I know how to get at it. Your song was all careful little effects. Well, good enough. But mine had one powerful effect. It had the proper muhd."

Monica was now sufficiently accustomed to Molloy's way of speaking to recognize that this was his way of saying "mood".

"The muhd's everything. Get it, and you'll get the rest. If you don't get it, all the *fioriruri* and exercises in agility and *legato* in the world'll be powerless to make a good singer of you. The muhd's at the root of all. And that's what I teach my beginners, and my advanced pupils, and some who've gone out into the world and made big names, but who come back now and again for a brush-up or some help with special problems. And mostly it all boils down to the muhd."

"That's what I'll teach you. You'd better come five days a week for a while. Ben says money's no object in your case, praise God! I think we'll get on—*simpatico*. And the muhd'll do wonders for you. Actually makes physical changes, in a lot o' people. Funny thing, I've known it to clear up terrible cases o' halitosis almost overnight. Not that that's your trouble. But you're stiff as a new boot and you've an awful Canadian accent as I suppose you know. It banishes regional accents completely."

As Monica ran down the stairs and out into Coram Square it did not occur to her to wonder why the muhd had not banished Molloy's very marked Irish accent. And in justice to him, it must be said that it was greatly diminished when he sang. She knew only that she was where she wanted to be, in the hands of a great teacher. She would master the secrets of the muhd. She would be a bardic singer like Murtagh Molloy. And if it involved having her waist hugged, and hugging his stomach in return—let it be so.

(2)

IN THE MONTHS of hard work which followed, Monica's enthusiasm never failed. Even during the preliminary six weeks when Molloy would not allow her to sing at all, in any sense which she understood, she was obedient. For an hour a day, five days a week, she stood before him, striving as best she might to follow his instructions.

"Feet a little apart. Let your neck go back as far as it will—no, don't move it, *think* it and and let it go back itself. Now, *think* your head forward and up *without* losing the idea of your neck going back. Now you're poised. Get the muhd, now—this time it'll be joy. Think o' joy, and *feel* joy. Open your lungs and let joy pour in—no, don't suck breath, just let it go in by itself. Now, with your muhd chosen, say "Ah", and let me hear joy.—Christmas! D'you call *that* joy! Maybe that's the joy of an orphan mouse on a rainy Monday, but I want the real, living joy of a young girl with her health and strength. Again—Ah, your jaw's tense. Get your neck *free;* think it free, and your head forward and up, and your jaw *can't* tense. Come on, now, try it again."

It was a technique for learning to command emotion—or, as Molloy preferred to call it, muhd. It became apparent to Monica that her range of emotion was small, and her ability to manifest it in sound, infinitesimal. This was dismaying, because she had been used to thinking of herself as a girl with plenty of emotional range; she could *feel* so much. But Molloy had his own way of extending the range of feeling and expression in his pupils.

"Your emotional muscles are weak, and what y'have are stiff. D'you go to the theatre? Well, you should. In fact, you must. Go to the Old Vic; go to any Shakespeare—any big stuff at all. Watch the actors. Working like dogs, when they're any good. Muhd, muhd, muhd, all the time; lightning changes, and subtleties like shot silk, winking and showing up new colours every second. Without a command o' muhd the work'd kill 'em. But it doesn't; they thrive on it. Never sick, and live to massive ages. And why? Because muhd's life, that's why. D'you know the Seven Ages o' Man, in *As You Like It?* Well, here, take this book and get it by rote for tomorra."

Work on the Seven Ages of Man became, under Molloy's enthusiastic direction, a riot of muhd.

"We start off calmly—the philosophic vein." Molloy's face was suffused with an appearance of weighty thought, and his stumpy frame took on the characteristic pose of those statues of nineteenth century statesmen, to be seen in municipal parks—one foot advanced, and a hand outstretched as though quelling the applause of an audience.

> All th' world's a stage,
> And all the men and women merely players.
> They have their exits and their entrances,
> And one man in his time plays many parts,
> His acts being seven ages.

Here Molloy underwent a startling metamorphosis; with knees bent, swaying gently from side to side, he hugged an imaginary baby to his ashy waistcoat.

> At first the infant,
> Mewling and puking in the nurse's arms.

"Ah, the wee soul!" said he, then like lightning banished the infant, and put on an expression which suggested a sick chimpanzee.

> Then the whining schoolboy, with his satchel
> And shining morning face, creeping like snail
> Unwillingly to school.

The chimpanzee gave place to something very airy, with hands clasped over its heart.

> And then the lover,
> Sighing like furnace, with a woeful ballad
> Made to his mistress' eyebrow.

Working on these lines, Molloy breathed the muhd of the soldier, the justice, and the Pantaloon—this last such a picture of trembling, piping eld as even the Comédie Francaise has never attempted. And his final portrait of dissolution—

> Sans eyes, sans teeth, sans taste—sans everything—

seemed to couple senility with the last ravages of paresis in a manner truly frightening.

It was not ham acting. It was something more alarming than that. Into each of these shopworn clichés of pantomime Molloy injected a charge of vitality which gave it a shocking truth. Vocally his performance was powerful, if in bad taste; physically it was rowdy and grotesque; but his meaning was palpable. To Monica it was a revelation; she had never seen anyone carry on like that before. She admired, and loyally fought down the embarrassment which rose in her. She was quite sure, however, that she could never do it herself.

Such resistance was like catnip to Molloy. Part of his profession was to prove to people that they could do what they believed to be outside their powers. Monica was put to work, exhorted, bullied and cajoled until, in a week or two she could cradle the baby, whine, sigh, roar, dogmatize (stroking an imaginary beard), shake like the Pantaloon, and at last, with eyes closed and hands hanging limp like the paws of a poisoned dog, await the stroke of death. Compared with Molloy's Protean performance hers was the merest shadow, but it was far beyond anything that she had ever dreamed she might achieve.

"Now we're beginning to get somewhere," said Molloy on the day when, at the third time of repetition, Monica had excelled herself. "Y'know, between ourselves, the stage people are always after me. A lot o' them come for lessons, y'see, and they say, 'Murty, you're a born director, and there's a dearth of 'em; how about it?' But I say, 'Boys, if it was only a question of speech, I'd do it like a shot, but I've no talent for the tableau side o' the thing. I've th'ear, but I lack th'eye'."

This was the process of vocal and spiritual unbuttoning which Sir Benedict Domdaniel had said would be accomplished by Murtagh Molloy. From the Seven Ages of Man they progressed to the First Chorus from *Henry V*, and at the beginning of each lesson Molloy would say—"Right; now let's have it—*O for a Muse afar!*" Obediently Monica would set her feet apart, poise her head on her neck, breathe a muhd commensurate with England's martial glory and declaim—

O, for a Muse of fire—

and so to the end of the speech, with horses, monarchs, and apologies for the inadequacy of the Elizabethan theatre, all complete. She was becoming quite pleased with herself, torn between her pride in being able to satisfy Molloy, and a sense of shame in the amount of noise and strutting which that involved.

In these declamatory exercises she was not permitted to speak the words in her accustomed way, and at first she used her true ear to copy Molloy's own accent. But when she did this he astonished her by declaring that she was speaking with a pronounced Canadian twang, and compelled her to adopt a tune and colour of speech which certainly was not English as she heard it spoken by Mrs. Merry, or by any of the people she met in chance contacts, but which she learned to identify in the theatre, at the performances of classical plays to which she was constantly being urged by Molloy. It was not the "English accent" mocked by Kevin and Alex, and forbidden by her mother, but it was not Canadian either; it was a speech that Garrick would not have found very strange, and of which Goldsmith would have approved.

Going to the theatre was, at first, a lonely business, and she did not like it. She had studied one or two of the plays of Shakespeare in school, but she had never associated them with any idea of entertainment. Nor was her first visit to the Old Vic a happy one, for the play was *The Comedy of Errors*, very cleverly transformed by a young director with his name to make into a mid-Victorian farce, in which the two Antipholuses, in chimney-pot hats and Dundreary whiskers, and the two Dromios, in identical liveries, rushed up and downstairs on a twirly scaffolding which was called Ephesus, until at last they were united with an Aemilia and a Luciana in crinolines and ringlets. Several critics had said that this treatment illuminated the play astonishingly, but for Monica it remained a depressing mystery. She was happier when, in a few weeks, it gave place to *Romeo and Juliet*. Peggy Stamper, dirtier than before, had hunted her up, and they went together. Afterward they discussed the play in detail at a Corner House and Monica expressed strong disapproval of the conduct of Friar Lawrence; if he had not tried to be so clever, everything might very well have been straightened out, and the lovers made happy. But then, said Peggy, where would the tragedy have been? And was it not better that Romeo and Juliet should have been unhappy, and tremendous, than happy, and just like everybody else? Monica would not have this; common sense, said she, was surely to be expected of everybody. But if you fill the world with common sense, countered Peggy, there'll be precious little art left. Art begins where common sense leaves off. And, perhaps as a result of Molloy's unbuttoning process, Monica had to agree that this was so.

Without becoming intimate with Peggy, Monica saw a good deal of her, and they did much of their theatre-going together. She met some of Peggy's friends, who were all art students and not particularly articulate or interesting, inclining to shop-talk, dirt, corduroys, beer and fried foods. But in their company she visited some of the galleries (for Molloy had urged her to study gesture and bodily posture in paintings and sculpture, as visible evidences of muhd) and learned enough from them to realize that she had no taste, and was unlikely ever to develop any. Peggy kindly attributed this to her musical interests, and Monica reconciled herself to possessing, like Molloy, th'ear but not th'eye.

These casual acquaintanceships were not enough to keep Monica from being very lonely and often in low spirits. Except for her visits to Molloy most of her days were long and dull. True, she went every morning to Madame Heber for a lesson in French, which she shared with two dry young men who were preparing for the Civil Service, and every afternoon at five o'clock she had a lesson in German from Dr. Rudolph Schlesinger, in the company of a spotty girl who was mastering that language so that she might read Freud in the original. Language study, and the exercises which Molloy ordered, filled up much of the time she spent in her rooms in Courtfield Gardens. But she still had plenty of time in which to be lonely. The few sticks which she and Mr. Boykin had purchased had made her rooms convenient, though far from luxurious, and she had learned how to feed herself economically and fairly well. She was even able to keep almost warm, though the gas-meter was remorseless in its demand for shillings. And, as winter wore away and spring came she began to see some of the strange, irregular beauty of London. But loneliness would not be banished, and Sundays were an endless weariness. Against all Thirteener custom, she began to go to Sunday movies.

Her cold resisted treatment, and became a sullen catarrh. Molloy refused to recognize its existence. "It's nothing at all," said he one day when she apologised for a coughing fit; "it's the dust in the air. You'd probably never get rid of it unless you took a long sea-voyage—maybe not then. Lots o' people have a congestion like that all their lives. Now me, for instance: I'd spit y'up a cupful o'phlegm any morning in the week. But I don't let it bother me." And so Monica decided that she would not let it bother her, either. But it did bother her, and particularly at night.

Her work with Molloy was the only life-giving element in her existence. Little by little he satisfied himself that she had some rudimentary notion of what muhd was, and could summon a small amount of it at will. It was true that Monica found it difficult to make love to a chair, which he regarded as an important test.

"Garrick could do't," said he; "time and again he'd astonish his friends that way. And it's all a question of muhd. To th'artist, with his imagination at command, and his experience of life to draw on, making love to a chair is just as possible—not as easy, maybe, or as pleasant—but just as possible as making love to a pretty girl. Now watch me: I'm going to make love to you."

The somewhat severe and admonishing expression which Molloy usually wore when he was teaching gave way to an alarming leer, and he approached Monica with youthful step. Seizing her hand he dropped on one knee and pressed it to his lips. "My darling," said he and, rising, pressed her to him with many variations on this simple endearment, which appeared to be the only one he could think of. When it seemed that he must inevitably kiss her he suddenly broke away, and looked sternly into her eye.

"Y'see? That's the way it is with the living subject. Now—what d'you say to this?"

And with a sudden turn he addressed himself to an armchair, caressed its dingy upholstery, knelt to it, entreated it to be his, praised its hair and complexion, called it his jewel, and swore that he could not live if it spurned him. Monica could not laugh, for unquestionably Molloy had the muhd, and however ridiculous his behaviour might be, the power in his voice might not be denied.

Nor could she rid herself of a feeling that Molloy liked showing her how to make love. He never missed a chance to feel her diaphragm, or gauge the expansion of her ribs at the back. And now, in these exercises with the chair it was always hard to know what he might do next. Obedient and teachable, Monica would do her best to pour out adoration for Molloy's unappetizing armchair.

"It's feeble," he would say. "Now you're not going to tell me that a girl like yourself doesn't know what love-making is. Eh? Don't blush; if you expect to be an artist you must get your feelings at command. Work on it at home, and show me what you can do next day."

Part of Monica's inability to enter whole-heartedly into these scenes of passion with the chair sprang from a feeling that other eyes than Molloy's were upon her. There were two doors in his teaching-room, one of which led to the landing, and the other, which had a glass transom over it, presumably to his private apartments; it was from this latter door that occasional rustlings and soft thumpings were heard while lessons were in progress. And one day, as Monica was leaving, she met a short, grey-haired woman on the landing, who gave her a gimlet look through a pair of steel-rimmed spectacles—a look which, from a stranger, was surprising indeed. As soon as the woman had disappeared into Molloy's apartment a sound of voices raised in high and unamiable converse broke out, and was audible until Monica had gone down the stairs and into the street.

(3)

IT WAS LATE in her first spring in London that Monica visited
Lorne and Meg.McCorkill in South Wimbledon. She never fully
understood how they came to know of her existence, although
they explained it at length; but as they both talked at once, the
chain which led from a friend of theirs in Salterton, who knew a
Thirteener who had obtained her address from Pastor Beamis,
and who had (the Salterton friend, that is to say) mentioned it
in a letter to—no, no, not the McCorkills, but to another Saltertonian, now resident in London—who had passed it on to them:
she had never fully understood it. But it was a beautiful spring
day, when she had been wishing that George Medwall wrote
better letters, less concerned with the inner politics of the Glue
Works, that a letter arrived for her, written in an unknown hand,
which addressed her thus.—

Dear Monica,
    You don't know us, but mutual friends in Canada have told
us about *you*, so Hi and all that stuff. Lorne and I have been
over here in the Great Frost for over two years now, and we
know just how tough it can be for a lonely Canuck. So why don't
you come out and have a real Canadian meal with us some night
next week, Friday maybe? We are always home, so if Friday is
no good; pick your own night. You can just get on the Underground at Earl's Court and come right to the end of the line.
Anybody will direct you from there. Better let us know by mail
when you are coming because Gawd only knows what will happen
if you try to phone in this country.

Be seeing you—
MEG McCORKILL

Beaver Lodge
Hubbard Road
Wimbledon, S.W. 20

Thus it was that a little after six on the following Friday evening Monica walked down Hubbard Road looking for Beaver Lodge. It was not hard to find, for on the gate was painted the name in rustic lettering which simulated sticks of wood, and at one of these a painted animal, not too hard to identify as a beaver, was gnawing. The woodwork of the semi-detached villa was bright with new paint, and a man on a ladder was dabbing delicately at a second-floor casement. He spied Monica as she came in the gate, and with a shout of "Hi!" he climbed down and hurried forward to greet her.

"Good to see you," he roared; "certainly good to see you. Can't shake hands—all over paint; just grab me by the wrist. Hey Meggsie!—I'm Lorne McCorkill; just call me Lorne. This is Meg. And where's Diane? Hey, Diane!"

"She's playing with that Pamela, and I suppose we'll have to get an earful of what Pamela's Mothaw's been saying," said Meg McCorkill, who had appeared in a very gay and brilliantly clean apron. "Hello dear, it's certainly great to see you. Come on in."

They bustled Monica into Beaver Lodge, which was a beautifully clean and bright little house—so clean and bright, indeed, that Monica was startled, for her eyes had become accustomed to the dinginess of Mrs. Merry's, the comfortable but seedy furnishings of Molloy's teachingroom, and the downright-squalor of the Heber and Schlesinger quarters.

"Isn't this lovely," said Monica; "it's like being at home!"

"Aw, you poor kiddie!" said Meg McCorkill. "Did you hear that, Lorne? Oh he's gone to change out of his paint-clothes." She raised her voice to a piercing shriek. "Lorne, didja hear what Monica just said? The minute she set foot in the door she said this was like home. How's that, eh?"

Lorne returned; he was wearing moccasin slippers, and was struggling into a sweatshirt which had the name of a western Canadian university printed across its chest. "That's swell," he said; "just swell. That makes up for all the trouble it was to get this paint here. Because let me tell you kid," said he, very emphatically, "every wall and piece of woodwork in this house is covered with real Canadian rubber-base paint. None of this English oil-base stuff for me. We brought it over, and fought it through Customs, and now it's on, and at least we know it isn't all going to shale off in wet weather. And that's something you can certainly count on here, boy—wet weather. Now how's about a real drink. Do you have yours straight, or on the rocks, or with water?"

Monica had been brought up in strict abhorrence of alcohol in all forms, but mixing with Peggy Stamper's friends had taught her to drink beer, in very small quantities. Meg saw her hesitation.

"Make us a Canadian Lyric, Lornie," said she. "Monica's too young for straight hard liquor."

They were in the kitchen, a gleaming room with a Canadian electric stove and a Canadian refrigerator in it; in a corner a Canadian washing-machine, with a round window in its middle, spied on them with this Cyclops eye. While Lorne worked with ice and bottles, Meg explained that they had imported these kitchen articles into England, because they could not possibly make do with the inferior local products. And what a trouble it had been! Everything electric had to be altered to accord with English notions of electrical current. And as for repairs—it was lucky that Lorne was able to turn his hand to pretty nearly anything—a real Canuck in that respect. God! cried Meg (who was very free with strong language, but did not seem to mean anything much by it) English women certainly put up with murder in their kitchens. Frankly, in their place, she'd just tell some of these English husbands where they got off at. But then, the poor mutts never knew anything better, so what was the use of telling them? They just seemed to be born sloppy. Their clothes! Had Monica ever seen anything like some of the comic Valentines you met just walking around the streets? In Medicine Hat—she and Lorne were both Westerners—they'd be taken in charge by the police.

By this time Lorne, with much shaking and measuring, had composed the Canadian Lyric, a cocktail made of equal parts of lemon juice and maple syrup, added to a double portion of rye whisky, and shaken up with cracked ice.

"The trouble we had getting real maple surrp!" said Lorne. "But I ran it down, finally, in a dump in Soho—a grocery that gets all kinds of outlandish stuff—and here it is, with that real old Canuck flavour! Boys-o-Boys! Just pour that over your tonsils and think of home! Say, where is Diane, anyway?"

Perhaps it was lucky for Diane that she made her appearance at this moment. She was a pretty little girl of about ten, with a fresh complexion.

"Sorry to be late, Mummy," said she; "I was playing with Pam, and I forgot."

"Hear that?" said Meg to Monica, as though expecting her to notice some serious symptom of disease in her child. "That's what we're up against, all the time. Of course, she hears it in school, and it's sure tough to fight school. Now, Little Pal," she said, directing her attention to Diane, "how often does Mom have to tell you to call her Mom, or even Mommie, but not that awful *Mummy?* Jeez, you make me sound like something in a museum."

"Sorry, Mom," said the child.

"I just can't bear that awful mush-mouthed way they have of talking," said Meg to Monica again. "If she takes that home, she'll be a laughing-stock."

Monica, not knowing what else to do, agreed.

As the evening progressed, she found herself agreeing to many other things, for in Beaver Lodge not to agree in any criticism of England was to be a traitor to Canada. Monica had never given much thought to Canada, as an entity, before; she was a Canadian, and if she had been challenged on the point she would have said that she was proud of it, but if the challenger had probed further, and asked her upon what foundations her pride rested, she would have been confused. But at Beaver Lodge there were no uncertainties: England was a compost-heap of follies, iniquities and ineptitudes. A great country—well, at one time, perhaps—but its greatness was passing. How could a country, where fish was offered for sale on marble slabs, perfectly open to dust and dirt, expect to hold a position of supremacy? The dirtiness of the English, in the eyes of Lorne and Meg, was their greatest crime.

Such conversation was apparently intended to lend savour to the meal, which consisted of tomato juice out of a can (they had their juices sent to them from Canada, every month) and real Western Canadian beef.

"You couldn't touch the beef here," said Lorne, as he carved. "It'd be criminal to feed it to Diane. This country, I tell you—their herds are riddled with T.B."

"What's T.B., Daddy?" asked Diane.

"It's an awful disease you get from dirt, honey," said Lorne. "You know how Daddy tells you to always hold your breath when you're passing a drain in the road, and it's steaming? The cows breathe dirt, and they get T.B."

Having eaten the safe beef, they had a banana-cream pie which was, in part, a traitor, for although the lard in the pastry was from Canada (as was the flour too, of course) the bananas were purchased in England, and were from the Canaries, and thus not the large plantains to which Canada is accustomed. The meal concluded with coffee, made in what Meg declared was "the real, old-fashioned Canadian way" in an electric percolator; it was very good coffee, and Monica was grateful for it.

She ventured to ask how it was that the McCorkills were able to get so much of their food from home?

"Lorne's work makes it possible," said Meg. "And if it didn't I don't know where we'd turn. He's with the marketing board, you know, and we can make arrangements which probably wouldn't work otherwise. And, frankly, if we couldn't get most of our stuff from home, I'd kick right over the traces; I wouldn't risk feeding Diane the stuff they have here. I've warned her not to accept food in the houses of any of the kiddies she plays with.

It's not an easy rule to enforce, but if a kiddy knows just what germs she may be taking into her system, she uses her head."

It was when Diane had gone to bed that Meg confided one of her chief worries. "She was less than eight when we left home," said she, jerking her head upward to indicate the child, "and more than two years is a long time for a kiddy. In spite of all we can do she's just getting to talk like all the kids around here, and the other day she said, 'Mommy, when are we going back to America?' *America!* Get it! Well, I just dropped everything, and I must have talked to her for fifteen minutes about home, and how she must always make it clear to the people here that there's all the difference in the world between Canada and the U.S. But where do you suppose she picked up an expression like that? From her teacher, of course! Gosh, they don't seem to be able to distinguish—I mean, you'd think they'd realize we were part of the Commonwealth, wouldn't you? I mean, when we're the granary of the world, and all through the war we were the Arsenal of Democracy, and everything?" Meg became almost tearful as she thought of this instance of British indifference to Canadian individuality.

"Diane's young," said Monica, trying to think of words of comfort for these exiles. "You won't have to worry about her; she's so pretty; I don't know when I've seen such a pretty complexion. There's something good that England has given her; all the children here have a lovely high colour."

"Yeah, and they've got broken veins in their cheeks by the time they're thirty," said Meg, who was so plainly resolved not to take comfort in anything that Monica decided not to try again.

After the conversation had passed through an embittered discussion of the scandalous price of fruit in England—"Didja ever try to buy a peach in Fortnum and Mason's? Half-a-crown each, and taste like wet kleenex! We bring everything in from home" —the McCorkills turned their attention to what Monica was doing in this desperate land. To her surprise, they did not assert that she could have learned to sing just as well in Canada; when

she told them about Sir Benedict Domdaniel, and about Murtagh
Molloy and his insistence that she should be able to call up the
memory of any emotion at will (she did not tell them about making love to a chair) they were impressed, and said what luck it
was that she should have a chance to study with such people. In
the realm of the unknown they were quite happy to acknowl-
edge English, or European, supremacy: it was in the things
which touched their daily life that they were impossible to please.
It came to Monica suddenly, in the midst of a tirade about the
utter impossibility of eating English bread—they baked their
own, though it was a nuisance—that the McCorkills' vast dis-
relish for England meant no more than that they were uprooted,
afraid, and desperately homesick. It was not a very remarkable
flash of insight, but she was only twenty-one, not at all accustomed to knowing things about people which they had not
fully recognized themselves, and it did much to soothe her self-
esteem, which had been badly bruised during her five months
in London.

Monica was not, in fact, accustomed to thinking anything
which was contrary to the opinion of any older person with whom
she was talking, and it was the McCorkills who first made this
adult luxury possible to her. Thus it was that, when Lorne had
walked her back to the Underground Station—"You should never
walk around in this city by yourself at night. Do you ever look
at the Sunday papers? God, the things that go on! And even
ministers in awful cases! Wouldn't it just rot your socks, though?"
—she was in high spirits and very well pleased with herself. She
had enjoyed the accustomed food, and the cleanliness, and the
genuine kindness and warmth of heart which Lorne and Meg
had shown her, but she did not feel in the least committed, on
that account, to acceptance of their opinions. A Thirteener upbringing had until now denied her the delights of social hypocrisy, and these came with a special sweetness. She had even let
the McCorkills think that she would join them at some future
meeting of a Canadian Club of which they were members—

"Hard to keep it going, though; so many people seem to lose interest, or they get mixed up with people who live here, and don't seem to want to get together with their own folks"—though she was determined in her heart that she was not going to spend another evening talking about English dirt and wondering why the English could never learn to make coffee. This new freedom to say one thing and think another came to Monica all the more sweetly for coming late, and she liked the McCorkills all the better for not feeling it necessary to agree with them in her heart.

During her long ride back to Earl's Court on the Underground she felt happier than at any time since leaving home. The warmth of the late spring night and the beauty of the city were hidden from her as she sped through the earth in the rattling tube, but she felt them in her heart. If it was to be a fight between England and Canada for the love of Monica Gall, she knew that England would win. Some of the folk songs that she had latterly been studying with Molloy were so powerfully present in her mind that she had to sing them under her breath, unheard by the other passengers because of the noise of the train.

> William Taylor was a brisk young sailor,
> He was courting a lady fair—

William Taylor had probably eaten a lot of fish that had been exposed to the air on marble slabs, too, but it had not apparently diminished his joy in life.

> As I went out one May morning,
> One May morning betime,
> I met a maid, from home had strayed,
> Just as the sun did shine.

This maid unquestionably had one of those superb strawberries-and-cream complexions which degenerated into broken veins after she was thirty, but at the time dealt with in the song she was breathing a wonderful, fresh muhd, and that was what really mattered.

From the Underground Station Monica walked slowly to Courtfield Gardens, happy in the moonlight and without a thought for the clerical rapists who might lurk in every areaway.

> *How gloriously the sun doth shine,*
> *How pleasant is the air,*
> *I'd rather rest on a true love's breast*
> *Than any other where.*

Thus sang Monica, and when two men returning from a pub called "very nice" from the other side of the street, she waved her hand to them, feeling neither shy nor frightened. It was the first time, since coming to England, that she had sung simply because she was happy. She was not thinking of George Medwall. He came into her mind once, but she dismissed him. He would not do here. He was not a McCorkill, but he did not fit into the new world which she had decided to make her own.

(4)

AT THE END OF JUNE a report was forwarded to the Trustees of the Bridgetower estate by Jodrell and Stanhope, as follows:

In re the Bridgetower Beneficiary

Dear Sirs and Madam:

As reported to you in our communication of January 3 the beneficiary of the Bridgetower Trust, Miss Monica Gall, is comfortably lodged at 23 Courtfield Gardens, S.W. 5. In reply to the specific enquiry of Miss Laura Pottinger, Miss Gall is visited on the first business day of each month by our Mr. Boykin, who reports that the landlady, Mrs. Merry, says that Miss Gall has at no time entertained a visitor in her quarters other than a Miss Margaret Stamper, a student at the Slade School of Art. If it is thought necessary to appoint a moral guardian for Miss Gall, we cannot undertake such duties, though we will approach Sir Benedict Domdaniel in this matter if so instructed by you.

Attached is a report on Miss Gall's musical studies from Sir Benedict Domdaniel (Encl. 1) and also a statement of dis-

bursements made by us on your behalf (Encl. 2). Assuring you
of our advice and service at all times,

Yours truly,

Miles Peter Andrews

(For Jodrell and Stanhope
Plough Court
Fetter Lane
London E.C. 4)

The first enclosure may be given in full:

To the Bridgetower Trustees
Salterton, Ontario,
Canada.

Sirs:

Since your protégée, Monica Gall, came to England to work
with me, I have seen her twice. On the first occasion I heard her
sing, and was frankly not as impressed with her possibilities as
I was when I heard her in Toronto. The voice was very muffled
and somewhat lifeless. Therefore I sent her to a first-rate coach,
Mr. Murtagh Molloy, who has been working with her several
days a week since then, and who has been able to do a good
deal with her. I heard her again about a week ago, and her voice
is at last beginning to declare itself.

It is a good soprano—promises to be really good—but is somewhat 'veiled' or 'covered'—Humphrey Cobbler can explain these
terms to you—for a little more than an octave in the lower part.
But the range is a fine one, from b below middle C to g'''.

However, as you are well aware, there is more to singing than
the possession of a pleasant tone and a big range. The voice must
be interesting, and this is a matter of brains, or temperament, or
both, and so far Miss Gall, though a nice girl, has not shown
anything out of the ordinary in either of these departments. Perhaps her biggest handicap, as I believe I said to you before, is
that she has virtually no general cultivation, and though she
seems to have some imagination, she has had nothing with which
to nourish it.

With a view to remedying this difficulty I am packing her off to Miss Amy Neilson, who lives in St. Cloud—an American lady who takes two or three girls into her house for coaching in history and literature, and shows them a good time in Paris—sights, shopping and whatnot. I have known Miss Neilson for many years and can vouch for her. Three months there should make a great difference to Monica; I have written to Amy, asking her to give special attention to the girl's musical background, and have had a copy of Grove's *Dictionary of Music and Musicians* sent there for that purpose. When she returns in the autumn we shall see what we shall see.

Murtagh Molloy, on whose judgement I place great reliance, says that Monica is young for her age and needs waking up. We shall see what can be done.

Yours sincerely,
BENEDICT DOMDANIEL

Dean's Yard
Westminster S.W. 1

It was Enclosure 2 which startled the members of the Bridge-tower Trust, assembled one hot July night to consider these communications.

"I must say they're very cool about our money," said Solly, who had been having trouble meeting some bills, and was sore on the subject.

"We may rely on Jodrell and Stanhope," said Mr. Snelgrove, sticking up for the profession.

"Perhaps we may, but what about Domdaniel?" said Solly. "He's 'packing her off' for three months in France without so much as by-your-leave. Have we given him an absolutely free hand?"

"Yes, and look at this," said Miss Puss, who had secured the itemized account as soon as Snelgrove had laid it down. "Grove's *Dictionary of Music and Musicians,* forwarded from Bumpus to France—nine volumes, twenty-seven guineas—one hundred and fifty dollars! For books, of all things! Can't she learn from anything less than that?"

"Not a hundred and fifty dollars, Miss Pottinger," said Snel-grove; "you are forgetting the rate of exchange."

"So far as I am concerned, a five-dollar bill and a pound note are the same thing," said Miss Puss. "If there is any drop in the value of the pound, I am sure it is merely temporary."

"And look what Domdaniel is paying himself," said Solly. "He's seen her twice, and he's soaking us ten guineas a time. And this fellow Molloy—five lessons a week at three guineas each! Sven-gali would have been glad of such fees. We'll have to protest. This is ridiculous."

"We're making a beggar on horseback of this girl," said Miss Puss, "and she'll ride to the Dee. Mark my words."

It was Dean Knapp who undertook the ungrateful task of being the Voice of Reason.

"We must bear in mind that we are simply appointed to carry out the terms of the Trust," said he, "and the income from your mother's estate, Solomon, is very large. Indeed, if what is spent to maintain and instruct the girl during the next six months is no more than we shall have to pay to settle this statement, it will not disperse one-quarter of the total in a year. Have we any right to accumulate money?"

"We have no right to accumulate funds at all, except what might be dictated by common prudence," said Mr. Snelgrove. "Certainly we cannot withhold money. When Mrs. Bridgetower made this will I tried to reason with her, but I am sure you all know how effective that would be. She was determined that her beneficiary should not be stinted."

"Not stinted!" said Solly. "And here I am pushed to the very edge of my bank account to settle a bill for a hundred and thirty-two dollars for repairs to mother's old car, when I've already had to sell my own to get ready money! It's intolerable!"

"It is the law," said Mr. Snelgrove. "We are not empowered to build up any large surplus. I fear that we shall have to tell Jodrell and Stanhope to spend more—and get Sir Benedict to spend more. Discreetly, of course. The girl need not actually know."

"As I understand it, we have to spend the income on roughly a million dollars, which is invested in three and four per cents, and with taxes deductible," said the Dean, and when Mr. Snelgrove nodded, he looked for a time at the ceiling, and then spoke what was in all their minds. "More than any of us is ever likely to have for himself."

"That is one of the difficulties of being a trustee," said Mr. Snelgrove; "that is why trustees often behave so strangely."

That night Miss Puss was very severe with her old housekeeper, who had left a light burning needlessly, and Solly went to bed drunk, to Veronica's great distress. Though the difficulties of their marriage had been many since they came under the Dead Hand of Mrs. Bridgetower, this was something new.

Six

"THERE YOU HAVE IT", said Sir Benedict. "Orders from headquarters: we must spend more money. I must spend more on having you trained. You must spend more, presumably, on your way of living. The lawyers here are doubling your personal allowance."

"O dear," said Monica. "I wish they wouldn't do that."

"Why? Didn't you learn anything about spending money in Paris? I particularly asked Amy to give you a few pointers about that."

"She did. She was wonderful to me, and told me a lot about clothes and make-up and hair-dos and things. But, please, Sir Benedict, I don't want to get involved in all that kind of thing. It's not what I'm here for."

"But apparently it is what you're here for. These Bridgetower people want their money spent, and it's your job to spend it. Most girls would jump at your chance."

"No, no. I'm here to be trained as a singer—a musician, I hope—"

"Why the distinction?"

"Amy took three of us to a party in Paris that some musical people were giving, and a string quartet played, and afterward I was talking to them, and said I was training to be a musician, and when they found out I was a singer, they laughed. One of them said, 'Music is a very nice hobby for a singer; it gives him a complete change from his profession'."

"I know; musicians are full of jokes about singers. Justified, most of them. But we'll try to make a musician of you, as well. What's that to do with all this extra money which must be got rid of?"

"Well, I can't escape a feeling that it will make it harder for me to do what I want to do. I mean—it seems to cushion life, somehow. It cuts you off from people, and experiences, and that's just what I need. I found that out in Paris. Those girls at Amy's; they were awfully nice, and I had a fine time, but they weren't serious. They're just dabblers—in the nicest possible way—but still dabblers. I'm serious. I want to be a professional. If possible I want to be an artist."

"And you're afraid having plenty of cash will cut you off from that?"

"Yes. Don't you agree?"

"Look around you, I'm far from rich, but I'm pretty comfortable, and I take care to keep my fees high. But I'm rather widely regarded as an artist."

"Of course. But you've made your way. You didn't begin with all this."

"My family were well-off; I was born with a very good weight of silver spoon in my mouth. In my student days I never missed a meal or wore a shabby suit, and I worked just as hard and agonized just as much as the fellows who hadn't sixpence. All money can do for a musician is keep him from discomfort and worry about bills—and that's a very good thing."

"Those girls in Paris were all ambitious, until it meant real work. But they all knew they didn't actually have to work, and that made all the difference."

"Had they any talent?"

"I don't know. But how do I know that I've any talent myself?"

"You don't, but you're industrious. Murtagh says you work like a black. But that has nothing to do with money. You really must shake off these fat-headed nineteenth century notions you have about musicians being romantic characters who starve in garrets, doing immense moral good to the world through the medium of their art. Now look here: money alone can't hurt you. If you're a fool, or if you haven't any talent, or not enough, it will influence the special way in which you go to the devil. Money is a thing you have to control; it must play the part in your life that you allot to it, and it must never become the star turn. But take it from me, too much money is less harmful than too little. Wealth tends to numb feeling and nibble at talent, but poverty coarsens feeling and chokes talent, and feeling and talent are the important things in your job and mine."

"Yes, but—I don't know whether I have any talent, and neither you nor Mr. Molloy will say anything one way or the other. And I do know that I haven't much feeling. Mr. Molloy says so, too. He's always at me to express more, but I haven't much to express."

"What would you have to express—at twenty-one?"

"Surely if I have any feeling, any insight into music, it ought to show itself by now?"

"Not necessarily. Some people are born with huge, gusty typhoons of feeling, all ready to be unleashed. Others have to learn to feel. And when they're both forty, you'd have a hard time telling one from the other. But when they're fifty the typhoons will be getting weaker, and the feeling which has been carefully nurtured and schooled may well be growing still. I don't suppose anybody ever told you that."

"Never."

"Look at your physical type. Medium blonde, northern-looking, good solid bones, strong as a horse, I'll bet, and with an excellent, good big head. You're not one of those little southern passion-pots, with a rose in her teeth and a stiletto tucked into her garter. *She's* got feeling; *you've* got intelligence. She's a sprinter; you're a miler. You'll have to learn, painstakingly, things that she seems to have known from her cradle. But because she's never had to learn them, they may desert her quickly—after an illness, or when her lover runs off with another girl, or something. Whereas you, once you've learned a thing, will cling to it like a bulldog, or like a snapping-turtle which is supposed never to relax its hold till sundown."

"I see," said Monica, who was overjoyed to be compared to a bulldog or a snapping-turtle under these circumstances.

"So get on with the job. Stop fretting because you're not worldly-wise and chock-full of Beethovenian *Sturm und Drang* at twenty. That's not your type at all. Stop fussing that comfort is going to knock the props from under your genius. Develop what you've got: make it possible for your emotions to grow. Get on with the job. Work, work, work. How are the languages?"

"Not too bad, Amy said."

"Well, work harder and make them damned good. And do what Murtagh tells you; if anybody can make a singer of you, he will. And you may take it from me that you'll get all the experience you want, soon enough. Most people reach a point where they're wishing experience would stop crowding them. Anyhow, it isn't what happens to you that really counts: it's what you are able to do with it. The streets are crammed with people who have had the most extraordinary experiences—been shipwrecked, chased out of Caliph's harems, blown sky-high by bombs—and it hasn't meant a thing to them, because they couldn't distill it. Art's distillation; experience is wine, and art is the brandy we distill from it.—Now, you'll have to go. I've a man coming about some music for a contemporary composers' series. And don't worry; we'll think of some ways to spend the Bridgetower money.—By the way, did you ever know this Mrs. Bridgetower?"

"Oh no; she was an invalid for years, I think. Anyway—I wouldn't have known her."

"She sounds like a loony. This Trust of hers is silly. Still, if the money has to be spent, we'll spend it."

(2)

EXPERIENCE—WELL, PARIS HAD BEEN experience. Amy Neilson had taught her a lot about eating, for instance. It had been a surprise to Monica to find that her very best manners weren't the thing at all, according to Amy, and she had had to modify them, not in the direction of more gentility, but less. And the gay little laugh with which she had been accustomed to pass off any social difficulty—Amy had quickly rooted out that little laugh. There had been, well, dozens of things that Amy had discouraged, always in the kindest possible way, and Monica had been a quick learner. Her clothes had been reformed in the direction of plainness; some rings and earrings, which were certainly not expensive, but which she had once thought very pretty, had been discarded; a tendency toward cuteness in dress and manner had withered under Amy's hint that to be cute was not the whole end of woman.

Yes, that was all experience. But shallow, surely? Not the raw material for one of Molloy's muhds. What else? That party to which Amy had taken her in that wonderful apartment on the Rue Scheffer—just like the movies, with a view which included the Eiffel Tower—that had been experience. For it was a very musical party, to introduce the work of a promising young composer, and Monica had gone to it in a reverential spirit. And what had happened? The assembled musicians, and patrons and critics and concert agents had listened far less intently and politely than the audience of the Community Concerts in Salterton would have done; some of them, sitting on a stair which led to a gallery above the salon, had actually *talked*, in loud whispers, and not about the music, either! That was experience, surely—to discover that in Paris, of all places, real music-lovers could be so rude as to talk while music was being played? She had mentioned this to Amy, and Amy had laughed. "You don't have to be serious about it all the time," she had said. But surely you did have to be serious about it all the time? Wasn't that what Sir Benedict had just been telling her?

But Sir Benedict wasn't very serious. He just shot off a lot of talk which seemed to be serious, and turned suddenly into jokes —the silly kind of jokes the English seemed to like so much. Still, a visit to him always made Monica feel that music was something even better than being serious—it was exciting. And what a marvellous person! So tall, and with a wonderful figure, even though he was fifty-three (she had checked him in *Grove*) and it didn't matter a bit that he was so bald and had really an uncommonly big nose. Her attitude toward him was worshipful, but she did wish he would explain himself a little more fully. His remark that she was intelligent, for instance. Why couldn't he have expanded that? If she was intelligent, why couldn't she summon up more muhd for Molloy?

What had he meant when he said that some people had to learn to feel? Surely that was a contradiction? And all that about distilling experience from the wine of life. What experience had come her way that could be distilled? Did he mean that everything was experience?

As Monica pondered, a large, middle-aged nun, with a schoolgirl in her charge, entered the bus and sat down beside her. The nun composed her vast skirts, and fished a rosary of workmanlike appearance from their depths. "Come along now, Norah," she said in a loud, cheerful voice to the girl at her side, "never waste a minute; let's say a rosary for the conversion of the people on the bus."

Was that experience? Could it be made into anything? Did it add anything to her?

Distilling thus, Monica went back to Courtfield Gardens, buying some special cakes for her tea on the way, to celebrate having spent half an hour with the exciting Sir Benedict.

(3)

OCTOBER PASSED IN MORE WORK with Molloy. A splendid combination gramophone and radio had arrived one day at Courtfield Gardens for Monica, with a note from Sir Benedict urging
her to make good use of it, and to buy as many records as she
wished. It was unfortunate that on the very day of the arrival
of this glossy monster, Peggy Stamper and one of her dirty young
men in corduroys dropped in.

"Cool" said Peggy, surveying it in wonder; "have you bought
that?"

"I suppose so," said Monica; "it's to be part of my training."

Peggy and the young man commented freely, and not without
envy, on the kind of training which demanded so costly an object,
and it was plain to Monica that the radiogram put her, so far as
these two were concerned, in a different world from themselves.
They were poor on principle; it was part of their creed that nobody who was serious about art ever had a bean, and those of
their group who had allowances from home took good care not
to offend against this tenet. When they left, Monica knew, without anything having been said about it, that her position on the
fringe of Peggy's group had become even more remote. They
had nothing against her, but obviously she was rich, and that was
that.

Without being aware that she was doing so, she salved her
wound in a manner common to the rich; she bought a lot of expensive albums of recordings, some swansdown cushions for her
divan, and some luxurious things to eat; these expenditures
numbed, but did not remove, her sense of loss. So she increased
the dose of her anodyne; she bought some new clothes—really
good ones, of the kind that Amy approved for the well brought
up young girl, and a quiet but expensive winter coat. If she had
lost her place in the corduroy group, she might as well be thor-

oughly out of it. The clothes and the pleasure of listening to the machine insulated her against loneliness for almost a fortnight. But she knew, every night, and as she prepared her breakfast each morning, that another bout of that terrible destructive despair which had seized her on her first arrival in London was imminent, waiting for an opportunity to descend. It would not be quite the same, for her circumstances had changed, but it would be of the same essence.

Sometimes she had to fight hard against panic. Should she confide in Meg McCorkill? Yes, but confide what? That she was afraid that money was cutting her off from serious work and the people who might be her friends? How silly it seemed when put into words! That the English winter, which was now beginning, filled her with dread? That pegging away at French and German made her feel like a schoolgirl, without a schoolgirl's resilience against the boredom of study? Meg would have a ready and immediate remedy for both those ills—frequent visits to Beaver Lodge. But three months in Paris, and the English spring, had put a barrier between her and the raw simplicities of Beaver Lodge which seemed to her to be insurmountable.

Of course she had Molloy's unfailing method of summoning and controlling emotion. She had only to breathe a happy and confident muhd, and serenity and confidence would certainly follow. But it didn't work. She determinedly set about it on two occasions, and both ended in crying fits. Real heaviness of heart could not be budged by such imaginative effort.

(4)

RELIEF CAME SUDDENLY. One day, at the end of a lesson in which Molloy was particularly exacting, he said: "Sir Ben wants to hear you tomorrow, and he's coming here. So be on your best behaviour and do me credit."

Half an hour of the next day's lesson had passed before Sir

Benedict Domdaniel appeared; in Monica's eyes he seemed more elegant than ever against the background of Molloy's shabby teaching-room, and beside the stubby figure of the Irishman. He heard her sing some of her folksongs, and declined Molloy's earnest request that she be allowed to recite some passages of Shakespeare for him.

"Done much about scales, Murtagh?"

"Not yet, Ben, but I'm goin' to get at them right away. She's ready for a good grind on exercises. But you know my way; the exercises must be linked with some real music, or you'll get nothing but a technical voice. But now the voice is warmed up, I can see where we're goin'."

"You've done a good job. Better voice than I thought it might be." He smiled at Monica. "Are you pleased with yourself?"

"I can't say," said she. "You must be the judge."

"Yes, but you know that you sing better than when you came here, don't you?"

"It feels better; I didn't know I had such a big range."

"Your voice is beginning to declare itself. Some technical work will make it very useful. But at present you haven't much to say with it, have you? And that's really what I've come about; it's time you went to another coach."

"Leave Mr. Molloy!"

"Oh no, not at all. He'll continue the work on your voice, make it agile and strong and give you a sound technical equipment. But I think you ought to go to another man to learn something about music generally, broaden your musical experience. You don't want to be just a singer; well—you must learn something more than singing."

"Aw, now, Ben I'll give her all o' that she can take," said Molloy; "I've started her already on some Shakespeare, and if you'd only let her show you what she can do, you'd get the surprise of your life. Come on, give him the Seven Ages—"

"Murtagh, I don't want to hear the Seven Ages or anything else. I know exactly what I want her to do, and if you'll listen—"

"Ben, some day you'll insult me once too often. Are you suggesting that I'm not capable of giving this girl a good cultural training? Is that what you mean? Because if so—"

"You're the best voice-builder in London. I tell you that, and don't forget I got my training with old Garcia, and I know what I'm saying. Isn't that enough for you?"

"You want to snatch a promising pupil away from me and give her to God knows what charlatan—"

"She's not your pupil; she's my pupil, and I'm responsible to the What's-Its-Name Foundation for her. I'm doing the best I can for her. That's why I sent her to you in the first place, Murtagh, and if you weren't so damned stubborn you'd know it. And I'm not taking her from you; I just want to send her to Revelstoke for some coaching in things you probably haven't time for."

"What in the name o' God are you sending her to Revelstoke for?"

"Excellent reasons, my dear Murtagh; excellent reasons. Let's say that it's to broaden her musical expérience, and leave it there."

"It'll do that. That fellow's worthless, Ben, and you know it."

"On the contrary. I have been working on some of his things for my series of contemporary music broadcasts, and he has been most helpful. And I'll tell you more: he's one of the best of our younger composers."

"Ha! Quite the little genius."

"Yes, quite the little genius."

"But an impossible fellow to get on with."

"Exactly what he says about you, so it's a draw. Now you mustn't take away the character of Monica's new teacher before she's even seen him, Murtagh, so shut up. And it's no good shouting any more, because I've settled everything. Monica, tomorrow at four o'clock you are to call on Mr. Giles Revelstoke; he lives at 32 Tite Street—on the top floor. He'll be expecting you, and he'll undertake some general musical training for you. And that's what you need."

After a little further pacification of Molloy, Sir Benedict carried Monica off in his car, and went some distance out of his way

to leave her at Courtfield Gardens. As they were parting, he said:
"By the way, I made rather a bloomer last time we were talking;
I re-read the letter from the lawyers afterward, and I don't think
I should have told you that we had to spend more money on you.
Apparently you're not supposed to know, though I don't really
see how it's to be kept from you. I'm a terrible chatterer—my
little vice. Anyhow, it's not my business to fall in with lawyers'
schemes like that. It's a fact; more money must be spent. That's
why I feel we can afford Revelstoke now. You'll like him. Delightful chap."

(5)

THIRTY-TWO TITE STREET was a gloomy house across the road
from a large Infirmary, from whose windows came an unceasing
sound which Monica at first thought was the weeping of baby
chicks, but which she later learned was the crying of infants in
the nurseries. A rack of cards in the hall told her that Giles Revelstoke was on the top floor, and she was about to press the bell
beneath his name when she heard someone coming down the
stairs very rapidly and noisily, shouting "Sorree, sorree" in a loud
voice. It was a very tall young man with tousled hair, who arrived beside her as her finger was poised to push.

"You want Giles?" said the young man. "Don't ring; don't
dream of ringing; you'll cut him to the heart if you ring. Go right
up, and right in without knocking, and if you don't see him about
give a cooee. Most informal fellow in the world. Hurry up, old
girl; up you go."

Monica had dressed herself elegantly for this first meeting with
her new teacher, and had worked up a sense of the dignity of the
occasion. She did not want to burst upon him without all the
proper formalities. But the tall young man was not to be gain-
said, so she went up two flights of long dark stairs, and found a
door at the top which opened into what was plainly a studio, an
extremely crowded and untidy room furnished with a large work

table and an upright piano, and beyond that nothing recogniz-
able as furniture, but with heaps of books, papers and music
piled on the floor and all the other flat surfaces. The only pleasing
thing about the room, apart from a large black cat asleep on the
piano top, was a dormer window set in the sloping roof which
gave a view, through chimneypots, toward the Thames.

Should she sit down? But where? She stood for a few minutes,
then picked her way through the debris on the floor to the window and looked out of it for a while. But she was disturbed by
the sense that she was in somebody else's room. She must not
make free. But where was Mr. Revelstoke? Had he forgotten that
she was to come at four? The tousled young man had said that he
was at home. This was quite unlike a visit to Molloy, who was as
punctual as the clock, or to Sir Benedict, whose valet was always
at hand to take her at once to the great man. What had Molloy
called Revelstoke? "Quite the little genius". This looked like a
genius's room. But how to inform the genius of her presence?

She coughed. Nothing happened. She coughed again, and
walked about heavily, making a noise with her feet and feeling a
fool. Should she go downstairs again, and ring the bell?

No; she would play the piano. She seated herself and played
what came first into her head, which was her one-time favourite,
Danse Macabre. The cat roused itself, yawned at her, and slept
again.

She had played for perhaps three minutes, when a voice said
very loudly behind her, "Stop that bloody row!" She turned, and
standing in the doorway was a man. He was utterly naked.

Nothing in Monica's previous experience had prepared her for
such a spectacle, and it was the most shocking sight, within the
bounds of nature, that could have confronted her. The Thirteeners, and everybody else with whom she had ever been intimately
acquainted, thought very poorly of nakedness. Courtships, even
when carried to lengths which resulted in hasty and muted weddings, were always conducted fully dressed. The intimacies of
married life were negotiated in the dark, under blankets. Shame
about nakedness was immensely valued, as a guarantee of high

character. It is true that, when in Paris, Monica had been taken
to the Louvre several times by Amy Neilson, and she had learned
to look at naked statuary—even the Hermaphrodite—without be-
traying the discomfort she felt in the presence of those stony,
bare monsters; but that was art and idealized form—no preparation for what she now saw—a naked man, not especially graced
with beauty, coloured in shades which ranged between pink and
whitey-drab, patchily hairy, and obviously very much alive.

He was smiling, which made it all worse. He seemed quite at
his ease; it was she—she who was in the right, she the clothed,
she the outraged one, who was overset. Monica had never fainted
in her life, but she felt a lightness in her head now, an inability
to get her breath, which might well rob her of consciousness.

"You're the Canadian Nightingale, I suppose," said he. "I forgot you were coming. Hold on a jiffy, while I get some clothes.
But don't play that trash any more."

And a jiffy it was, for he was back again almost at once, wearing flannel trousers, and with his bare feet thrust into worn slippers, buttoning his shirt; he went behind the piano, picked up a
bundle of woman's garments and threw them through the door
into the next room, shouting, "Come on, Persis, you lazy cow, get
up and make us some tea." The reply, which came through the
door in a rich and well-bred contralto, was brief, and couched in
words which Monica had never heard spoken in a woman's voice
before. "Shut up," replied Revelstoke, "can't you behave yourself
when we have company—a distinguished guest from the Premier
Dominion, our mighty ally in peace and war? Be a good girl and
get some tea, and we shall have music to restore our souls."

He took the cat in his arms and stroked it, as he turned again
to Monica. "You mustn't mind a degree of informality here which
you haven't met in the elegant environs of Sir Benedict Domdaniel. Brummagem Benny, as we sometimes call him in the
musical world—without a hint of malice, mind you—likes to do
himself very well. And properly so. He must keep up a position
commensurate with his great and well-deserved reputation. But

I, you see, am a very different sort of creature. You are now in the editorial offices of *Lantern*, undoubtedly the most advanced and unpopular critical journal being published in English today. The significance of the name will not escape you. *Lantern*—it is the lantern of Diogenes, searching for the honest, the true and the good, and it is similarly the lantern, or lamp-post, referred to in the good old Revolutionary cry "A la lanterne!"—because from this *Lantern* we suspend the hacked corpses of those whom we are compelled to judge harshly; you will not miss, either, the allusion to that Lantern Land which Master Francis Rabelais describes in his *Pantagruel* (with which I presume that you are amply acquainted) and which was the habitation of pedants and cheats in all branches of the arts; we allude to it slyly in our title by a species of gnomic homophony which will at once be apparent to you. This is a workroom, and workrooms are apt to be untidy. This will soon be your workroom, too, if we get on as well as I hope we shall. You had better meet my friend, Pyewacket, a delightful but musically uncritical cat."

He was interrupted by the entry, from the bedroom, of a tall girl of twenty-three or four, wearing a not very fresh slip and nothing else; her long dark hair was hanging down her back and she had the tumbled look of one who has risen from bed.

"Match," said she to Revelstoke. He found one on the table and gave it to her.

"Allow me to introduce Miss Persis Kinwellmarshe, daughter of Admiral Sir Percy Kinwellmarshe, retired, now of Tunbridge Wells. Miss Kinwellmarshe is one of my principal editorial assistants. We have been engaged in a type of editorial conference known as scrouperizing. You do know Rabelais? No? Pity!"

Monica disliked Miss Kinwellmarshe on sight. She had Bad Girl written all over her, and in addition she was extremely handsome, with a finely formed nose, through the crimson-shadowed nostrils of which she now seemed to be looking at Monica.

"It's a pleasure to meet any acquaintance of Mr. Revelstoke's," said she.

Monica knew when she was being mocked, but Amy's prime injunction—"You can never go wrong by being simple, dear"—came to her rescue. So she bowed her head slightly toward Miss Kinwellmarshe, and said "How do you do?"

Miss Kinwellmarshe, taking the match, turned and went to the kitchen. *She's got a butt-end on her like a bumble-bee,* said the voice of Ma Gall, very clearly, inside Monica's head,—so clearly that Monica started.

"Now, let's do some work," said Revelstoke, who appeared to have enjoyed this encounter. "You've been with the ineffable Molloy for a while, Sir Benny tells me. An admirable coach, with a splendid, policeman-like attitude toward the art of song. Sing me a few of the things he's taught you."

Unlike Molloy, he made no move to accompany her, so Monica sat at the piano and sang half-a-dozen English folksongs. She could not have explained why it was so, but the knowledge that Miss Kinwellmarshe was within earshot had a tonic effect on her, and she sang them well.

"The accompaniments are charming, aren't they?" said Revelstoke. "Cecil Sharp had a delightful small talent for such work. But of course folksongs are not meant to be accompanied. Just sing me *Searching for Lambs* without all that agreeable atmospheric deedle-deedle."

So Monica sang the song again. *If he thinks I've never sung this without accompaniment he certainly doesn't know Murtagh Molloy,* she thought.

"Not bad. You have a true ear, and a nice sense of rhythm.— Ah, here is dear Miss Kinwellmarshe with the tea. I won't ask you to take a cup, Miss—I forget for the moment—yes, of course, Miss Gall, but you shall have one when you've finished singing. Now, Brum Benny tells me you have a special line in Victorian drawing-room ballads—such a novelty, and so original of you to have worked it up in a time when that kind of music is so undeservedly neglected. I understand that Tosti's *Good-Bye!* is one of your specialties. I can hardly wait. Will you sing it now, please.

You won't mind if we have tea as you do so? The perfect accompaniment for the song, don't you think?"

Miss Kinwellmarshe had laid herself out voluptuously on the work table, pillowing her head on a pile of manuscript and permitting her long and beautifully wavy hair to hang over the edge; the splendour of her figure in this position was somewhat marred by the dirtiness of the soles of her feet, but it was clear that she aimed at large effects, and scorned trifles.

"I haven't sung that song for several months," said Monica. Indeed, she had learned to be thoroughly ashamed of Tosti under the rough but kindly guidance of Molloy. How could Sir Benedict have mentioned it! These English! Sly, sneaky, mocking! You never knew when you had them.

"But after we have put a favourite work aside for a time, we often find that we have unconsciously arrived at a new understanding of it," said Revelstoke, and he was smiling like a demon.

"I'd really rather not," said Monica.

"But I wish it. And I dislike having to remind you that if I am to teach you anything, you must do as I wish." His smile was now from the teeth only.

He just wants to roast me in front of that grubby bitch, thought Monica. I'll walk out. I'll tell Sir Benedict I won't bear it. I'll go home.

But she met Revelstoke's eyes, and she sang. She was angrier than she had ever been in her life. She hated this man who dared to show himself naked, and whose talk was one smooth, sneering incivility after another; she hated that nearly naked tart lolling on the table. She hated Sir Benedict, who had been making fun of her behind her back. She was so full of passionate hatred that her head seemed ready to burst. But she had not spent six months with Murtagh Molloy for nothing. She took possession of herself, she breathed the muhd, and she sang.

She finished, and the seven bars of *diminuendo* regret on the piano were completed. There was silence. The first to break it was Miss Kinwellmarshe, and her comment was a derisive, dismissive, derogatory monosyllable.

"Not at all," said Revelstoke; "and let me remind you, Persis, that I am the critic here, and any comment will come from me, not you. Take yourself off, you saucy puss, and do some typing, or wash up, or something." Rising, he hauled Miss Kinwellmarshe off the table and pushed her toward the kitchen, giving her a resounding slap on her splendid buttocks. She repeated her previous comment with hauteur, but she went.

"Now," said he, "let's get down to business. What's that song all about?"

Monica had occasionally been questioned in this way by Molloy, and she always hated it. A song was a song, and it was about what it said; it was almost bad luck to probe it and pull it to pieces, for it might never regain its shape. But Revelstoke had made her sing against her will, and she knew that he could make her speak. Might as well give in at once and get it over.

"It's about people saying good-bye."

"People?"

"Lovers, I suppose."

"Why are they saying good-bye?"

"I don't know; the song doesn't say."

"Doesn't it? Who wrote it?"

"Tosti."

"The music, yes. When did he live?"

"Oh, quite recently; Mr. Molloy once saw him."

"Who wrote the words?"

"I—I don't know."

"Oh, then I assume that you consider the words of small importance in comparison with the music. Do you think it is good music?"

"No, not really."

"How would you describe it?"

"A sort of drawing-room piece, I suppose."

"Yes, yes; but technically?"

"A ballad?"

"No, not a ballad. It is hardly a tune at all—certainly not a hummable sort of tune like a ballad. It's what's called an *aria parlante*. Know what that means?"

"A sort of speaking song?"

"A declamatory song. So there must be something to declaim. The words were written by a Scottish Victorian novelist and poet called George John Whyte-Melville. I see that your copy of the song gives his initials as 'G.T.' and robs him of his hyphen; just shows what the firm of Ricordi thought about him. Ever heard of him?"

"Never."

"An interesting man. Quite successful, but always underestimated his own work and was apt to run himself down, in a gentlemanly sort of way. Wrote a lot about fox-hunting, but there is always a melancholy strain in his work which conflicts oddly with the subjects. His biographer thought it was because his married life was most unhappy. Does that seem to you to throw any light on that song?"

"It's very unhappy. You mean that perhaps it wasn't lovers, but himself and his wife he was writing about?"

"I am charmed by your implied opinion of the married state. Married people are sometimes lovers, and lovers are not always happy. Why are they unhappy, do you suppose?"

"Well, usually because they can't get married. Or because one of them may be married already."

"There can be other reasons. Read me the first verse."

In a constricted tone, and without expression, Monica read:

> *Falling leaf, and fading tree,*
> *Lines of white in a sullen sea,*
> *Shadows rising on you and me;*
> *The swallows are making them ready to fly*
> *Wheeling out on a windy sky—*
> > *Good-bye, Summer,*
> > *Good-bye.*

"You see? A succession of pictures—the fall of the leaf, the birds going south, a rising storm, and darkness falling. And it all adds up to—what?"

This is worse than Eng. Lit. at school, thought Monica. But she answered, "Autumn, I suppose."

"Autumn, you suppose. Now let me read you the second verse, with a little more understanding than you choose to give to your own reading—

> Hush, a voice from the far away!
> 'Listen and learn', it seems to say,
> 'All the tomorrows shall be as today.
> The cord is frayed, the cruse is dry
> The link must break and the lamp must die.
>> Good-bye to Hope,
>> Good-bye.'

What do you make of that?"

"Still Autumn?"

"An Autumn that continues forever? Examine the symbols— lamp gone out, chain broken, jug empty, cord ready to break, and all the tomorrows being like today—what's that suggest? What is the warning voice? Think!"

Monica thought. "Death, perhaps?"

"Quite correct. Death—perhaps: but not quite Death as it is ordinarily conceived. The answer is in the last verse—

> What are we waiting for?
>> Oh, my heart!
> Kiss me straight on the brows!
>> And part—again—my heart!
> What are we waiting for, you and I?
> A pleading look, a stifled cry—
>> Good-bye forever,
>> Good-bye!

There it is! Plain as the nose on your face! What is it all about? What are they saying Good-bye to? Come on! Think!"

His repeated insistence that she think made Monica confused and mulish. She sat and stared at him for perhaps two minutes, and then he spoke.

"It is Death, right enough, but not the Death of the body; it is the Death of Love. Listen to the passion in the last verse—passion which Tosti has quite effectively partnered in the music. Haste—the sense of constraint around the heart—the pleading for a climax and the disappointment of that climax—What is it? In human experience, what is it?"

Monica had no idea what it was.

"Well, Miss Lumpish Innocence, it is the Autumn of love; it is the failure of physical love; it is impotence. It is a physical inadequacy which brings in its train a terrible and crushing sense of spiritual inadequacy. It is the sadness of increasing age. It is the price which life exacts for maturity. It is the foreknowledge of Death itself. It is the inspiration of some of the world's great art, and it is also at the root of an enormous amount of bad theatre, and Hollywood movies, and the boo-hoo-hoo of popular music. It is one of the principal springs of that delicious and somewhat bogus emotion—Renunciation. And Whyte-Melville and old Tosti have crammed it into twenty lines of verse and a hundred or so bars of music, and while the result may not be great, by God it's true and real, and that is why that song still has a kick like a mule, for all its old-fashionedness. Follow me?"

Monica sat for a time, pondering. What Revelstoke had said struck forcibly on her mind, and she felt that it would have opened new doors to her if she had fully understood it. And she wanted to understand. So, after a pause, she looked him in the eye.

"What's impotence?"

Revelstoke looked at her fixedly. Ribald comment rose at once to his tongue, but Monica's seriousness asked for something better than that. He answered her seriously.

"It is when you want to perform the act of love, and can't," he said. "The difficulty is peculiar to men in that particular form, but it is equally distressing to both partners. The symbolism of the poem is very well chosen."

There was silence for perhaps three minutes, while Monica pondered. "I don't see the good of it," she said at last. "You take an old song that hundreds of people must have sung and you drag it down so it just means a nasty trouble that men get. Is that supposed to make it easier for me to sing it? Or are you making fun of me?"

"I am not making fun of you, and I have not done what you said. I have related quite a good poem to a desperate human experience which, in my opinion, is the source from which it springs. If you think of a poem as a pretty trifle that silly men make up while smelling flowers, my interpretation is no good to you. But if you think of a poem as a flash of insight, a fragment of truth, a break in the cloud of human nonsense and pretence, my interpretation is valid. When you sing, you call from the depth of your own experience to the depth of experience in your hearer. And depth of experience has its physical counterpart, believe me; we aren't disembodied spirits, you know, nor are we beautiful, clear souls cumbered with ugly indecent bodies. This song isn't about 'a nasty trouble that men get'—to use your own depressingly middle-class words; it is about the death of love, and the fore-knowledge of death; it is an intimation of mortality. As you say, hundreds of people have sung it without necessarily looking very deeply into it, and thousands of listeners have been moved without knowing why. Poetry and music can speak directly to depths of experience in us which we possess without being conscious of them, in language which we understand only imperfectly. But there must be some of us who understand better than others, and who give the best of ourselves to that understanding. If you are to be one of them, you must be ready to make a painful exploration of yourself. When I came in here just now, you were playing a rather silly piece in a very silly way. You sang your folksongs like a cheap Marie Antoinette pretending to be a shepherdess. Domdaniel wants you to be better than that, and so he has sent you to me."

"Do you think Sir Benedict thinks about songs and poetry the way you do?"

"Sir Benedict dearly loves to play the role of the exquisitely dressed, debonair, frivolous man of the world. But he's no fool. And he thinks you are no fool, too. He told me so. Here's your cup of tea that I promised you."

It was very nasty tea. Monica drank it reflectively. After a time, during which Revelstoke had stared intently at her, he said—

"What are you thinking about?"

"I was thinking that you're not really *simpatico*."

"I've no time for charm. Many people think me extremely unpleasant, and I cultivate that, because it keeps fools at a distance."

"Mr. Molloy says you're quite the genius."

"Mr. Molloy, in his limited way, is quite right.—Well, are you coming to me for lessons?"

"Yes."

"All right. Give me thirty shillings now, for your subscription to *Lantern*. Here's a copy of the latest number. And next time you come here, have the politeness to ring the bell. It'll spare your blushes."

(6)

IF MONICA HAD BEEN in danger from loneliness and boredom before, she would now have found herself in danger of being exhausted, had it not been that, as Sir Benedict had said, she was as strong as a horse. She thoroughly enjoyed the excitement. Molloy continued to take her association with Revelstoke as an intentional affront offered to his own powers as a teacher by Domdaniel, and he worked her very hard on exercises designed to develop those two characteristics of the voice which he called, in his old-fashioned nomenclature, "the florid and the pathetic", and which Sir Benedict preferred to call "agility and legato". He imparted his infallible method to her in a sort of pedagogic fury, nagged ceaselessly about the importance of breath and posture in the control of nervousness, and enquired searchingly about what she ate, and how much. In a veiled manner, he enquired about the regularity of her bowels. The poise of her head and the relaxation of her jaw become obsessions with him, and sometimes she woke in the night, startled to hear his voice shouting "Head forward and up—not backward and down—lead with your head!"

Revelstoke said very little to her about the production of her voice, and it did not take her long to discover that he knew little about it. "Let the ineffable Murtagh teach you the mechanics," said he, "and I'll take care of your style." But he led her on to tell him what Molloy did and said at lessons, and she, finding that imitations of the Irishman amused him, could not resist the temptation to oblige, now and then, though she felt rather cheap afterward. Molloy was so truly kind, so unstinting in his efforts on her behalf, and yet—it was not easy to resist a young and clever man who wanted her to make sport of the older, exuberant one. She salved her conscience by telling it that she meant no real unkindness, and that everybody, including Sir Benedict, laughed at him.

With Revelstoke she toiled through a great amount of the literature of song, not studying it for the purpose of singing but, in his phrase, "getting the hang of it." Nevertheless, this process was hard work, and involved excursions into poetry in English, German and French which taxed and expanded her knowledge of those languages.

She knew no Italian, and Revelstoke urged Sir Benedict to find a teacher for her. This added to her day's work considerably, for Signor Sacchi was a zealot, yearning to get her into Dante at the first possible moment.

It was with English, however, that she had most trouble. Molloy, as good as his word, had moderated her Ontario accent to a point where she had occasional misgivings that her mother would consider her present speech "a lotta snottery". But it would not do for Revelstoke. He condemned much in her new manner of speech as "suburban", and insisted on a standard of purity of his own. Her former models, the actors at the Old Vic, he dismissed out of hand; their speech reeked, he said, of South London tennis clubs.

"English is not a language of quantities, like Latin," he said, over and over again, "but a language of strong and weak stresses. A faulty stress destroys the meaning and flavour of a word, and distorts the quality of a line of verse. Without a just appreciation of the stresses in a line of verse, you cannot sing it—for singing is first, last and all the time a form of human eloquence, speech raised to the highest degree."

His manner of teaching was confusing to Monica's straight-forward intelligence, for she never knew when he was joking. She had been accustomed in her schooldays to teachers whose jokes were infrequent, and clearly labelled. But after a few weeks she learned to identify certain tones of voice which signi-fied irony, and even to enjoy it, though hers was by no means an ironical cast of mind. It was the variety and apparent depth of his knowledge which principally amazed her, and she never be-came accustomed to his ability to quote from the Bible, though it was obvious that one who lived so evil a life (Miss Kinwell-marshe's garments were forever turning up in unforeseen places) must be an unbeliever.

One day, after he had talked to her for half an hour about Schubert's settings of poems by Müller, and of the ability of a poet of very modest achievement to inspire a musical genius of the first order, she ventured to thank him, and to say that it was wonderfully educational. He understood that the clumsiness and seeming patronage of the phrase concealed a genuine humility of feeling, but he uttered a warning which lodged itself in her mind.

"I know what you mean," said he, "but I wish you wouldn't use words like 'educational', which have grown sour from being so

·much in the wrong people's mouths. What we are doing isn't really educational. It's enlightening, I suppose, and its purpose is to nurture the spirit. If formal education has any bearing on the arts at all, its purpose is to make critics, not artists. Its usual effect is to cage the spirit in other people's ideas—the ideas of poets and philosophers, which were once splendid insights into the nature of life, but which people who have no insights of their own have hardened into dogmas. It is the spirit we must work with, and not the mind as such. For 'the spirit searcheth all things, yea, the deep things of God'."

Thus, rather quickly, all things considered, Revelstoke persuaded Monica to give up her determination to learn like a parrot, and to imitate her masters without really understanding what they did, and brought her to a point where she could feel a little, and understand, respect and cherish her own feeling.

(7)

"OLD GILES IS ONE of the best; it's a treat to know him—but it's his bloody menagerie that kills." Thus spoke Bun Eccles to Monica a few weeks after her lessons with Revelstoke began, as they were having a drink in the saloon bar of The Willing Horse. Monica agreed heartily.

In fairness she had to admit in her own mind that Eccles himself was a prominent and disturbing element in Revelstoke's menagerie. John Macarthur Eccles was the young man whom she had met coming down Revelstoke's stairs the first day she visited him; he was an Australian painter, always called Bun, which was an abbreviation of Bunyip. Very early in their acquaintance Monica asked him indignantly why he had urged her to go up without warning, knowing what he knew. His answer was characteristic: "Well, kid, I'd just dropped in on 'em and they were as mad as snakes, and I wanted to find out what you'd all do."

Bun was grandiloquently called the Art Editor of *Lantern*.

He did woodcuts and ornamental spots for the magazine, and
was supposed to take care of its typography, but as he understood little of this craft, and rarely knew what day of the week
it was, the work was usually done by the printer. *Lantern* was
printed by a very good firm, Raikes Brothers, because a nephew
of the senior Mr. Raikes was interested in it, and sometimes had
his satirical verses printed in it. Raikes Brothers also looked after
the mailing of copies to subscribers, because nobody else connected with the magazine had a complete list of those fortunate
creatures, though there was a shoe box somewhere with index
cards in it, upon which Miss Kinwellmarshe had written the
names and addresses of some of them. *Lantern* was without a
business manager, although it had an impressive list of editors
and contributors. It also lacked any facilities for dealing with
possible advertisers, though two or three extremely persistent
publishers and musical firms had sought out some responsible
person at Raikes Brothers, and positively insisted on buying
advertising space.

It was *Lantern* which accounted for Revelstoke's menagerie.
The copy which he gave to Monica on her first visit mystified
her completely; it resisted her most earnest attempts to find out
what it was all about. It was handsomely printed, and contained
several articles which were manifestly very angry and scornful
on a high level, and some photographs and caricatures. But
everything in it seemed to presuppose a special body of knowledge in the reader, and to allude to this private preserve of indignation and disgust in a way which shut out the uninitiated.
It was not for some time that she learned that *Lantern* really was
a very special publication. It was devoted in a large part to
criticism of critics—of literary critics, theatre critics, critics of
painting, and music critics. These critics were, it appeared, without exception men of mean capacities and superficial knowledge;
it was the task of *Lantern* to show them up. Of course, if you did
not read the popular critics in the first place, *Lantern* meant
nothing to you.

Revelstoke wrote about music himself, and was one-half of
the editor-in-chief; the other half was a frail, gentle creature
called Phanuel Tuke, who looked after the literary side. Tuke
was not particularly indignant; his long suit was critical sensibility, and he was always discovering masterpieces which
coarser critics had overlooked, or finding beauties in books which
the rough fellows in the Sunday papers and middlebrow week-
lies had condemned as tripe. It was widely believed in his circle
that stupendous integrity was lodged in Tuke's meagre frame,
and that he was unquestionably the foremost wit of his day in
London. His wit was of the sort which is called dry; indeed, it
was so very dry that Monica could not detect any flavour in it at
all, smack her lips as she might over some of his most valued
remarks and apt rejoinders. But she was sure the fault was hers.
Apart from the elusive quality of his wit, she liked Tuke, who
was a decent little man and needed mothering, even by young
virgins.

Tuke's constant companion and defender was a plain, square
Irish girl in her early thirties, called Bridget Tooley; she was
always on the lookout for a chance to fight somebody for Tuke.
She wrote, in some sense that was never clearly defined, and apparently her stuff was too good to be published very often. When
Tuke was late with his material for *Lantern* it was always Miss
Tooley who stumped up the stairs and broke the news. For no
very good reason Revelstoke's flat was the headquarters of the
publication, to the great alarm of his landlady, Mrs. Klein. She
had come to England as a refugee, and had never accustomed
herself to English law as it relates to lodgings and apartments;
in consequence she was perpetually in dread that the police
might descend upon her and charge her with permitting a business to be conducted on her premises, without having an appropriate licence. Poor soul, she could not comprehend how little
like a business *Lantern* was, and so she appeared from time to
time, like the wicked fairy in a ballet, and made pitiful scenes.

Nobody was particularly rude to Mrs. Klein except Odo
Odingsels, the photographer. He was a very tall, loose-jointed

man of some northern European stock which was never identified; he had beautiful, liquid brown eyes, but his appearance was
spoiled by his unusual dirtiness, and by a form of spotty bald-
ness from which he suffered, and which made his head look as
though it had been nibbled by rats. It was his unpleasant way
to shout loudly at Mrs. Klein in German, which made her cry.
This was embarrassing, but it was widely admitted that Odingsels was a genius with a camera, and must be allowed his little
ways.

These were the principal visitors to the flat in Tite Street—if
the term visitor may be applied to someone who may come at
any hour of day or night, and stay for anything up to ten hours
at a stretch. It was not uncommon for Monica to have a lesson
with Revelstoke while Tuke and Tooley whispered over a manuscript in a corner, and Odingsels ate fish out of the tin almost
under her elbow. Pyewacket contended with her at every lesson
for the master's attention. But Revelstoke's concentration was
complete, and she learned to disregard external distractions while
they were working. All external distractions, that is to say, except
Miss Persis Kinwellmarshe.

"You got the wrong ideas about Old Perse," Bun Eccles told
her. "She's just supplying something Old Giles needs; sheilas are
his hobby. Never without a girl; can't leave 'em alone. Now me,
for instance, I like a squeeze and a squirt now and then, same as
the next chap, just to make sure everything's still attached to the
main, but beer's my real hobby. But Old Giles—he's never had
enough. And it's the same with Perse; she likes it. But apart from
that all there is between 'em is a sort of intellectual companionship, you might call it. Old Giles is a genius, you see, and that's
what Perse really wants. Her home, you see—well, her Dad's an
ex-admiral, wears a monocle, still wishes the *Morning Post*'d
never folded up—and she's in revolt against all that. Doesn't
want to be a lady in Tunbridge bloody Wells. Maybe she's over-
done it, but she's a decent old cow, is Perse."

"She doesn't need to be so dirty about her appearance," said
Monica, thinking this was safe ground for criticism.

"Aw, now kid, she does; it's revolt, see? And she's one of the lucky ones that looks just as good dirty as clean. She's a real stunner. I know. Anatomy. All that stuff. Perse is damn near perfect, but not poison perfect, you know, like those bloody great stone Greek sheilas in the Louvre. Have you looked seriously at her knees? Cor stone the crows, kid, that's perfection!"

"Knees! I'm surprised that's all you've seen."

"Aw now, stow that, Monny. That's small-town stuff. Sure I've seen all there is to see of Perse; she's posed a bit, as well as her hobby. But good knees are very, very rare. And when you get past all that pommy lah-di-dah she's a real nice girl."

"I'll bet!" said Monica. It was not irony on the level of *Lantern*, but it was heartfelt. "Next thing you'll be telling me she has a heart of gold."

"Well, so she has."

"Bun, that girl's a tramp, and you know it."

"Aw now, Monny, that's not like you. Perse is a wagtail, nobody denies it, but what's that to you? You don't have to be like her, if you don't choose. But don't come the Mrs. Grundy around the *Lantern*; it's the wrong place for it. I'll get you another half-pint, to sweeten you up."

Monica had taken to going to The Willing Horse every day with Bun Eccles, but she could never rid herself of a feeling of guilt. There she was in a pub—what would have been called a "beverage room" at home—drinking beer. By the standards of her upbringing she was on the highroad to harlotry, but no harm ever befell her, and Eccles seemed to look on her as a friend, and to ply her with half-pints for no reason other than that he liked her. She even reached the point of paying for drinks herself, as it seemed to be quite all right for girls to do so in *Lantern* circles. Amy had told her, "You don't have to drink, dear, but never make a fuss about not drinking." And here she was, drinking like a fish, by her reckoning—often two and three pints of beer in a day—and the admonitions of Ma Gall and the adjurations of Pastor Beamis grew fainter in memory.

It was interesting, however, that some of her mother's saltier remarks kept intruding themselves into her mind, spoken in her mother's own tones, especially in connection with Miss Kinwellmarshe. Monica had not realized that there was so much of her mother in her. The feeling which often plagued her that she was drifting away from her family in speech and outlook was complemented by the realization that some of the mental judgements she passed on the people around her were unquestionably her mother's, and couched in her mother's roughest idiom. It was frightening; sometimes it seemed like a form of possession. For what she wanted most was experience, that experience which is supposed to broaden and enrich the soul of the artist, and what could Mrs. Gall conceivably have to do with that?

To her surprise, she quickly gained a place in the *Lantern* group, for she possessed accomplishments alien to them. She could work a typewriter, and produce fair copy even on the senile portable Corona which was all the magazine owned. None of the others could use more than two fingers, and Miss Tooley and Miss Kinwellmarshe always fought bitterly about which should undertake this degrading work. Tuke wrote illegibly in pencil; Revelstoke wrote an elegant Italian hand, but so small that it was a penance to read much of it. Monica's professional speed seemed like magic to them. She could also keep books in an elementary fashion, and though *Lantern* had only one misleading petty cash book, she could come nearer to making it balance than anyone else. This was power, and Monica, who badly wanted to be indispensable to this glittering array of talent, was not slow to recognize it. She became more and more irregular in her visits to Madame Heber and Dr. Schlesinger, for Tuke was happy to talk to her in French, and Odingsels and Mrs. Klein provided her with plenty of practice in German. She could not elude Signor Sacchi, for she was a beginner in Italian, and she did not want to miss any of her lessons at Coram Square, where Molloy was working so hard to show himself the superior of Revelstoke. But there were days when Monica spent six and eight hours at a stretch in the flat in Tite Street typing, talking, accounting and learning. She became as familiar as Miss Kinwell-

marshe with the small and disorderly kitchen; she lost her shame
about going downstairs to the w.c. on the second floor landing
(for Revelstoke's bathroom consisted of tub and basin only and
was, as a usual thing, full of imperfectly laundered and extremely wet garments belonging to himself and Persis Kinwellmarshe). She was useful, she was wanted, and if she had been
able to banish her hot gusts of disapproval of Persis, she would
have been completely happy.

(8)

THE BRIDGETOWER TRUSTEES had little, in these days, to draw
them together, and their meetings were infrequent. After the
June meeting in which they received the melancholy news that
they would have to spend more on Monica, they did not meet
again until the 21st of December, the second anniversary of the
death of Louisa Hansen Bridgetower. There was not much for
them to do except to hear Mr. Snelgrove read two letters, of
which the first was from the London solicitors, presenting their
account of disbursements and expressing the hope, in a joyless,
legal kind of way, that they were spending enough money. The
other, and as usual the more interesting, letter was from Sir
Benedict, and read thus:

> Your protegée has been faring much better since her return
> from Paris where, as I expected, Miss Amy Neilson was able to
> do a great deal for her. She learns readily and is sensitive to
> atmosphere, and she now comports herself in a way which will
> smooth her path in the secondary, but important, social side of a
> singer's career.
> In addition to her work with Mr. Molloy, and her languages
> (to which Italian has been added) I am sending her to Giles
> Revelstoke for coaching in the literature of song, and some of
> the general musical culture which she so badly needs. You may be
> familiar with some of his work; he is, in my opinion, one of the

most promising composers to appear in England for many a decade, and is especially gifted as a song-writer in a period when the real lyric gift is extremely rare. He speaks well of her progress.

You will be interested to know that I have taken upon myself to bring Monica to the attention of Lady Phoebe Elphinstone, who does a great deal of admirable work in introducing Common-wealth and American students to English families with whom they spend holiday periods which might otherwise find them at a loose end. Lady Phoebe has arranged that Monica shall spend the Christmas vacation period with a Mr. and Mrs. Griffith Hop-kin-Griffiths of Neuadd Goch, Llanavon, Montgomeryshire. They are delightful people (Lady Phoebe assures me) and a taste of country-house life will be a pleasant experience for Monica, with whose character and talents I am increasingly impressed, and quite in line with the desires expressed for her by her late patroness, Mrs. L. H. Bridgetower.

"Well!" said Miss Pottinger. "Country-house life! I only hope she has the gumption to take an appropriate house-gift. Should we cable her about it, I wonder?"

"I had gained the impression that there was no country-house life left," said Dean Knapp; "but then, in Wales probably things are on a much humbler scale."

"That is really all we have to consider," said Mr. Snelgrove, "except expenditure. In spite of what Jodrell and Stanhope have been able to do, the money keeps piling up at the bank. It is unlikely that there will be any official questioning of our hand-ling of funds, at least for some time, but we must bear in mind that we can be called upon for an accounting by the Public Trustee at his discretion."

When the meeting was over, Veronica served the Trustees with coffee and Christmas cake, using the fine Rockingham ser-vice which Auntie Puss regarded as her own.

"And how have you been keeping, Veronica?" said that lady, eyeing her speculatively.

"Very well, thank you, Miss Pottinger," said Veronica, but

she wore a look of strain which was becoming habitual. Nearly two years had passed since the reading of Mrs. Bridgetower's will, and so far there was no sign that she might have a child, and retrieve the Bridgetower money for her husband.

(9)

IT WAS ON THE 21st of December that Monica set out from Paddington, travelled to Shrewsbury, changed her train and crossed the border of Wales to Trallwm, and there took a local to Llanavon. She had in her luggage a suitable house-gift (a large and expensive—but not embarrassing—box of candied fruits of appropriately Christmas-like appearance) so Miss Pottinger need not have feared for her on that score. But she carried in her heart misgivings about country-house life which were all that Miss Pottinger could possibly have desired. Everything that she had ever read, or seen in the movies, or heard, about the county gentry of Great Britain came back to her: would she have to hunt foxes? would she be despised because she could not ride a horse? what about the inevitable awesome butler? what about the equally inevitable heiress of broad acres, a picture of British hauteur and beauty (Miss Kinwellmarshe was cast mentally for this role) who would make her feel like a crumb, while being exquisitely but coldly polite all the time? Lady Phoebe Elphinstone had been perfectly wonderful and not a bit awesome, on the one occasion when Monica had met her, and Lady Phoebe's secretary, Miss Catriona Eigg of Uist, had been helpful and kind in every possible way, even to suggesting the box of fruits, but neither of these benign presences was on the train with her as she moved, at the deliberate pace of Welsh trains, from Shrewsbury to Trallwm.

There was, however, a man in the same carriage whom she had seen get on the train at Oxford, and who had, like herself, changed at Shrewsbury. A young man, apparently English from his clothes and his easy way with porters; a shortish, plumpish young man with a high colour (incipient broken veins in the cheeks?) and short dark hair very neatly brushed. As well as a large valise he carried a briefcase crammed with books, which he kept close to him on the seat as though its presence were a comfort. In his hand he had an orange-bound pamphlet, which he read with great concentration, moving his lips as he did so, and occasionally making phlegmy noises, apparently clearing his throat. But the farther they travelled from Shrewsbury the greater his excitement became, and the less he worked over his book; at times he hung right out of the window, and gaped at the landscape. As a castle became fleetingly visible, nesting among trees, she thought he muttered "Peacock". When the train drew up at a tiny station labelled Buttington he threw open the door and said in an awed voice, under his breath "The Battle of Butt-ingtune, 893", and stared in all directions at small holdings and distant hills until the guard locked him in again. He sank back on the seat, and stared at Monica with unseeing eyes. "An old and haughty nation, proud in arms," he whispered, and then re-peated it, with greater emphasis. When the train drew up at Trallwm he hastily consulted his yellow pamphlet, leaned well out of the window, and fixed a porter with his eye.

"Arrgh!" he cried, in accents of despair. "Arrgh!"—but no further utterance came.

"Yessir? What can I do for you, sir?" said the porter, and the young man fell back upon the seat, deflated.

Monica, with the inflexible determination of women travelling, snatched the porter for herself, and had her luggage transferred to the local for the coast which would take her to Llanavon. She took good care to get into a carriage far from the afflicted young man.

But when, half an hour later, she dismounted at Llanavon sta-tion, he did so too, and when a girl of about Monica's own age approached them and said "For Neuadd Goch?" it was he who said, "Yes, thanks, I'm John Scott Ripon."

Monica had never heard the name of her destination pronounced by a Welsh tongue. Lady Phoebe and Miss Eigg of Uist had tended to hurry over it and avoid it.

"Miss Gall?" said the girl. "I'm Ceinwen Griffiths; you're going to my uncle's, aren't you? I've brought the trap, because it's a fairly clear day, and I thought you might like to ride that way. Mr. Lloyd'll take care of your luggage, and somebody'll bring it up in an hour or so."

She led the way to a pretty governess-cart, drawn by a pony. Monica had never seen such a thing before, and Ripon was delighted with it. He couldn't, he said, have possibly hoped for anything better.

Introductions left Monica somewhat flattened. John Scott Ripon, it appeared, was not English, but an American Rhodes scholar, and he seemed to get on very easy terms with Miss Ceinwen Griffiths in a matter of minutes. She was a girl who, without being pretty, was uncommonly attractive, for she had a soft and winning air, beautiful legs, and quite the loveliest speaking voice that Monica had ever heard; everything that she said was so beautifully articulated, and so charmingly stressed, that it was a kind of music. This was not the habitual downhill tune of English speech, or the tangle of stressed and unstressed syllables upon which Revelstoke insisted, but a form of speech-play—a delight in sound and words for their own sake. It was fascinating, and it struck Monica mute. But not Ripon.

"I made a terrible boob of myself on the train," said he, as they set off in the pony-trap. "I was trying to speak Welsh to the porter at Trallwm. I'd been studying this book, you see—*Welsh in a Week*—and I wanted to say 'A wnewch chwi edrych ar ol fy nheithglud?'—thought I'd surprise him. But it all died in my throat. Of course I knew he'd speak English, but I thought I'd try it. I always like to try everything. Much Welsh spoken around here, Miss Griffiths?"

"No, hardly at all. A little on market days, when the people come in from the hills. And they wouldn't have spoken to you, except in English; it makes Welsh people shy, hearing it spoken by English-speaking people."

"Do you speak it at all?"

> 'Annhebig i'r mis dig du.
> A gerydd i bawb garu;
> A bair tristlaw a byrddydd
> A gwynt i ysbeiliaw gwydd;—do you follow?

"No, but it sounds great."

"That's a comment on today's weather by one of our old poets; you won't find it in *Welsh in a Week*. But I'm not a fair example. My father's quite a well-known Celtic scholar."

"Oh, that's wonderful! Then it'll be an even greater pleasure to meet him."

"You won't meet him. I'm staying with Uncle Griff and Aunt Dolly; they're dears, too, but not the least bit Celtic scholars. You'll see."

"But it was an understandable mistake. You see, I've looked your uncle up in *Burke's Landed Gentry*. Terrific ancestry, so I thought he might be very hot on Welsh history, and customs and whatnot."

"You've been doing your homework, haven't you? Uncle Griff will talk to you about genealogy all night, but any Welshman will do that. No, Uncle Griff's not a scholar, but he's a landed gent."

"Unbroken tenancy of the Neuadd Goch estate since 1488, the book said."

"Oh, how beautifully you say Neuadd Goch!"

"No kidding?"

"Well—not very much kidding."

Miss Ceinwen Griffiths, it appeared, was not only very attractive but an accomplished flirt. Monica began to feel reservations about her.

They had mounted a steep hill, and were now driving along a ridge. Because the pony cart was high, they could see over the hedges on both sides of the road, toward England on the right, and toward the mountains of Wales on the left. It was such country as Monica had never seen before, rolling, gentle, quiet in its winter sleep, yet with an air of mystery which could not be explained. Perhaps it was the quality of the light, which varied so greatly within the range of her vision. Where they were it was not quite so fine a day as Miss Griffiths had said; as the pony trotted through the lanes the air was wet and chilly on their faces. But a mile or two away on the English side of the ridge the sun shone in golden patches, moving slowly across the side of another hill. On the Welsh side it seemed to be raining in the middle distance, for there the land was purplish, as though it had been bruised, but near these darkened patches were stretches of grey obscurity, which occasionally stirred and heaved, for it was mist. But beyond the purple, and the mist, and a few pools of tearful sunlight, rose mountains which caught a little wintry glory from an unseen setting sun, and were otherwise deepest blue-black. Their heads were in cloud.

"On a good day you can see the two peaks of Cadeir Idris from here," said Ceinwen, "but not often in winter."

"Marvellous!" said Ripon. "Just the country·for *Morte d'Arthur.*"

"We like it very well," said Ceinwen.

"Oh, come on, Miss Griffiths, that won't do! It's absolutely terrific, and you know it. Leave understatement to the English. I'm an enthusiast; they say all Americans are, but it's not true. But I am. I enjoy things while I've got 'em. I'm a romantic. Don't discourage me."

"I won't. Wales always seems very beautiful to people when they first come to it. Perhaps we try to restrain our own feelings so as not to seem to be boasting. Now we leave the Cefn, and drop into this little wooded place. It's called Cwm Bau."

"Cwm, a valley, and bau—let's see, wait till I get out *Welsh in a Week*—or will you tell us?"

"In English it means the Dirty Dingle—though why nobody

knows, because it's very pretty, as you see. And then we go·up
the hill on the other side to Neuadd Goch. You haven't said anything, Miss Gall; I hope you don't find your first sight of Wales
disappointing?"

"I'm an enthusiast, too," said Monica; "but I'm not very good
at words. I think it's the loveliest landscape I've ever seen."

"I truly hope that it will be kind to you."

(10)

LIFE AT NEUADD GOCH was kind indeed. Monica knew nothing
of country life; in Canada she had had the usual experiences of
cottage life at lakesides with the joys of insects, privies, boiled
water and the thunder of rain on the roof, but an ordered and
comfortable existence in the midst of natural beauty was utterly
new to her. In this house there was no window which did not
look out upon a view of the beautiful valley on one lift of
which it stood, and the variations of light changed these views
from hour to hour, and sometimes from minute to minute. The
farms and cottages in the landscape, thatched and built of white
plaster and blackened oak beam, were so picturesquely pretty
that she could not believe that they were real farms at all, for
her only experience had been of the plain-faced farmsteads of
her own part of Ontario. She fell immediately and deeply in love
with North Wales, and in this affair she was rivalled by John
Scott Ripon. As for the family at Neuadd Goch, they were everything that was kind and charming. No awesome butler, but two
maids so obliging that Monica suspected them briefly of hypocrisy, managed affairs. She liked Ceinwen better than any girl
she had met since leaving home, and desperately wanted her
as a "best girl friend"—but Ceinwen was not aware of this
North American relationship, and was quite as flirtatious in her
behaviour toward Monica as she was toward Ripon. And Mr. and
Mrs. Hopkin-Griffiths were very old hands at entertaining house

guests, and knew that the art lies in leaving them to themselves a great part of the time. Monica and Ripon arrived on the afternoon of the twenty-first of December; by tea time the day following they felt as though they had been at Neuadd Goch for a glorious year, and on the morning of the twenty-third they were such seasoned country folk that they went for a walk after breakfast, wonderfully happy. Ripon was bursting with talk.

"I've got it straightened out now," said he. "Ceinwen is the daughter of Professor Morgan Griffiths, who is only a half-brother of our host, who is Hopkin-Griffiths, and very big stuff in this part of Wales, and a timber man in a large way. That's where the money comes from. He doesn't seem to work, but that's his craftiness. Dolly was a widow when she married him; she's English and has a son—that's the son she's always talking about who may come for Christmas. The Squire seems very fond of the boy, but I think I detect a note of worry in his voice when he talks about him. It makes it interesting, I think, everybody being halves and steps. Now in my family we're all fully related, and I can't say it makes either for interest or good feeling. What about your family?"

"Oh my family hasn't got any specially interesting relationships. It seems to make them interesting, being Welsh. When I was a child I sometimes used to wish we had a romantic foreign strain of some sort, to cheer things up."

"That's what I don't understand. Ceinwen seems to make a lot of being Welsh, but the Squire, who is the real thing, and can trace his ancestry back to Bleddyn ap Cynfyn, takes it very lightly. You heard what happened last night when I asked him about it at dinner; he just laughed and said he supposed it was true, but that it had never made much difference one way or another. He likes me calling him 'Squire' though, especially when I explained about my fondness for *Gryll Grange* and Squire Gryll. I was astonished he'd never heard of it. D'you know, Monica, I don't think these people understand or value what they have. I don't suppose it's twenty-five miles from here to the Mary Webb country, but would you believe that when I asked Mrs.

Hopkin-Griffiths about it, she had never heard of Mary Webb? And they've lived all their lives close to Shropshire, but they don't seem to know anything about Housman. George Herbert? Unknown! Of course I don't mean that they ought to develop those things as we do in the States. God forbid! But you'd think they'd know about them, wouldn't you? I mean, what do you suppose gives shape and focus to their lives?"

"Do books give shape and focus to your life?"

"Why certainly. Don't they yours?"

"No. You must be a very literary sort of person."

"I wouldn't say that. But you have to see and feel life in terms of something. Think; what makes you tick? What shapes your life?"

"Music, I suppose."

"Well, there you are."

"But not quite the way you mean. I hear music all the time. I've always done so, even though I've tried very hard not to."

"Why did you do that?"

"When I was very small I once told my mother about it, and she said I must break myself of the habit, or it would drive me crazy. So I tried, but I didn't succeed. The music is always at the back of my mind. It's not particularly original, but on the other hand it isn't anybody else's. It's just that I feel in terms of music. And when I can be quiet enough to get at what's going on in my mind, the music is what gives me a clue."

"Have you ever tried to write it down?"

"Oh no. And I don't want to try. I'm not a composer. It's just that music is a part of my way of feeling things. I only realized that a few months ago. And do you know that when I finally discovered that my mind worked that way, it set me free from that fear of going mad. And until I was free of the fear, I hadn't really admitted to myself that it was there. But for years I had been listening to my inner music guiltily. It was like—oh, like being let out of a jail! You're the only person I've ever told about that."

"I'm glad you told me, and I'll keep it to myself. Look at that

view! Now I'm appreciating it in literary terms, and you're interpreting it in some kind of inner music which is incomprehensible
to me. So I ask you again: what does it mean to the people who
live here? By what means do they interpret it to themselves?"

"Do you know, I've just had the most extraordinary experience? Look at these hedges; do you know what they are?"

"Of course I do; they're holly."

"Yes, but—I've never seen holly before. Oh, I've seen a few
sprigs, imported to Canada for decoration, and I've seen imita-
tion holly. But this is the real thing—miles and miles of it—just
growing beside the roads as a hedge. All my life I've associated
holly with Christmas, but I never really knew till this minute
why. I never understood that it was something real. I've seen it
on paper wrapping, and in pictures, and I never knew why it
went with Christmas, except that it was pretty. But here it is, in
December, green leaves and red berries and all! It's like suddenly getting a mysterious piece of a jigsaw puzzle to fit into
place."

Ripon solemnly removed his hat. "This is a sacred moment,"
said he. "Sacred to me, anyhow, as a student of literature. You
have just made the great discovery that behind every symbol
there is a reality. For years you have accepted holly as a symbol
of Christmas, unquestioningly, like a true Anglo-Saxon believer.
And now, in a flash, you know why it is so. It is because, in this
land which gave you your Christmas, holly is at its finest at this
time of year. Perhaps we should cause a carved stone to be
erected on this spot, to identify forever the place at which, for
one human being out of the whole confused race, a symbol
became a reality."

They were standing in the lane which traversed Cwm Bau,
and at this moment Ceinwen rounded the corner, leading an
aged donkey, across whose back two large willow-work panniers
were fixed.

"We've been admiring the holly, as only North Americans
can," said Ripon.

"Good," said Ceinwen; "then you can come with me and

gather a lot of it. I thought I might catch you, so I brought plenty of gloves and two broom-hooks. I know where we can get mistletoe, too."

It was idyllic to gather holly and mistletoe with Ceinwen, to take it back to Neuadd Goch and hang it in festoons on the staircase, to put sprigs of mistletoe in places where, Griffith Hopkin-Griffiths assured them, mistletoe had been hung for as long as anyone could remember.

Neuadd Goch was not an uncommonly old house, though it stood where two very old houses had preceded it. The older, which had been built before the Welsh Tudors had sought their fortune in England, had been supplanted by a Jacobean house which, after a fire in the first decade of the nineteenth century, had been replaced by the present building. It was not the sort of house which attracts the attention of connoisseurs, for it had no special architectural distinction; but it was wonderfully pleasing and comfortable. Its park and its gardens were pretty, but not remarkable. It was not large enough to be a mansion, but it was quite large enough to hold its owners, their servants, and ten or twelve guests without crowding. It was fully and admirably what its name said—it was the Red Hall at Llanavon, modestly appropriate.

Whether it took its character from its owners, or whether they became like it, nobody could say. Mr. Hopkin-Griffiths certainly was as red as his own house. His face was brick red, round, and wore a look of surprise allied to firmness; his hair was of a red which had faded from its original foxy shade to a browner tone. His hands were red and covered at the joints with red hair. As with so many of his race, a few red hairs grew capriciously out of the tip of his nose. He gave an impression of bluntness in his speech and manner, but those who knew him were not deceived; he came of a family which had foreseen the time for getting out of goats and going into sheep, in the fifteenth century; had dropped sheep for cattle in the eighteenth; and had added timber to cattle in the nineteenth. His neighbours respected Mr. Griffith Hopkin-Griffiths as a smooth man.

Dolly, his wife, was a charming, walking monument to her own beauty as it had been thirty years ago; she had not changed her way of dressing her hair, and though she had yielded a little in matters of clothing she still looked more like the 'twenties than the 'fifties. She even made up according to the methods she had perfected in her youth, and it was a credit to the good qualities of her face that the effect was not grotesque. Seen at a distance, by a short-sighted man, she was a pretty, frivolous ghost from the period immediately following the First World War; seen closer, there was about her the pathos of the woman who has not quite grown as old as her years, either in body or mind.

She came upon them as they were hanging the last of the Christmas greens.

"Mistletoe!" she cried. "Oh, what fun! You'll be absolutely worn out with gallantry, Mr. Ripon. Oh, I do so hope Gilly can come. Don't you, Ceinwen? Yes, I'm sure you do! It'll be no sort of Christmas without at least two young men."

Monica and Ripon were by now very familiar with this hope that Gilly, her son, would be able to get away from his work in London to join them at Christmas. By many broad hints Mrs. Hopkin-Griffiths implied that Ceinwen must be especially anxious for his presence; Monica and Ripon were happy enough to fall in with this notion on the part of their hostess. The young are usually, out of sheer good nature, ready to indulge the sometimes clumsy romantic ideas of their elders.

If it was idyllic to hang the Christmas greens, it was Dickensian to drive the twelve miles to Trallwm and buy Christmas gifts. The rule at Neuadd Goch was that gifts exchanged among guests and family must not cost more than a shilling. It was on Christmas Eve that they made the journey, Monica, Ripon and Ceinwen in the Squire's serviceable Humber.

"The sheer bliss of this robs me of speech," said Ripon. "Here we go, on Christmas Eve—get that, Christmas *Eve*—to buy Christmas presents. If I were at home, I would have finished my Christmas shopping a full two weeks ago; I would have wrapped everything in elaborate paper, and tied it with expensive plastic twine. I would approach the great festal day prepared for everything but a good time. But here I go, prepared to squander ten shillings at the utmost on the very eve of the day of giving; for the first time in my life I have got Christmas into focus. Tomorrow I shall worship, I shall feast and—quite incidentally, I shall give and receive. And that's how it ought to be. It's Dickensian. It's Washington Irving-like. It's the way Christmas ought to be."

They spent all day making their purchases, for the shilling rule had been made in a time when a shilling bought a bigger variety of possible gifts than it does now. But Ripon persuaded a bookseller and stationer to let him rummage among some old stock, and produced a wonderful variety of paper transfers, Victorian post-cards, and works of edification which had once been sold as Sabbath School prizes. And in an outfitter's he got a dicky for ninepence, and an almost forgotten oddity—a washable "leather" collar—which he said would be just the thing for Mr. Hopkin-Griffiths. Monica, who did not want to be outdone, turned up some cards of pretty old-fashioned buttons in a wool-shop and, after much pondering, bought another copy of *Welsh in a Week* to give to Ripon, who had been mercilessly teased by their hosts and Ceinwen about his earlier adventures with that work. At mid-day Ripon took the two girls to lunch at The Bear, where they ate fat mutton with two veg. following it with prunes doused with a custard of chemical composition, and some surly cheese. But even this did not crush their spirits.

Driving back to Llanavon, Monica and Ripon agreed that it had been one of the happiest days they had ever known. Their protestations of pleasure made Ceinwen shy at first, then effusive, and the drive ended in an atmosphere which a cruel observer might have described as maudlin, but which was in truth full of genuine, warm, though possibly facile feeling.

They rushed into the house in time for tea, hungry from the

asperities of The Bear, and hungry too as only emotion can make one. Mrs. Hopkin-Griffiths scampered out of the drawing-room to meet them.

"Oh darlings, it's too, too wonderful. He's been able to come! I never quite dared to hope, but he's here. Gilly's come! It's going to be a perfect Christmas!"

Swept forward by her excitement they burst into the room. There, before the fire, stood Giles Revelstoke.

(11)

THAT NIGHT, HAVING made herself ready for bed, Monica went to the bathroom to clean her teeth, a maiden; in slightly less than fifteen minutes she returned to her room, her teeth clean, and a maiden no more.

There was only one bathroom at Neuadd Goch. It had formerly been a bedroom, and was a chamber of considerable size, in a corner of which was a very large and deep bath, encased in mahogany and standing on a dais; there was also a large and ornate marble basin, a full-length cheval-glass with candle-brackets, an armchair and a side chair, and a set of scales upon which it was possible to weigh oneself by sitting on a large, padded seat. There was a couch of the type familiar in the best-known picture of Madame Récamier, with one arm and a partial back. The two large windows were richly curtained to the floor. This splendid chamber was for ablutions only; the water closet was housed in mahogany splendour in a smaller room nearby; it had a bowl in the agreeable Willow pattern.

If Monica had not been a North American her fate might have been very different; in each bedroom was a washstand, with ewer and basin, and night and morning a copper pitcher of boiling water. But she had been accustomed all her life to clean her teeth in running water, and so she went to the bathroom in her dressing-gown, her toothbrush and a tube of paste in her hand. She would only be a minute, thought she, so she pushed the door around, but did not bolt it. It was not quite closed, and less than a minute later Giles Revelstoke, towel in hand and in his dressing-gown, pushed it open.

"Oh, I'm sorry," said he.

And then, because Monica looked so attractive with her hair brushed out, and her mouth foaming slightly with pink dentifrice, and because the lamplight in the bathroom was so charming, and because the couch was so conveniently at hand, and probably also because it was Christmas—because of so many elements so subtly combined, Monica returned to her bedroom in just under a quarter of an hour, much astonished and even more delighted.

As always when something important had happened, she wanted a time of quiet in which to think about it. But that was not to be hers just yet. As she was opening her door, a figure hastened to her side out of the darkness of the stairs. It was Ripon.

"Want to talk to you for a minute," said he, and hurried into the room after her.

Monica's bedroom was large, and as the electricity at Neuadd Goch—a private system—operated only on the ground floor, it was lit with a large oil lamp by the bed. She and Ripon were in a rich gloom, but it was plain that he was excited.

"You get into bed and keep warm," he said. "I'll sit here. Listen; Ripon the sleuth has done it again! I just got the lowdown on this whole situation from Ceinwen; she's a bit put out that this chap Revelstoke has turned up—she was hoping against hope that he wouldn't, and Mrs. H.-G. was aching that he should. We've been misled by Mrs. H.-G.; Ceinwen does *not* look on this Giles as Prince Charming. And do you know why? It's a fantastic deal among the older generation. Ceinwen is to marry Revelstoke; Mrs. H.-G. wants it because she is keen for him to settle down, live a quiet life in the country, and be a good boy. It appears that he isn't a very good boy in London. She's got quite a bit of money, you see, left her by her first husband, who was a stock-broker, of all things. And the Squire wants the marriage because he will then leave this house and estate to Ceinwen, on condition that they change their name from Revelstoke to Hopkin-Griffiths, thus continuing the name at Neuadd Goch. And Ceinwen's father, Professor Griffiths, wants it because he wants her to have Neuadd Goch, which he thinks ought to be in his part of the family anyhow, and the marriage will make him retroactively county gentry, instead of just a well-known scholar. Did you ever hear anything like it?"

"No," said Monica. "But surely it all depends on what Ceinwen and Giles want?" It was fortunate that it was dark in the room for it was the first time she had ever called him Giles, and she blushed deeply.

"Ah, that's what you'd think, and what I'd think, but it's not what these people think. And that's what makes it fascinating. It's like finding oneself in a Victorian novel. I've got to re-adjust all my thinking about the set-up here. You see, I had it all worked out on the Hamlet-theme; I asked myself why Mrs. H.-G. was so wild to have her son come home, when there seemed to be so much doubt about it. I mean, nobody ever said he couldn't come; they just said he mightn't. Well—it was plain as a pike-staff. Revelstoke was a Hamlet-figure, unconsciously jealous of the Squire, identifying himself strongly with the late Revelstoke, and bitter against his Ma. It sees itself, doesn't it? I was crazy for him to come home, because I've never had a chance to observe a man in the Hamlet-situation at close quarters. But how wrong I was!"

"You certainly do see life in terms of literature, Johnny."

"Well—just look at the fun I have! But now, you see, I'm bang in the middle of one of those terrific novels about Who Gets the Dibs; the next thing to be decided is—are we in a Jane Austen situation, or a Trollope situation?"

"Does it have to be one or the other?"

"But you can't call it a modern situation?"

"Well, it's happening now, isn't it?"

"Only in a very limited sense. There are whole climates of thought and feeling which aren't really modern; I can't see a situation where two people are being pushed toward marriage in order to save family name, and family pride, as modern."

"Go on; I bet it happens all the time."

"You're just being feminine and perverse. Anyhow, you said you felt in terms of music; I feel in terms of literature."

"All right, then; where do we fit into the plot?"

"Frankly, I don't see that you come into it at all, except as a fringe-figure—Nice Girl for Christmas Purposes. But for myself —well, I don't mind telling you that I go for Ceinwen in quite a big way."

"So soon?"

"Don't be naive. I have the feelings of a poet. There's a remarkable quality about her, don't you think? Sort of figure in a poem by Yeats? Or really more like one of those wonderful women in the poems of Dafydd ap Gwylim. You know that Welsh verse she recited to us the first day, when we were in Cwm Bau? That was Dafydd ap Gwylim. I asked her, and then I read up on him in the encyclopaedia. Wonderful, warm, infinitely fascinating women, full of passion yet teasingly chaste."

"Johnny, you've got a really bad case."

"It's not anything that can be described as a case. Here she is, being sacrificed to ideas which don't really come into her climate of thought and feeling at all; she's in the wrong book. The thing is, can I get her into the right book?"

"Johnny, I want to go to sleep. And if anybody hears you talking at the top of your voice in my room, you won't get Ceinwen into any book at all. You go to bed now."

Monica leapt out of bed and fetched a small parcel from her chest of drawers.

"Just so you won't think I'm unsympathetic, here's your Christmas present now. Don't open it until morning. It's something that will be useful to you in getting Ceinwen back into the right book."

She pushed him out of the door, bearing her gift, which was, of course, another copy of *Welsh in a Week*.

Rid of Ripon, she was able to attend to her own affairs, and her first act was to fetch the lamp, and set it on the floor beside the full-length mirror which formed part of the front of the large wardrobe. Then, chilly as it was, she took off her night-dress and studied herself in the mirror with satisfaction.

By the laws of literature which meant so much to Ripon, her first experience of sex should have been painful, dispiriting and frightening. But it had been none of these things. She had been too confused and surprised to take great heed of the physical side of the encounter; it had all been so strange—the nearness, the intimacy of the posture, the inevitable and natural quality of the act itself; though new to her, it did not seem utterly unaccustomed, but rather like something dimly but pleasurably remembered from the past—and this in itself was strange. What had moved her more than these things were the endearments which Revelstoke had whispered, and the kindness and gentleness with which he had carried out his purpose. Nobody had ever spoken to her in such a fashion before. She had been kissed once or twice in a very tentative way, but that was nothing; this had touched the tender places of her spirit, caressed and stirred them, bringing her a fresh consciousness of life. And again this was not utterly strange, but like the resumption of something once cherished, and lost for a time.

She should feel evil, depraved—she knew it. But, miraculously, at this moment when she should have stood in awe of her mother, and Pastor Beamis and the whole moral code of the Thirteeners, she felt, on the contrary, free of them, above and beyond them as though reunited with something which they sought to deny her. She knew something which they could never have known, or they would not have talked as they did. If Ripon had known about it, he would have said that she had moved into a new climate of feeling.

Gazing at her naked body in the mirror she stretched, and

preened, and looked at herself with an intent and burning gaze. She was, by the standards of her upbringing, a ruined girl, and she had never looked better or felt happier in her life.

She slipped again into the nightdress, blew out the lamp and jumped into bed. Almost at once she was asleep. But not before a new and warming Christmas satisfaction rose from the deeps of her mind: What a smack in the eye for Persis Kinwellmarshe!

(12)

Did the morrow bring remorse? It did not. When Monica ran into the diningroom the squire told her that she looked fit as a fiddle, and gave her a smacking Christmas kiss. Ripon followed his example; he was a literary kisser and presumably his salute had some inner significance which was not to be apprehended by the unlettered. When Ceinwen entered a moment later, and was kissed by her uncle, Ripon did not have quite the courage to go on, and shook her warmly by the hand. But Monica had still to be kissed by Revelstoke, and he saluted her in a friendly fashion which could not have aroused suspicion in the most observant mother; it was precisely the sort of kiss, which, a moment later, he gave Ceinwen. Monica was inwardly amused; nobody knew what she knew!

"Gilly, there's the most awful thing happened," said Mrs. Hopkin-Griffiths to her son. "Mr. Mathias has sent up a message that Mr. Gwatkin is too ill to play at the service this morning. Rheumatism, poor old thing—real arthritis; he hasn't really been able to do anything with the pedals for years, and now it's in his hands so badly he simply can't manage. Will you be a dear and play for Morning Prayer?"

"But mother, I'm not an organist."

"But dear, you'll be quite good enough. Everybody knows you can play anything. Why, when you were just a lad, I remember how you did wonders with a coach-horn after only an hour or two. It's a very small organ."

"I know, and it's a very out-of-tune organ too, I'm sure. I'd rather not."

"Now dear, don't be disappointing. Mr. Mathias is counting on you."

"But I don't know what music he wants, or anything."

"We always have very simple services. You're sure to be able to manage. And think what a thrill it will be for everybody! They all know your things have been broadcast; they'll think it wonderful, whatever you do."

"I know, that's what's so embarrassing. I don't want to impose on their ignorance; it's immoral."

"Oh Gilly what nonsense! Very well then, don't play. I've promised Mr. Mathias you will, but I suppose I must just swallow my pride and go to him before service and say you won't. It's humiliating, but of course I wouldn't ask you to put yourself out."

The upshot was that under this maternal blackmail Revelstoke played, and did things with the organ of St. Iestyn's Church which would not have been approved by a Fellow of the Royal College of Organists but which sufficiently astonished and delighted his hearers, who had not heard the pedals of the parish instrument for some years past; Revelstoke even essayed pedal chords from time to time, and contrived a few impressive roars at moments of climax, and was altogether satisfactory. Mr. Mathias beamed from the vicar's stall, and threw in an extra hymn, just to make the best of the occasion. But the triumph of the morning was after the service when, as an organ postlude, he improvised a medley of Welsh airs; the difficulty was that, so long as he continued to play, the congregation would not leave the church, so in the end he had to stop and indicate with a wave of his hand that there would be no more.

His mother was delighted. She stood happily at the door of the Church, beside Mr. Mathias, ostensibly to wish everyone a

Merry Christmas, but in reality to garner compliments on the brilliance of her son. The Neuadd Goch party walked home bright with reflected glory. Even Ripon recovered from having been given three copies of *Welsh in a Week* (Monica's, and one from the squire, and one—unkindest cut—from Ceinwen) and said that he had loved every minute of the service, and felt much nearer to Washington Irving than ever before, but wasn't the singing a little under par for a Welsh congregation?

"It's a lie that all the Welsh can sing," said Mr. Hopkin-Griffiths; "the truth is that some can sing but they can all yell. And they were quiet this morning because they were listening to our Canadian visitor; I never was told that you could sing like that, my dear. We'll want to hear more from you this afternoon."

"I'm a pupil of Giles', which should explain it," said Monica, and once again Mrs. Hopkin-Griffiths launched into an account of the fine things that had been said, and how well he had played, and how, perhaps, after all, there might be some sense in his treating music as a profession.

"Mind you, Griff and I couldn't be more sympathetic about Gilly's music," she said to Monica and Ripon, who were walking with her. "We've always said it was a wonderful gift, ever since he became so serious about it at school. There was a master there in his time who was wonderfully gifted—quite professional, really. And Gilly has made friends among musicians—one of them is this Sir Benedict Domdaniel, and I've heard he's charming, though of course a Jew—but Jews are wonderfully gifted, aren't they, and we must always remember it and particularly at Christmas. And some of his things have been broadcast, which is awfully good, too. And of course he's so deep in this magazine—*Lantern*, isn't it—and we thought that might lead to a job with a publisher, or something like that. And even a pupil! You know dear, you could have knocked me down with a feather, as the people say around here, when you came in yesterday, and knew Gilly, and he was your teacher. When Lady Phoebe gave us your name, it meant nothing to us—just that you

were a Canadian studying in London, and of course I thought
from the London School of Economics, because that's where the
Canadians all seem to go, and the dear knows why, because it
seems to make them so gloomy and farsighted about nasty things.
Gilly was thunderstruck. Thought I'd asked for you on purpose.
He so resents any interference from me in his London life you
know. But it was sheer chance; though Lady Phoebe always
seems to think we're musical, though I don't know why. But
music as a profession—well, nobody we know has ever done it,
and one hears about the risks, and everything. What do you
think, dear? Of course it's different for you; you're wonderfully
gifted—oh, don't say you aren't, because I can tell just by looking at you. And also I expect you've your way to make. But Gilly
could have such a different life, if he chose, and one does so
want one's son to make the right choice. Tell me what you really
think."

Monica could not conceive of anyone who had it in him to be
a composer being anything else, nor was she interested in pro-
moting a marriage between Revelstoke and Ceinwen. Her reply
was a model of modesty and tact; she was not a proper judge,
she said, but she knew that Sir Benedict had a very high opinion
of Giles' work, and especially his songs. She could have spared
her breath, for Mrs. Hopkin-Griffiths was not really listening;
she had her eyes on Revelstoke and Ceinwen, who were ahead
of her, and who seemed to have nothing to say to one another.

After luncheon the squire and Mrs. Hopkin-Griffiths retired to
their rooms, he for a frank sleep, and she for what was more
delicately called "my usual rest"; Ripon was doing his best to
find the way into Ceinwen's climate of feeling, and Monica was
too full of happiness to want to disturb them, for her adventure
of Christmas Eve had made her generous and charitable; she had
some hopes of a talk with Revelstoke, but he too vanished, so she
went for a walk by herself, up the hill behind the house, and
over a moor which was wild and romantic enough to satisfy the
most eager heart. She wandered there for almost two hours,
thinking over and over again that she was now a woman, and

that she had a lover, and that life was sweeter than she had ever known it to be. Not a thought had she for the Galls in Salterton, who would at this time be sitting amid the ruins of Mrs. Gall's calorifically murderous Christmas dinner, fighting, in the name of Christian charity, a losing fight against their mounting ennui and repletion. She returned to Neuadd Goch just in time for tea, and found herself the only member of the party who was in a really good temper.

After tea the squire asked her to sing. "Music at Christmas, always," said he; "I well remember as a boy, in this room, my pater always sang at Christmas—just one song, Gounod's *Nazareth*. Wonder if anybody sings it now? And my Aunt Isobel sang *The Mistletoe Bough*. Can't have Christmas without music."

Somewhat to Monica's surprise, Revelstoke moved to the piano to play for her, which was not his custom at lessons. She sang *The Cherry Tree Carol*, which she had learned from Molloy, and he improvised an accompaniment of considerable beauty, using the simple tune as a point of departure for harmonies remote from any that might have been expected by a conventional ear, but evocative of an atmosphere wonderfully congruous with the simple legend of the song. To Monica it was a delight, and she sang well, but the listeners received it with apathy. She sang *Blow, Blow Thou Winter Wind*, and this time Revelstoke confined himself to a piano part which respected the intentions of Dr. Thomas Augustine Arne. But Monica wanted to return to the adventure of improvisation, so she sang *Jésu Christ en Pauvre*, trying to interest the Hopkin-Griffiths by saying that it was a folk-song of her native land.

"Really, dear?" said her hostess, "and I suppose it reminds you of home and familiar things. How sweet."

"Yes, it does," said Monica. It was the first in a series of lies which she was to tell during the next few days, all calculated to throw her Canadian past into a pleasing and romantic light. For she had never heard *Jésu Christ en Pauvre* until she learned it from Molloy, and certainly the singing of wistful French-Canadian folksongs had never been a Christmas pursuit of the Gall family, or anyone they knew. But pretence is wonderfully stimulating to the artistic mind, which is why some people lie for fun, rather than from necessity. The tender feeling and insight with which Revelstoke had illumined *The Cherry Tree Carol* he brought in greater measure to the naive, spare little legend of Christ disguised as a poor man, and when the song was done he and Monica were well content with it.

"Good, good," said the squire, in a voice which made it plain that he had felt and understood nothing. "Now, Ceinwen, tune your pipes. Let's have a Welsh song. Always like a Welsh song at Christmas."

"Where are those Welsh songs I sent you last year, Uncle Griff," said Ceinwen; "I'll sing you one of those."

A brief search discovered them in the music bench. "I wanted you to have them because I helped edit these two collections," said she. "My name is in the introduction—'Our thanks are also due to'—me, along with a few others. So you see you're not the only one to get your name on a bit of music, Gilly."

This was plainly meant to be a pleasantry, but Giles was not willing to take it so. "More weeping little modal tunes; I can't bear the way the Welsh folk-song people arrange their stuff," said he.

"We heard what you like done with Welsh tunes this morning," said Ceinwen, without good humour.

She sang *Y Gelynen*, explaining that it was in praise of the holly bush; her voice was small, pure and sweet, and prettily suited to the rippling, trilling refrain of the song. She did not sing in any way as well as Monica, but there was an individual quality and a justness of musical feeling about her singing which gave it charm. From Revelstoke's expression as he played it was plain that he did not like the accompaniment, and by the fourth verse he had begun to guy it, so slightly that only Monica noticed.

Next Ceinwen sang a Christmas carol, *Ar Gyfer Heddiw Bore*, and this time he treated the accompaniment to please himself. Ceinwen was put off by his improvisation; she was a good singer, but she was not up to that. And it was clear to Monica that Revelstoke's treatment of the theme was clever but unsympathetic; he was not helping the singer, he was showing off. The colour had left Ceinwen's cheeks, and her green eyes seemed to darken.

The squire beat time to the Welsh songs with his hand, and nodded from time to time to show that, while he might not understand the words, he was sure they were full of Welsh Christmas cheer.

"The last song I'll sing is a particularly fine one," said Ceinwen; "it is called *Hiraeth*."

"Aren't you going to tell us about it?" asked Ripon. "Please do. This is wonderful, really it is. I'm living in a novel by Peacock," he said, beaming at the squire, who accepted the remark with a smile, having learned by now that it was a compliment.

"It is about the longing for what is unattainable, which is called 'hiraeth' in Welsh. The singer is someone very old, who begs the wise and learned men of the earth to say where hiraeth comes from; all the treasures of the earth perish, gold, silver, rich fabrics and all the delights of life, but hiraeth is undying; there is no escape from it even in sleep; who weaves this web of hiraeth?"

"Splendid," said Ripon; "real Celtic magic."

"Oh I don't know," said Revelstoke. "The Welsh make a fuss about their hiraeth as if they'd invented it; it's common to all small, disappointed, frustrated nations. The Jews have used it as their principal artistic stock-in-trade for two thousand years. It's the old hankering to get back to the womb, where everything was snug. Whimpering stuff."

"Now that you've made it seem so delightful, I'll sing it," said Ceinwen.

The accompaniment was a simple but effective succession of chords, played in harp-like style, against which the tune appeared almost as declamation. Revelstoke played it thus for the first verse, and then he began to experiment; his arpeggios whined, they groaned, they shivered piteously. It was cruel caricature of the deep feeling of the words and the simple beauty of the air, and it made Monica's flesh creep with embarrassment. Ripon, though no musician, could understand the import of this right enough, and even the Hopkin-Griffiths knew that all was not well.

What will she do, thought Monica. He'll break her down. There'll be tears in a minute, and what had I better do?

Ceinwen was not the weeping sort. She finished the song, and, as Revelstoke was bringing his accompaniment to a close in a series of sour chromatic progressions she whipped off her left shoe and hit him over the head with it. Then she struck at his hands again and again, bringing from the old Broadwood yelps and twanglings which mingled with his extravagant and astonishing curses.

There was an alarming scene, in which everybody accused and nobody apologised. There was a general withdrawal to bedrooms, and some slamming of doors. But to the amazement of Monica and Ripon everyone turned up at dinner apparently in excellent spirits, and Ceinwen and Giles pulled a cracker together with that extra, clean-hearted goodwill which is seen in people who have had a thoroughly satisfactory quarrel.

After dinner they rolled up the rug in the drawingroom, the maids and outside men came in, and there was dancing to the gramophone.

"The Welsh are rather a hot-tempered race," said Revelstoke to Monica, as they danced.

And that was all that was ever said about it.

(13)

THE WEEK WHICH FOLLOWED was passed in walks, visits to neighbouring country-houses, and motor jaunts to special places of beauty, including a day of great glory when the young people drove through Gwalia Deserta and explored the gorge at Devil's

Bridge; Monica sat in the front seat of the car with Revelstoke all that day. She met several Welsh people, and was astonished by the vivacity and genial spite which they brought to social conversation, and which was unlike anything she had experienced among the people of England. But Monica was more astonished by herself than by anything external. She began to talk about her family; she was often alarmed by what she said, for she found that she was weaving a legend around the Galls.

The Welsh had a national character, or at least they were strongly under that impression. Very well; if they chose to play the Celt, she would play the Canadian. She spoke of Canadian Christmasses, finding in them pleasing and picturesque qualities which would surely have astonished her mother, or even those nationalist zealots, the McCorkills. She deepened the snow, intensified the cold, and enthused retrospectively about winter sports in which she had never taken part. Driving in cutters on the frozen waters of the harbour at Salterton, for instance; she had never done it, but neither did she claim to have done so; she simply described it as if at first-hand. And ice-boating—there was excitement! When she talked of these things her tongue ran away with her, and though she spoke no clear untruths, she implied a whole world which had no counterpart in her past. She did not suppress the Glue Works or the Thirteeners; she simply did not feel a necessity to mention them.

"What a liar you are!" she said one night to her image in the mirror. But the next day her resolve to guard her tongue vanished; she wanted to be as interesting as Ceinwen, whom she liked but whose rapid alternations of temperament began to excite her jealousy. The girl was playing the Celt all over the place, muttering in Welsh to please Ripon, and teaching him Welsh objurgations, as one might teach a parrot to swear. That affair was going swimmingly, but Revelstoke had not said an intimate word to her since Christmas Eve.

It was what she did to her family which most alarmed Monica in her soberer moments. Ma Gall began to appear as a wonder-

fully salty character, a lady, of course, but with the strength of
pioneer ancestry behind her. Ma Gall was, she told Mrs. Hopkin-
Griffiths, a natural gourmet, delighting in food and bringing to
it family secrets which produced dishes of incomparable savour,
unknown in the British Islands. This tower of mendacity was
erected on the trifling foundation of a rather dull Indian Pudding
which Mrs. Gall had learned to make from her mother.

Of course, those who embark on such a game as this must be
trapped into lies at last.

Monica's entrapment, and her punishment, came almost at the
end of her stay at Neuadd Goch. It was at dinner, on New Year's
Eve, the night of the County Ball, a festivity which was to be the
crown of the entertainment provided by the Hopkin-Griffiths for
their guests. Ripon, who was filled with true gratitude toward his
hosts, had made them a graceful speech before dinner, saying
that their kindness would never be forgotten while he lived, and
that he hoped that at some future time he might pass it on, in
the same spirit, to visitors to his own land. He did it well, and
keeping away from talk of climates of feeling, created an atmosphere of open-hearted friendliness which inevitably led to talk
of the bonds which united the English-speaking world. Monica
could not contain herself.

She spoke of her admiration for and debt to the British people, and did it in such a way that there was nothing pompous or
unseemly about it. But she could not leave it there. This feeling,
she said, was not only her own, but had long been that of her
family. The Galls, she asserted, were of United Empire Loyalist
stock.

This fell rather flat, for nobody present seemed to know what
United Empire Loyalists were. So she explained that they were
those loyal subjects of King George III, who at the time of the
American Revolution, deserted their worldly goods and migrated
to Canada, in order that they might keep the inestimable privilege of living under the British flag. Though she did not say so, it
could be understood from her words that the descendants of

these people formed a vigorous, splendid, but unassuming core of leadership—a kind of democratic aristocracy—in Canada.

In the high and charged atmosphere of the moment—the climate of feeling—this would have been acceptable enough, but Revelstoke fixed her with a sardonic eye.

"What's so remarkable about that?" said he. "Why should they do otherwise than leave the country if they didn't like the Revolution? Are you asking us to admire them simply because they were loyal? Surely that's the least Britain could have expected of them. Honouring people for being loyal is like honouring them for being honest; it's a confession of an essentially base and cynical attitude toward mankind. It's either that or it's just sentimental silliness."

Perhaps Monica should have hit him on the head with her shoe. But she was, beneath the superficial part of her mind which was boasting and prattling, so conscious of the untruth of what she was saying, that she felt disproportionately rebuked. She felt that everybody at the table was disgusted with her, and ashamed for her, as a foolish little braggart. She felt that she had been sharply and contemptuously put in her place. Of course there was no such general feeling. Mrs. Hopkin-Griffiths was thinking how distinguished Giles looked when he was nicely washed and had on his dress suit, and hardly heard what was said. The squire thought the boy was much too rough on the little Canadian; loyalty ought to be encouraged, or where would we all be? Ceinwen thought: well, there's her reward for laying herself out to charm Master Giles, the dirty English pig (though as she thought this in Welsh the last term was not quite so stinging as it seems in translation). Only Ripon guessed at the truth.

The County Ball was held in Trallwm, in the Assembly Rooms, which was a grand term given to a largish public-hall-of-all-work, and the corridors and anterooms surrounding it, in the Town Hall. It was prettily hung with holly and Christmas decorations, and had been furnished for the occasion by a local dealer with some really handsome antiques, and so it was a pleasant setting for an occasion when most of the guests brought a genuine spirit of gaiety with them.

It was a mixed assemblage of county gentry, well-to-do farmers and townspeople, and it was ostensibly in aid of the hospital. The squire could well remember—and never ceased reminding everyone he met of the fact—the days when a velvet rope divided the dancing floor, and the county danced on one side, and the lesser folk on the other. But those days were gone, and everybody said, with varying degrees of sincerity, that they were glad of it. The Neuadd Goch party were disposed to enjoy themselves, except Giles, who hated the music but had not quite enough determination to stay at home.

Balancing the ballroom, at the other end of the main corridor of the Town Hall, was the Court Room, which had been arranged as a sitting-out room; it was splendidly suited to such a purpose, for it was a maze of fenced-in compartments, wells and cubby-holes which allowed sitting-out couples quite enough privacy, if they wanted it. It was here that the kindly Ripon led Monica, and as they could not, in the gloom, find anywhere else that was not taken by a seriously whispering couple, they climbed into the prisoner's dock, which was high and surrounded by a fence of spikes—presumably to keep felons from leaping into court and menacing the learned counsel. They sat on the little bench inside it.

"Don't take it so hard," said Ripon, after a few moments of silence.

"Eh?"

"What Revelstoke said at dinner. You've been dragging your wings ever since. He's a bastard; he likes to take it out of women. Look what he did to Ceinwen at Christmas."

"But, Johnny, this was different."

"Yes, I know it was."

Monica began to weep. Ripon gave her his handkerchief, held her round the shoulders, said soothing and not very coherent things, and after a time restored her to some sort of order.

"It's not the end of the world. You've just got to see it as it was. You'd been boasting, and he slapped you down. It was nasty of him, but that's all it was."

"I'd been making a perfect fool of myself. I've been doing it ever since I came here. You must all despise me."

"No, no. I'll be frank; you've been giving us quite a line about Canada and your people and all that, but anybody with half an ear could tell that you were only asking to be patted. It wasn't even boasting. It was just putting a best foot forward. Nothing to be ashamed of. These people invite it, you know."

"Welsh people, you mean."

"All the people in these islands. They're so self-satisfied. You have to hate them, or you have to try to pull yourself up even with them. I know all about it. When I'm at home I'm not terrifically American, but over here I have to act a part, or disappear. You were just trying not to disappear; and because you're such a hell of a good singer it would easily have passed as the rather charming egotism of the artist, if dear Gilly hadn't stuck his knife into you. You were just the tiniest bit silly; but he was intentionally brutal."

"Do you mean that, Johnny, about having to act a part, and the people here being so strong in themselves, and that?"

"Of course I mean it."

"It's not just something you got out of a book?"

"What would be wrong with it if I did get it out of a book? As a matter of fact, it's in lots of books. Have you read any Henry James?"

"No; did he write about that?"

"Sometimes. We've been living in a kind of Henry James climate for the past few days. The American getting the works from Europeans was some of his favourite themes. 'This arrogant old Europe which so little befriends us', he called it. But your mistake was that you didn't act a part; you were trying to make yourself believe it, and that never works. That's bad art."

"Well, what should I do?"

"Why don't you try passing as white? You know about the light-skinned Negroes in the States, who move North and live among whites as one of themselves? The only way to get on in peace with the people over here is to conceal as well as you can that you're not one of themselves—pass as white. Minimize the differences; don't call attention to them. This country's full of Canadians, Australians, New Zealanders, yes and Americans, all passing as white, because if they let it be known what they are, the natives will patronize the living bejesus out of them. They don't really mean to be unkind; they just have this wonderful sense of being God's noblest work.—Now it's getting near the New Year. We must go back to the ballroom. Pretty soon all these Welshmen and Englishmen will be singing one of the most pedestrian verses of Robert Burns, and kissing each other. I wouldn't miss it for worlds, and if you won't be offended, I'll hunt up Ceinwen. Happy New Year, Monica darling!"

Seven

PHANUEL TUKE SWITCHED OFF Monica's radio-gramophone.

"Well," said he, "if fate is unkind to my verse, I shall at least be known to posterity as the man who provided Giles Revelstoke with the words for his first work of undoubted genius."

Revelstoke's menagerie was assembled in Monica's living-room because she had the best wireless set among them. They had been listening to a broadcast on the Third Programme of his *cantata da camera,* called *The Discoverie of Witchcraft.* Tuke had not written the words, but had selected them; the libretto was made up of recitative passages chosen from Reginald Scot's *Discoverie,* verses from Ben Jonson's *Masque of Queens,* and a witch-trial or "process" adapted from *Malleus Malleficarum.* Monica knew the words well; she had typed them many times, for the singers to study, and for the seemingly endless needs of the broadcasting people.

"I still think Brum Benny should have let Giles conduct," said Persis Kinwellmarshe. She was not sufficiently musical to venture any opinion on the composition itself, but she had found plenty of matter for vehement partisanship in the politics surrounding the broadcast.

"Now Perse, give that a rest," said Bun Eccles. "Giles himself admits he's no hand at conducting. Why risk a good chance like this just to wave the stick? He can't manage an orchestra and even you know it."

"He'd be perfectly all right if Benny didn't hang over him all the time and offer advice and fuss him."

"Benny's responsible to the B.B.C. you know that. He got them to do *Discoverie;* he has to deliver the goods. Giles said so himself."

"Giles may have said so to you, Bun dear, but I know damn well what he thinks. It's the old story: young man of genius under the wing of old man of talent—and the old man will bloody well see that he stays under his wing. Tonight will settle all that, though. It ought to put Giles right on the top of the heap."

"Does anyone know what he will get for this broadcast?" said Odo Odingsels. He had tucked his lean length into a corner and all through the music had been eating the food which Monica provided.

"There won't be much left of his fee when all the costs are paid," said Bridget Tooley. "The expense of copying the scores will eat up most of it. But of course he'll have them for subsequent performances, and over the years the rentals might amount to a good deal."

"Can't count on that," said Odingsels. "This isn't going to be a popular work. No use pretending."

Odingsels was the only one of the group who knew much about music. Giles had friends, but no intimates, among musicians. Odingsels knew what he was talking about, and ordinarily the others deferred to him. But Persis would not do so now.

"Why not?" said she. "You've heard it. Isn't it the most exciting thing in this contemporary music series?"

"I don't know," said Odingsels; "I haven't listened to any of the others. Have you?"

Miss Kinwellmarshe had not.

"It's good, mind you," said Odingsels. "In parts it's wonderfully good. I didn't mean that it wasn't. But it's hard to perform. The music is difficult; it sounds simple, quite a lot of the time, but just you look at the score. It's an inconvenient size. It isn't a song cycle, that any singer and his accompanist can carry round

the world in a music-case. And it isn't a big work that an amateur choral society can chew on for two or three months. It calls
for soprano and bass-baritone soloists, a double-quartet of better
than average choral singers, and an orchestra consisting of string
quartet and double-bass, with piano, oboe and French horn. Just
the size to be neglected."

"I suppose a good deal will depend on what the critics say,"
said Tuke.

"A little. Not much." Odingsels seemed determined to be discouraging. "Critics of any importance aren't likely to commit
themselves heavily on a new score that they haven't examined
by a composer they don't know. Giles won't find himself made
over-night. It's only in the more trivial arts like literature, and
theatre and ballet that critics wield that sort of power." He
grinned irritatingly.

"Giles will be ready for them," said Persis. "He's been wal-
loping them in *Lantern* for three good years. I don't suppose that
will make them like him, but it will let them know that he will
have a reply for anything they want to say. I don't expect for a
minute that he'll get his due from them, but they'll have to be
civil."

"Why?" said Odingsels.

"I've told you. Because of *Lantern.*"

"How many critics do you think read *Lantern?* Who do you
suppose takes it very seriously except ourselves? How many well-
known or influential names are on the subscription list? Sometimes I think we are deceiving ourselves about *Lantern.* In my
really sane moments I know it. How lucky that none of us has
to live by it."

"Odo, why are you being so bloody-minded tonight? Is it because Giles has had a wonderful work performed? I know you
hate anybody else's success, but is it necessary for you to be so
completely poisonous?"

"Persis, my pretty darling, I am a realist. Giles has had a very
good piece of music performed. A lot of people will have heard

it. Some will have liked it, others will have hated it, and some others—perhaps the biggest number—will not have paid any particular attention. Of those who have liked it, perhaps half will remember Giles' name. It is slow work, becoming known as a composer. What has Giles done? He's written perhaps fifty songs and a couple of suites for small orchestra; he's had a few things done publicly, and I believe four years ago he gave a small recital of his own stuff to which not one critic of the first rank turned up. This is his real beginning—tonight. In ten years, if he works hard, he may be quite well known as a rising young composer."

"Oh, come; sooner than that, surely," said Tuke.

"Giles is a slow worker. This piece has been on the stocks for a good eighteen months, to my knowledge. He spends so much time on other things." Odingsels cast a leer at Persis.

"Too true," said she. "He has far more than his share to do on *Lantern* and of course he has to waste his energies teaching, and doing musical odd jobs, to keep the pot boiling."

"He isn't the only one on *Lantern* who has personal work to attend to," said Miss Tooley. "If you are insinuating that Fanny and I don't pull our weight, I'd like to say that you should be the last person to criticise; you do nothing at all, except provide occasional cups of indifferent tea. And of course keep your eye peeled for cracks in the ceiling."

"Now girls, stow that," said Bun Eccles. "We all know what Odo meant; he meant Giles spends a lot of time playing bunny-in-the-hay with you, Perse, but maybe that's why he writes good music. Why don't you look at it that way, and be happy?" He raised his glass of beer toward Persis, and drank to her.

"If he doesn't want to teach, I don't suppose he has to," said Monica. "And if I take up his time being taught, I certainly save it getting the *Lantern* accounts out of tangles."

"Oh, we know you're quite the little woman of business," said Persis. "But unfortunately he can't give up teaching; he has to have the money. If that tight-fisted old mother of his would give him whatever you pay him for lessons, he wouldn't need to bother."

"Doesn't he have family money?" said Tuke.

"He's got a tiny income from some money his father left him directly. Otherwise not a bean. His mother's terribly rich; she could easily let him have a very good allowance. She lives someplace in Wales, in a tremendous house, with every luxury, and now and then she sends him a few quid, for birthdays, or something. It's a shame people like that can't die, and let their money do some good. But no, she thinks not having anything will make him get a steady job. I suppose she sees him leading the municipal orchestra at Torquay, or someplace. Mothers! I think the most disgusting and immoral relationship is between mothers and sons—no, on second thoughts, between fathers and daughters. The old ones just want to eat the young ones up."

Persis knit her dark brows and looked very beautiful, brooding on the psychological horror of Mrs. Hopkin-Griffiths and Admiral Sir Percy Kinwellmarshe.

"It is of course utterly unrealistic to suppose that reputations in literature are made overnight," said Tuke, who had been brooding on Odingsels' hard words. "One despises egotism, of course, but one instances oneself; one can give Giles a few years, and one is perhaps more *engagé*, but one has certainly not been overwhelmed with recognition. As for music being, *au fond*, more serious than letters, well—one feels perhaps that those who are committed to an art are the best judges of its limits."

"Better judges than technicians, however capable," said Miss Tooley, bridling. Everybody knew that when Tuke began to refer to himself as "one" Bridget would do battle for him. "Particularly when their own stuff appears so seldom."

"My best work is for connoisseurs of really imaginative photography," said Odingsels, grinning. "I don't have to publish to get recognition."

The menagerie was working up for one of its periodical ugly fights, but at this point Monica brought in another plate of sandwiches, and Bun Eccles went the rounds with more beer. The greedy could say no more while this lasted, and Tuke, who had a gift for talking and eating without missing a chew or a syllable, gained a great advantage. He proceeded to contrast the powers of music and poetry, being scrupulously fair, but, as he knew very little about music, not especially enlightening, though extremely strong on sensibility.

Monica went back to her bedroom, where she made the sandwiches, to be sure that the supply should not fail; she knew that when Revelstoke was not present, the menagerie could only be controlled by heavy sedation with food and alcohol. They quarrelled astonishingly, and about things which she rarely understood in detail, though she knew by her native good sense that jealousy lay at the root of it. Every time an issue of *Lantern* appeared there was one of these pow-wows, and the pattern was fixed; Tuke was offended by Odingsels, and Miss Tooley and Odingsels fought bitterly; Eccles, who was thoroughly a painter, and bored by men of words, lost patience with them all, and got drunk; Persis Kinwellmarshe asserted that there would be no *Lantern* without Revelstoke, and was called whore for her pains by Bridget; Revelstoke laughed and cursed at them all. At last Mrs. Klein would appear and complain that her other lodgers were discommoded by the noise, and Odingsels would make her cry. On one occasion Monica could bear it no more, and took Mrs. Klein's part; to her astonishment her display of temper put them all in great good humour, and improved her position in the group. After one of these brawls, which she found tiresome and exhausting, but which they seemed to enjoy, Revelstoke would marshal the *Lantern* forces again and work would proceed once more in its ill-organized, imperfectly understood fashion.

But Revelstoke was not at hand now, to keep all their bad-tempered egotism in check. And Monica was afraid that Mrs. Merry would not take the attitude of Mrs. Klein, who always managed to say, at some point in her complaints—"I'm full of sympasy for ze artist; I am grateful to have ze artist under my roof"—a protestation invariably greeted by Odingsels with a shout of "Halt die Schnauzel" Mrs. Merry was not full of sympathy for anyone, except perhaps herself, and would certainly complain of any noise to Mr. Boykin on his monthly visit with the rent. Monica wished heartily that she had not asked them to listen to Giles' broadcast on her receiving-set.

Yet it had seemed such a chance to get in with them, to strengthen her position. She was not so simple as to think that she had no place in the *Lantern* group; the finances of the magazine, such as they were, were understood by her alone, and Raikes Brothers had of late shown a tendency to call her when they wanted a decision about anything. She had been in the happy position of having two pounds ten to lend to Tuke on an occasion when he needed that sum very badly, and Revelstoke himself had been her champion a few weeks later, and had compelled the poet to pay back the ten shillings, which was all he could afford. She had a place, but it was the bottom place. And here it was six weeks after that encounter in the bathroom at Neuadd Goch, since when he had not so much as kissed her!

Why? Why could he not see that she loved him? She was not a ninny; she did not sigh and lallygag like Juliet; she put herself heart and soul into the business of *Lantern,* and although it could not be said that its position was any better than before, it was certainly clearer. She managed to get his attention for fifteen minutes one day and explained the whole financial situation to him. He had been bored, and had told her in a huff that if people hadn't enough wit to appreciate *Lantern,* he could do nothing about it. He wrote for the bloody magazine, didn't he? What more did she expect him to do? Hawk it on street-corners? But Monica would not believe that this expressed his true feeling; if he was really committed to the publication—and he was—he must desire its financial success; it was axiomatic. So she troubled him no more about it, and plunged into even more discouraging talks with Raikes Brothers, who were beginning to want something on account.

Not that she expected to win him by a flashing display of business method; she was not so foolish as that. But what better approach had she, what more effective way of showing that any-thing she had in the way of skills or talents was at his com-mand? Her heart was full of love, but externally she remained neat, silent, and perhaps a little too quick at producing pencils and pieces of paper; once or twice she sensed that it is con-venient, but perhaps not wholly romantic, to be the person to whom everyone turns for a clean bit of india-rubber. She could not hope to be useful to him musically; was she not his pupil? How, then, could she serve except with the typewriter and the account-book, in the use of which she was more expert than any-one else in the group? She wanted desperately to be one of the menagerie. She tried to swear, but it was a failure. She could not use filthy words, as Persis did; a Thirteener upbringing and, she felt, a native fastidiousness, prevented her; she had also a grudg-ing recognition that what suited the opulent sluttishness of Per-sis did not appear so well in her. However, she sought to liven up her conversation with a few bloodies until one day she caught Odingsels' ironic eye on her, felt deeply foolish, and tried no more.

They never thought of her as one of themselves. She thought of them as Bohemians, though they would have hooted at so romantic and unfashionable a word, taking it as further evidence that she was an outsider. But under their Bohemianism they were very English. No, ridiculous! Odingsels—nobody knew quite what he was, but he was certainly not English. Bridget Tooley's father was a lawyer in Cork; she was Irish as—Ma Gall's expres-sion came pat to memory—as Paddy's pig. Bun Eccles was an Australian, and abused the English as Pommies. Revelstoke him-self was English, of the Eton and Oxford variety, and of course the hateful Persis—

Ah, Persis was the one! There was a creature who managed to have the best of two or three worlds! To be the draggle-tailed gypsy, with all the advantages of great and apparently inde-structible beauty, and at the same time to be able to come the well-bred English lady—that was having it with jam and syrup at once. She was the one who created the atmosphere which excluded Monica. She was the one who did not have her speech corrected by Revelstoke. She was the one who did not have to know that "glory" was a trochee, instead of a spondee, which was what both Monica and Eccles made of it. She was the one who did not have to do anything about *Lantern*, though she was always in the way when the work was most pressing. And why? Because she was Revelstoke's mistress, his recreation, his hobby, his—

Monica, who was cutting bread, sawed savagely at the loaf. Filthy abuse that was pure Ma Gall rushed up into her throat, her head hurt and her eyes seemed to fill with blood. She had to sit down on the bed to recover herself.

Oh, it was so unfair! Why couldn't she be to him what Persis was, and at the same time a helper and a constructive influence in his life? She was better than Persis. She was; she was! Why couldn't he see it? How could he stand that creature, who took baths now and then for fun, but not to get clean, and who kept tufts of long hair in her oxters because she said real men liked it? Monica was clean (though Amy had taught her not to talk about "personal daintiness") and cleanliness ought to count. She would do anything for Revelstoke, be anything he wanted. And he had turned to her once. He must have some feeling for her. It could not be otherwise.

Meanwhile the noise from the other room was increasing. Two or three guests had made journeys to the watercloset down the stairs, shouting their contributions to the discussion as they went up and down. There had been some rapping on the ceiling by the lodger below, to which Eccles had replied with a few hearty stamps. Persis was developing the theme of parental stinginess in her extremely carrying voice. Monica knew that she would have to go in and shut them up. She held a cool bottle of beer to her forehead for a couple of minutes, and went back to the living-room.

She entered just as Mrs. Merry came in from the hall. The landlady wore a look of aggrieved hauteur, and when she spoke her accent was more refined and wholly diphthongal than usual.

"Miss Gall, I am really compelled to ask your guests to leave," she began, but got no further, for behind her appeared Revelstoke, and with him Sir Benedict Domdaniel. The menagerie greeted them with a roar.

The appearance of the great conductor created a difficult situation for everyone. Mrs. Merry was in a particularly ticklish spot, for she had to reconcile her landlady's indignation with her elation at having a celebrity (and a titled one, too) under her roof—and there were the promises she had made to the lodger downstairs to drive the rowdies out into the street. Persis, who had been making very free with Brum Benny's name, was revealed as one who had never met him personally, and had not quite the brass to be insulting when she was introduced. Monica, who had been thinking passionately of Revelstoke as a lover, had now to greet him timidly as a guest, feeling the very least of his menagerie; she was uneasy, also, about Domdaniel, who had not encountered the menagerie before, to her knowledge and who, at this moment, contrasted strangely with them, like a royal personage photographed among the survivors of some disaster. But Domdaniel managed the whole thing very well.

"We seem to have come at the peak of the party," said he, smiling affably at Mrs. Merry, and bending so low over her hand that she thought, for one golden but panic-stricken moment, that he was about to kiss it. "A very great occasion, and I'm sure you'll understand; our friend has been covering himself with glory." It was this easy, glossily splendid manner, which had won him the name of Brummagen Benny among the envious; unable themselves to rise to such heights, they took revenge by recalling his plebian origin. And a severe critic might have said that his manner was not thoroughly well-bred; it was too accomplished, too much a work of art, for mere "good form". He presented Revelstoke, who greeted Mrs. Merry with proprietary charm, as though she were his guest. At the same moment Odingsels bowed his piebald poll toward Mrs. Merry's startled face, and put a glass of beer into her hand.

"The last thing of which I am desirous—" she began, with immense graciousness, but was unable to sustain this fine beginning, and went on—"It would ill become me to—it is certainly not my desire to intrude a note of solemnity into such an occasion as this, but you will understand my position *vis-à-vis* Mrs. Porteous who occupies the flatette below, and whose advanced years and habit of life—" She floundered.

"Mind your manners," said Revelstoke to the menagerie, and they obeyed, to the point of congratulating him in stagey whispers.

"Oh, please, please!" cried Mrs. Merry, laughing throatily, and gesturing with her glass of beer, like some marchioness in an old-fashioned musical comedy, "don't feel that you must whisper. That I could not bear! Please, Sir Benedict, beg them not to whisper." She bent upon Sir Benedict a look of arch agony. With him at her side, looking so gallantly into her eyes, Mrs. Merry would have incited the party to dance clog-dances upon the head of Mrs. Porteous.

"I have a proposal which I think will settle everything," said he. "Suppose we all go to my house, and continue the party there. I've lots to drink, but if you've any food, Monica, perhaps you'll bring it along. And as we have inconvenienced you, dear lady, I hope that you will forgive us and make one of the party."

Smiling his most winning smile, he gazed deep into Mrs. Merry's eyes, mentally signalling to her—Say no; say no; you can't leave the lodgers; say no. But Mrs. Merry was not susceptible to telepathy; she was borne aloft on a cloud of social glory; this was as it had been when that worthy solicitor, Maybrick Merry, was alive, and they had invited three couples to dinner every second Thursday, and once an M.P. had come. "Yes, yes," she carrolled; "I'll run and get my wrap."

It was quite ten minutes before Mrs. Merry had changed her clothes, put on all her rings, and run a darkening stick through the grey patches in her hair. Monica had plenty of time to line her rubbish pail with *The Times* and put the food in it, and Bun

Eccles providently carried the beer downstairs, in case Sir Benedict should have overestimated his supplies. Sir Benedict had gone down to wait in his car, and Revelstoke admonished the others to come quietly. And, upon the whole, they did so, except that Odingsels insisted on carrying Persis downstairs pick-a-back, and tickled her legs as he did so, making her squeal. And it was unfortunate that Eccles, who insisted on carrying both the food and the drink, caught his heel in a worn bit of stair carpet, and—determined to save the drink—allowed the rubbish-pail to go crashing down to the landing.

A door opened and somebody—almost certainly Mrs. Porteous —poked a parrot-like head, adorned with an obvious wig, into the hall. "Well," she gobbled, "this is the first time that anything like this has ever happened here, and if it is what comes of giving shelter to Commonwealth students—"

Odingsels, with Persis on his back, lurched toward her.

"Shh!" said he. "We are taking this lady to a nursing-home for an abortion, and I must ask you please not to make so much noise." Down the lower flight he went at a gallop, with Persis shrieking and fizzing like a soda-syphon on his back. Bun retrieved the food, and, acting on sudden inspiration, pushed a sandwich into Mrs. Porteous' hand, then crammed the remainder into the pail, and raced after him. It was Monica who heard the last of Mrs. Porteous' unflattering comments and prophecies.

On the pavement there was a slight resurgence of ill-feeling, for everyone wanted to crowd into Sir Benedict's handsome car, which was manifestly impossible. Odingsels would not be parted from Persis, and Mrs. Merry, with the superior cunning of middle age, got the front seat next to the great man for herself; at last Revelstoke and Tuke were crammed into the back seat, and Monica and Bun were left to follow in a taxi with a disgruntled Miss Tooley.

"Fanny can't resist luxury," she said, "and as soon as he smelled that real leather upholstery he was done for. Not a terribly nice characteristic, really."

The house in Dean's Yard was empty, for the servant did not sleep in, but Domdaniel quickly found glasses, and in five minutes the party had been resumed. Odingsels and Persis had changed from quarrelling to silent, intimate pawing, and they needed a sofa to themselves. Miss Tooley was being distant toward Phanuel Tuke, which involved standing quite close but with her back turned partly toward him. Sir Benedict moved about, making them at home, but he soon found how needless this was; the menagerie was at home wherever it was assembled. But Mrs. Merry had a highly developed, indeed a swollen, social sense; unquestionably she thought of herself as "the senior married woman present" and she set to work to establish a high tone of behaviour. She pursued her host, she complimented him on the taste in which his house was furnished; she confided that she could judge people instantly by the glassware they used; she sincerely hoped that they were to be favoured with a little music later on, as it would be such a treat; she let it be known that when her husband was living they had several times met Madame Gertrude Belcher-Chalke, whose renditions of Scottish songs were such a delight, and who must certainly be known to Sir Benedict; and, well, yes, she would be glad of the teeniest drop of Scotch—no more than a drop, mind—and plain water.

Monica, who had had no opportunity to recover from her nerve-storm, soon found the kitchen, took the hacked loaf—fetish for the hateful Persis—from the rubbish-pail, and began once more to make sandwiches. The capacity of the menagerie for food was boundless and she, true daughter of Ma Gall, had bought in ample viands. It soothed her to make sandwiches, and it kept her away from the others.

But she had not been long alone before Sir Benedict slipped quickly through the door.

"I'll have a quiet drink out here with you," said he. "I can't convince your landlady that I don't play the piano at parties."

"I'm terribly sorry," said Monica; "it was wonderful of you to rescue us, and terribly kind to ask her. She's having a marvelous time."

"I told her to persuade Revelstoke to improvise something," said he. "A dirty trick, but self-preservation, and so forth. Have a drink. You look as if you needed one. What's the matter?"

"Nothing. We heard the broadcast."

"What did you think?"

"I thought it was wonderful. But you know what my opinion is worth."

"Don't hedge. Did you like the work?"

"I don't know. It's awfully strange. Not as strange as lots of modern music; not so sort of repellent. It doesn't fight the listener. But mystifying. I wish you'd tell me about it."

"I've done so; I conducted it. It's quite a solid piece of work, though I wish he'd study with a really first-rate man on composition for a while. He can't completely say what he means, yet, in orchestral terms. Most of the instrumental writing is brilliant, but there are a few passages of awful muddle that I couldn't persuade him to change. What he does best, of course, is write for the voice, and that lifts him above all but a few today. This isn't an age when many composers seem to care about the voice; they want to use it in all sorts of queer ways, and often they do marvelous things, but it's not really singing, you know. It's abuse of the voice. But his stuff is wonderfully grateful to sing and that, combined with a modern musical idiom, gives it great individuality."

"I suppose a lot depends on what the critics say?"

"A bit. Not too much, really. Far more depends on what chaps like me say."

"Anyhow, he'll be able to deal with the critics in *Lantern*."

"That's precisely what I'm afraid of. He wastes too much time on that nonsense."

"Nonsense?"

"Yes. What's the good of fighting critics? Mind you, some of them are very able, particularly when judging performances. But only a few can form any opinion of a new work. Most of them are simply on the lookout for novelty. They hear too much, and they hear it the wrong way. They get like children who are peevish from having too many toys; they are always tugging at the skirts of music, whining 'Amuse me; give me something new.' Giles hasn't shown them anything particularly new. He's not an innovator. But he has an extraordinary melodic gift. Now you just watch the critics and see how many of them are able to spot that."

"You don't think much of *Lantern?*"

"My dear girl, these little reviews and magazines of protest and coterie criticism come and go, and they don't amount to a damn. They're all right for what's-his-name—Tuke and that formidable female bodyguard of his—but Revelstoke is a serious man; he ought to be at work on music. You've rather involved yourself with this Lantern thing, haven't you?"

"I help a bit with the accounts."

"Good enough. You're what—twenty-two? It's all right for you. Gives you a taste of that sort of thing, and we're all the better for a taste. But Revelstoke is thirty-three. Time he was over all that, and down to serious work."

"Do you think teaching is a waste of his time?"

"Not if it brings in money he needs. But this *Lantern* is just an expense of spirit in a waste of shame."

"Shakespeare. Sonnet something-or-other."

"Bright child. He's making you do some reading."

"Yes.—And *Lantern's* not the only waste."

"You mean that gang in there? They're no more a waste than any other pack of friends, I should say. Many fine things are written about friendship, and there's a general supersition that everybody is capable of friendship, and gets it, like love. But lots of people never know love, except quite mildly; and most of them never know friendship, except in quite a superficial way. Terribly demanding thing, friendship. Most of us have to put up with acquaintanceship."

It was flattering to Monica to be enjoying, for the first time, a conversation with Sir Benedict which was not about music, and which was not crowded by the press of his engagments. She fell into a trap; she tried to be impressive; she tried to be his age.

"But don't you think people like that, who live such irregular lives, are terribly exhausting? I mean, they must drain away a lot of his vitality, which should be saved for music. I don't want to gossip, but it's common knowledge that he's terribly taken up with that girl in there—the dark one—and I don't know when he finds time to do any work. Do you think he ought to get off into the country, somewhere, and really slave at his music?"

"No; I don't. When I was your age I might have thought so, but I know better now; you can't write music just by getting away from people. Slavery is for the technicians, like you and me; we thrive under the lash. But creators must simply do what seems best to them. Some like solitude: some like a crowd. As for the girl, why not? When I was a student in Vienna my teacher told me how often he had seen old Brahms, when he was all sorts of ages, strolling meditatively home from the house of a certain lady who lived in the Weiden. Couldn't matter less. Nothing, nothing whatever really stands in the way of a creative artist except lack of talent."

"You don't think a disorderly life matters?"

"Wouldn't suit me. I couldn't answer for anyone else."

"Then you don't think that Shakespeare was right—about the expense of spirit in a waste of shame?"

"It's only shame when you feel it so. And he obviously doesn't feel it. You are the one who feels it, and there can be only two explanations of that: either you're more of a missionary than a musician, or else you're jealous of that girl with the black hair and blue eyes."

Monica turned back to her bread-cutting. She had never been much of a blusher, but she knew that her appearance had changed in many tell-tale ways.

"Am I right?" said Sir Benedict, taking a pull at his drink. "Well, falling in love with one's master is recognized practice in the musical world. Even in his eighties I can remember old Garcia having to fight 'em off, to protect his afternoon nap. Well, go ahead by all means. Anything to broaden your range of feeling."

Monica turned toward him, and her expression was so angry, her eyes so brilliant, and the bread-knife in her hand so menacing, that Sir Benedict skipped backward.

"I hate you damned superior Englishmen!" said she. "Murtagh Molloy tells me I have no emotion; Giles Revelstoke treats me like the village idiot because I haven't read everything that's ever been written, and you tell me to fall in love because it will extend my range of feeling! To hell with you all! If I haven't got your easy, splattering feelings I'm proud of it. I'll throw this all up and go home. I won't stay here and be treated like a parrot, and learn to say 'Polly wants a cracker' in just the right accent and with just the right shade of feeling! I hate the whole pack of you, and I hate your rotten little Ye Olde Antique Shoppe of a country. I'd rather go home and be a typist in the Glue Works than take your dirt for another day."

Sir Benedict looked thoughtfully at her for a full minute, then he said: "You're perfectly right, my dear, and I apologise." Monica made a dreadful face, snorted painfully, and burst into tears. She had never been a pretty weeper.

Sir Benedict had for many years made it a habit to carry two handkerchiefs, one for his own nose and one for other people's; he produced the second now, shook out its folds and gave it to Monica just in time to hide a very messy face. Then he sat her down on the kitchen table and sat beside her, holding her tenderly.

"You mustn't mind us," said he; "it's just a way of going on that we have carried over from the nineteenth century, when we really ruled the waves. Molloy would be terribly hurt if he knew you had called him an Englishman. As for me, I'm English, right enough, but not really out of the top drawer; there is a large grandpaternal pop-shop in Birmingham which it would be ungrateful of me to deny. Revelstoke is English, too, and I don't mind telling you that I worked it that you should go to his mother for Christmas. Not that she, or Giles, knew, of course; I

cooked it up with Miss Eigg, who is an old friend of mine; I
thought it might be more friendly for you. Weren't they nice
people? Surely Giles must have relaxed a little, in his own home?
Of course he plays the great man with these silly hangers-on of
his, but it's only mannerism.

"I didn't realize you had any really strong feeling for him. But
what I said was quite sincere, and not meant to be hurtful. A
love-affair, if it is anything more than a tennis-club flirtation,
does enlarge one's range of feeling. Of course that isn't why one
does it, but you must understand that I was speaking as your
teacher and advisor, looking at the thing from outside. And of
course what looks unique and glorious to you, at your age—and
is so, too, of course—has a rather more accustomed look from my
age and my point of view. The terrible truth is that feeling really
does have to be learned. It comes spontaneously when one is in
love, or when somebody important dies; but people like you and
me—interpretative artists—have to learn also to recapture those
feelings, and transform them into something which we can offer
to the world in our performances. You know what Heine says—
and if you don't I won't scold you: 'Out of my great sorrows I
make my little songs.' Well—we all do that. And what we make
out of the feelings life brings us is something a little different,
something not quite so shattering but very much more polished
and perhaps also more poignant, than the feelings themselves.
Your jealousy—it hurts now, but if you are as good an artist as
I begin to think you are, you'll never have to guess at what
jealousy means again, when you meet with it in music. And love
—don't ask me what it *is*, because I can't tell you anything more
than that it is an intense and complex tangle of emotions—you'll
have to feel that, too. Everybody claims to have been in love, but
to love so that you can afterward distill something from it which
makes other people know what love is or reminds them forcibly
—that takes an artist. Do you feel a little better now?"

"Gluh."

"Good. And you won't go back to the Glue Works tomorrow?"

A shake of the head.

"Then perhaps we should return to the others, or they will think that I am up to no good with you, and although that would be flattering to me, in a way, I don't think it really desirable."

But at this moment Mrs. Merry came into the kitchen. She wore a splendid, elevated look, more like a martyr than Monica had ever seen her; her teeth were bared in a smile which suggested that the first flames of the pyre were licking at her toes.

"Sir Benedict, I must leave you now," said she. "It is quite time—indeed it has been made obvious to me that it is far past time—that I quitted the gathering." She gave a slight, refined hiccup, and burst into tears.

For the first time in his life Sir Benedict had no clean handkerchief to offer. But Mrs. Merry, a lady even in grief and liquor, fished one out of her bosom, and held its lacy inadequacy to her lips.

"My dear lady, has anyone ill-used you?" said he. In perfect fairness he should have sat Mrs. Merry on the table and held her, but he did not.

"My fault," she quavered. "Intruded. Went too far. Artist—high strung. Should have remembered."

Sir Benedict took the glass from Mrs. Merry's hand and hunted in a cupboard where the cooking things were. He found a bottle of cherry brandy, and poured a generous slug. "Drink this, and tell us all about it," said he.

"Mr. Revelstoke—a genius, of course. And fresh from a great success.—Well, if you insist. Oh dear, I shall never be able to drink such a lot!—Well, I ought to have known. Madame Gertrude Belcher-Chalke was just the same after a concert—*elevée*, indeed one might say utterly *ballonée*—and hardly civil for hours. I meant no harm. Asked him to play. Well, I mean—a musician? Surely he *plays*? He said no. I pressed. I mean, they *expect* to be pressed. Nono. Press again. Nonono. I entreat the others to support my request. That man with the nasty picked-looking head shouts something in German. Then Mr. Revelstoke rushes to the piano and says—'For you, for you alone, you lovely creature!' And plays." Here Mrs. Merry's bosom heaved as no bosom has heaved since the heyday of the silent films. She drained the cherry brandy to the dregs. "He played *Chopsticks!*" she cried and hurled her glass dramatically into the sink.

Sir Benedict proved amply that a conductor of the first rank is not only a notable interpretative musician, but also a diplomat and an organizer of uncommon ability. He soothed Mrs. Merry. He shooed Monica upstairs to his own bedroom to wash and restore her face. He enlisted Eccles to help him bring champagne up from the cellar. He brought the party to some semblance of unity and enjoyment. And, finally, he went to the piano.

"Giles and I want to play something for Mrs. Merry," said he. "It is called *Paraphrases,* and it is what all musicians play when they are happy."

Drawing Revelstoke down at the piano by his side, Domdaniel compelled him to join in a duet; with great verve and gusto they played the twenty-four variations on *Chopsticks* which were written by Liszt, Borodin, Cui and Rimsky-Korsakov. Mrs. Merry, very much at the mercy of her feelings and with her remaining self-possession disappearing beneath the champagne, managed to get to the piano, against which she posed, smiling soulfully at Sir Benedict until, suddenly, all meaning disappeared from her face and she fell heavily to the floor.

Eccles, expert in such affairs, lifted her head and fanned her. Mrs. Merry opened her eyes, and she smiled blissfully. "Put me to bed and don't bend me," said she. And thus the party ended.

(2)

ON STAGE AND SCREEN the business of getting a drunken person to bed is always represented as uproariously funny. Monica, Revelstoke and Eccles found it merely laborious. Mrs. Merry was a

Junoesque woman in her late fifties; as a deadweight, she was not easily budged. It seemed that they had no sooner stuffed her untidily into a taxi at Dean's Yard, than they had to haul her out of it at Courtfield Gardens. The men held her upright while Monica paid the taxi, and while they hoisted her up the steps, Monica retrieved her shoes, which fell off in that process. When they got her inside, there was the problem of the stairs. It was not that she was so heavy (though she was substantial) as that she offered no handholds. They made a Boy Scout chair with their hands, but in her satin gown she slipped twice to the floor before the first step was mounted. At last they were compelled to take Mrs. Merry up her own staircase as if she were a piano; Eccles crawled up the steps on his hands and knees, with Mrs. Merry on his back, steadied, and to some extent borne, by Revelstoke and Monica. It was slow, noisy and toilsome. When they reached the landlady's room they tumbled her into bed with everything on but her shoes, and climbed on to Monica's quarters, greatly exhausted.

"Good thing I liberated this," said Bun, pulling a bottle of Sir Benedict's champagne out of one of the large poacher's pockets in his jacket. "Don't suppose you've such a thing as a bottle of brandy, Monny?"

Monica had not. Eccles was philosophic. He removed the wire from the bottle and then, seizing the bulbous part of the cork in his teeth, he gave a tremendous wrench; when the champagne spurted he checked it dextrously with his thumb. "Here," he said, passing it to her, "stab yourself and pass the dagger."

Monica had had only one glass of champagne at the party, and Revelstoke, who never drank much, had taken little more. They were both glad of a refreshing pull at the champagne, but did not want more than a gulp or two. He was still in high spirits, which he could support on excitement alone; he had enjoyed the party, springing as it did from his personal success; the only annoyance he felt was with Persis, who had vanished with Odingsels. Monica was too much elated at having him in her living-room, almost to herself, to want other stimulant. But Eccles was a hardened and persistent drinker. When his turn at the bottle came he did not take it from his lips until it was empty. Then— "I want a bath," said he; "humping the old trout upstairs has brought me out in a lather." He rose, belched cavernously, waved a casual farewell and went. They heard him go down the stairs; the bathroom door was slammed and its noisy bolt pressed home; water ran, and the whole house hummed with the rumble of pipes.

"I hope he doesn't come to any harm," said Monica.

"Not Bun," said Revelstoke, "but he may have a doze in the tub."

What now? Girls in books and plays always seemed to know what to do when left alone with the men they loved; Monica hadn't an idea in her head.

"Would you like something to eat?" she said.

He wanted nothing to eat.

Silence that went on for minutes.

"It was wonderful of you and Sir Benedict to rescue me. I was afraid Mrs. Merry was going to throw us out."

"Would have served them right. They have no manners."

"It would have been a shame, though, just as you came. We wanted to celebrate the broadcast."

"You saw how they celebrated."

"They all said you were a genius."

"I wish I had their certainty."

"I thought it was magnificent."

"Did you really?"

"Of course I don't know much about it. You know that. But if you won't laugh, I'd like to say that I think you have an extraordinary melodic gift."

"Oh? How do you mean?"

"Well, of course you know that I'm no judge of modern music, or any music, really, but I think I have a feeling for it, and it seems to me that so many modern composers write for the voice without having any real understanding of it, or love for it. And all the vocal part of *Discoverie* seemed to me to be so wonderfully singable. The idiom was modern, of course, but the feeling was—you know, the feeling you get with Handel, the feeling that you are in expert hands. The singers could settle into their parts, without having to be getting ready all the time for the next bit of acrobatics. A certainty of touch, I suppose you would call it."

"That's very shrewd of you. The others don't really know anything about music, and what they say doesn't matter. Odingsels knows a good deal, but he's terribly jealous of anyone who makes a mark, you know. That's why he's pinched Persis for tonight; wants to take me down a peg."

Monica had heard all her life that Opportunity knocks but once. But when Opportunity knocks, the sound can bring your heart into your mouth. No use dithering. She plunged.

"Do you think she'd have behaved like that if she really loved you?"

"I've never thought for an instant that she loved me."

Opportunity had a foot in the door and was thundering on the knocker. Now was the moment. She felt awkward and plain; her head was light and seemed to be thumping. But, beneath these discomforts, she was elated. She was alive as never before.

"If I had Persis' chance to show that I loved you I could do things for you that she can't. You're a genius. I know it and she doesn't. I care about it and she doesn't. I'm ignorant and silly, and I made a fool of myself at your mother's house at Christmas, boasting and pretending. You must have despised me. But I wanted to impress you. I suppose I ought to have known better, but I didn't. And you had shown that you had some feeling for me. And there it is."

As she finished this speech, sitting bolt upright on the uncomfortable day-bed, looking at the carpet, Monica's mind was almost entirely filled with a sense of having taken an irrevocable step, of having gone beyond the bounds of modesty which had been established for her in twenty-two years, of having burned her bridges: but there was room also for a sense of wonder, and indeed of admiration, for herself, and a pleased recognition that she had spoken plainly and well. She was ashamed of these latter sensations, and tried to banish them, but they would not go. Very far at the back of her mind a triumphant Monica was exulting, *I've done it, I've done it, I've brought it to the point!*

Revelstoke looked at her for a time, smiling, and twisting the ring which he wore on his left hand. He looked as he had looked when first she saw him, when he interrupted her playing of *Danse Macabre*.

"If you love me, prove it," said he.

He means going to bed with him, she thought. Well, I knew that. I'm ready.

"I know that sounds hatefully egotistical," he went on, "but I have always wondered what people meant when they talked about love. My mother has always told me that she loves me, but it's astonishing how little she will do to show it; the love between us always seems to mean great concessions on my part, and very little ones on hers. And there have been girls— quite a few girls—who were sure they loved me, and whom I thought I loved, but it never seemed to go beyond what was pleasant and flattering to themselves. Once they had me, as they thought, under their thumb, they wanted great changes in me. I do not propose to change to anybody's pattern. That is the charm of Persis; she doesn't expect changes in me, and she certainly doesn't mean to make any in herself. She knows that I am no Darby, and certainly she is no Joan. Now, I have a suspicion —and I know it is caddish of me to mention it at such a tender moment as this—that you want to reform me, and make me better. Am I right?"

"No."

"Don't you want to make a quiet haven for me, in which I shall write immortal music, while you keep bad influences from the door, and do wonders with our tiny income?"

"No. You must do whatever seems best to you."

"You have no notions about marriage?"

"I hadn't thought about it."

"Swear?"

"I swear."

"Then let me tell you a thing or two. Our meeting at Neuadd Goch was a shock to me, and when I thought you had planned it, I hated you and determined to do you a very bad turn for it. But when I found out from my mother that it was all quite unplanned, I was delighted to find you there, and our encounter in the bathroom was proof of it. You were silly, bragging about your family; I don't know anything about them, but every word you said was palpably false. And what were you trying to do? You wanted to impress *my* family. Why? Did you think them so marvellous that you couldn't live without their admiration?"

"They were kind to me; I don't know any other people like that. I wanted to be a little bit like them, I suppose."

"You think you are devoted heart and soul to music, but you will waste so much effort and stoop so far to impress the first examples of our declining county gentry you meet? Well, never mind. Now listen: I don't love you. Is that understood? But if ever I do love you, I'll tell you. I'll be absolutely honest with you. But because I fall short of loving you, that doesn't mean that I don't want you, and that I am not sometimes extremely fond of you. Meanwhile, you think you love me. Shall we act on that assumption?"

He led her into the bedroom, and there the atmosphere which had so enraptured Monica at Neuadd Goch was created again. Giles would not say that he loved her, but that was only a form of words; could he treat her so if he did not? She would not believe it.

He undressed her, and an incident occurred which she was to remember always. She stood in her slip, shy and unaccustomed, and as he began to remove his own clothes, she turned to get into the bed. But he caught her by the arm, and, removing the slip, stepped backward and looked long at her nakedness.

"You must get used to being looked at," said he. "It is beautifying to be seen naked by those we love, and the body grows ugly if it is always huddled under clothes. Nakedness is always honesty, and sometimes it is beauty: but even the finest clothes have a hint of vulgarity. Never make love with your clothes on; only very common people—really common people—do it."

It was a long night of love, and when at last Revelstoke slept, Monica lay beside him feeling triumphant and re-born. He was hers. Though he had spoken coldly to her, and bargained, and said flatly that he did not love her, she was confident. She would win him at last. He should be brought to say it. He would love her, and tell her so.

(3)

WHAT THE CRITICS SAID was a matter of concern to all of the menagerie, and it was during the week that their opinions appeared, and were chewed over at Thirty-two Tite Street, that Monica's new relationship with Giles became apparent to the inner circle of *Lantern*.

It was Persis who was first to learn of it. The day after the party in Dean's Yard she strolled round to Tite Street at about four o'clock in the afternoon, expecting a brief quarrel and a reconciliation. But when she climbed the stair to Giles' apartment she found the outer door closed.

This was something unknown to her. Giles never closed that door except as a signal that he was working, and was not to be disturbed under any circumstances. Since she had known him, he had never closed it except when she was in the flat, and very rarely then. She could not conceive that it was meant to exclude her, so she tried the handle. The door was locked. This certainly did not mean that Giles was from home, for he seldom troubled to lock his flat. She knocked, peremptorily. There was a stirring inside, so she gave the door a hearty kick. It opened, and Monica appeared in the crack, dressed in slacks and with a scarf tied around her head; in her hand was a mop.

"Shhh!" said Monica, laying a finger to her smiling lips.

"What d'you mean, 'Shh!'"

"I mean Giles is sleeping, and you'll disturb him."

"Sleeping! And what are you doing, may I ask?"

"Cleaning the kitchen," said Monica; "somebody's left it in an awful mess. If you like to come back later this evening, I'm sure he'll be pleased to see you."

The door closed. If Persis had been the swooning kind, she would have swooned with rage. As it was, she gave the door a few more kicks, and stamped down the stairs.

The encounter gave a new dimension to Monica's happiness. She had driven Giles from Courtfield Gardens that morning before seven o'clock, for she did not want him to be found there by Mrs. Merry, and she had no idea how long the landlady would sleep. Shortly after the shops opened she had followed him to Tite Street in a taxi, bearing with her brooms, soaps and cleansers, as well as the necessaries for a splendid breakfast. She served him his food on a tray, kissed him, and told him to go back to sleep, as she meant to be busy for several hours. He was too astonished to resist.

"My God, I have fallen into the hands of a Good Woman," he said, as she left the room, but she merely smiled as she closed his door.

Then began such a ridding-out as the flat had never known since Giles had lived there. All Ma Gall's hatred of slopdolly housekeeping, transfigured by love, was unleashed in Monica; she shook things, beat them, scrubbed and scoured them, rubbed, polished and dusted them; wearing rubber gloves, and using lye and a knife, she scraped the rancid and inveterate grease out of the stove; she washed every dish; she got rid of a large, reeking jam-pail, which had been the flat's principal ash-tray for some months and had never been emptied. She washed Pyewacket's dish, to the cat's astonishment and displeasure. She raised an extraordinary dust, and worked miracles. When she was finished, after six hours' toil, the flat was only moderately dirty—which was cleaner than it had been since she had known it. It smelled better. It looked better. But except for the dirt, nothing in it was altered.

Monica was too wise to move things about, or attempt to impose order on Giles' chaos. She was content to clean up the chaos, but not to alter it. Music and books still heaped the top of the piano, but they no longer blackened the hands. The large trestle table which was covered with *Lantern* papers was still heaped high, but the heaps were neater around the edges. The bathroom was gleaming, and some underthings of Persis', which customarily hung on a piece of twine from corner to corner, had been removed, and were awaiting removal in a bag in the kitchen. And the kitchen—its stench no longer caught at the throat, the dirty linoleum and the foul grey mess beneath it had been removed from the drying board; two tins of cleanser had gone into the waste-pipe so that when it belched (as it did whenever water went down it) it belched a harsh, carbolic smell, and not a breath from the charnel-house. All the things for which Giles cared nothing had been cleaned and put straight; all things for which he cared had been cleaned and left in familiar disorder.

And to cap it all, Persis had come and been repulsed. Monica was happy as any bride in her dream house. She drew a bath in the clean bathroom, lay down in it, and sang a few snatches recollected from *The Discoverie of Witchcraft.*

> '*I have been gathering Wolves' hairs*
> *The mad Dog's foam, and the Adder's ears;*
> *The spurgings of a dead man's Eyes,*
> *And all since the Evening Star did rise.*'

It was not ideal as an outpouring of the joy of love (though it was not without some reference to her house-cleaning work) and she did not sing it in the hope of catching Giles' ear. It was a simple burst of delight. But Giles put his head around the door.

"Didn't know you could sing any of that," said he.

Remembering his words of the night before, she did not make a show of concealment, but lay still in the water.

"I can sing all the soprano part. Do you want tea? I'll be out in a minute."

She could not bring herself to use the unpleasant towel, nor yet the shower curtain, so she had to dry herself on her head-scarf and her handkerchief, and remain damp where these would not suffice. She did not care. She sang as she mopped, patted and fanned herself dry:

> 'A Murderer, yonder, was hung in Chains,
> The Sun and the Wind had shrunk his Veins;
> I bit off a Sinew; I clipp'd his Hair,
> I brought off his Rags, that danc'd i' th' Air.'

"You've been busy," said Giles, when she took tea into the workroom.

Monica made no reply. She had made several resolutions as she worked, and one of them was that she would never draw attention to anything she did for him, or seem to seek praise. Patient Griselda was only one of the parts she meant to play in the life of Giles Revelstoke and it was certainly not the principal one. Nor did she mean to camp in that flat. So when she had fed him the sort of tea he liked—large chunks of thickly buttered bread smeared with jam, strong tea and soggy plumcake—she said that she would have to go, as she had work to do for Molloy.

"There'll probably be people looking in during the evening," said she. "Shall I get the papers and see if there is anything about the broadcast? Persis was here earlier, and I gathered that she will be back again."

"Very likely," said Giles. But as soon as she had gone, he burst into loud laughter. He was thinking of Persis.

(4)

WHEN MONICA RETURNED at nine o'clock, the menagerie was assembled, and it was characteristic of them that they all said they wanted to see the papers, but none of them had bought any. When she appeared with all the principal ones, fresh and clean, they fell upon them eagerly, and rumpled them, and read pieces aloud derisively, to show how superior they were to the events of the day. But of the lot, only two papers had brief references to the broadcast.

By the following Sunday, when all the papers which might be expected to say anything about *The Discoverie* had made their appearance, there was a creditable total of seven notices. They ranged from two brief, cautious comments on the quality of performance through four others, which were complimentary in a pleasant but unimportant fashion about the work itself, assuring the public that Giles was "promising" and "original" and that his score was "musicianly". But the longest, and most impressive, in the most influential of the Sunday journals, was the one by Stanhope Aspinwall.

It would have delighted most composers. It treated *The Discoverie of Witchcraft* seriously, complimented Giles on the fine sense of form which it revealed, praised the splendid melodic gift which Domdaniel had mentioned, and also called attention to the inferiority of the purely instrumental passages, though it said that they were interestingly laid out for the small group of instruments used. But it was the two final paragraphs which made Giles angry. They read:

'In spite of the high quality of the work as a whole, and the brilliance of many pages, the hearer who hopes for great things from Mr. Revelstoke may be disturbed by a quality in *The Discoverie of Witchcraft* which can only be called "literary". The choice of theme is strongly romantic, and none the worse for that

—but it is a literary form of romance. The portions of the text which are not by Ben Jonson are drawn from two seventeenth century books on witchcraft which have no particular grace of style but which have, from time to time, roused the enthusiasm of amateurs of literary *curiosa*. Even the skill of the musical treatment of this matter cannot persuade us to take the theme—witchcraft—seriously. In another composer this would cause no concern; we should be sure that he would grow out of it. But Mr. Revelstoke is known—indeed, principally known, at present —to the musical world as a musical journalist. Though musical gifts and literary skill have often gone hand in hand there comes a time when one or the other must take the lead. Mr. Revelstoke will forgive me if I point out that, as Schumann, Berlioz and Debussy in their time had to give up their avocation as writers to embrace their fate as composers, that time has also come to him. In brief, he must give up what he does well and devote himself to what he does best.

'What he does best is to match fine poetry with eloquent, graceful and seemingly inevitable melody. The cantata form of the composition under review is commandingly used, and it is this sense of drama, even more than the lyric passages, which make *Discoverie* an important new work; there is a foreshadowing here of that rare creature, a real composer of opera. But Mr. Revelstoke must find his way toward opera not through his present literary enthusiasms, but by clearing the literary rubbish from the springs of his musical inspiration.'

"But it's a rave, old man," said Bun Eccles when he had read it. "You said he'd given you a rocket, but it's a ravel He says you're marvellous, and all you've got to do to be twice as marvellous is to get down to work. Cor stone the bleedin' rooks, you don't know what a bad notice is! Why, I've seen chaps— painters—really chewed up in the papers; told to go and find some honest, obscure work, and trouble the world no more— that kind of thing. I don't understand what's eating you."

"I will not be school-mastered, and lectured, and ticked off by Mr. Bloody Aspinwall," said Revelstoke. "I will not be told to stop writing criticism of critics by a critic. I will not be known-best-about by a man who knows nothing of me except what he reads in *Lantern*."

"He just wants to shut you up," said Persis. "You've probably exposed him so often as an incompetent that he's taken this way of revenging himself. You're dead right, Giles; you'd be a fool to pay any attention."

This was the opinion of Tuke and Tooley, as well. They did not want Giles to lose his enthusiasm for *Lantern*. They knew that if he withdrew from the magazine it could not survive another issue, for not only did he supply the workroom and most of the enthusiasm, but he also supplied Monica, whose secretarial work had made the production of the magazine much easier.

"Of course you have it all your own way," said Tuke; "you have only to reply to this in *Lantern*, and that will be the end of Mr. Aspinwall. It will be one of the few times when a creative artist has been able to answer a critic quickly and finally."

Monica could understand nothing of this. She thought Aspinwall's notice wonderful. And when she found opportunity, she looked through the back numbers of *Lantern*, and found no attack upon that critic whatever from Giles' hand. What she did find, in an early copy, was a suggestion in one of Giles' articles that he admired Aspinwall's judgement alone among the London critics of the day. It made no sense to her. Giles' ravings against Aspinwall seemed sheer perversity.

But she did not say so. A week, during which their intimacy had grown every day, had taught her that contradiction was not the way to reach Revelstoke's heart, or his head. He could not bear to be crossed in anything. He could only be reasoned with about matters which were of no importance to him. And so she kept silent about what she thought until she had either ceased to think it, or had banished her disagreement to the depths of her mind, as disloyalty. She did not join very readily in the general condemnation of Aspinwall; she did not, as the witty Persis did, refer to him always by an obscenity which somewhat resembled his name; she did not speak as though he were an enemy of everything that the *Lantern* group stood for. She had resolved that she would not try to make Giles anything other than what he was. And her compliance was showing results.

"Quite plainly there is a new *maitresse en titre*," said Tuke to Tooley one day as they climbed the stairs. And Bridget Tooley, who had already changed her attitude toward Persis, marvelled once again at how long it took even Phanuel Tuke to see what a woman saw at once.

(5)

THE WORD "mistress", insofar as she had thought of it at all, had always held a dark splendour for Monica. Because of her beauty, even Persis had not spoiled this notion that women who lived with men out of wedlock breathed a special, exciting and romantic air. But now she was a mistress herself, and although it had its excitements and rare, deep satisfactions it was by no means what she had, dimly, foreseen. It was very agreeable to be deferred to by Tuke and Tooley, and to see the baleful glint in Persis' fine eyes, but there was a lot of hard work about it.

Giles liked comfort, though he had no intention of supplying it for himself, and once the flat was running in a reasonably orderly manner, he wanted it to continue that way. And *Lantern*, now that she had a bigger say in its production, took more of her time. Giles made a pretext to ask Domdaniel to cancel her German and Italian lessons, so that this time would be provided. And he began to work her mercilessly at her singing lessons. The success of *Discoverie* had raised his ambition as a composer to a new pitch. He hunted out and revised his songs—which were far more numerous than Odingsels' estimate of fifty—and it was her task to copy the new versions neatly; under his tuition she became a quick, deft and pleasantly ornamental copyist. But he also began to write new songs, and as she was at hand, he arranged the *tessitura* of these new works to suit her voice, making them inconveniently high for the majority of singers. His choice of lyrics tended toward poets not widely popular and usually dead; his settings of modern verse were few. His sensitivity to poetry, and to the rhythms of English, was reflected in all his songs, but in the new works it expressed itself in complications of time, and in prolongations of phrase, which made them very hard to study, though wonderfully easy to hear. It was Monica's delight, and also her despair, to slave at these songs through countless revisions, while the composer visited upon her all the irritation and dissatisfaction which he felt with himself. Giles never praised her. When a song had reached its final form, and she had sung it precisely as he wanted it, he would sometimes say, "Got it now, I think." But it was of himself that he was speaking.

The flat ceased to be the hang-out of the menagerie, for Giles was too busy to be bothered with them, except when *Lantern* work was to be done, or when he wanted conversation and a party. Of course they blamed Monica for coming between him and his old friends. And of course they wondered what on earth he saw in her.

Sometimes she joined in this wonder herself, for as a lover Giles was fully as demanding as he was when he was teaching her to sing what he had written. Indeed, the two kinds of experience were uncomfortably similar. He could be tender, but he could not be patient. He was experimental and ingenious, demanding for himself aspects of pleasure which she could not comprehend, and therefore could provide only by happy accident. If luck was not with her he might scold; worse, he might laugh at her. Once, after what had seemed to her a wonderful, ecstatic afternoon in the pokey little bedroom of the flat, she had turned to him, certain that the moment had come, whispering, "Do you love me?" He had replied, "What if I say no?" The sardonic glint in his eye warned her not to press the matter.

She could not conceal her hurt, so she rose, dressed herself, and made him the stodgy, jammy tea-meal which he liked. She knew better than to ask that question again.

She did not spend the nights at Tite Street. She did not dare, for fear that Mrs. Merry would tell Mr. Boykin, who would tell Mr. Andrew, who would tell the Bridgetower Trust—who would tell her mother. But except for her lessons with Murtagh Molloy she spent almost all of her waking hours there. Her first decision to preserve some aloofness from Giles had quickly weakened; the harder he worked her, the more he nagged her about the most minute details of her singing, the more tyrannous his demands as a lover, the less was she able to keep away from him.

Bun Eccles alone of the menagerie seemed to have any true estimate of her relationship to Giles.

"You've certainly got it bad, kid," said he to her one day as they sat in The Willing Horse.

"Worse than bad," she replied. "It's abject."

"Well, cheer up. You'll get over it."

"Only when I'm dead."

"Bad as that?"

"Yes; bad as that."

It was Bun who sent her to a physician.

"You got trouble enough, Monny, without getting landed with a baby. You can't expect Giles to do anything about it. He belongs in the great nineteenth century tradition, when geniuses littered the earth with stupider-than-average kids. So you just cut along and see my friend Doc Barwick; I'll tell him you're coming, and why, and he'll put you wise. Self-preservation is the first law of fallen women and a couple o' quids' worth of prevention is better than fifty guineas' worth of dangerous cure."

And thus a new and unwelcome complication was introduced into her love for Giles. Monica had been brought up with a Fundamentalist's horror of this particular interference with Nature, and with an ill-defined but strong notion that if the consequences of sin were avoided now, some triply-compounded exaction would be made at last. She faithfully did as Eccles' friend bade her, for she feared open disgrace, but she added immeasurably to her sense of guilt by doing so.

By the irrational account-keeping of unhappy love, the humiliations and labours which she underwent for Giles made her love him the more; and the more she loved him, the more inevitable it seemed to her that some day he must recognize the burdens which she had incurred on his account, and love her for it. He could not know the truth, and still withhold his love from her. Such indifference could not be reconciled with her estimate of his character.

Easter fell late, and it was the beginning of March when Molloy said to her, one morning—"Got a message for you from His Nibs; wants you to study the *St. Matthew Passion* thoroughly and in a hurry—which can't be done, as he well knows. But he's conducting the Oxford Bach Choir in a performance on the first Sunday in April, and he wants you to be one of his London soloists. Oh, nothing tremendous, so don't think it! You'll be the soprano False Witness—seven glorious bars in your part. But he thinks it's time you got a smell of public performance, and here's your chance. You're to bone up on the whole job, sit in the choir, sing your bit, and get your expenses paid. Know any Bach?"

"I've been through the *Anna Magdalena Notebook* with Revelstoke."

"Ever look at the *Passion?* Ever hear it?"

"Never."

"We've a month; we'll scratch the surface."

It seemed to Monica that they did much more than scratch the surface; she slaved at it, and Molloy even made her study the full score, so that she might have some acquaintance with classical orchestration. He forbade her jealously to seek help from Giles. "What would a fellow like that know about this sort of music?" he demanded, unreasonably. It was not Giles' musical competence he doubted, but his moral worth. Molloy had a cult for the *Passion* which astonished Monica, for she had not supposed him to be a deeply religious man. "If the Bible was divinely inspired, so was the *Matthew Passion*," said he; "you've not only to know it note for note and rest for rest—you've to feel it in the furthest depths of your soul." It was in this spirit that they worked.

The effect on Monica was deeply unsettling. As the great music took possession of her, it became a monumental rebuke to the life she was living. Without having done so consciously, she had moved far from the Thirteener faith; the altered conditions of her life shoved it into the background, and when she thought of it at all, it was the crudities of its doctrine, the sweaty strenuosities of Pastor Beamis, and the trashiness of its music which recurred to her. Not that she condemned it in such clear terms, for to have done so would have been to condemn her family, and her own former self. Loyalty was as strong in Monica as it had been when she declared to George Medwall that nothing would make her untrue or ungrateful to her home. Fifteen months was not long enough to shake that resolve, though it was long enough to give quite another colour to the situation. The Thirteener faith was like a shoddy and unbecoming dress which she had ceased to wear, but had not yet thrown out.

The bigotries of Ma Gall, and the palaverings of Beamis were not the whole of Monica's religious experience, however. Christian myth and Christian morality were part of the fabric of her life, dimly apprehended and taken for granted behind the externals of belief. And it is what is taken for granted in our homes, rather than what we are painstakingly taught, which supplies the bones of our faith. Monica believed, as literal truth, that her Lord had died on the cross to redeem her, Monica Gall, from the Primal Sin of Adam; a life of devotion to His will was her duty and her glory; strict adherence to the Ten Commandments was the whole moral law; her sins were fresh wounds in the body of her wounded Lord. Because of the special nature of the Thirteener faith—the notion that historic time was an illusion, and that it was possible to "make contact" with Christ by living a godly life—Christ seemed at times to be awesomely and reproachfully present and palpable, grieved because she could not break through the prison of her own imperfection and exist fully with Him. She had not been much troubled by this sense of His imminence since she was sixteen, when she had been somewhat worried by sexual fantasy, but it returned to her now, with new strength, as she worked over the pages of the *Passion*.

The noble utterance of Bach wakened in her a degree of religious sensibility of which she had never previously been conscious. She had outgrown the Thirteeners and in one or two daring moments had thought of herself as finished with religion; but in the presence of this majestic faith she was an unworthy pygmy. She was overwhelmed, frightened and repentant. It seemed to her that there was something ominous and accusatory in the fact that Domdaniel had chosen her to appear as a False Witness.

"But why?" she asked Molloy. "It says in the score that the part is to be sung by an Alto, and it's plain enough that I'm no alto. Has there been a mistake? Should we tell him?"

"No mistake at all," Molloy replied. "You can sing the notes all right, and the other Witness is a very light tenor, so the balance will be better than if he was paired with some girl with a big, bosomy note. Ben knows what he's doing; it's that covered, *chalumeau* effect of your lower register that he wants—hints at something a bit spooky."

Revelstoke was quick to see the change in her, and it was characteristic of him that as Monica's reluctance to yield increased, so did his demands as a lover.

"I like you much better in this Lenten mood," he said one afternoon, as she lay beside him, very near to tears. "For a while I had begun to doubt if you could make love in anything but the key of C Major, but this is a far, far better thing. Mr. Revelstoke is pleased to report to the Bridgetower Trust that the pupil is making steady progress."

Wretched and guilty as Monica had felt, these words filled her with a piercing delight. If this were sin, how sweet it was!

(6)

In the front row of the Oxford Bach Choir sat Monica, soberly
dressed and self-possessed, a professional in the midst of amateurs. Behind her rose the ranks of undergraduates, dons male
and female, dons' wives and daughters, which comprised the
Choir; before her was the orchestra, part local and part brought
down from London, and ranging in demeanour from the splendid calm of the concert-master and the aloof grandeur of the
harpsichordist to the fussy eccentricity of the player of the *viol
da gamba*. High above them, and inconveniently placed for the
conductor, was the organ-loft, into which the ripieno choir of
boys had been packed. The Sheldonian Theatre was crowded
with a university audience, so much odder and frowsier than a
London audience, so young in the main, so long of hair, so forti-
fied with scores of the *Passion*. Monica was conscious that many
eyes had found her, and that she was looking very well. And
why not? Had she not been made free of the room in the Di-
vinity School where the London artists made ready for the performance? Had not Miss Evelyn Burnaby, the great soprano,
spoken to her in the pleasantest terms, when Domdaniel had
introduced them, and asked for help with a difficult zipper on
the back of her gown? Monica felt every inch a professional,
and concealed her surprise that the Sheldonian Theatre was not
a theatre at all, as she understood the word, but a kind of arena
which looked as though it might be used for some sort of solemn,
academic circus. The ceiling was beautifully painted, and she
had to check herself from gaping upward at it; everywhere in
the building there were odd little balconies, pulpits and thrones;
part of the audience was very high up, almost under the roof.
Altogether a wonderful place in which to make one's first, real
professional appearance as a singer. Nothing at all to do with
the Heart and Hope Quartet.

It was five minutes past eleven, and by that curious instinct

which audiences have, silence fell suddenly and Sir Benedict
Domdaniel, elegant in morning dress, walked to his place, raised
his baton, and the introduction to the *Passion*, rising majestically
from its first deep pedal-point, began. Monica's knowledge of
this music was intimate but remote, for she had heard it only
as it sounded on Molloy's piano and her own. She had rehearsed
once with Domdaniel in London, again with a piano, but she
had no conception of how it would sound with the heavy forces
of organ, double orchestra and continuo, and the double choir.
The mighty, ordered grandeur came from everywhere about her,
and she seemed to shake and vibrate with it. It was a glorious
and alarming experience. In her capacity as a very minor soloist
she rose and sat with the choir, and sang with the sopranos, keeping her voice well down, both that she might not make mistakes
through lack of rehearsal, and that its superior quality should
not singularize it among the amateur choristers. Standing in the
midst of these voices and instruments, she was conscious as
never before of the power of music to impose order and form
upon the vastest and most intractable elements in human experience.

She was conscious also, and for the first time, of why Domdaniel was regarded as a great man in the world of music. He
conducted admirably, of course, marshalling the singers and
players, succouring the weak and subduing the too-strong, but
all that was to be expected. It was in his capacity to demand
more of his musicians than might have been thought prudent,
or even possible—to insist that people excel themselves, and to
help them to do it—that his greatness appeared. With a certainty that was itself modest (for there was nothing of "spurring
on the ranks" about it) he took upon himself the task of making this undistinguished choir give a performance of the *Passion*
which was worthy of a great university. It was not technically
of the first order, but the spirit was right. He had been a great
man to Monica, for he could open new windows for her, letting
splendid light into her life: but now she saw that he could do

so for all these clever people, who thought themselves lucky to be allowed to hang on the end of his stick. Without being in the least a showy or self-absorbed conductor he was an imperious, irresistible and masterful one.

At one o'clock the performance halted, to be resumed again at half-past two. As soon as she left her place in the choir Monica was claimed by John Scott Ripon who bore her off to the George restaurant for lunch.

"Poached salmon and hock," said he. "Fish is the only possible thing during the *Passion*, don't you agree? And hock, to keep your pipes clear for your solo bit—just a single glass, because we don't want you to be not only false but drunk. Now tell me all your news. How's the ineffable Giles? Still the same old Satanic genius?"

"He's well. Why do you enquire about him in that sneering way?"

"Well, Monny, you're surely the last person to ask that, considering how he behaved toward you at Christmas. I've been doing a bit of research on him. Reading *Lantern*. Dreadful muck, most of it. Who's this twit Tuke? I mean, how second-rate can you get? But Giles' stuff is very good—very good, that's to say, considering how old hat all that sort of thing is now."

"Old hat? You think it's old-fashioned?"

"Monny, it's not as good as old-fashioned. It's just plain out-of-date. All that preciosity belongs to the 'twenties. The modern line for little mags and reviews is frightful dyspeptic anger and working-class indignation and despair and shameless gut-flopping self-pity—real Badly Behaved Child stuff. *Lantern* belongs to a much earlier, more romantic time, the Wicked 'Twenties, when every Englishman of the intelligentsia was ashamed of himself because he wasn't a Frenchman; it belongs to the era when chaps boozed on absinthe, when they could get it, and wished they had the guts to take drugs. No, *Lantern's* an oddity; I suppose there's a public for it among chronic harkers-back and hankerers-after, but it is not going to attract anything really

first-rate. Except for Giles. He can really write. Of course out-
smarting the critics is always good fun, and popular, too. Nobody
likes critics, and I seriously doubt if there is an artist of any kind
worth his salt anywhere who wouldn't poison every critic if he
could. I mean, why not? You create something—it's your baby.
Then along comes some chap, quite uninvited, and points out
to the world what a puny, rickety little shrimp it is. Of course
you want to kill him. Critic-baiting is very good fun, and they're
easy game. But Giles does it in a rather old-fashioned style, all
the same. He's a man of the 'twenties. A Satanic genius, as I said."

"You mean he poses?"

"Certainly. Don't we all? He just does it a bit more obviously
and consistently than most."

"You're quite wrong, Johnny. His music isn't a pose. It's very
fine. And that's not just my own opinion."

"Oh, quite. I don't deny it for an instant. You saw what Aspinwall said about his broadcast piece? When Aspinwall takes him
seriously, it's important. Aspinwall is one critic that Giles can't
make a fool of. But that's what's so silly about Giles; he's
obviously a real genius—whether first, second or third-rate I don't
know, but certainly more than just a competent chap. But he has
to act the genius, as well. And the way he plays the role isn't
the modern way. And maybe he isn't play-acting. Ceinwen says
that all that bad temper and sardonic laughter and nonsense is
quite natural to him. It would be hard luck to look like a fake
when you were simply being yourself, wouldn't it?"

"You've been seeing Ceinwen?"

"Not seeing. Writing. But I am going to see her in the Easter
vacation. Her father has asked me to stay for a bit."

"Is it serious, Johnny?"

"Yes, it is, really. But I don't know—I can't imagine her in
Louisiana, standing with her back against the wall of the family
shoe factory."

Monica found herself in the role of confidante, and being
young she had little patience with it, unless she were given an

opportunity to confide in return. It was over the coffee that she told Ripon about herself and Giles, and said a little about the religious scruple which was troubling her. His reply had that clarity, objectivity and reasonableness which is possible only to advisors who have completely missed the point.

"If it makes you unhappy, break it off. You're a charmer, you know, Monny, in your quiet way; it's a quality you have of looking as if you could say a devil of a lot if you chose, but had decided not to—a kind of controlled awareness; so you don't have to behave as if Giles was the only pebble on the beach. You'll have dozens of chaps after you. What if he is a genius? Being a genius doesn't excuse being a bastard. Not that we should be too hard on him. I mean, how would you like to be the son of Dolly Hopkin-Griffiths, who doesn't know one note from another, and wants you to settle down to honest work? And I'm sure he hates old Griff, though Ceinwen says not. But it's a Hamlet situation, as I told you at Christmas. And what he's taking out on you is his resentment against Dolly, for being unfaithful to Daddy.

"But the religious business—I'd pay it no mind, if I were you. You're an artist, Monny. You'll have to shake off that Fundamentalist stuff. If you are of a religious temperament, be religious like old Bach, not like a grocer with a hundred thousand recollections of short-weight chewing at his vestigial conscience. No, no; live in the large, Monny; dare greatly; sin nobly." Johnny had finished the bottle of hock, and was shouting a little.

No, Johnny simply did not understand. Be religious like old Bach! As the afternoon session of the *Passion* got under way the religion of old Bach seemed more than Monica could bear. The pathos of the Prologue to the Second Part worked searchingly within her, as the voice of the contralto soloist (Miss Emmie Heinkl, herself, if the truth were known, the mistress of a director of the Midland Bank) repeated—

> *Ah, how shall I find an answer*
> *To assure my anxious soul?*
> *Ah! where is my Saviour gone?*

Quickly followed the recitative in the Court of Caiaphas, then the chorale begging for defence against evil, and then—Christ's Silence Before Caiaphas, and the False Witnesses! She could not stand; she could not sing; she was unworthy, and what might be forgiven in others could never be forgiven in her! Terror seized her. She must not sing; she was unworthy!

But when the moment came she stood, she sang—and sang well—and sat again. For the remainder of the *Passion* her head throbbed, she was in misery, and she feared that she might burst into tears.

She was surprised when, after the performance, Sir Benedict offered her a seat in his car for the drive back to London; she was still more surprised to find that no one else was to drive with them.

"You were very nervous," said he, as they sped toward Abingdon.

"I didn't think I could utter."

"But you did. That's Molloy's training. That's being a pro."

"I was afraid of the music."

"Well you might be. So was I."

"Oh no!"

"Oh yes. Not of the choir or the orchestra, or anything like that, of course. But I never conduct the *Passion* or the *B Minor* without a sensation that the old Cantor is listening. It's not the kind of thing I readily admit to, because if publicity people got hold of it, the result could be very sticky. But I'm telling it to you, because this was your first public performance of any consequence, and I think it may be helpful to you. Don't make sloppy nonsense of it, but remember, sometimes, when you sing, that if the composer were listening you'd want him to be satisfied with you. Don't presume to guess what his answer might be. Don't conjure up silly visions of him nodding his peruke and saying 'Well done!' But use it as an exercise in humility. That's what all of us who perform in public must pray for at dawn, at high noon, and at sunset—humility."

"It was humility that nearly finished me today. Sir Benedict, may I ask you a very personal question? I don't mean to be impertinent, but I truly want to know."

"Yes?"

"With the *Passion*, does it make a very great difference to you —not being a Christian?"

"Ah, I gather that the widespread notion that I am a Jew has reached you. As a matter of fact, I'm the second generation of my family to be baptized and safe in the respectable bosom of the Church of England—just like that eminently respectable fellow Mendelssohn. But to speak honestly, I'm nothing very much at all, which is reprehensible on all counts. Theologians and philosophers are terribly down on people who are nothing at all. But I find it's the only thing that fits my work. I tackle the *Passion* like a Christian—quite sincerely; but I don't carry it over into my fortunately rare assaults on *Also sprach Zarathustra*. One's personal beliefs are peripheral, really, if one is an interpreter of other men's work; Bach was devout, but it is far more important for me to understand the quality of his devotion than to share it."

"Mr. Molloy says you must feel the *Passion* in the very depths of your soul."

"Quite true, but don't interpret Murtagh simple-mindedly. He knows perfectly well that you can feel *Hamlet* without believing in ghosts."

"I see. At least, I think I see."

"But what about you—for I assume that this enquiry about me is leading up to something about yourself. What about you and the *Passion*? You've been brought up something tremendously devout and Bibliolatrous, if I recollect aright. You mentioned humility nearly wrecking your performance today. Of course it couldn't have been humility. What was the trouble?"

"I'm in a muddle about my personal life."

"Still in love with Revelstoke?"

"Yes, I am."

"Is it serious?"

"As serious as it can be."

"And I take it from your manner that he doesn't reciprocate?"

"He doesn't feel as I do."

"How does he feel? Now please don't cry. And what has this got to do with humility?"

"The music—I'm afraid I'm living a very wrong sort of life— and the music made me feel despicable."

"I'm driving, and I simply can't do anything about it if you're going to cry. However, you will find a handkerchief in my left-hand topcoat pocket, and there are others in my portmanteau. But I most earnestly beg you not to cry, but to listen very carefully to me. First, despising yourself isn't humility; it's just self-dramatizing. If you're living in what is pompously called sin with Revelstoke, you'd better be sure you are enjoying it, or you will soon find that you have neither your cake nor your penny. I've seen a great deal of sin, one way and another, and the biggest mug in the world is the sinner who isn't getting any pleasure from it. I'm not taking your situation lightly, though you may think so. I'm talking sense, but I'm too old to get any pleasure out of playing the sage, and making heavy weather with my trifle of worldly experience. My best advice to you is: clarify your thinking about your situation, and act as good sense dictates. Don't torture yourself with vulgar notions about what the neighbours will think, but get this maxim into your head and reflect on it: chastity is having the body in the soul's keeping —just that and nothing more."

They talked all the way to London in this strain. Monica explained, and Sir Benedict advised, but nothing new was said. When at last he stopped at Courtfield Gardens he summed up:

"Remember: you must clarify your thinking. I know it's the last thing you want to do, but you must do it. If necessary, take a couple of weeks off and go to Paris. Get away from him, and see things in perspective. And when you've made up your mind, stick to your decision. And finally, don't suppose that I'm going to allow this to wreck your work, because I won't."

Within an hour, Monica had gone to Tite Street, and discovered Giles in bed with Persis Kinwellmarshe. There was a quarrel of proportions and ferocity of which Monica had never dreamed. It ended with Giles telling her that her chief trouble was that she had no sense of humour.

Two days later she flew to Paris.

(7)

PARIS IN SPRING is not an easy place in which to nurse a grudge against oneself. Monica arrived with a long face and a heart full of what she conceived to be self-hatred, but her spirits began to rise almost as soon as she was in Amy Neilson's pretty house in St. Cloud, and before the first evening was over she had confided her trouble to that wise and capable woman. She had not meant to confide; she had fully meant to grapple with the problem alone. She was humiliated by her readiness to spill her story to anyone who might be sympathetic; it seemed so weak. But Amy was an American and a woman, and might understand better than Ripon, who was a man, or Domdaniel, who was English. A little to her surprise, Amy came down flatly on the side of conventional morality.

"These affairs don't do," said she. "Particularly not with girls of your temperament. Their tendency is always to harden you, and what would you be like if you were hardened? You'd be very much like your mother, my dear. Oh, different in externals, I'm sure, but very much like her. And in spite of all the nice loyal things you've said to me about her from time to time, I don't think that will answer. What was it you said he told you—that you had no sense of humour? Lucky for him. A woman with a sense of humour would never have taken up with him in the first place. He sounds an impossible person. Oh, a genius, perhaps. Benedict is always discovering geniuses; it's a craze with him; he's terribly humble about not being a composer himself, and he's always exaggerating the talent of young men who show promise. But suppose Giles Revelstoke is a genius? Geniuses are not people to make a woman happy. The best he could do for you would be to marry you and make a drudge of you. No, you've done the right thing. Get over him as fast as you can."

"But perhaps that's what I'm for—to drudge for somebody far above me. I'm nothing very much, and I know it."

"Benedict says you can become a very good singer. That's something. Let me be very frank, dear. You're not what I call a big person. It's not just being young, it's a matter of quality. You've got a fair amount of toughness, but essentially you're delicate and sensitive. You must preserve that. It's true you have no sense of humour, but very few women have. You should be glad of it. It's not nearly such a nice or important quality as silly people make out. Wit and high spirits and a sense of fun— yes, they're wonderful things. But a sense of humour—a real one —is a rarity and can be utter hell. Because it's immoral, you know, in the real sense of the word: I mean, it makes its own laws; and it possesses the person who has it like a demon. Fools talk about it as though it were the same thing as a sense of balance, but believe me, it's not. It's a sense of anarchy, and a sense of chaos. Thank God it's rare."

"Maybe what Giles has is a sense of humour."

"You may be right. He sounds like it. But my advice to you, dear, is to get yourself out of this before you're hurt worse than you are—which isn't nearly as badly as you think, I dare say. It isn't sleeping with a man that makes you a tramp; that's probably healthy, like tennis or yoghourt. But it's having your feelings hurt until they scar over that makes you coarse and ugly. You're not the temperament to survive that sort of thing."

And thus the pattern of Monica's Easter in Paris was set. She was getting over Revelstoke. Amy did not refer to the matter again, but she kept Monica busy with French conversation, French literature, shopping, and visits to plays and sights. And Monica, who was beginning to recognize the chameleon strain in her nature, seemed most of the time to fit very well into the stimulating, pleasant, sensible atmosphere which Amy created.

But in her inmost heart she was hurt and puzzled by the failure of all her advisors to comprehend anything of her feelings. They seemed to know what was expedient, and self-preservative, and what would lead to happiness when she was fifty, but they appeared to have no comprehension at all of what it was like to be Monica Gall in love with Giles Revelstoke. Even Ripon, who was not more than a year or so older than herself, could marshal all the facts and make a judgement about them, but not even Domdaniel could grasp the irrationalities of the situation. Must one live always by balancing fact against fact? Had the irrational side of life no right to be lived? The answer did not have to be formed; the irrational things rose overwhelmingly from their deeps whenever she was not strenuously bending her mind to some matter of immediate concern.

Did she want to be a singer? She had been assured so often that it lay within her power to be one, but not since she left Canada had anyone thought of asking if that were truly her desire. What was it, after all, to be a public performer of any kind? One morning, when Amy was busy elsewhere, Monica strayed into the museum of the Opéra to pass the time. She had been there before, but under Amy's firmly enthusiastic guidance; she had been told to marvel, and she had obediently marvelled. But now, alone, she looked about her. How dreary it was! So many pompous busts of Gounod; Gounod's real immortality was through the wall, on the great stage. But here was the monocle of someone called Diaghilev; Amy had said something about him, but who was he, and what had he done? Where was his immortality? And these pianos of the great—how small they seemed; they bore about them a suggestion that they must have been played by very small men. And these worn-out ballet shoes to which names, presumably great, were attached—was this trash all that the darlings of the public left behind them? There were things here which had belonged to great singers, bits of costume and pitiful, dingy stage jewellery. This was what remained of people who had breathed the muhd as she could hardly hope to breathe it; was this worth the struggle? Would it not be better to be Revelstoke's drudge and his trull, contributing thereby to something which might live when they both were dead?

She brought herself near to tears with these gloomy broodings. She looked out of a window across the Rue Auber, where a sign caught her eye; it said "Canada Furs", and suddenly she was sick with longing for the cold, clean, remorseless land of her birth. Why had she ever come away, to get herself into this mess?

Luncheon raised her spirits, and she was a little surprised to discern that what she had really been thinking about, and longing for, was immortality—and a vain, earthly immortality at that, the very kind of thing which the Thirteeners (who were in no great danger of attaining it) condemned so strongly.

Ah, the Thirteeners! After that shaking hour in the Sheldonian, when she had sung her seven bars, and felt herself sealed of the seal of Bach, she could no longer be one of them. But what, then, was she? A whirligig, like Domdaniel, who confessed that he took the colour of whatever work he was engaged on at the moment? But that was unjust to a man whom the world called great, and who was certainly the greatest man in every way that she had ever met. It was, indeed, a moral judgement. And what was it that Domdaniel had said to her, on that drive from Oxford, concerning her own harsh judgement on herself?—"Moral judgements belong to God, and it is part of God's mercy that we do not have to undertake that heavy part of His work, even when the judgement concerns ourselves." But wasn't that just gas? If you didn't make moral judgements, what were you? Well, of course Domdaniel said that you were an adult human being, and as such ought to have some clear notion of what you were doing with your life. Clarity, always clarity. The more she puzzled, the less clear anything became.

Reflection, even on these somewhat elementary lines, was hard work for Monica, and it made her very hungry. After her lunch, she continued her wandering through familiar tourist sights, putting in time until she should meet Amy again, and return to St. Cloud. Her wanderings took her to the Panthéon.

A vivid imagination is not of great use in the Panthéon, unless one knows much of the earthly history of the great ones who lie buried there, and can summon splendid visions of them to warm the grey, courteous unfriendliness of its barren stones. In spite of Amy's cramming, Voltaire was not a living name to Monica, nor was Balzac, or any of the others who gave the place meaning, and everywhere the bleak, naked horror of enthroned Reason was ghastly palpable. Within five minutes she had left the place, and wandered on a few paces into the church of St. Étienne du Mont.

All she knew of this church was that it possessed a remarkable rood-screen which Amy, stuffing her charges with culture like Strasbourg geese, had insisted that she see and admire. And there it was, its two lovely staircases twining upward toward a balcony surrounding the High Altar; Monica, as upon her first visit, longed to climb one of them and look down into the church; she yearned, for no reason that she could define, to see that balcony filled with singing, trumpeting, viol-playing angels. She sat down in a corner, and stared, trying to see what existed only in her imagination.

She saw no musical angels, but she became conscious of the windows, so strong and jewel-like in colour. She was warmed and soothed by the dark splendour, and some of the pain in her head—the fullness and muddle—began to go away. She hated thinking, and was ashamed of hating it. But thought was like the Panthéon. Here was feeling, and feeling was reality. If only life could be lived in terms of those windows, of that aspiring, but not frightening, screen! If only things and feelings existed, and thoughts and judgements did not have to trouble and torture!

She was conscious of movement and sound nearby, but it was not for some time that she looked to see what it was. Quite close was a canopy, not very high, of stone, under which was a tomb, not particularly impressive. A grille surrounded it, but an old woman was reaching through this fence, as she knelt, and as she prayed she rubbed the stone gently with her arthritic hand. Tears stood in her eyes, but did not fall. A Negro came near, knelt until he was almost prostrate, prayed briefly, and left.

What could it be? Monica found a sacristan, and soon had her answer. It was the tomb of St. Geneviève, the patroness of the city of Paris.

"Formerly in the Panthéon," said the man, "but it was taken from there and publicly burned when the church was re-dedi-cated to Reason; the ashes and relics were brought here when all that foolishness was over."

Then, in the darkness beneath the canopy, there was some-thing of a saint? A saint who had found a haven here after the persecutions of Reason? She had never considered saints before. But, with a sense of awe and wonder that she had never known, Monica went to the tomb and, when no one was near, knelt and stretched her hand through the grille.

"Help me," she prayed, touching the smooth stone, "I can't think; I can't clarify; I don't know what I want. Help me to do what is right—no! Help me—help me—." She could not put any ending on her supplication, for none would express what she wanted, because she did not know what she wanted.

Nevertheless, when she met Amy at the end of the afternoon, she seemed in splendid spirits, and Amy was convinced that she was forgetting Giles Revelstoke, and that the whole thing had been one of those fusses about very little, which were so com-mon among girls who matured late.

(8)

WITHIN THREE HOURS of her return to London, Monica was at the flat in Tite Street; her excuse was that it was hopeless to try to reach Revelstoke by telephone, and she must make her own arrangement about future lessons, or else give an embarrassing explanation to Domdaniel. Giles greeted her more warmly than he had ever done.

"I've something that I think you'll like," said he, handing her a bundle of music paper. It was a *solo cantata* for a soprano voice with piano accompaniment. She looked quickly through it; the manner was very much his own—the old *solo cantata* form, recitatives alternating with melodic passages, but in a modern idiom; she saw immediately that the *tessitura* of the lyric passages was unusually high and that the recitatives lay in a lower register. Yet it was for one voice.

"You haven't looked at the title," he said.

It read

KUBLA KHAN
a setting of Coleridge's poem, by
GILES REVELSTOKE
for MONICA GALL

"A present," said he. "We'll work on it, and you'll sing it the first time it's heard which, if my plans don't fall through, will be quite early next autumn—Third Programme again."

She did not dare to ask if this were an amends for the quarrel before Easter. And what did it matter? She did not dare to ask if this meant that he loved her; even that did not seem to matter, now. The great fact was that he was in better spirits than she had ever known, and that they were to work together again. *On something written specially for me*—it was that voice which she had heard within herself before, that voice of which she was afraid, because it spoke so selfishly and so powerfully.

But—Oh, Saint Geneviève, was this your doing?

"There's another thing," said Giles. "I've been approached— only approached, mind you—by the Association for English Opera; they wanted to know if I had anything in their line. It was *Discoverie* that interested them; they were very complimentary."

"Giles!"

"Yes, I know. I can't tell you what it was like, talking about it to people who really knew, and could understand what was implicit in it, as well as what was staring out of the score. The upshot of it was, they want something. Now don't go off the deep end, because it's all very tentative. I haven't anything—not on paper—but I've been tinkering with a notion for years. So I'm to make a sketch, and rough out some of the scenes, and they'll hear it. Wait, wait—don't exult too much; there's a sticker even if they like it. They're broke. They can't commission a new work, but they can do one if it's up to standard. Production here; perhaps production in Venice. But I don't see how it's to be done."

"But it must be done! It's unthinkable that it shouldn't. Why can't you do it? Would it take too long? How long does it take to write an opera?"

"Well, Rossini used to knock one off in three weeks, when he was in form. It can also take any number of years. The one sure thing is that you have to live and eat while you're doing it. If I'm to do this, I must give up all teaching—not that it brings in much—I'd have to give up everything else—bits of film work, editing, the lot. I'm a fairly rapid worker, but an opera is a backbreaker—worse than a symphony in lots of ways. And the costs can be staggering; copying the parts can eat up a packet. The Association is long on prestige, short on cash. I can't expect help from them."

"Would your mother help?"

"I've asked her, and she has sent me fifty pounds and a lecture, saying that there will be no more, and couldn't I find a professorship in a conservatoire, or something. The worst of it is, Raikes are getting rough about the *Lantern* bill and I had to give them the fifty to keep them quiet."

"Giles, with this on hand, you'll have to give up *Lantern*."

"That is what I positively refuse to do. Nothing would please Aspinwall better. He wants to kill *Lantern*, and I am not going to oblige him."

"Giles, listen to me. Do you really think *Lantern* is so good? Why must you sacrifice to it? Because it is a sacrifice. People I know say it's—only one of a lot of small magazines, and not the best, except for your things; everyone agrees they're wonderful. Why can't you give it up?"

"Because it is a personal mouthpiece which I value. I know that a lot of the stuff in it is tripe; do you suppose I really thrill to the off-key twanglings of Bridget Tooley's lyre? Or even to Tuke's tosh? You can't tell me anything about *Lantern* that I don't know. But I have said my say in it for four long years and I want to go on. I might have dropped it if Aspinwall had not so clearly revealed that he wants me to do so, but I shall keep it on to spite him, even if the opera goes up the flue in the process. No, if I write *The Golden Asse*, it must be done with *Lantern* still in existence."

"*The Golden Asse?* It that what it's called? You have a story?"

"I have one of the oldest and best stories in the world; it is *The Golden Asse*, by Lucius Apuleius. I have been haunted by it since boyhood, and any operatic jottings I have done, have been done with it in mind."

They talked long and eagerly, for Giles was off his guard as Monica had never known him to be. He was enthusiastic; he forgot to play the genius; he was—she was ashamed of herself for admitting the phrase, even mentally—almost human. But talk as they might, the ground never changed. He wanted to write his opera: he must somehow get money to live while doing so, and to pay the heavy costs involved: he would not give up *Lantern* because he was convinced that somewhere in London a malignant demon named Stanhope Aspinwall was consumed with the desire that he should do so.

"But it's lunatic," cried Monica, in exasperation; "I don't suppose Aspinwall really gives a damn."

"I know what I'm talking about," said Revelstoke, and as he seemed about to close himself up in his unapproachable character again, she let that matter drop.

Of course this conversation led at last to the pokey bedroom, where Monica, for the first time in her life, really enjoyed what passed—enjoyed it not because it gave pleasure to Giles, or because it was a sign that she held some place in his life, or because it was a proof of her freedom, but because it gave pleasure to herself, and because it was herself, and not Persis, to whom he had confided his great news. It was plain enough that Giles needed her.

He should need her more. Monica conceived a great plan. She would find the money which should make possible the writing of *The Golden Asse.*

(9)

HER FIRST PROPOSAL was that she should go to Sir Benedict, and ask him to lend Giles enough money to keep him going for a year. Giles vetoed this plan at once; his attitude toward Domdaniel was an unpredictable mingling of admiration for his great gifts as a conductor, and contempt for his success. "I'm not going to give it to him to say that he made it possible for me to write anything," said he; "if I'm to have a patron it won't be Brummagem Benny." And from this position he would not budge. It was pride, and Monica admired him for it, though she could not have analysed it.

Nevertheless, if she could not go to Domdaniel, Monica's list of possible patrons was at an end. She knew no moneyed people. She confided her trouble to Bun Eccles, as they sat in The Willing Horse.

"Why don't you finance it yourself?" he asked.

"Me?" said Monica, incredulous.

"Well, Monny, you know your own affairs best, but you look to me like a pretty flush type."

"Oh, Bun, I'm a church mouse. I've always been poor. I mean, Dad had to leave school at sixteen, and we've always just managed, you know. All I've got now is this scholarship thing."

"It seems to amount to a good deal. You've got some pretty expensive clothes, Monny, and all kinds of costly junk in that flat at Ma Merry's. Are you sure you're really poor, or are you just one of those people who assume that they're poor? Have you ever gone without a meal? Ever had less than two pair of shoes? I have, often, but I don't consider myself poor. I mean, I'm not telling you what you should do. I'm just asking. But the menagerie thinks you're rolling."

It took Monica a full two days to comprehend this, but in the end she was forced to admit to herself that she was not really poor—was, indeed, very well situated. She had all her bills paid; she could buy things on tick; she got five hundred a year, now, as pin-money. The idea was breath-taking; she did not want to be well-off—that was something one said of people against whom one felt an honest working man's grudge. People who had more than enough money (with a few splendid exceptions like Domdaniel) were for that very reason morally suspect. But at last she accepted the reality of her situation.

Once again she sought Eccles' advice, and then began such a complication of chicanery as Monica had never dreamed possible. Eccles had a genius for the finance of desperation, and assuming that she wanted as much money as possible, he gave himself a free hand. Within a week he had sold her expensive radio-gramophone and her collection of records. ("They are going to Mr. Revelstoke's for a time," she explained to Mrs. Merry, and the landlady was impressed.) He sold some of her personal luggage, including the fitted case which she had been given by the Thirteeners; it was gone before she realized what was happening. He persuaded her to dispose of quite a large part of her wardrobe. He even got ninepence for *War and Peace*, which had been unopened for fifteen months. All this was done in an ecstasy of haggling and what he called "flogging".

"This clothes caper is absolutely endless, Monny," he explained. "We can go on and on. You buy a few smart things every month, charge 'em, wear 'em once and turn 'em over to me. I flog 'em. Good for eight or ten quid. These lawyers aren't going to snoop through your cupboard. Go right ahead till they squawk."

Well, thought Monica, Sir Benedict said they wanted me to spend more money.

She had a few pounds in hand, left from the money she had received for her visit to Paris. Eccles pounced on it.

"You can save a lot on food," said he, "and you'd better let me have a look at your gas-meter. Those things eat shillings. There's a little jigger inside that controls how much you get for a bob; I'll just bring over a tool I have, and put yours right. I don't doubt Ma Merry's been swindling you; the only fair thing is to make an adjustment right now. Pity you don't have your own electric light meter; I've a sweet little trick with a magnet that does wonders with one of those. Still, can't be helped. Oh, you'd be amazed what money you can raise when you know how!"

Monica was indeed amazed, and the uneasiness she felt was shouted down by her pleasure in being able to put a substantial sum of money—nearly two hundred pounds—in Giles Revelstoke's hand. He was delighted.

"You're keeping me!" he shouted.

"No, no; it's a loan, or an investment, or something like that. You mustn't mind."

"But I don't mind. I love it. I've never been kept by a woman before."

The situation seemed to gratify something perverse in him. He knew how Monica came by the money, and he delighted in calling it "her immoral earnings". But she very soon discovered that it had been a mistake to give him the money, for he had no idea of how to keep it, or use it sparingly. He did not want things for himself, particularly, but he gave Raikes Bros. another fifty pounds on the *Lantern* account, and he gave a party for the menagerie, to whom he confided, as the best joke in the world, that he was now Monica's kept man. Monica was so torn between shame and exultation that, for the first time in her life, her digestion troubled her. All the better, said Bun Eccles; she'd want less to eat.

The menagerie thought it all wonderful, and Tuke and Tooley courted Monica embarrassingly, seeing in her the saviour of *Lantern*. It was true that Miss Tooley, who kept Tuke (but in a sublimated, disciple-like way) made a few veiled references to the iniquity of diverting trust funds: and it was also true that Tuke, who was deeply hurt because he was not to make the libretto of *The Golden Asse* (which Giles was adapting himself) was a little bitter about artists who sold themselves for money. Persis was jealous, because she could not afford to keep Giles; it would have been such a sell for her straight-laced parents if they had discovered that she kept a man. But she shut up when Eccles suggested to her that she might try her luck on Piccadilly, and put her earnings into the general fund. Though there were undercurrents, it was accepted among them that Monica was a heroine.

Eccles had no money, but he gave his talent to the acquirement and husbanding of anything that Monica could lay her hands on. There was only one source of income which he ruled out.

Odingsels approached Monica one evening, and sitting beside her, so that his unpleasant head was very close to hers, said: "If you really want money, I can always pay you for work—though I can't afford to contribute anything for nothing. But I do figure studies—the nude, you know—oh, nothing unpleasant and very well thought of by judges; the right models are always a problem, and it so happens that you have an excellent figure, of just the sort I require. You know me, Monica, and I am sure you have no silly ideas about such things. I could run to ten guineas a sitting, and I could make use of you quite often."

Monica was willing; after all, if Persis could take off her clothes for Odingsels, so could she. But Eccles was firm.

"No you don't," said he.

"But he says it's not dirty pictures. And it's ten guineas a time.

I don't mind. Why, Bun, you know you employ models yourself. What's the fuss?"

"Monny, some day that fellow is going to be in very bad trouble. And when he is, you don't even want to know about him, see? Now don't argue. You're not going to do it."

And although Monica was rebellious, she obeyed.

The fact was that the small engagements and sources of income which Giles gave up to work on his opera—some examination of manuscripts for a music publisher, some arranging of music for the B.B.C., scores for documentary films, and some occasional critical writing outside *Lantern*—might have brought him twenty pounds or so a month. Monica was providing him with about twice that sum, but it all vanished without anybody seeming to be better off. The same hand-to-mouth methods of finance continued; for Monica, who understood the management of money best, was not asked to take charge of it. Nor did it ever seriously occur to her that it should be so.

Monica never thought of herself as keeping Giles; she thought of it as financing the creation of *The Golden Asse*, which went swimmingly. Giles worked very hard, and during the time when he should have been teaching her (and he was still sending his bills to Domdaniel for her lessons) she kept up her work for *Lantern*, and provided him with food, comfort and companionship in bed. But other people thought of the situation quite differently, as she discovered within a few weeks.

Ripon had written to her soon after their meeting in Oxford, to ask her to go with him to the Vic-Wells Ball; he had been asked to go with a party, and wanted a partner. She grudged the money for the costume-hire, but when Ripon called for her, not very happily disguised as a toreador, she was ready in an outfit which included a large panniered skirt and a tricorne hat, which the costumier called a Venetian Domino.

The ball was held in the Albert Hall, not very far from Courtfield Gardens, and when they arrived the floor was well filled with those characters inseparable from such occasions. There were soldiers and sailors of all sorts, whole tribes of gypsies, Harlequins and Columbines in all shades, and platoons of Pierrots; there were fifteen or twenty head of Mephistopheleses, and quite as many Gretchens; Cavaliers and Roundheads abounded. These were the staples, the bread-and-butter, of disguise. In addition there were the lazy people who had come as monks, or simply as robed figures, and the over-zealous people who had come in costumes so ingenious and original that they could neither sit down nor dance, but wandered the floor smirking self-consciously, and hoping to be admired. The saddest of these was a gentleman whose costume consisted of a clever arrangement of Old Vic and Sadler's Wells programs; people kept stopping him to read the fine print, and to debate about what it said, quite as if he were not inside it. There were homosexuals in pairs and singly, their eyes—they hoped—speaking volumes to understanding hearts. A few Lesbians swaggered menacingly in very masculine costumes, smacking their riding-boots with whips. A pitiful little man, dressed with loving care to resemble Nijinsky in *L'Après Midi d'un Faune*, crept about in a contorted posture, meant to remind the beholder of the best-known picture of the great dancer in that part; but it was pathetically apparent that he had a crooked spine. Like all costume balls, it was a fascinating study in self-doubt, self-assurance, thwarted ambition, self-misprision, well-meaning ineptitude and, very occasionally, imagination or beauty.

Monica found it dull. A year ago she would have exulted in such an affair, but tonight she thought it rather silly, and was annoyed that Ripon had to wear his spectacles with his costume if he were not to trip over things and tumble on the stairs.

When he had gone to fetch drinks, she stood in one of the upper corridors, wondering how soon it would be before she could decently ask to be taken home. She was conscious that the door of a box near her had been opening and shutting indecisively, but she was taken unawares when a stumpy Mephistopheles burst from it, seized her arm, and dragged her inside.

They were at the back of the box, which was otherwise unoccupied, and at a little distance, over the railing, the full rampaging splendour of The Veleta was to be seen. The Mephistopheles snorted within his mask for a moment, then seized Monica and kissed her.

She was too surprised to resist, conscious chiefly of the hot-buckram-and-glue smell of the mask, and when the Mephistopheles clutched at her again, she stumbled backward into a chair, bearing him down with her.

"It's about time," snorted the figure, in a Cork accent which could only belong to one person known to Monica.

"Mr. Molloy!" she cried.

"You'd better call me Murtagh," said the Mephistopheles, tearing off his mask, and showing a very red face. "We've some business together, my girl, that's waited long enough." He made another dart forward and thrust his hand deep into the bosom of the Venetian Domino. It was an inexpert move, too vigorous; the hooks on the back of her gown burst, and his hand stopped not far from Monica's stomach. She seized his arm and removed it.

"Whatever is wrong," said she. "Are you ill?"

"B'God I'm not ill, but I'm fed up," said Molloy. "Seein' you day after day, growin' lovelier and lovelier and—oh hell! Monica, you've got to be good to me; that fella'll ruin you, and never think the toss of a button about it. I could love you—I could teach you—God, there's nothing I'd not do for you! You'll say I'm old, but it's not the truth. I could be young for you, my darlin', I could! Be kind to me; I'm begging you!"

He looked almost ill, as he squirmed on his knees on the floor in front of her, and he seemed to be in a torment of passion that was partly physical desire, for at one point he seized Monica's right leg beneath her skirt and kneaded it painfully. He smelled of drink, but it was not drink that ailed him.

"Mr. Molloy, what can I do for you? You mustn't go on like that. Tell me what's the matter. No! Stop that, or I'll have to go away."

He raised a terrible, tear-swollen face to her, and groaned. "I want you," he said. "I love you."

"But—you mustn't; it won't do."

"Oh, it won't do, won't it? Well, if you don't want to be decent, b'God we'll be indecent! And no surprise to you, either. It won't be the first time for you, nor the tenth, nor the hundredth, so shut up and keep still!"

So this is rape, thought Monica, strangely cool, as she was dragged down upon the fusty carpet of the box. The Venetian Domino outfit included a large lace fan, mounted on heavy sticks, a formidable bludgeon; she cracked Molloy smartly over the skull with it, as he snuffled and puffed above her. His face grew small with pain; all its features seemed to draw together; she gave him a shove and he rolled over on the floor, still too hurt to utter.

"You shouldn't have done that," said Monica, in what she felt to be a schoolmistressy way. But what was there to say? "What ever made you do such a beastly thing?"

But Molloy could not answer. She wriggled over the floor, impeded by her large panniered skirt, to a point where she could hold his head in her lap and nurse it. After a time he was able to open his eyes. And again she asked him: "What made you do such a thing?"

"I love you," he sobbed, with tears of pain and despair running down his cheeks. "Oh God, you can't know what I've been through, with the thought of you and that fella.—And now they say you're keepin' him; your fancy-man.—Shouldn't I have known what was goin' on, the way your lower octave kept gettin' stronger and richer?—If you're meat for him, why the hell aren't you meat for me? I could do miracles for you. I could make you famous. I wouldn't drag you down and ruin you.—But I'm just an old fella to you—an old fool. Aw God, that's the hell of it."

He wept, and Monica wept with him, but it cannot be pretended that they understood each other. Two puritanisms were in conflict, and could not meet. But under that, in a realm below the morality which was bred in the bone, they wept for the sadness of all unrequited love, all ill-matched passion, and the prancing rhythm of The Veleta mounted to them like the indifference of a world where all loves were happy.

The door of the box opened a crack, and someone peeped in; then it opened fully, and admitted a short figure in a purple domino and a mask. Outside the mask it wore a gleaming pair of steel-rimmed spectacles.

"Get up outa that, Murt, and come on home," said the figure.

Molloy started. "Norah!" said he.

"Myself," said the purple domino. "Did you think you'd given me the slip, my fine wee fella? Come on now, and don't trouble Miss Gall any more."

Molloy got unsteadily to his feet, helped by Monica. The purple domino, hands on hips, offered no assistance. He was a sorry figure, for one side of his moustache was gone, and the paint on his eyebrows had run down his face in streaks. Without a word to Monica he went through the door.

"You'd better not come for any more lessons till you hear from me," said the purple domino. "He won't be himself for a few days. Och, these artists! You'd better be married to a barometer; up and down, up and down all the time."

"Are you Mrs. Molloy?"

"I am. And I've no word of blame for you, my girl, though I advise you to watch your step in future with himself. He can't resist a good pupil; wants to run away with 'em all. But I've always kept him respectable, and please God I always will. Which isn't light work, in the line we're all in. But it's lose that, and lose all."

And such is the power of anything which is said with a sufficient show of certainty that Monica, who was robbing her benefactors to maintain her lover, nodded solemnly in agreement as the door of the box closed behind the purple domino.

Eight

"I AM ENTIRELY AGREED that Miss Gall should come home if this family crisis demands it," said Miss Pottinger, "but you have not yet fully convinced me that it is the duty of the Bridgetower Trust to pay her expenses."

The other trustees groaned in spirit. During the three years of the Trust's existence Miss Puss, contentious by nature, had grown even more insupportable. She fancied herself in the role of a keen woman of business, husbanding money which these foolish men would have squandered; she demanded elaborate and repetitive explanations of the obvious; she made notes in a little book while the others were speaking, thereby missing much of the point of what was said; she pawed through all the bills and lawyer's statements, demanding explanations and comparing costs with some standard of expenditure adopted by herself in her youth, and now invalid. Although she was believed to be nearly eighty, she had an appetite for committee-work which exhausted Solly, the Dean and Mr. Snelgrove. They all, in their various ways, hated her.

It was half-past ten, and the Bridgetower house, now so meagrely heated by Solly, was growing colder; since half-past eight they had been chewing away at a single decision. Mr. Snelgrove decided to allow himself the luxury of a calculated loss of temper.

"Let me repeat once more that I fully realize that I am merely the solicitor and legal adviser of this Trust," said he, "but I urge

you with all the force at my command to seize this opportunity
of spending some of the Trust money. If it is not done willingly,
you may find yourselves compelled to do it unwillingly. I have
told you repeatedly that the Public Trustee is disturbed by the
way in which your funds are accumulating. Unless you want an
investigation, and all the disagreeable circumstances which will
come with it, you had better snatch at this chance to spend two
or three thousand dollars. Miss Gall's mother is reported to be
seriously ill; she fears that she may die, and she wants to see her
daughter. If she dies, and it comes out that you have denied her
daughter the means of visiting her, you will not like what people
will say. You will not like it at all."

"Has Miss Gall no funds in hand?" demanded Miss Puss. "She
has received a very substantial allowance, and of late her expenditures have been remarkably heavy—far heavier than can
be justified by a student life. I have said that she may come home
for a time, so far as I am concerned. But we are empowered
under the will of the late Louisa Hansen Bridgetower—whose
memory seems to be growing very misty in your minds—only to
spend money on her artistic education. Can this jaunt be justified on those grounds? That is what I want to know."

"Personally I do not care the toss of a button whether the
journey is educational or not," said Snelgrove. "But you had
better understand this: Mrs. Bridgetower left, when all charges
were paid, rather more than a million dollars to this Trust. As
invested, that brings in roughly $31,000 a year to be spent on
this wretched girl, after all taxes on income and property are
paid; spend as she will, and reckoning my own expenses and
those of my London colleagues, and the money for travel abroad,
and the fees of the teachers, there is still about $45,000 of un-
spent money in our funds, to which we have no right. The Public
Trustee wants to know when we are going to spend it, and he
wants it spent as soon as possible."

"Whose money is it?" asked Solly, a light in his eye.

"It is Monica Gall's money," said Snelgrove, "and the sooner
we get it off our hands the better I shall like it."

"You are surely not suggesting that we give it to her in a lump sum," said Miss Pottinger. "We are instructed to educate the girl, not to debauch her."

"Must we suppose that she would use the money foolishly?" said Dean Knapp. "I have seen little of her, but what I saw, and the reports from Sir Benedict, certainly do not suggest that she is an imprudent girl. With some guidance by us such a sum might be put aside by her for future expenses incidental to her career. Everyone knows of cases in which a little money in hand has tided people over difficult times, and greatly smoothed their way."

"It is not a little money," said Miss Puss. "It is a great deal of money. Certainly it would never occur to me to call it a small sum. Of course, I have always had to manage rather carefully."

This was a hint at the $3,500 a year which the Dean's wife received from her father's estate, a sum which, added to the Dean's stipend, was supposed to make the Knapps unbecomingly worldly. Miss Pottinger, who had lived on inherited money all her life, was a positive socialist about the inherited money of other people.

"Big or little, I wish I had it," said Solly. He looked shabby and sharp; his hair wanted cutting, and his grey flannel trousers wanted pressing. He could have afforded to make himself tidy, but tidiness did not accord with the character of Wronged Son which he now played regularly at the meetings of the Trustees. "Still, I agree that it is quite a lump to throw into her lap all at once. Surely this could have been foreseen? Why haven't we made it over to her, or banked it for her, every quarter? Isn't this rather late in the day to tell us about it?"

Mr. Snelgrove looked at Solly for a little time before he spoke, choosing his words.

"The delay was my fault, Solomon," said he. "I had some hopes, as you had yourself, that this Trust would not be of long duration. When we all heard the good news that you and Veronica were expecting a child, I said nothing about the matter, because I thought it might all be adjusted more agreeably when that child was born, and the Trust perhaps ended by that event. I accept any blame there may be. My intention was of the best."

The Dean, always tactful, struck in.

"I suggest that we wire Miss Gall to come home at once, to relieve her mother's mind. When she is here we can talk to her and make some arrangement which will satisfy the Public Trustee. And of course the Trust should bear all expenses."

Thus it was decided, for even Miss Puss quaked at the bogy of the Public Trustee.

(2)

Through the long night which divided Canada from England, Monica was carried fifteen thousand feet above the ocean in the humming Limbo of a luxury aircraft. Mr. Boykin had brought the word to Courtfield Gardens: "Your mother is seriously ill, and the Bridgetower Trustees think you had better go home for a time. I've made all arrangements, and everything is in this envelope. Can you be at the terminus tonight at six-thirty? Good. Now, you really mustn't distress yourself." Mrs. Merry, whom Mr. Boykin had fearfully enlisted as his ally in delivering this news, also urged Monica not to distress herself. As they seemed to expect it, she did her best to be somewhat distressed, and the thought of leaving Revelstoke gave her the necessary fuel for a show of concern. But she had no feeling of reality concerning the news about her mother. None of the Galls ever thought seriously about sickness or health, and death was a theological, rather than a physical, fact to them. Ma was ill. Well, Ma was always up and down but the strength of her spirit, in elation or depression, remained constant. She would find Ma depressed, no doubt, and in bed, but she would persuade Ma to feel better again, as she had done so often before. What might seem to be serious illness to outsiders was a different thing when you knew Ma.

But to return to Canada! As the plane sped on through the darkness it was as though a limb, long numbed, regained its feeling. She had had so much to do since Revelstoke began his work on *The Golden Asse* that even her perfunctory letter-writing had fallen far behind. She had so little time to write, she told herself; in her more honest moments she recognized that she had so little to write that would have made any sense to her readers at home. That had always been the trouble about letters —finding things that her family would be interested in, and of which they could approve. She was no writer. How could she make what she was doing real to her parents? How much could she reveal without bringing, in return, their mockery or a scolding?

The visit to Neuadd Goch, for instance, which was now more than a year behind her. She had told Ma something of it—a very little, really—about the beauty of the countryside, the charm of the house, and the kindness of the Hopkin-Griffiths. Ma's reply had been sharp enough about "your swell new friends" and strongly disapproving of the news that Monica had been to a Christmas service as offered by the Church of England—"Does this mean you are changing your religion? What do you expect to get from that?" On the whole, it had been politic not to mention her small part in the *Matthew Passion*, or the perplexities and anguish which it had brought. That was the trouble; you couldn't tell Ma anything really important without running a risk of hurting her. And it went without saying that her sharpness arose from hurt feelings; question that, and you might find yourself thinking that it sprang from ignorance, jealousy and meanness, which was inadmissable; loyalty could not permit such thoughts.

Loyalty! Monica had not forgotten her protestation of loyalty when George Medwall hinted that she might want to abandon some of the beliefs and attitudes of her family. She had meant it then, and she still meant it. But she had not realized how costly such loyalty might be. She had not foreseen that it could mean keeping two sets of mental and moral books—one for inspection in the light of home, and another to contain her life with Revelstoke, and all the new loyalties and attitudes which had come with Molloy, and particularly with Domdaniel. To close either set of books forever would be a kind of suicide, and yet to keep them both was hypocrisy. As Monica pondered her problem she felt that she was perplexed and tormented unendurably; but anyone looking at her on the plane might well have thought that she looked uncommonly animated and happy.

Letters were no good as a means of communication. She had written as faithfully and as fully as she could, but there were things which did not belong in letters, and which she would now have a chance to tell her mother face to face. And if her letters were poor and thin, what about the ones she received? Ma's letters were a record of small facts . . . "thought I'd go to church this morning but did not feel I could tackle the stairs . . . your Dad is patching the linoleum in the upstairs hall, but it don't hold the tacks like it used & guess will have to think of new . . . Donny is growing like a weed & is cute as a fox & says Ganny plain as plain." And food, always food! Mrs. Gall was a Sunday afternoon letter-writer, and every week contained a description of the Sunday menu . . . "Guess you don't get eats like that over there Eh Monny?"

More informative were the letters of her sister Alice, now Mrs. Charles Proby. Chuck Proby was getting on faster in the service of his bank than he had expected, and he had taken Alice to wife, and abandoned his idea that religion was a lot of crap at the same time. Religion had an important place in a young man's progress. The Probys, however, had taken a long upward step in the religious world, for they had left the Thirteener fold and associated themselves with the United Church, where a vastly superior group of people were to be met. Their union had been blessed with a son, Donald, and snapshots and detailed accounts of the progress of this wondrous child made up the bulk of Alice's letters. There was still room, however, for a general, nagging discontent to assert itself. Alice had Chuck and Donny; Chuck had a safe job and prospects; but life did not move quickly enough for Alice, who felt the need for a bigger house and a more important husband and an apparently endless list of labour-saving household devices. She frankly envied Monica, whose luck had been so good, and who had no problems, and nobody to consider but herself.

George Medwall wrote now and then, but less frequently as the months went by. He was getting on. He was saving money. He was sick of boarding-houses. He hoped she was keeping well. He had seen her father, who looked okay. Far, far better were the very rare epistles which Kevin and Alex wrote together, and illustrated with funny pictures. But they were tactful, and urged her not to think it necessary to write in return, though she did so.

Worst of all, when it came to answering them, were the letters from Aunt Ellen, so long, so kind, so loaded with a tremulous curiosity about the richly musical world in which Monica was now living. Aunt Ellen was dying to know all about it and to share it as far as possible. But everything she said made it so plain that Aunt Ellen had hold of the wrong end of the stick, and that the musical world she imagined was that intense, genteely romantic world of *The First Violin.* And she wanted Monica's life to be cast in that mold, wanted it so badly that it would have been inexcusable cruelty to disillusion her. There was the danger, too, that nothing must be told to Aunt Ellen which had not also been told to Ma, for Ma was sure to find out, and make trouble. Thus Monica was forced to deny Aunt Ellen the romantic crumbs which she might otherwise have afforded her. If Aunt Ellen knew that Monica was in daily association with a man who was writing an opera, she would be transported; it would give her a real and abiding joy. But if Ma knew, Ma would simply want to know why she saw him every day, and if he slept at the same place that he worked. It was bitter hard work writing to Aunt Ellen.

As Canada drew nearer, however, all of these considerations

gave way to excitement and anticipation. Coming down at Gander—wonderful! The coffee was not what the McCorkills would have called "real Canadian coffee", being that characterless grey drink common to lunch counters in all countries; the Quebec carved figures, and the factory-made beaded moccasins, spoke of no Canada which Monica had ever known; but the genuine uncivil Canadian fat woman behind the counter, and the excellent quality of toilet paper in the Ladies were home-like indeed. And the air, the cool, clear air, which had not been breathed and re-breathed by everybody since the time of Alfred the Great—that was best of all.

On to Montreal and Dorval airport. On to Montreal's Windsor Station, that massive witness to the love-affair between Canada and its railways. Thence to a train which would carry her to Salterton—a real Canadian train, smelling of carpets and stale cigar-smoke, which toiled and rumbled through the country-side whistling, and ringing its bell, and puffing defiance at anyone who might dare to suggest that it was not really going very fast. Monica rode in the parlour-car, gazing rapturously at the snowy landscape, even while eating her luncheon of leathery omelet and cardboard pie. Yet to her it was the food of the gods, for this was an omelet of Canadian leatheriness, a pie of real Canadian cardboard!

Salterton! But nobody at the station to greet her. Well, of course telegrams which you sent to announce your arrival did have a way of appearing, with every show of smart efficiency, after you had well and truly arrived. She took a taxi to her home.

Dad answered her ring at the bell. He looked older, thinner and very weary.

"Oh God, Monny, it's good to have you here," he said. And then, breaking into the tears which he had so long held back—"It looks like we're goin' to lose your Ma!"

(3)

IF IT WERE STILL the fashion to see ghosts (and it may be asked
if such revelations are not a matter of fashion or, if a more pre-
tentious phrase is demanded, of intellectual climate) Veronica
Bridgetower would very often have seen the ghost of her mother-
in-law, Louisa Hansen Bridgetower. While she had lived, Mrs.
Bridgetower had worn her large, ugly house close about her,
like a cloak. Her spirit was in every room; her will in some way
influenced every thought and action on her premises. In his
bachelor days Solly had tried to escape her by making an eyrie
for himself in the attic; there his bedroom and his workroom and
a little washroom had provided him with a complete kingdom;
he had but to close the door at the foot of the stair and his
mother could not pursue him; her ailing heart had prevented her
from mounting those stairs for ten years before she died. But she
was there, none the less, and he had always known that every
creak of a bedspring and every scrape of a chair was heard and
considered by her sharp ears. When he had married, he had
brought Veronica to this house. Mrs. Bridgetower had pleaded,
with the sweet self-abasement possible only to those who are
completely sure of their power, that her son and his wife should
make their home with her—for if they were to leave her, might
she not be frightened in that large house, alone except for her
two old servants?

Alone; yes, she would have been alone in the sense that one is
alone in a familiar, comfortable garment. She, frightened, there?
She had Solly and Veronica in her pocket, and well she knew it.
They had lived with her. How, they asked each other, could they
refuse?

I have never had a home of my own, thought Veronica, as she
lay beside the sleeping Solly. The January wind roared around
the house, making the storm-window outside the bedroom rattle

fiercely, as though to rebuke this rebellion against Fate. Though of course I've been terribly lucky, she added, hastily placating whatever, or whoever, might be listening to her thoughts.

Lucky? Oh, yes, for was she not the daughter of Professor Walter Vambrace, who had written a book on the Enneads of Plotinus? And was it not a privilege to grow up in the atmosphere of strenuous thought which that austere scholar created? And to realize that Father was a cousin of the Marquis of Mourne and Derry, and if eight people had died young and childless Father would have had the title? It was true that Father and Mother never quite got on together, chiefly because he was such an aggressive free-thinker, whereas Mother was a devout Catholic. But Mother had always been so sweet, so abstracted, so truly kind. It was sad that since her marriage she saw her parents so seldom, though they lived not much more than a mile away.

But then, her marriage with Solly had been so beset with difficulties on both sides. And although the Vambraces and Mrs. Bridgetower had made the best of it when it was plain that it could not be prevented, there had been clear indications that they were doing precisely that—making the best of it. Solly had tried to keep it secret from her that his Mother thought their marriage a great mistake. How like him it was to try to spare her! But of course she knew. How could anyone who lived with Mrs. Bridgetower help knowing? Her mother-in-law's opinions were as palpable in that house as was the smell of heavy upholstery.

It could not be pretended that she had been made at home in Mrs. Bridgetower's house. She had learned all the rules—what chairs not to sit in, what doors to close and which to leave open, what books and papers might be read, and when, and her mother-in-law's long rosary of pills, which had to be worked through every day—but she had never learned the spirit of the house, because it was Mrs. Bridgetower's spirit. She had tried with uttermost patience and submission to be a good daughter-in-law. She had even dressed Mrs. Bridgetower's body for burial, arranged her hair and painted her face—Ah, there it was again, the thought that would not down! Years ago, at a children's party, Veronica had been blindfolded and asked to identify a group of objects on a tray; one of these was a kid glove which had been stuffed with paper, and thoroughly soaked; she had dropped the chill, damp object with a shudder, and only the self-control which her father had instilled in her had kept her from weeping with fright. Painting the face of her dead mother-in-law had revived and hideously prolonged that sensation, and she had not wept on that occasion, either. She had done her best to be a good daughter-in-law because it was part of being a good wife, part of her love for Solly. Why, then, would his mother not leave her alone, even after death?

Mrs. Bridgetower was everywhere in this house. Across the hall was the room in which she had died. Below, in the drawing-room, was her chair. Everywhere, all was as she had left it, and her watch-dog, Miss Laura Pottinger, took care to see that nothing was changed. This was not Veronica's house, and her husband's; it was the property of the Bridgetower Trust, and they lived in it simply as caretakers—caretakers who paid the big coal bills and tried to keep it clean.

Why could they not go elsewhere? But she had never even asked Solly why, and she would never do so now. For it was Veronica's terrible secret that Mrs. Bridgetower owned her husband, as well as everything else in the house. He, who had been high-spirited and amusing in his ironic, undergraduate way before their marriage, had become more and more like his Mother since his Mother's death. A severity, a watchfulness had grown on him, and all the more quickly since the birth of the child.

She had never seen the child, but the nurse had told her, against doctor's orders, that it had been a fine boy. It was the boy which might have broken the Trust, might have given them Mrs. Bridgetower's fortune, might have enabled them to sell this hateful, haunted house, might have delivered them from this bondage. But the boy had been born with his navel-cord tight around his neck, strangling as he moved toward the light.

Had that been Mrs. Bridgetower's work, also? If she had drawn the spiteful will, if she still possessed this house, might she not also be capable of that?

Solly had wept with her, had taken her away for as long a holiday as they could afford, and then—had promised that there would be more children. He had meant to be kind and courageous, but Veronica feared the thought of more children. The doctor said that there was not the slightest reason for fear. But the doctor was not Mrs. Bridgetower's daughter-in-law; she could not tell him that she feared the vengeance of a dead woman whose son she had stolen.

Solly had become grimmer, and they had grown poorer, trying to keep up the house, and old Ethel, on his modest university lecturer's salary. It was not that they seriously lacked money; it was, rather, that all the appurtenances of an income far greater than their own, and all the habits which went with money and a large house, hung around them, and they were both poor managers. Their poverty was illusory, but it was perhaps the more destructive and humiliating for that. And here she lay, fearing the future—fearing, more than she dared admit to herself, the man whom she so much loved, who was passing more and more into the possession of the woman who had so much hated her.

Still, was this not better than that year which had followed Mrs. Bridgetower's death—the year when Solly had hoped that they might have a son, and halt the whole business of forming the Trust? She had borne patiently with his first flogging of himself to beget a child; they had pretended to each other that it was a joke—but they knew in their hearts that it was no joke. And as time passed, and nothing happened, Solly grew frightened and suddenly could make love no longer. He sought medical advice; the doctor said that there was nothing wrong with him, and suggested in the easy way of doctors that he must relax. Yes, relax. Rest would work a cure.

That rest-cure had been a troubled time. If a man is trying to recover from impotence, when is he to assume that he has refrained long enough? The deceptions and mockeries of Solly's body distressed them both, for Veronica longed for him, and could not always dissemble her longing. Both felt the Dead Hand of Mrs. Bridgetower; its chill had frozen the very fountain of their passion, brought winter to the garden of their love.

Then, as the doctor had said he would, Solly recovered, and with a new determination and greater caution they sought an heir—no, a son. And, after the months of pregnancy, with the chances that it would be a daughter at least evenly weighed against them, the stillborn son had come to mock their hopes. Veronica had endured it all, and could endure anything the future and—if it were indeed a fact—the posthumous malignancy of her mother-in-law might bring, if only she did not lose Solly. But so often now it seemed that he was possessed by the spirit of his mother at least as much as by the nature which she so much loved, and it was this that brought her, in such nights as this, a terror which was desolating and bleak.

More children! Sometimes, when Solly made love to her, she could have wept, could have shrieked with misery. For in the very climax of love he might have been struggling with the spirit of his Mother, so oblivious did he seem of Veronica. And did he want a child, or was it rather vengeance on his tormentor, and the recovery of her money, which he sought to plant in his wife's body?

Who could say that Louisa Hansen Bridgetower was dead? Freed from the cumbrous, ailing body, freed from any obligation to counterfeit the ordinary goodwill of mortal life, her spirit walked abroad, working out its ends and asserting its mastery through a love which was hate, a hatred which was love.

—Suddenly Solly started up in the bed, his eyes staring, muttering hoarsely. He often had bad dreams now. Quickly she woke

him. He smiled, looked very young, kissed her and laughed at
himself.

"Let's go and get something to eat," he said.

In the large kitchen, in expiation of her gloomy and almost
disloyal thoughts, Veronica made toast and scrambled eggs.
They liked to eat in the middle of the night, childishly defying
old Ethel and the solemn spirit of the house.

"The Gall girl's been home almost a week now," said Solly, as
they ate.

"What do you hear about her mother?"

"Improving, apparently. Knapp has been keeping in touch.
He's very kind about such things."

"What ailed her?"

"Gall, appropriately enough. A really bad go of gallstones.
She's more frightened than hurt, I gather. They'll operate and
she'll be all right in a few weeks. People are extraordinary; apparently they were all convinced that she would never pull through;
she's never been seriously ill before. Getting Monica home has
brought her round."

"Good. It'll be a load off Monica's mind."

"Yes. Old Puss is beginning to hound her about giving a recital
here before she goes back. To show what's been done with our
money, presumably. Well, it'd better be good."

(4)

DR. JAMES COBBETT was widely considered in Salterton to be
a promising young man, but he was still at that delicate stage of
his career when people called him "*young* Dr. Cobbett"; however,
this meant that when he wanted advice he could readily turn
to his father, "*old* Dr. Cobbett". He did so in the case of Mrs.
Gall.

"She ought to be in hospital, but they're all scared to death of
hospitals," said he: "fantastic to run into such prejudice now-
adays. She ought to have a cholecystotomy as soon as possible,

but they won't hear of it. The family have no regular doctor, though this woman has been having what she calls bilious attacks for at least a couple of years; I'm sorry they got hold of me. They seem to think if I can 'tide her over' as they call it, she'll be able to manage. She's sworn she'll diet, live on slops—anything. The old man even asked me if there wasn't some way of melting gall-stones by taking medicine. They're just scared of the knife."

"What are you doing?"

"Usual thing. Got two nurses on. The daughters and the husband sit with her at night. Morphia—though I can't do too much with that, because I suspect fatty degeneration of the heart—she's probably twice her optimum weight. She's in the static stage now, but it can't last long. They're kidding themselves that she's getting better, but of course she isn't."

"No, no; of course not."

"Well, what do I do?"

"I don't see that there is anything more that you can do. What do you think is the real trouble? Have they some kind of religious scruple about surgery?"

"No. They're Thirteeners, whatever that means. But the preacher was at the house the other day when I called—a fellow named Beamis—and when I explained the situation to him he was perfectly reasonable. Tried to persuade her to go to hospital. Did everything he could, really. But the old girl kept sobbing and moaning 'Don't let 'em take me; please don't let 'em take me'. I felt like a fool."

"There's no need for you to feel like that, Jimmy. You've given the best advice—the only advice, really. If they don't take it, you can throw up the case, but I wouldn't, if I were you. If people are determined to commit suicide by the long and painful course of going against medical opinion, it's hard to watch, but I don't think you want to be known as the kind of doctor who throws up cases."

"I had a little hope until this week. The younger daughter is home, now. You've heard of her; she's the girl that's being educated with old Mrs. Bridgetower's money. They insisted on putting off a final decision till she came. She's far above the rest of them, and she's certainly not scared. I've talked to her very frankly; she knows exactly what'll happen. I got her to the point of saying that her mother should go to hospital. 'I'll tell her myself', she said, and we went into the room together. But the old lady must be a mind-reader. She snatched the girl's hand, and began to scream. 'Monny, don't let 'em take me; Monny, don't let 'em get me in that place', she shrieked, over and over again. The girl looked dreadful; I was really sorry for her. Her mother made her swear, then and there, with a Bible in her hand, that she should not be taken to hospital. 'You see how it is', she said to me, and I suppose I do, in a way. But she said a funny thing to me, as I was leaving. 'You realize that your decision may be bringing about your mother's death?' I said—"

"Now Jimmy, that was a mistake."

"Yes, I know it was, but I was mad. It's all so senseless! But she looked me straight in the eye and said: 'My decision *may* do so, Dr. Cobbett, but your decision would do so beyond any doubt. My mother lives by the spirit as well as by the flesh; if I kill the spirit by delivering her, frightened and forsaken, into your hands, what makes you think that you can save the flesh?' Now what do you make of that? A layman ever dare talk to you in that way?"

"Speaking after more than thirty years of practice, I think the girl is right. Under stress, you know, Jimmy, people sometimes speak wiser than they know. I suppose if the girl had said yes, you could have doped the mother enough to get her to hospital and operate on her. But it would have been a serious risk. And—I don't know—if the whole cast of her mind, and her level of intelligence, and everything about her is against having her life saved by science, I question if we've any cast-iron moral right to save it."

"The job of the profession is to preserve life, under all possible circumstances."

"Oh, I know. I was taught that, too. And as long as you never learn anything but medicine, you'll probably continue to think so."

"I'm sorry you take it like that, Father."

"Don't be hurt, Jimmy. I'm sorry you've got such a miserable case. But they do turn up, from time to time. Hang on; it's your duty, and it can't last long."

(5)

MRS. GALL'S ILLNESS HAD already lasted for two weeks and two days when Monica came home. The first violent onset had utterly demoralized Mr. Gall, who fully believed his wife's agonized protests that she was dying. He had no experience of illness, except for occasional coughs and colds, and the Galls had no physician, now that old Doctor Wander, who had attended to the children, had died. He had called Alice, and Alice had called young Dr. Cobbett. But she did not call him until morning, heeding the widespread complaint of doctors about night calls, and had been scolded by Dr. Cobbett when he arrived, for not calling him sooner. By that time Mrs. Gall had discovered that if she lay very still, with her knees up, and breathed as shallowly and as slowly as possible, her pain was less. But she was deeply frightened.

She was only a little less frightened when the doctor disposed of her fear that she had cancer. This was her secret dread, which she had hugged to herself for years. But if it were not cancer, what was it? Dr. Cobbett talked in big, unfamiliar words, but it emerged that he did not know what it was, either. Myocardial infarction; what could that be? Acute pancreatitis; an obstructive neoplasm; volvulus of the small intestine? Young Dr. Cobbett was kindly and able, but he was not above astonishing the simple. When Mrs. Gall, feebly supported by her husband, showed strong resistance to going to the hospital, he astonished them even more, in the hope of breaking down their determination. But it was useless, and as he could not put Mrs. Gall in hospital by force, he had to leave her at home, and get Nurses Gourlay and Heffernan to take care of her. The nurses were a much affronted as he by the Galls' refusal to accommodate themselves to the needs of medical science, and they let their displeasure be felt. Nurse Gourlay, indeed, made no secret of the fact that if she had her way, there would be a law to compel people to do what the doctor said was best for them.

Mrs. Gall was down, but she was not out. Pain and fright lent her courage, and she gave Nurse Gourlay a piece of her mind; for Nurse Heffernan, a softer sort of woman altogether, she reserved her fears that she might die, and her dread that her ailment might yet turn out to be cancer. Nurse Heffernan seized the chance to say that if only Mrs. Gall would go to hospital, like a good girl, they'd have her leppin' like a goat in a couple of weeks. But Mrs. Gall was firm: no hospital.

Her resolution was strengthened by morphia, which Dr. Cobbett ordered in doses sufficient to control her pain. But in her morphia dreams there detached itself from some submerged mass of fear and floated upward into Mrs. Gall's consciousness a notion that she was being held against her will in a bawdy-house, which was also a hospital, and where the wildest indecencies were demanded of her. She had too much cunning to confide these dreams to Nurse Heffernan, who would certainly have derided them, because of her professional stake in hospitals; she told them instead to her daughter Alice, during the eight hours of the night when neither nurse was on duty.

It was Alice who insisted that Monica should be sent for. She was not a bad or unkind daughter, but she took her duties as Charles Proby's wife heavily, and she was impatient of what she considered "nonsense". Not to go to the hospital was nonsense. To have delusions of being in a bawdy-house was nonsense. There were times when Alice was very close to thinking that being ill, which involved claims upon the time and charity of busy, ambitious young matrons, was nonsense. Nonsense had to be stopped. And why should she carry the weight of all this nonsense when Monica was living abroad, free of all care, thinking of nobody but herself?

"Every tub must stand on its own bottom," said Alice, and went to see Mr. Snelgrove. It was on the sixteenth day of Mrs. Gall's illness that Monica arrived home, and was greeted by her father with his pathetic cry of fear that Mrs. Gall might die.

Dr. Cobbett and the nurses seized upon Monica as a new ally. By this time Dr. Cobbett was virtually certain that Mrs. Gall had acute cholecystitis and might die even if she were now moved to the hospital. But it was his task to do everything in his power to save her, and he would have risked an operation at an even later date: it must also be admitted that he loved to have his own way, and wanted to beat down this insurrection against the righteous forces of Hygeia.

Monica would not be bustled. She was a strange figure now in the stuffy little house. Her manner of speech, her clothes, her demeanour were all at odds with it. Nurse Gourlay did not dare to bully her; Nurse Heffernan, who had a feudal streak in her, accepted Monica as the mistress, to be heeded right or wrong. Monica took on the night nursing.

"Monny, are you there?"

"Yes, Ma, right here."

"Monny, you won't let 'em take me to that place?"

"No, Ma; don't worry."

"I've been there. I was there this afternoon. But I run away. I run away in my night-gown. A couple o' fellas in the hall seen me, and they tried to grab me. Was it bad?—Monny, was it bad?"

"Was what bad, Ma?"

"Was it bad they seen me in only my night-gown?"

"No, no; not bad. It was only a dream."

"It wasn't a dream. I was there. Monny, when they get you in there they make you do awful things. It's a bad-house. There

was girls there I used to know. Kate Dempster was there, flirtin'
her tail just like she used when we was girls. Kate's a bad girl.
Am I a bad girl, Monny?"

"No, Ma, you're a good girl."

"Are you a good girl, Monny?"

"Yes, Ma, I'm a good girl."

"Then why do you talk so funny? You're talkin' all the time
waw-waw-waw so I can't make you out. You ain't Monny!"

"Yes, yes dear, I'm Monny. You mustn't upset yourself. I'm
Monny and I'm right here."

"No you ain't. Monny don't talk like that. You've sent Monny
away! And I'm a bad girl, and they'll put me in the bad-house!"

"Quiet, dear. Let me give you a sip of this. Just a sip."

"I'm a bad girl.—Monny, will I die?"

"No, dear, of course not. You had a very good day today."

But it was not a good day. It was what Dr. Cobbett called "a
remission."

The period of remission lasted for seven days. To the nurses
the vomiting, the bloating, the wasting away of flesh, the groaning and the recurrence of pain were the accustomed circumstances of serious illness. To Alfred Gall, who had never seen
his wife in such straits, it was an agony for which he could find
no expression. Morning and night he would go to the door of
her room, look at the inert form in the bed and listen to its
heavy breathing, after which he would creep away, his face
marked with fear and loss. Only his sister Ellen had power to
raise any hope in him. Alice was impatient of his spiritlessness;
it was her temperament to talk about troubles, and to find relief
in talk; she had no understanding of her father's stricken silence.
Monica was gentle with him, but her energies were saved for the
long vigils at her mother's bed-side.

Not all of their talks in the night were coloured by Mrs. Gall's
semi-delirium. True, most of what was said was in the pattern of
fear and delusion, countered by love and reassurance. But for
Monica her mother's rational spells were more exhausting than
her wanderings, for in them it was emphasized and re-empha-

sized that to her mother she was now in part a stranger. Her manner of speech had changed, and Mrs. Gall could not be comforted easily in the new, clear, warm speech which Monica had been at such pains to learn; but she could not undo it, could not go back to the speech of her home, for the new speech had become the instrument of the best that was in her mind, and heart. It seemed to her cruel and shameful that it should be so, but she was forced to admit the fact; it was so. To speak as Ma wanted her to speak was not only difficult, but it was a betrayal of Revelstoke, of Domdaniel, of Molloy and all the poets and musicians who stood behind them in time. Did she love these things more than her own mother? She put the question to herself, in those words, many times, but never dared to give either of the possible answers. Loyalty demanded that she give love, and she gave it as fully as she was able.

Loyalty demanded truth. But Mrs. Gall, fearing death, returned again and again to incidents in her own life, at which she could only bring herself to hint, though in delirium their nature was revealed a little more clearly. She was convinced that she had sinned unforgivably, and that her sins were sexual in their nature. She named no names, spoke of no incidents; perhaps there had been none. But during her lifetime the only morality to which she had ever given a moment of serious thought, or to which she had ever paid solemn tribute, was a morality of sexual prohibition; she felt now that she had not been true to it, yet she could not confess her transgression or give clear expression to her remorse. Instead, she accused herself vaguely, and suffered in the tormented images of her morphia dreams.

She was specific in her demands and exhortations to Monica, however. Was Monica a good girl? The question came again and again when she was partly conscious, and thus phrased, from Mrs. Gall, it could have only one meaning. Monica had no intention of saying that, in her mother's terms, she was not a good girl. But she had to meet the question in her own mind. Was she? To say yes was disloyal to home, to the woman who was in such distress at her side. But there were seven of these weary nights, and before the last Monica was sure of her answer. She was a good girl. Chastity is to have the body in the soul's keeping; Domdaniel had said it, and everything in her own experience supported it. And this decision, more than anything else, divided Monica from her mother when her mother most needed her. Her mother's ideas of good and bad would not do for her.

If these ideas were invalid for her, what else that was valid had her mother to give her? Nothing, thought Monica; not with any sense of freedom, of breaking a lifelong bondage, but sadly and with pity for her mother and herself. But on the sixth night, after a brief period of sleep, Mrs. Gall opened her eyes, and looked at her daughter more clearly than she had done since her homecoming.

"I been asleep."

"Yes, Ma. Do you feel a little rested?"

"Was I talkin' foolish a while ago?"

"The hypodermics make you dream, dear."

"And I guess I go on pretty wild, eh?"

Monica was about to deny it, but she looked into her mother's eye, and saw a twinkle there. Mrs. Gall laughed, feebly but unmistakably.

"Yes, you were pretty wild, Ma."

"You bet I was. I've got quite an imagination. That's where you're like me, Monny. Always remember that. You got that from me."

Tears came into Monica's eyes; they were tears of happiness, for at last she shared something with her mother. She wept, and laughed a little, as she said—

"Yes Ma, I got that from you. We're very alike, aren't we?"

"Yes, I guess we are."

The period of remission ended, unmistakably, a few hours later, on the morning of the seventh day, and Dr. Cobbett said that peritonitis, which would certainly be fatal, had come, as he had expected it would under the circumstances. The family last saw Mrs. Gall, leaden gray, with eyes partly closed and seemingly already dead, though the doctor called it "shock". She died at four o'clock the following morning. Only Monica was with her then.

(6)

"I THINK IT IS MY DUTY to emphasize once again that this need not have happened," said young Dr. Cobbett as he prepared to fill out the certificate of death.

"My mother was always used to having her own way," said Monica, "and there is no point in discussing that now. The decision was mine, made according to her wishes, and if you feel that this matter should be carried any further, I shall be ready to answer any official questions."

Dr. Cobbett did not want to pursue the matter. All he wanted was an admission that he had been in the right, and he saw that he was not going to get it. So he continued.

"How old was your mother?"

Monica did not know. It had always been understood that it was "bold" to want to know the ages of one's parents; it was like uncovering their nakedness, in the Bible. When Aunt Ellen was consulted, Monica was surprised to learn that her mother was fifty-six. Then when Monica was born, Mrs. Gall had been thirty-three—ten years older than her own age, attained last December. Mrs. Gall, fat and toothless, her hair streaked with gray, had somehow seemed to be without age—a mother.

"I guess living with Dad wasn't much incentive to her to keep herself up," said Alice.

After her first outburst of grief, Alice was unpleasantly practical. Mr. Gall could not be sent off to work on such a day, but neither could he be endured in the house, which must be made ready for the funeral. It was Alice who packed him off to her house, with complicated instructions about what he was to do for little Donald. Aunt Ellen, too, stayed away from her work, and it was Alice who put her at the job of calling and telegraphing the necessary relatives, from her own home. This, Alice explained to Monica, was more convenient and meant also that Aunt Ellen would pay for the telegrams; it could be her share of the funeral expenses.

At nine o'clock on the morning of their mother's death, Alice prepared coffee for herself and Monica, and sat down to make plans.

"The funeral can be from Queen Street United," said she; "I'll get Reverend Calder on the phone right away."

"But why?" said Monica; "Why not from the Tabernacle? Mother never had anything to do with Queen Street United."

"Monny, let's face it. Do we want Ma's funeral to be a Thirteener circus, with Beamis spreading himself all over the place? You remember old Mrs. Delahaye's funeral?—Well?"

"But that was her church, Alice. That's what she'd want."

"What makes you so sure? I've heard her say things about Beamis that certainly didn't sound as if she had much use for him."

"But wouldn't it seem odd?"

"Not half as odd as a Thirteener funeral. Chuck and I go to Queen Street United. We could arrange it."

"I don't see it that way, Alice."

"What's it matter to you? You're independent. You'll be away out of this as soon as you can get. But I've got to live here. Listen Monny—Chuck's boss will probably be attending this funeral. I don't want him coming to the Thirteener Tabernacle, and getting the idea that those are the people we associate with."

"Alice, you're a snob!"

"Who's talking? Lady Haw-haw-haw; even when she was out of her head Ma used to make fun of you, right up till the last. Snob? Listen, I've got my own way to make. I'm not being carried by anybody else's money. And I'll tell you another thing, just while we're speaking our minds: I think Ma ought to have been put in the hospital, so there."

"Then why didn't you put her in yourself, before I came home?"

"Because Dad insisted on waiting for you. You've always been the Big Mucky-Muck around here, and now you've got this Trust behind you, Dad and Ma were scared of you. It had to be Monny's decision. Well, you decided, and a fine mess you made of it. If you'd used common sense Ma would be well and strong now, and not dead upstairs. If you want my straight opinion, you killed Ma."

"Alice, you're over-excited. I did what I did out of kindness; I swear it."

"I never said you didn't. But Ma won't be the first one that's been killed by kindess."

But the final arrangement was for a funeral at the Thirteener Tabernacle. It was not a complete victory for Monica. Pastor Beamis, who knew nothing of Alice's desire to displace him as spiritual adviser to the family, took his position for granted, and began to plan a service; he wanted Monica to sing a solo, and preferably two; he wanted to get the Heart and Hope Quartet together again, to make a special re-appearance at the graveside; it would draw a record crowd, he said, and what a comfort that would be to Brother Gall. Monica did not refuse without consideration; she fought with herself for the greater part of a day, but in the end she refused. Her reason was that she did not feel that she could control her voice well enough to sing upon such an occasion. But the inner voice, increasingly powerful in her thoughts, said: *Don't be a hypocrite; you're ashamed of them.*

The inner voice was cruel. So often it put the worst construction on everything, and in that respect it was like a conscience. But it spoke no morality which Monica could associate with a conscience—unless, somewhere, she were developing a new conscience, suited to her new needs. But if that were the case, why was the voice so often cruel? Sometimes it spoke with the unmistakable tones of her Mother, but in this instance it used the voice of Giles Revelstoke.

The three days before the funeral were tiring, after the long trial of Mrs. Gall's illness. Ineffectual as he was, decency demanded that Mr. Gall be consulted about the more important arrangements, and it was his wish that the funeral be held partly at the house and partly at the Tabernacle. Alice wanted it to be at the undertaker's chapel which, she pointed out, was so undenominational that you could imagine yourself anywhere. But in this last bid for social advancement she was defeated.

She and Monica bickered all the time, and quarrelled at least once a day. Their worst encounter was at the undertaker's, when they were choosing a coffin.

"Can you show us anything in oak?" said Alice.

The undertaker could show them something in oak; he mentioned the price.

"I don't think we want anything as expensive as that," said Monica.

"Who's we?" said Alice; "I think it's very nice."

"It's too expensive. Dad shouldn't be burdened with that on top of everything else."

"Who said Dad's going to be burdened? Who do you think is paying for this?"

"We all are, I suppose; we'll have to arrange some system of shares."

"Listen, Monny, we're all paying according to what we have. Aunt Ellen has done telegrams. Chuck and I are looking after flowers at the house and the church. Dad'll have all he can manage settling up for the doctor and nurses, even with his insurance. That means that this is your share. See?"

"You mean I'm paying for the funeral?"

"None of the rest of us have got a sugar-daddy."

"But Alice—the Trust money isn't for private expenses. Mr. Snelgrove would never allow it. I had no idea you were thinking like this!"

"If you don't know how to get money without saying what it's for by this time, you'd better learn. Chuck'll tell you, if you want; he's a banker and he knows how these things are done. Now get this through your head; you're not going to bury Ma on the cheap. You're the rich one; well, you can just spend some of it on Ma. It'll be the last thing you can do for her and you'd better just make up your mind to do it right. It'll be sure to get around if you don't: you can depend on that."

Monica protested, but she could not do so with much vigour. If she could rob the Trust for Revelstoke, why not for Ma? There was no answer to that question—not even such an answer as the uncomfortable inner voice could give. But it was a bitter blow to her to discover, as she did very soon, that not only Alice, but Dad and Aunt Ellen, were looking to her to pay all the heavier costs of this occasion. It was not wholly that they wanted money; it was that her supposed possession of money made her, in their eyes, the head of the family. Not moral authority, or age, but hard cash was what decided the matter. She could never again be a child in her father's house, because she had more money than he.

The funeral came, and passed. Eleven relatives from out of town arrived, and were fed; seven of them were given overnight lodging at the Gall house and at Aunt Ellen's. They were all Gunleys, relatives of Mrs. Gall, and like her they tended to be fat and sardonic. The night before the funeral they assembled for a family pow-pow, and Mr. Gall and Alice, between them, gave a dramatic account of Mrs. Gall's last illness. Alice tried to weight the story a little by emphasizing the doctor's assertion that Mrs. Gall need not have died, and that Monica's decision that she should not go to the hospital was the deciding factor. But she got nowhere with the Gunleys.

"Ada always liked her own way," said Aunt Bessie Gunley; "stubborn as they come."

"Yep; independent as a hog on ice," agreed Noble Gunley, a second cousin in the hardware business.

They appeared to glory in Mrs. Gall's defiance of the entrenched powers of the medical world; she had died as she lived, a Gunley through and through.

Pastor Beamis did not extend himself at the funeral as much as he could have wished, but he respected the desire, put to him strongly by Alice and Monica in their different ways, for conservatism. He was conservative, by his lights. He prayed for the family, in turn and by name, and managed to give Almighty God an excellent capsule account of Monica's high associations abroad. He spoke eloquently of the late Mrs. Gall, informing a somewhat surprised group of listeners that she had been open-handed, devout, courageous, a lifelong lover of all that was beautiful (this tied in neatly with his prayerful reference to Monica) and a constant source of inspiration to himself in his pastoral work. Accompanied by Mrs. Beamis on the piano, and his son Wesley on the vibraphone, he sang *Swinging Through the Gates of the New Jerusalem*. But by comparison with some of his more unbuttoned efforts, it was conservative.

Chuck Proby's boss did not come, after all. He sent the head accountant, as the most suitable person to represent the august entity of The Bank at the funeral of the mother-in-law of a promising, but still junior, employee. The Bridgetower Trust was represented by Dean Knapp, who declined Pastor Beamis' pressing invitation to sit on the platform, but who behaved himself beautifully, even when his sensibilities were most outraged, and spoke with real Christian kindness to the Gall family afterward.

Not that Alfred Gall noticed who spoke to him. The light which, however it may have appeared to the outside world, had been sufficient to fill his life, had gone out, and he was in darkness. All through the funeral he sat like a man carved in wood.

Alice wept copiously. She had a valuable talent for allowing her grief free play when it was most wanted, and suppressing it at need. But, certainly in her own estimation, at least, she wept in the same spirit as Dean Knapp prayed at her mother's funeral —sincerely, but not as a Thirteener.

Monica lacked Alice's ability to present her feelings suitably.

She had wept for her mother at the time of her death. At the funeral she found herself lifted up by a wave of emotion which she knew to be optimistic, and which at first she thought was relief that the long ordeal was over at last. But as Beamis prayed, she heard the inner voice, speaking this time not as her mother or as Giles, but in a voice which might have been her own, and it said: *You are free. You did your best for her, and now you are free. You will never have to worry about what you can tell her, or what would hurt her, again.*

(7)

THE DAY AFTER THE FUNERAL Monica found herself in a disordered and neglected house which she was apparently expected to put in order, and keep indefinitely for her widowed father. It was plain that Alice meant to do nothing, and Aunt Ellen had her job. She made a beginning, and quickly tired of it. Doing domestic work for Revelstoke was one thing; this was a very different matter. Should she call in a cleaning-woman? No, that would be unwise on several counts. It would encourage the family to think that she had cash in hand, and in reality she was very short; she had left all she could spare with Revelstoke. It would also defer the time when some permanent arrangement was made for Mr. Gall, and that was pressing; she wanted to get back to London as soon as she could. She must be diplomatic.

Her new position in the family, that of the moneyed daughter, made diplomacy easier than she had foreseen. It was so easy, indeed, to persuade her father to fall in with her suggestions that she was a little ashamed of herself, and of him. At a family council she made it clear that she must return to London; much depended on it, she said. She meant *The Golden Asse,* but did not say so. The family, assuming as people without money are wont to do, that all the affairs of moneyed people concern money, agreed. How was Dad going to manage? To everyone's surprise, Dad himself had a plan; Alice and Chuck and little Donald should move in with him. Alice was quick to quash that proposal.

"Three generations in one house never works," said she. "You see it everywhere. I think it'll be far better if every tub stands on its own bottom."

After much beating about the bush it was finally agreed that Miss Gall should give up her pretty little house, and move in with her brother. That was what Monica wanted; that was, indeed, what she had decided to arrange. But it hurt her, nevertheless, that Miss Gall had to be the sacrifice. Aunt Ellen was the only one of them who was not toadying to her because of her supposed riches; that good woman was simply and extravagantly proud of Monica because she was gaining a place in the world as a singer, and she would have laid her head on the executioner's block without complaint, if thereby she could have advanced her niece's career.

Still, now that Ma was dead, it was possible to confide more fully in Aunt Ellen, and Monica spent many nights in the pretty, crowded sitting-room of her aunt's house, where she had learned her first lessons in music. She sang for Miss Gall; she sang Revelstoke's songs to her, which Aunt Ellen did not really like, but which filled her with pride none the less. She sang the folk-songs and the songs in an older musical idiom which she had learned from Molloy, and these delighted the little woman. She said, quite truly, that she had never heard anything so fine before. And when Monica asked Aunt Ellen's advice about her program for the Bridgetower Recital, her cup was full and brimming over. This, at last, was the real musical life!

For there was to be a Bridgetower Recital. The members of the Trust had advanced the idea very delicately, fearing that Monica might be too prostrated with grief at the death of her mother to sing for some months. They were surprised, but gratified, by the resilience of her spirits. Yes, she said, she would be happy to sing for any audience they chose to assemble. Yes, she thought that Fallon Hall, at Waverley University, would be an excellent place for a recital. No, she was not in the least dubious about filling it with her voice; she had sung in the Sheldonian Theatre, and at Wigmore Hall, and size did not alarm her. Certainly, she would plan a program in the course of a few days. The question of mourning? Well, would it not be possible to include in her program a short group of songs of a devotional nature? She would like to do so, as a form of memorial to her mother. The Trust thought this most suitable and proper, and were delighted with her for thinking of it.

Miss Puss was particularly pleased by the whole notion of the recital. Indeed, she revealed a romantic strain in her character which the others had not suspected, but which came out clearly at a meeting held, with Monica present, to discuss all the details of the great affair.

"There is a point which I wish to raise," said Miss Puss, positively blushing, "which may seem—I hardly know how to phrase it—fanciful to you gentlemen, and which may at first seem strange to our protégée, Miss Gall. It has long been the custom of singers, when embarking upon their careers, to choose a name for professional use—a *nom de guerre*. The instances of Melba and Nordica arise at once to mind; Melba was Helen Mitchell—an honorable but scarcely inspiring title—and Nordica was Lillian Norton. Nor must we forget our own dear Marie Lajeunesse, which we shall certainly not do if we think of her as Madame Albani. They chose names, you see, which were remarkable for euphony, and ease of recollection. Mind you, I do not say that a name with a certain, well, asperity about it is a barrier to success. Who has forgotten Minnie Hauk? Well—I put it to you, Minnie Hauk! But the exception in this case strengthens the rule. Consider the great Yendik—born Kidney! Well, you will have gathered by now what I am driving at. Our dear Monica—(Monica's eyes opened to their uttermost to learn that she was dear to Miss Puss, but she was becoming inured to surprises)—has a lovely Christian name. But Gall? A name honoured in Ireland, certainly, but is it quite the thing for the concert platform? Can one imagine it on posters, programs? Can we be of assistance in finding something more suitable—more euphonious and easily memorable? I confess that I have pondered over this matter a good deal during the past few days, and what I want to suggest"—and here Miss Puss positively glowed—"is that the forthcoming recital would be a most suitable place for the assumption of a new name. And the name I propose—a name compounded of parts of Monica and Gall, a sort of anagram—is Gallica."

Up from the depths of Monica's memory floated the name of Monique Gallo; how long ago that was—more than two years! How she had changed.

"It is wonderfully kind of you, and I can't tell you how much I appreciate your thoughtfulness," said she, "but I think, all things considered, I had better keep my own name. You see, I have sung twice for the B.B.C. as Monica Gall, and I have sung at Wigmore Hall in a recital of new work by Giles Revelstoke, which attracted a good deal of attention. I have sung for Sir Benedict under my own name, as well; so perhaps it would be a mistake to change it now, just when it is beginning to be known."

How oily I am getting, she thought. That sounded just like Giles imitating somebody he despised.

Aunt Puss was quick to swallow her words.

"I had no desire to seem arbitrary or intrusive," said she; "I only wished to draw attention to a recognized professional custom."

"I think it is a custom which is falling into disuse," said Solly.

"That may not be entirely a good thing," said the Dean. "A career in art must often mean great changes in personality—much abandoned in the past, and much learned. I've sometimes thought we might all be the better for taking new names when we discover our vocations." He looked kindly at Miss Puss, who was flustered and cast down. One of the few flashes of romance in her life had been quenched.

Poor old chook, thought Monica. She wants to make something; she wants to create, and Gallica would be in some measure her creation. She would be particularly nice to Miss Puss when the meeting was over, to salve the wound.

It was at this meeting that Monica was told of the substantial sum of money which the Trust had on hand, and which was legally hers. It was Mr. Snelgrove who explained it to her, and when he reached the point where he had to say that she could have it and do as she pleased with it he could hardly bring the words to his lips. As a lawyer he knew what the position was, and in that capacity he had been urging the Trust to get the money off its hands; but Mr. Snelgrove was also a man—a dry, conservative, stuffily prudent, snobbish old man—and the thought of turning over so much money to a girl of very common background, who might commit the Lord only knew what follies with it, deeply shocked him. Nor was he without heart; the sight of young Solomon Bridgetower sitting in what ought to be his own house, looking as though he had bitten a lemon, while this strange girl was given money which might have been his, hurt Mr. Snelgrove's sense of justice—which a life devoted to the practice of the law had not wholly eroded away. But at last Mr. Snelgrove was done with his humming and hawing, and his meaning was clear.

"Of course I am very much surprised," said Monica, "and more than ever grateful to the late Mrs. Bridgetower. You need have no fear that the money will be wasted, or frittered away in trivial spending. Indeed, I can tell you now that I should not dream of using it for purely personal benefit. With your approval, I should like to use a small part of it—a few hundred dollars—to settle my mother's funeral expenses. I shall pay it back as soon as I am able, out of my own earnings. The remainder will be used exclusively for musical purposes of which I shall give you a full account when the time comes."

She spoke soberly, but her heart was singing. From the minute she understood the drift of Mr. Snelgrove's harangue, she knew precisely what she was going to do with that money. It would be more than enough to close the gap between what the Association for English Opera could afford to spend in producing *The Golden Asse*, and what was necessary to do the job properly, and with a decent margin for unexpected needs. She would now be able to make it possible for Giles to take a giant step in his career, and she could do it decently, without robbery, padding of expenses, and selling second-hand clothes. Like many people when they suddenly get their own way, she saw the hand of God in it. But she was not so lost to discretion as to talk of her plan to the Trust, until she actually had the money.

The Trustees were somewhat surprised, and the Dean at least was relieved, that she did not take the news of her windfall in a frivolous or greedy spirit. They badly wanted to know what she was going to do, but pride forbade them to ask. So they passed on to a discussion of the invitations to the Bridgetower Recital. For of course it was to be an invitation affair, and they meant to get the utmost possible glory out of it for themselves. Glory was all that they stood to get from the Bridgetower Trust, and having parted, though vicariously, with $45,000 they badly felt the need of something in return.

(8)

THE PERIOD DURING WHICH Monica was preparing herself for the recital was enlivened for the whole British Commonwealth, and several millions of interested people in the U.S.A., by what was known as the Odingsels Obscenity Scandal. Odo Odingsels, described to Monica's astonishment and private amusement as "a fashionable Mayfair photographer," was arrested on charges of selling, at very high prices and to a small but constant clientele, indecent photographs of men and women highly placed in society and politics. The nature of these photographs, the newspapers said, was of an obscenity to astonish the most hardened libertine, for not merely were they filthy in themselves but they brought into disrepute people for whom the whole world had the utmost respect and affection. The man Odingsels was plainly a criminal lunatic of horrifying depravity; employing models sufficiently like his subjects (though as a usual thing younger and more pleasingly formed) he put the heads of the victims on them by brilliant photographic trickery, employing photographs purchased from news agencies and portrait photographers. The newspapers dwelt with well-simulated horror on the lifelike and astonishing effects which this perverse combination of artistry and technique produced. The Old Bailey had been cleared while the jury examined the monster's work, and the Judge had admonished them to secrecy. Nevertheless, it was said on sufficient authority that European Royalty, British Royalty, the White House—nay, the very Vatican itself—were spattered.

Ransacking its recollection for some yardstick of enormity to apply, the press came up, not very appositely, with the Oscar Wilde case, and a bright young journalist, remembering that Wilde had once lived in Tite Street, made great play with the fact that Odingsels frequently "resorted" there, to the editorial offices of a publication called *Lantern*, run by a Chelsea group which was made out to be as unsavoury as the laws of libel would permit. Another point of similarity with the Wilde affair was that Odingsels showed no proper dismay in the dock, but grinned and sometimes laughed outright when evidence was given that he had received as much as one hundred guineas for a single exclusive print.

Odo's counsel, a celebrated silk, attempted to defend him on the ground that many of his ingenious photographs, representing celebrated figures in world affairs, were essentially political in subject, and satiric in intent. They were, he said, the modern counterparts of the vigorous, sometimes savage, and often suggestive political caricatures of Rowlandson and Gilray. He created a sensation in court when he produced a list of Odingsels' clients and began to read it; extraordinary as it seemed, some of the photographer's victims were themselves purchasers of obscene portraits of other eminent people. The Judge did not permit the reading of the list to go far, but read it himself, de-

clared it to be, for the present, irrelevant, and no more was
heard of it. But the eminent silk had read enough to set the
newspapers buzzing; it was, Fleet Street agreed, the liveliest
thing since the great hue and cry after homosexuals a few
months before. Leaders appeared under such headings as "Curiosa In High Places". Much was made of the fact that the learned
Judge, after looking through a portfolio of Odingsels' work, said,
"These things would make a vulture gag." He also said that the
models who lent themselves to the production of such filth
should be discovered and dealt with appropriately.

"Thank God for Bun Eccles," said Monica, drinking this in
with her breakfast coffee, "or I might have to stay here for a
few months. I wonder if they'll get Perse? A girl with as many
moles as she has oughtn't to be hard to identify—but the slops
can't strip every tart in London, matching up shapes."—From
which it may be seen that Monica did not phrase her private
thoughts as elegantly as she did her speeches to the Bridgetower
Trustees.—"I wonder who I would have been the body of, if I'd
gone to him? I always knew he was no good. I just hope Giles
has enough sense not to try to go to his rescue by appearing as
a character witness, or something."

For five days the wonder raged, and at last a shuddering
smudge appeared in the newspapers which was described as a
radio-photograph of Odo Odingsels being escorted from the
Central Criminal Court by twelve police, while a crowd of five
hundred angry women tried to slaughter him with umbrellas
and rotten vegetables. His offence was such a strange one, and
the law relating to it so various and confused, that the best the
Judge was able to do for him was to send him to prison for five
years, three of which were to be spent in hard labour.

Much was made during the trial of the unsavouriness of
Odingsels' appearance; the Judge and the newspapers were at
one in agreeing that his outward form was the true mirror of his
soul. Monica and everyone else learned that the type of mange
from which he suffered was called *alopecia areata*, and everywhere harmless, afflicted citizens wrote to the papers protesting

that this ailment was not a mark of turpitude. But the Odingsels Obscenity Scandal vanished as suddenly as it came.

There were two days when the name of *Lantern* was prominent in the news, and when people who had never seen a copy were writing of it as a scabrous and scruffy publication, when she had to be very firm with herself, to keep from sending a cable of warning advice to Giles. But she knew how furiously he would resent such interference; three or four weeks in Canada, domineering over her relatives, had awakened her considerable talent for bossiness, but she must not use it on Giles. Of late his touchiness had reached new heights; hard work on *The Golden Asse* raised his spirits, but drove him to new excesses of freakishness. And so much of it was directed against Stanhope Aspinwall! The critic had been favourable but pernickety in his judgement of *Kubla Khan* when it was broadcast; Monica was inclined to think well of him because he had written of her singing in terms of warm praise . . . "an artist still somewhat tentative in her approach but plainly possessed of uncommon abilities . . . combines vocal qualities usually considered to be mutually exclusive—extreme agility and brilliance in the upper register with a warm and expressive tone . . . a purity of English pronunciation and delicate interpretation of poetic nuance which recalls the late Kathleen Ferrier". Monica had suggested to Giles that, as he had taught her all she knew, this praise was for him, but he would not hear of it. "All these old critics go ga-ga about a new girl if she isn't a positive gargoyle," he had said, and had raged on about Aspinwall's criticism of the piano part of the cantata as unduly elaborated. And when, a few weeks later, Giles had given a recital of his work at Wigmore Hall, and Aspinwall had once again praised her warmly, and found some faults in the music, Giles became quite impossible.

He had procured a picture of Aspinwall (through Odingsels, it was now unpleasant to remember), had framed it and hung it in the water-closet which was one flight downstairs from his own apartment. He made a point of using the paper for which Aspinwall wrote in order to wrap his garbage; he bought several copies every week, cut out Aspinwall's signed articles, and hung them in the water-closet, as a substitute for the toilet roll, though Mrs. Klein and the other lodgers objected strongly. On one embarrassing occasion he took Monica to a concert and, finding that they were sitting behind Aspinwall (which he swore he had not arranged) he badgered the critic by tapping on the back of his seat, and making insulting remarks, just loud enough to be heard, in the intervals. He even began to write obscenely abusive letters to Aspinwall, but Monica and Bun Eccles intercepted them, and so far as they could judge, none had escaped their watch.

"Pay no attention," Bun had said when she confided her worry to him; "old Giles is a genius, and when he's working at full steam he gets ratty. Some of the things he does are a bit crook, Monny, but he's sound as the bank—too right he is. Wait'll he gets the opera done, then you'll see."

Well, she thought, the first thing is to get the opera done, and hope Aspinwall likes it. So she cabled Giles that the money difficulty was settled, explained it in detail in a letter, and worked even harder for the Bridgetower Recital.

(9)

WHEN THE DAY CAME Monica's nervousness, as always, took the form of depression, a sense of unworthiness, and a fear not of failure but of a spiritless mediocrity. By now she had some experience of this state, and recent reflection had convinced her that it was part of her heritage from Ma; her imagination, and her ups and downs of feeling, were Ma's. Well, she must not let them dominate her life, as they had dominated the life of Mrs. Gall.

But it is one thing to reason with depression, and another to lift it. All day she was gloomy. She had procured invitations for her own friends. Would Kevin and Alex draw attention to themselves in some unsuitable way? Would George Medwall, with whom she had had two or three brief, uneasy conversations, come at all, and would it bother her if she could not see him in the audience? The Canadian Broadcasting Corporation had asked to make a tape-recording of part of the concert; was that going to mean a microphone to fix her with its disapproving, steely face, somewhere directly in her view? Why, she wondered, did anyone want to be a singer?

Did she indeed want to be a singer? What singer whom she knew did she admire? In her present mood she could think of none. Singers! The creatures of a physical talent, constantly fussing about draughts in spite of their horse-like health—conscious that their voices might drop a tone if the room were too hot. Evelyn Burnaby, with whom she now had some acquaintance, and whom she admired as an artist—did she really want to be like Evelyn? So dull, except when she sang.

And Ludwiga Kressel—a genuine *diva*, that one, to whom Domdaniel had introduced her after a performance at Covent Garden. Ludwiga had dominated the party, a powerful, brass-haired woman, with a sense of humour as heavy as her own tread. She had compelled them all to silence while she told them of her experiences with the stage director at the Metropolitan. She had been unable to continue, convulsed by her own fun, yet protesting through her big-throated laughter, "However funny I am I cannot be so funny as Graf." She had got to the Metropolitan because she had previously secured an engagement in Vienna. "Byng is impressed by Vienna, but Vienna is nothing, nothing at all." Did she want to think like Ludwiga, who talked endlessly of "concertizing" and "recitalizing?" Did she want to live like Ludwiga, whose ferocious schedule of plane travel made it possible for her to cram the greatest possible number of appearances—operatic and concert—into a single season? No, no; not like Ludwiga.

By six o'clock she was in the depths, and wanted a drink more than anything else. No—obviously not more than anything

else, for a drink was easily within her reach; Kevin and Alex
had been discreetly keeping her modest needs supplied. But a
drink before a concert might disturb her voice, so it was out of
the question for her to have one. She knew very well, as she
denied herself, that she was by that abnegation settling her
shoulders to the singer's yoke.

The recital was to be at half-past eight, and well before eight
she was entering the artist's door of Fallon Hall. The artist's
door, in this case, simply meant the entrance to a poky little
room, piled half-full with folded wooden chairs and ferociously
over-heated by steam coils, at one side of the stage. But this was
what an "artist's door" meant in her native land—not the mysterious and somewhat furtive side-doors which led to stages in
England, nor the glorious, lamplit courtyard which led to the
stage entrance of the Paris Opera; she entered Fallon Hall itself
by just the same door as the public used; for after all, what had
an artist to conceal, or what marked him off from the general
public? Nothing, of course; nothing but a world of dedication.

Having failed to open a window, or find a janitor to do it for
her, Monica was fearful that she might take cold even before her
concert. The air was hot and dry, so she went into the corridor,
and at last found another room, dark and not so hot, where
faculty meetings were held, and here she concealed herself until
five minutes before the concert was to begin.

Her accompanist, Humphrey Cobbler, had not yet arrived,
and Monica worried furiously. But with a minute to spare he appeared, much rumpled and utterly unpressed, but in evening
clothes and plainly in very good spirits. During rehearsals she
had learned to know and like Humphrey very much, and so now
she was able to speak sharply to him about his lateness.

"But I'm not late," said he, smiling indulgently. "You don't
suppose they'll get going before eight forty-five? My dear, the
nobility and gentry, the beauty and chivalry, not to mention the
money and the stretched credit, of Salterton are assembling to
hear you. You can smell the moth-balls and the bunny coats

away back here if you sniff. And it's all for you. Don't fuss; glory in it."

"I can't glory. I think I'm going to be sick. Oh, Humphrey, this scares me far worse than the B.B.C., or anything I've ever done."

"But why?"

"Because it's my home town, that's why. You couldn't understand. You're an Englishman; you haven't got Salterton in your bones; you didn't grow up with those people out there meaning the larger world to you. So far as they know me at all, they know me as a stenographer at the Glue Works. And right now that's exactly what I feel like."

"Listen, poppet, it's very charming of you to love your home town, but now is the time to put that love in its proper place— which is right outside Fallon Hall, in a snowbank. Salterton can't be your measure of success or failure; what you think are its standards are just the standards of childhood and provincialism. You've been away long enough to recognize that your home town is not only the Rome and the Athens of your early life, but also in many important ways a remote, God-forsaken dump. Those people out there are just provincial professors, and bankers, and wholesale druggists who want to be proud of you if you give them half a chance, but who will just as readily take any opportunity you give them to keep you down. Now: don't try to dominate them; you're not a lion-tamer. Go out on the platform and do what your teachers have told you, and what you know to be right and best, and pay no heed to them at all, except when courtesy—the high courtesy of the artist—demands it. We'll walk up and down this corridor, you and I, taking deep but not hysterical breaths, until the head usher tells us that all the bunny coats are in their seats. Come on, Monica: head forward and up, back long and easy, and—what does Molloy say?—breathe the muhd."

(10)

THE FIRST PART OF THE Recital was over, and Cobbler returned Monica to the Faculty Room, shut the door and guarded it from outside. It had gone well. That is, she knew that she had sung well, and the audience, after a rather watchful beginning, was prepared to like her.

It was true, as Cobbler had said when she first discussed her program with him, that she was giving them something tough to chew. But—"It's a fine program," he had said, "and I'm delighted you're getting away from that fathead notion that music must always be performed in the chronological order of its composition. The audience here has had a thorough Community Concerts training; they'll be expecting you to start off with a Classical Group, putting your voice through its hardest paces while it's still cold and before you've really got the feel of the hall or the audience, and then a group of Lieder, to show that you know German, and a French group, to show that you know French, and then a Contemporary Group, consisting entirely of second-rank Americans, and topping off with a Popular Group, in which you really let your hair down and show how vulgar and folksy you can be. But this makes sense."

The program was prepared on a principle which she had learned from Giles; not the chronology of composers, but a line of poetic meaning, was the cord on which the beads were strung. And so she had begun with Schubert's *An die Musik,* and after that noble apostrophe she plunged straight into Giles' own *Kubla Khan* which was certainly tough chewing for a Salterton audience, as it took fifteen minutes to perform and without being in the mode of what Cobbler called "wrong-note modernism" was written in an idiom both contemporary and individual to the composer. Then, as relief, she had sung a group of folk-songs of the British Isles as she had learned them from Molloy. The folk songs had stirred the audience to its first real enthusiasm, for they all felt themselves competent judges of such seeming simplicity.

Now an interval, and then a group of three songs which the audience was asked, in a note on the program, not to applaud. These were the songs which Monica intended as her memorial to her mother. The oak coffin, the five black Buicks at the funeral, and the red granite tombstone, like a chunk of petrified potted meat, which Dad and Alice wanted, were trash. But in these songs she would take her farewell of Ada Gall.

First would be Thomas Campion's *Never weather-beaten Saile.* She would follow it with Brahms' *Auf dem Kirchhofe,* and if anyone thought it gloomy—well, let them think. And last, Purcell's *Evening Hymn,* noble and serene setting of William Fuller's words. Would any who had known Ma—Dad, for instance, or Aunt Ellen—find the reflection of her spirit which Monica believed to lie in these songs? During the night-watches at her bedside, Monica had thought much about Ma, and about herself. They were, as Ma had said in her last fully rational utterances, much alike. For in Ma, when she told tall stories, when she rasped her family with rough, sardonic jokes, when she rebelled against the circumstances of her life in coarse abuse, and when she cut through the fog of nonsense with the beam of her insight, was an artist—a spoiled artist, one who had never made anything, who was unaware of the nature or genesis of her own discontent, but who nevertheless possessed the artist's temperament; in her that temperament, misunderstood, denied and gone sour, had become a poison which had turned against the very sources of life itself. Nevertheless, she was like Ma, and she must not go astray as Ma—not wholly through her own fault—had gone. In these songs she would sing of the spirit which might have been her mother's if circumstances had been otherwise. Alice had not hesitated to say that she had killed their mother by giving in to her wilfulness. Well, it was not true; what was best in her mother should live on, and find expression, in her.

Monica had often heard of singers losing awareness of themselves while facing an audience—of losing the audience, and existing for that time only in their music. She had never quite believed it. But that was her own experience while she sang the three songs which she had, in her own mind, set aside as a memorial to her mother. She was back in the Faculty Room before she emerged from that inner calm. Humphrey Cobbler kissed her on the cheek and—sure sign in him of strong feeling—said not a word, but left her to herself.

Her tribute offered and her final peace made with the spirit, not departed but strongly present, Monica found the remainder of her recital pleasant and, all things considered, easy. She sang a group of settings of poems by John Clare, Thomas Lovell Beddoes and Walter de la Mare which Giles had written for her, and their sombre beauty led the hearers out of the memorial atmosphere which had been created, and left them ready for Berlioz' *Nuits d'été*, and the final group of songs, which was four Shakespeare lyrics, in settings by Purcell and Thomas Augustine Arne, which Giles had arranged from the gnomic and scanty original accompaniments. The audience had made up its mind after the memorial songs that it liked Monica—liked her very much and was proud of her—and the applause as she left the stage was warm, and mounting. There were even a few greatly daring, un-Canadian cries of "Bravo!" which Monica attributed, rightly, to Kevin and Alex.

"Sticking to plan?" said Cobbler.

"Yes; go back on the crest of the applause, and one good encore," said Monica. This was a piece of practical wisdom from Domdaniel; Giles hated encores because they disturbed the shape of his programs; Molloy believed in singing as long as one delighted listener remained in the hall; the balance lay with Sir Benedict.

So, as the applause mounted for fifty seconds, until there was actually some stamping—stamping in Fallon Hall, and from a stiff-shirt audience at that!—Monica remained out of sight, judging the sound. And when it seemed to her that it would go no higher, she returned to the stage, amid a really gratifying uproar. Ushers moved forward with flowers; a large and uncompromising bunch from the Bridgetower Trustees, a very handsome bunch from Kevin and Alex, a bouquet containing a card which read, "With Love and Pride from the Old Heart and Hope Quartet" (which made Monica blush momentarily, for she had havered a little about inviting the Beamises) and two or three others. Cobbler, greatly enjoying the fun, for such recitals did not often come his way, helped her to pile them all on top of the piano, and she sang her single encore.

"Never sing below your weight in an encore; try to do something you haven't done earlier in the evening; and try to sing something they'll like but probably haven't heard before." These were the words of Domdaniel, talking to her about public appearances several months before. So Monica had determined to sing Thomas Augustine Arne's *Water Parted*.

It was a song which she deeply loved, though Giles laughed at her for it. "'May this be my poison if my bear ever dances but to the very genteelest of tunes—*Water Parted*, or the minuet in *Ariadne*'," he would say, to her mystification, until one night when he had taken her to the Old Vic to see *She Stoops to Conquer*, and had nudged her sharply when the line was spoken. But he had prepared an accompaniment for it, for her special use, and had set it in a key which made the best use of what he called her "chalumeau register", as well as the brilliance of her upper voice.

> *Water parted from the sea*
> *May increase the river's tide—*
> *To the bubbling fount may flee,*
> *Or thro' fertile valleys glide.*
>
> *Tho' in search of lost repose*
> *Thro' the land 'tis free to roam,*
> *Still it murmurs as it flows*
> *Panting for its native home.*

She sang it very well, though this was the first time she had ever sung it in public. She sang it as well, perhaps, as she ever sang it in her life, though in later years her name was to be much associated with it, and audiences were to demand it in and out of season. She performed that feat, given to gifted singers, of making the song seem better than it was, of bringing to it a personal significance which was not inherent in it. But Monica always protested that the song was great in itself, and that she merely revealed in it what had gone unnoticed by others, too hasty to make a personal appraisal of a song by a composer usually dismissed as not really first-rate. She was already, under Revelstoke's guidance, developing a faculty of finding worth where others had missed it, and this was to give her repertoire a quality which was the despair of her rivals.

But there, in Fallon Hall, she sang *Water Parted* for the first time, and lifted her audience to an even greater pitch of enthusiasm.

"I think we may call it a triumph," whispered Humphrey Cobbler, as they bowed again and again.

(11)

"AN UNDOUBTED TRIUMPH!" cried Miss Puss Pottinger, as Monica was led by Cobbler into the Bridgetower home. The house was full of people—more people than had been in it since Mrs. Bridgetower's funeral—and they all appeared to be in that state of excitement which follows a really satisfactory artistic achievement. Their excitement varied, of course. There were those who talked of the concert, and there were those who talked of politics and the stock market; but all their talk was a little more vivacious, or vehement, or pontifical because of what they had experienced; music had performed its ever-new magical trick of strengthening and displaying whatever happened to be the dominant trait in them.

But Cobbler knew his work too well to allow Monica to be snatched from him. With the technique of a professional bodyguard he guided her to the stairway, rushed her up it, and into

the little second-floor sitting-room where Solly and Veronica
were waiting with food and drink.

Singers must eat, and there have been those among them who
have eaten too much. As amorousness is the pastime of players
of stringed instruments, and horse-racing the relaxation of the
brass section of the orchestra, so eating is the pleasure and sometimes the vice, of singers. After a performance, a singer must be
fed before he or she can be turned loose among their admirers,
or else somebody may be insulted, or even bitten. Cobbler had
told Veronica that Monica would need something substantial, and
preferably hot. So, in the upstairs sitting-room, a dish of chops
and green peas, a salad, a plate of fruit and a half-bottle of
Beaune were in readiness.

As Monica devoured them gratefully—for she had eaten nothing since mid-day, and had taken only a glass of milk at five
o'clock—a close observer might have thought that even more
than a meal had been prepared. When Solly had given Cobbler
a drink, he said that they really must go and talk to their guests,
and led the accompanist away, leaving Monica and Veronica
alone.

Veronica was a poor diplomat, and she had small relish for
the task before her; but she had undertaken it on behalf of her
husband, and she decided that the best thing was to jump in
with both feet, and get it over.

"Monica—I hope you don't mind me calling you Monica—
Solly and I want to ask a favour of you. A large favour, and it
isn't easy to ask. But—we're terribly hard up. And we wondered
if you could possibly lend us some money."

Monica looked up, not appearing to best advantage with her
mouth full. This was one development she had not foreseen.

"I know it must seem strange to you, but I suppose you have
heard about the conditions of my mother-in-law's will?"

Monica shook her head. "Not a whisper," said she.

"You must be one of the few people who hasn't heard something. But of course you've been out of the country. Still, I

thought your—some of your relatives might have written to you about it. It seems to us—to Solly and me—that everyone knows about it. Well, it's complicated, but it comes to this; the Trust which supports you has all Mrs. Bridgetower's money for its funds. When she died, my husband was left one hundred dollars, and that was all. It was a blow; I know you'll understand that. But it wasn't as though he was free. The money may come to him; it will come to him if we have a male child. Had you not heard anything of that?"

"Nothing," said Monica, and felt suddenly cold in the warm little room.

"Yes. If we have a male child, the Trust automatically ends. But till that time all the money goes to you. We had a child, you know—you didn't?—well, we had a son, but he was born dead. It was a sore disappointment. Not wholly, or even mostly, because of the money but—you do understand, don't you? We don't hold ill-will against you. After all, it might have been somebody else—anybody with talent. But we're chained to this house, which costs a terrible lot to keep up, even when the Trust undertakes to keep it in repair. And my husband is still only a lecturer, and even with Summer School fees, and what he can get by writing now and then for the radio, and so forth, we can't keep our heads above water. We're not merely broke; we're terribly in debt. Now, of course Solly knows that the Trust has just made over $45,000 of surplus funds to you.—I hate saying this, but under other circumstances that would have been our money. I'm asking if you could let us have ten thousand, to tide us over?"

Monica looked, but could not speak.

"You see, we have hopes. We hope for another child. But suppose it isn't a boy? Suppose there is never another boy? I don't want to let myself talk about my mother-in-law, but it's so cruell If we could get free of the house, we might snap our fingers at the whole thing, but we can't—at least we haven't quite gone so far as to sacrifice all hopes in order to get out of this net. And meanwhile—you understand, don't you, that I'm talking to you as a friend, and I'm not trying to wring your heart, really I'm not—I only want you to know how things are—our marriage is being twisted out of shape. Solly is a drudge, and I'm a baby-factory, bound to go on and on, until we have a son. It's a horrible vengeance—because she hated me—because I took her son—"

Veronica was not a weeping woman, but her mute distress was more terrible to another woman than tears could be.

Oh God, thought Monica, if only I had enough sense not to always tell everything I know! I've told Giles I've got $45,000, or close to it, when the funeral's paid for, and that's what he'll be counting on. If I go back with less—I couldn't explain it to him, ever. These people wouldn't be real to him. Nothing's real to him except the opera, and I'm real because I've been able to support him while he wrote it, and can help to pay to get it on. But what can I tell Veronica? Tell her that an artistic venture demands every cent of this money, when she and her husband think of it as theirs? What could a plan like that mean to people who are in this sort of mess? Tell her my lover must have every penny I can get, like a tart giving her earnings to her pimp, for fear of a black eye? How real would Giles seem to them? What can I say?

The silence between them was more than either woman could bear, and it was Veronica who broke it.

"It would be a loan, of course, a matter of business—we wouldn't dream of asking more than that. I mean, we'd have to arrange a rate of interest; we wouldn't expect you to lose by it."

Monica was frozen with discomfiture and pity, but she could not find anything to say. Veronica could not be silent, now; anything was better than silence. She continued:

"I know, of course, that what I'm asking you to do is quite illegal. Solly has tried to get loans out of the funds from Mr. Snelgrove, and it can't be done. If you let us have some money, we might all end in jail, I suppose. Or at best it would look terrible if anyone found out."

Monica had to speak.

"I wouldn't care how illegal it was, if I could help you," said she. "I just can't. There's a very good reason—I swear to you that it's a good reason—why I can't, but at present I'm unable to explain it. I will explain as soon as I can, and as fully as possible. But you must believe that it isn't greed, or stinginess, or because I don't admire you and your husband very much, and want you to think well of me. But I can't do it."

"I thought that would be your answer," said Veronica, without rancour; "Solly said you had spoken of a plan of some sort to the Trustees. But you see that I had to try, don't you?"

The noise of the party mounted to them, and Solly came to fetch his wife and Monica. A quick glance told him what he most wanted to know, and he did not allow his obligatory high spirits, as host, to flag. To lose all hope is, in a way, to be free, and it often brings with it a lightening of mood. Downstairs they went, into a sea of compliments, of enthusiasm, of success.

Much later, as Monica lay in her bed, she thought of the party with satisfaction, and yet somewhat remotely. It had been the occasion for an outlet of the enthusiasm which her recital had evoked, and which had not expended itself in the applause at Fallon Hall. She had done her duty. She had tried at first to bring Dad into the circle of enthusiasm; he had appreciated her solicitude, but it was doubtful if he really knew any more about the affair than that Monny had, in some mysterious way, made a hit with these big-bugs. It was not that he was stupid; he was dim, remote and, since the death of his wife, only partly alive. Aunt Ellen was quite different; it was not at all hard to find people for her to talk to; Cobbler had been very good to her. Alex and Kevin, astonishingly assured and competent at a party far above their accustomed welkin, had been kind about looking after Dad.

For Monica had not been able to do so. Everybody wanted to

talk to her. One or two had liked *Kubla Khan*, and said so; some
had spoken very kindly about the songs sung in memory of Mrs.
Gall. But *Water Parted* seemed to have impressed everybody.

Yet what strange things they found in it! "I wish I knew what
was in your mind when you sang that!" Over and over again she
heard that comment, differently phrased. Many, as soon as they
had said it, gave her their notion of what the song had meant
to her. A surprising number took it as a song of nostalgia for
Canada, cherished by her during her exile abroad—an idea
which had never entered her head. Some were convinced that it
was a love-song.

What did it mean to her? It meant what *Hiraeth* meant to
Ceinwen Griffiths—a longing for what was perhaps unattainable
in this world, a longing for a fulfillment which was of the spirit
and not of the flesh, but which was not specifically religious in
its yearning. It meant her surge of feeling at the tomb of St.
Geneviève. It meant the aspiration toward that from which she
drew her strength, and to which she returned when the concerns
of daily life were set aside. It was the condition of being which
lay beyond the Monica Gall who bossed Dad and Aunt Ellen
into living together, who quarrelled and lost her dignity with
her sister Alice, who spoke in honeyed words to the Bridgetower
Trustees, who denied poor Veronica Bridgetower the money
which might deliver her from a hateful bondage, who cheated
and scraped for Giles Revelstoke, and endured all his whims in
return for his absent-minded and occasional affection. It lay
through, but beyond, the world of music to which she was now
committed—the singer's bondage which tonight had so plainly
shown to be hers. It was the yearning which had been buried in
the heart of her mother, denied and thwarted but there, forever alive and demanding. It was a yearning toward all the vast,
inexplicable, irrational treasury from which her life drew whatever meaning and worth it possessed. It was the yearning for—?
As Ceinwen's song had said, not all the wise men in the world
could ever tell her, but it would last until the end.

(12)

"I TRUST THAT YOU WILL NOT THINK THAT I have acted unwisely, but that is what has been done with the large sum of money which you made over to me in February. I hope that the enclosed reports will persuade you that it has been well spent." Thus ran part of Monica's letter to the Bridgetower Trustees, which Mr. Snelgrove read to them at a meeting held in the following May.

"I'm sure Mother would have been greatly surprised to know that she had partly financed the production of a new opera," said Solly, and the others could only agree.

And such an opera! The criticisms which Monica had enclosed were all agreed that it was an extraordinary work, containing flashes of genius, but freakish in the extreme. That the principal tenor should have been transmuted into an ass, by sorcery, was part of the story. But that he should bray—musically, of course, but still undoubtedly braying—for the whole of the middle act, was certainly hard to swallow. Part of the audience had refused to take it seriously as a musical work, and had been tempted to boo. But Stanhope Aspinwall, in two long articles which he wrote about the new opera, rebuked them sharply. Here, he said, was the most original musical talent to emerge for many years, asserting itself—pulling the public's leg, perhaps, but that was the privilege of genius. His analysis of the work contained many criticisms which, he said, he had been obliged to bring against Giles Revelstoke's work on several occasions—lyricism at the expense of dramatic movement, conventional passages of orchestration which seemed to have been thrown together in a hurry and never revised, a sacrifice of musical to literary values in some sections—but judged as a whole, a work of splendid qualities.

All of the critics agreed that in Monica Gall, the Canadian

soprano who played the small but important role of Fotis, the serving-maid turned sorceress, the world of chamber opera had gained the most gifted singer of many years. She could not act particularly well, but that could be mended. It was good news indeed that the British Opera Association had chosen this work to perform in Venice, in September, at the Festival. There was even a kindly mention of the fact that some of the money for the excellently-mounted production had been supplied by a Canadian trust fund, founded for the furtherance of the arts; thus, the British critics agreed, the dominions were returning some of the loving care and cultural dower which had been lavished upon them in their early days by the Motherland. It was to be hoped that more might follow.

"Without knowing it, we seem to have covered ourselves with glory," said the Dean, laughing. But Miss Pottinger and Mr. Snelgrove agreed in all seriousness. "Certainly we made no mistake when we chose Monica Gall for the first beneficiary. I wonder if we shall have to choose another. May I say that I hope not?"

They all looked at Solly. They knew that since late April, Veronica had been pregnant.

"You cannot possibly hope that as fervently as I do, Mr. Dean," said Solly, with a laugh which took some of the bite out of the remark.

It was at about that same time that Chuck Proby (as Mr. Gall could not be persuaded to do it) went to the cemetery vault, where the body of Mrs. Gall was identified by him, and buried in the grave which the now soft ground permitted to be dug. The law demanded it, and someone has to do these things.

Nine

MONICA HAD BEEN five full days in Venice, and so far she had seen no more of it than could be glimpsed in flittings from her hotel to the theatre, and thence to Giles' favourite restaurant. True, she had been several times in a gondola, which might have been romantic if she had not always been accompanied by her portable typewriter, or the very heavy suitcase which contained the orchestra parts for *The Golden Asse*, or Giles himself in his anti-Venetian mood. The city was a tourist-trap, he told her, and its romance was spurious; the Venetians were all scoundrels; had they not launched income tax, the science of statistics, and state censorship of books upon the world? He laughed away her meek proposals that, when the long days of work were done, they might see some of the sights; he had seen the sights, years ago, and they were not worth having. They had not come to Venice to be tourists, but to work.

Monica, who had not seen the sights, would not in the least have minded being a tourist. Giles laughed still more, and said that she was provincial. Apparently this was a very dreadful thing to be, and she timidly asked Domdaniel about it.

"Giles is playing the man of the world," said he. "You mustn't mind. Everybody's provincial if you put 'em in the right spot to show it, and nobody more so than the man who won't be impressed, on principle. When we get this mess straightened out I'll show you the town; I know some very pleasant people here."

The mess to which he referred was *The Golden Asse*, which had been undergoing revision ever since its appearance in London in May. The work had revealed weaknesses in performance, and when Revelstoke had been convinced that the weaknesses were real, and had tried to correct them, the opera had seemed to collapse; its individual parts were still good, but they could not be made to stick together satisfactorily. Domdaniel had been reassuring; the commonest thing in the world, said he; always happened when a big work wanted revision; all that was needed was patience. But patience had worn thin, for *The Golden Asse* was to appear as part of the current Music Festival in Venice, and revisions had gone on, minutely but tiresomely, until yesterday. Most of the tinkering had been done on the orchestral interludes which linked the many scenes of the opera; Monica had copied, and re-copied, and copied again, principally because it was convenient for her to do so, being so close at hand, but also to save the money of the Association for English Opera—money which she had herself provided in substantial but insufficient amount. There is no such thing as enough money for opera, she had discovered.

The pattern of work was surprisingly regular. Domdaniel would find fault with a passage, and suggest how it might be re-cast: Revelstoke, after argument, would re-write the passage in his own way: Domdaniel, having first said that the new version would do splendidly, was likely to find in a few hours that it was—well, not quite right, and suggest further revision, usually along the lines he had originally proposed. Revelstoke would again re-write, producing something manifestly inferior to what he had done before. Domdaniel would then suggest that the earlier revision be used—with a few changes which he could easily make himself, to spare Giles trouble. But Giles did not want to be spared trouble; he wanted the music as he had written it in the beginning. There were shocking rows.

The parts which would shortly be distributed to the music desks in the orchestra were a muddle even for musicians, who are used to muddled parts. Over the neat script of the professional copyist were gummed countless bits of paper upon which were corrections in Monica's script, almost as neat. But over these might be further corrections, in Giles' beautiful but minute script, or in the bold hand of Domdaniel. Further revision appeared, in Domdaniel's hand, in red pencil. Yet, somehow, at orchestra rehearsals the players made sense of it all. Philosophical and usually patient men, they interpreted the muddle under their eyes, and brought forth beauty.

That was what made it all worth while. *The Golden Asse* was a thing of beauty. Giles' libretto followed faithfully the second century story of the unfortunate Lucius, whose meddling in magic caused him to be transformed into an ass, from which unhappy metamorphosis he was delivered only after he had achieved new wisdom. But the character of the music emphasized the tale as allegory—humorous, poignant, humane allegory —disclosing the metamorphosis of life itself, in which man moves from confident inexperience through the bitterness of experience, toward the rueful wisdom of self-knowledge. Where the music came from, not even Giles' most intimate associates— and this now meant Monica and Domdaniel—could guess, for as the work had progressed he had grown increasingly freakish, his moods alternating between one of morose incivility and another of noisy hilarity. There was nothing of the serene wisdom of his music to be discerned in himself.

The journey to Venice had been, for Monica, a misery. She had travelled with Giles and the stage director, Richard Jago. Giles had insisted that *wagon-lits* were an extravagance, so they had slept in their seats; nor would he hear of meals in the restaurant-car—they must picnic, it would be so much cheaper and jollier. So they had eaten innumerable hard rolls into which lumps of bitter chocolate were stuffed, fruit-cake, and cheese, with occasional swigs at a flask of brandy. Monica had not liked this stodgy diet, and had bought a few pears for herself; they had made her ill, as Giles, who had an English mistrust of fruit, had predicted, and after their arrival in Venice Domdaniel had had to dose her for a couple of days with Fernet Branca.

But it was not the physical discomforts of the journey which had made it so exhausting. Giles was in one of his hilarious moods, and insisted that she and Jago sing lewd rounds with him, for hours at a time. Giles was entranced by rounds and catches, especially those of the seventeenth and eighteenth centuries in which, as they were sung, simple-minded obscenities were revealed. And so, to the astonishment of their fellow-travellers (when they had any) they sped across Europe to the strains of—

> Adam catch'd Eve by the furbelow,
>   And that's the oldest catch I know;
>   Oho, did he so!

Jago, who was a mild and withdrawn young man, could never quite master the time of that one, and Giles abused him whenever they sang it. They had better luck with—

> I lay with an old man all the night;
>   I turned to him, and he to me;
> He could not do so well as he might
>   He tried and he tried, but it would not be.

But Giles' favourite was the most musically intricate and poetically inane of his large repertoire. It was a true "catch", and the words ran—

> I want to dress; pray call my maid,
>   And let my things be quickly laid.
> What does your Ladyship please to wear?
>   Your bombazine? 'Tis ready here.
> See here, see here, this monstrous tear,
>   Oh, fie! It is not fit to wear.

But when the "catch" made itself heard, he would enjoy it as heartily as any port-soaked member of an eighteenth century catch-club, and smack Monica resoundingly on her bottom as he sang "And let your bum be seen?"—as though there were some possibility that the point might be missed.

"For God's sake, Giles, will you stop acting the Beloved Vagabond for just half an hour? My head aches," Jago would protest.

"You have no zest for life," Revelstoke would reply. Or he might sulk for a time, or doze. But soon he would be at it again, insisting that they try once more to master Purcell's—

I gave her cakes, and I gave her ale—

which they never succeeded in doing, for Jago was not up to it. Monica was heartily glad, dulled though her senses were by the nausea which the bad pears had caused her, when the train crept through some dirty suburbs and Giles announced that they were at last sniffing the undeniable stench of the Queen of the Adriatic.

Still, that was all past now. The first Venetian performance of *The Golden Asse* in its revised version was to take place tonight, and Monica, at half-past four, was already in her dressing room, arranging and re-arranging her make-up materials, or lying on a sofa looking out at Venetian rooftops, so quiet under the September sunshine.

To be here, in a dressing-room all her own, in the celebrated Teatro della Fenice—was that not romance enough, without common, touristy sight-seeing? Yes, certainly it was. One must grow up some time, and would she not herself be, in a few hours, one of the sights of Venice? Yes, of course, that was the idea. And anyhow, after the first night was out of the way, Sir Benedict would take her sight-seeing.

At twenty-three, resting can be hard work. Monica was thoroughly tired of it. She ran down the broad, empty passages until she came to the large, gold-framed mirror which was fastened to the wall in the long gallery which gave the artists access to the stage, and passed through the door from daylight into the darkness of the huge stage itself. Above her was the soaring, dusty mystery of the flies, hung thickly with drop-scenes; somewhere, high in the lantern above the stage, a sunbeam penetrated the murk, touching the cobweb of fly-lines in a dozen places before it came to rest at last on one of the huge canvases

Once again Monica experienced the unfamiliar feel of a raked stage, so subtle in its enticement toward the footlights, so unexpectedly resistant in its retreat toward the back-cloth—for the single basic setting which served for *The Golden Asse* was already in place. One setting for an opera with eighteen scenes—it still seemed strange to her, nurtured on the elaborate naturalism in *The Victor Book of the Opera;* yet it was wonderful how well this unit-setting worked. She yielded to the slope, and stood directly in front of the prompter's box, looking across the orchestra pit toward the ornate music desk from which, in a few hours, she must follow Domdaniel's nuances of direction.

Then she raised her eyes, and became conscious that in the dimness of the beautiful theatre something was happening— some work was in progress. As she became accustomed to the gloom she saw that a work-party of those little old women who seem to be inseparable from European opera houses were busy hanging garlands of fresh flowers across the front of the first tier of boxes.

For an instant she felt, stronger than ever before, the mixture of elation and dread which she was learning to recognize as part of her professional life, part of her fate. It was exquisitely delicious and terrifying.

Then, suddenly, from the wings there came a slight draught, and hastily clutching a scarf about her throat she scampered back to the protective warmth of her dressing-room.

(2)

WHEN NEXT SHE STOOD upon that stage and felt the gentle urging of the rake toward the footlights, she resisted it, not only because she must go nowhere that Richard Jago had not told her to go, but also because she knew by now that crowding the footlights is not the best way for a singer to make herself heard; Domdaniel had given her the valuable tip that stage centre, fifteen or twenty feet from the footlights, is the preferred place on most good operatic stages, and Monica had learned all the polite ways of getting herself to that precise area. For the Association for English Opera was a very polite organization; no shrewishness, no temperament, no bluster marred its rehearsals as sometimes happens among the operatic stars of lesser breeds without the law; nevertheless, there were well-tried English ways of establishing that what was best for the individual singer was also best for the work, for the production, for the balance of the ensemble, and when the position of advantage was Monica's by right, she had no trouble in getting it. She shared it now with Amyas Palfreyman, the tenor who sang the part of Lucius; Mr. Palfreyman was a contradiction of everything that Ludwiga Kressel had said about tenors—that they were all fat, short, the possessors of too-small noses and an excess of female hormones; he was tall, lean, beaky of nose and, if not aggressively masculine certainly not effeminate; furthermore, he liked Monica and gave her all the help he could without compromising his own role. Monica was very lucky to be making an important early appearance with Mr. Palfreyman, and she knew it. Lucky, too, to be under the direction of the great Sir Benedict Domdaniel who, from his place in the pit, kept everything under his control, blending the ensemble of voices and orchestra with immense skill, so that the singers rested upon his conducting as gently and as confidently as gods in a Renaissance picture, resting upon a cloud. Ordinarily the Association for English Opera could not have afforded the services of Sir Benedict; he appeared in Venice, as he had done in London when the opera was first heard, at something like half his ordinary fee, because he wanted to advance the music of Giles Revelstoke.

Oh yes, Monica was very lucky, and she knew it, but during the performance she had no time or inclination to glory in her luck; she was too busy showing fortune that she was worthy of its favours. She had slaved to learn the craft of the opera singer; make-up, classes in posture, hours of toil with the demanding

Molloy—she had spared herself nothing. Not only was she able, now, to sound right; she could also look right. She had learned from Giles to be naked before him and to be neither ashamed nor brazen; it was not so very different to appear before a great audience with the same candour. Not that she was naked, though the costume which the designer thought fit for the entrancing servant-enchantress Fotis was a revealing one. "Not every day you get an opera singer who peels well," the designer had said, "so we may as well make the most of you." And that was what he had done. The mirror in the long gallery beyond the stage told Monica a pleasing tale. It was amazing, she thought, how well a rather sturdy girl ("strong as a horse", Sir Benedict had said) could be made to look. Oh, it was good to be as strong as a horse and yet, on a large stage, to look pleasantly fragile!

Domdaniel in the pit was not the only good angel who was watching over her. She moved about the stage in the pattern taught her by Richard Jago. She maintained the mental discipline —the dual consciousness of the actress, which enabled her to give herself to her part, and at the same time to stand a little aside, criticising, prompting and controlling—which had been so carefully imparted to her by Molloy. And as well as the feat of balance which enabled her to keep all these elements in control she still found a place in her mind for the humility of the interpreter toward the creator, of which Domdaniel had spoken as they drove from Oxford. It was not to the spirit of Bach, long-dead, but to Giles, very much alive and somewhere in the theatre, that she made her offering: would he be pleased?

He certainly should have been pleased, for the opera was very well received. It provided a kind of delight particularly pleasing to an Italian audience, for it gave almost unbroken opportunities for beautiful singing; modern enough in idiom, it was not modern in asperity and rejection of sheer vocal charm; but neither was it sentimental, a succession of musical bon-bons. It was, some of the critics who had descended upon Venice for the

Festival said in their dispatches to Germany, to Rome and to
Paris, a comic masterpiece—goldenly, sunnily comic, splendid
in its acceptance of the ambiguity of man's aspirations toward
both wisdom and joy. Musically it was somewhat novel to Italian
ears, for virtually all of its music was either for the ensemble or
for the orchestra; but, as the Italian critics pointed out, firmly
but kindly, this suited the English voices, which were fine instruments, governed by keen musical intelligence, but not of the
highest operatic order. Amyas Palfreyman was generously
praised, particularly for his musical braying in Act Two, when
he was transformed into an ass; and Monica Gall was mentioned
in all the notices as a new singer of great promise, freshness,
and uncommon agility and sweetness of voice combined with a
lower register which was striking in the scene where she figured
as an enchantress.

But these sweets were to be enjoyed later, after the critiques
had been collected. The immediate reward was the cheering at
the end of the performance, when the cast appeared again and
again in front of the curtains; when Sir Benedict appeared with
them, and called the orchestra to its feet; when Sir Benedict led
Giles Revelstoke forward for the kind of ovation which an audience chiefly Italian gives to a composer who has delighted it.

It was a great evening, marred a little by Giles' behaviour
afterward when Sir Benedict, who liked to keep up certain
princely customs, invited the company to have supper with him
at the Royal Danieli. The applause had affected Giles adversely,
and he was in his morose mood; he would not go, and he took
it ill that Monica did want to go. He thought she should have
been pleased enough to return with him to their very modest
hotel near the Fenice. She felt some concern for him, as he stood
apart, scowling at the party as it embarked in gondolas. But
when, half an hour later, she was sitting at Sir Benedict's left
hand on the terrace which overlooks the Grand Canal (the place
of highest honour, on his right hand, was understandably reserved for Lalage Render, the British *première danseuse étoile*

who danced the role of Psyche in the ballet of Cupid and Psyche which was one of the high points of the opera) she was not troubled about Giles, or about anything. She was perfectly happy, for she knew that she had done well, and (true Canadian that she was) she could enjoy her treat because she had earned it.

But the best was still to come. Sir Benedict took her back to her hotel by gondola, and although he may have found it slightly chilly, and though Monica was perpetually readjusting the scarf around her throat, it was romantic and moonlit enough. When he helped her ashore he thanked her for a delightful evening and kissed her hand. Monica started a little, and drew it away more quickly than was polite.

"What's the matter?" said Sir Benedict.

"Nothing; nothing at all. Only—this seems all wrong. I mean, I feel very much your pupil and—I don't know, I suppose I feel I ought to be thanking you—or something."

"You make me feel fully a hundred and ten," said Domdaniel, his bald head gleaming nacreously in the moonlight. "Still—good of you. I hope you'll be my pupil for a long time. But after tonight I'm very happy to think of you as a fellow artist, as well." And he kissed her hand again.

Monica was not at all sure how she found her way to bed.

(3)

THE OPERA WAS scheduled for only eight performances in Venice, and when the first of these was successfully over, Monica was free to see something of the city, which she did in the company of Domdaniel. He was an ideal sightseer, for he knew when to stop, had friends in the city, was acquainted with the best restaurants and thoroughly understood the first principle of aesthetic appreciation, which is that it can usually be doubled by sitting down. Monica, flattered by her new status as fellow-artist, had never enjoyed herself so much. Surely such attention from the great man meant that she had finally made the grade, and was counted among the Eros-men rather than the Thanatossers? Indeed, she began to wonder if she might not be something of a sex-squaller as well, for as she travelled about the city with Domdaniel she observed young men eyeing her and pulling furiously at their ear-lobes; a few of the more daring flung out their hands, with the index-finger leading, as she passed, and Sir Benedict explained that these were gestures of admiration, comparable to the wolf-whistles which she had heard (always for other girls) at home.

Giles remained sullen, and she saw little of him. On the fourth day Domdaniel said, as they were at lunch together—

"Giles has got his way at last. He's going to conduct tonight."

"Oh? Will we have to rehearse with him?"

"No, no; but keep your eye on him very closely. He's anxious to make a good job of it."

"Of course. But I didn't know he was scheduled to take any performances here. He never mentioned conducting to me. Are you going away?"

"No I'm not, and he isn't. But he wants to conduct very much, and he's persuaded me to persuade Petri that it will be all right—and I only hope it is."

"Are you worried?"

"Well, it's a difficult situation. You see, with my reputation, I'm rather a draw, and quite a bit of the preliminary seat-sale was based on that. People know that I do a good job with opera, and with a company which doesn't contain any other names of international reputation—except for Render, and she's not a singer—that's important. But I can't very well stuff that down Giles' throat. After all, he's the composer, and he's extremely touchy. But he really isn't a conductor."

"He's a marvellous accompanist."

"My dear girl, quite a different thing. Conducting opera is a first-class juggling trick, and Giles is no juggler. He fidgets and flogs his people. He radiates dissatisfaction. You know how singers are about atmosphere. Once a sense of strain has been created the whole thing can go to bits. Still, I had to put it to Petri, when Giles was so insistent on it, and Petri wasn't a bit easy to persuade. The trouble is, if I refuse to do this for him, he thinks I'm trying to keep him down."

"How awful! What a tangle!"

"Oh, not really. You should see what an opera company can create in the way of hell when it tries. Still, I feel responsible to Petri, who expected me to be on the job every night."

"Will you be there tonight?"

"Oh, I'll probably drop in."

Sir Benedict was there before the overture, in the back of a box, supposedly out of sight, though the singers were all aware of his presence. Signor Petri was very much in evidence, huge and imperial in evening dress, dropping into the dressing-rooms before curtain time to make trivial conversation in careful English, with very much the air of a man who is not saying what is on his mind. And Giles, taut and abrupt, visited every singer before the half-hour call, charging them to watch his beat, as there would be passages which he would take somewhat differently from Domdaniel.

And so he did, but for the first twenty minutes or so *The Golden Asse* went as well as usual. There was a different quality of tension on the stage, for singers were loyally determined to support their composer; but they could not rest confidently upon his conducting as they did upon that of the masterly Domdaniel. His beat was clear, and if his manner was peremptory and his face sometimes showed irritation (with what? with himself, the orchestra, or the singer? how can a tenor with his body working in one vast integrated effort to produce the best tone, allied with the suitable gesture, possibly be expected to know?) they had their own professional experience, and their own musicianship, to sustain them. But when the first of the important orchestral interludes came, it was clear that something was very wrong.

Of the fourteen hundred-odd people in the theatre, perhaps

a hundred and fifty really knew what the trouble was; another five or six hundred sensed that something was amiss but could not have identified it; the remainder knew only that the music which had been so melodious before, had taken on a queer turn which was probably attributable to some unfamiliarity of idiom. But for several bars a section of the orchestra would be at cross-purposes with the rest; or a vigorous entry would come a beat too soon, or too late; or sounds which no system of musical logic could account for would assert themselves, only to be subdued by the furious, quenching gesture of the composer's left hand.

As the performance progressed, it became nervous agony for the people on the stage, deeper mystery·for the listeners. The singers, upon the whole, fared well, for nothing completely disorganizing happened to their part of the score, though portions of accompaniment, faintly familiar, yet unaccustomed, rose to their ears. Yet, because they were the most exposed part of the musical forces, they suffered, and their occupational sensitivity to atmosphere worked strongly against them. The philosophy of the orchestra manifested itself in shrugs, which could be seen from the boxes and galleries. But the only outright fiasco of the evening was the ballet of Cupid and Psyche; the six dancers engaged in it were exposed, for the eight minutes of its duration, as men and women who seemed not to know what they were doing. Even Lalage Render, who was admired wherever ballet was understood for her classic perfection, seemed suddenly to be hopping arbitrarily and rather foolishly about the stage, at odds with the music.

The frequent variation of time signature, which was one of the chief characteristics of Giles' score, and which gave his music the variety and subtlety of nuance which was its chief beauty, seemed to be at the root of the trouble; the opera was not precisely as the company had learned it.

When, at last, the curtain descended, there was applause. For was not *The Golden Asse* the chief success of the Music Festival that year? And were there not many good people present who, having been assured that they were to hear a masterwork, were humbly ready to accept whatever they heard as belonging in that category? But it was not the kind of applause which had greeted the earlier performances. When Giles did not come at once from the pit to the stage, Amyas Palfreyman tried to find him, to appear before the curtain with the company. But the applause did not last long enough to make a thorough search possible. The company dispersed to their dressing-rooms greatly disturbed; they had taken a few calls, but they could not forget that at the end of the ballet of Cupid and Psyche there had been several hisses and some murmuring from the gallery.

When Monica went into her dressing-room, Giles was there, sitting on the sofa. His expression was furious, but she was not deceived; there was a forlorn look about him which she had never seen before, and it filled her with pity. She ran to him and tried to put her arms about him, but he pushed her away.

"Well—a fine bloody mess that was," said he.

"Giles, what was wrong?"

"That damned orchestra. Wouldn't follow the score, wouldn't follow my beat—absolute chaos! I explained the whole thing to them beforehand, and they said they understood—anyhow the first fiddle did—but they had no idea what they were doing. I could cheerfully have killed the lot of them!"

"Poor Giles."

"Don't 'Poor Giles' me. I saw you, shuddering and making faces, like Palfreyman and all the rest of them, whenever we got into trouble."

"We didn't. It was only that—"

"You did. You were all mugging like lunatics. Do you think I can't see? You were throwing the show away with both hands. I don't particularly blame you. You're nothing but a bloody little colonial greenhorn who doesn't know anything about professional conduct, but Palfreyman was flat for the last two acts, and he was glaring at me with his eyes sticking out like doorknobs. I could have thrown my stick at him!"

"I'm sure he was just trying to follow your beat, Giles. We all were, honestly. What was the trouble?"

"I've told you the trouble. I was trying to give *my* opera, instead of Brum Benny's, and everybody behaved as if I were demanding some obscene impossibility. I'm almost ready to believe you were all in cahoots to do it."

"Oh, Giles!"

"Yes, you're all hypnotized by the great Sir Benedict. What the composer wants is nothing; it's what Sir Benedict wants that counts. He's bought the whole lot of you with blarney and champagne suppers, and I'm just a stooge."

"No, it isn't like that a bit—"

"What's the good of saying that? D'you think I can't see? What do you supppose I've been doing since I came here? Fighting for my own music. And it appears I've lost the fight."

And so on; much more to the same effect, until there was a soft knock on the door, and Sir Benedict came in.

"Well, we ran into a spot of bother," said he, smiling.

"'We' didn't run into anything. I ran into something. I ran right smack into the fact that my music seems to mean less in this theatre than your ideas about it."

"But my dear fellow, why did you do it?"

"Is it so extraordinary that I should want a chance to conduct my own opera?"

"No. You know what I mean. Why did you try to revise the score at the last minute?"

"I did not revise it; I simply restored it to what I originally meant it to be. I've heard your version, with all the neat, conventional little bridges and re-writes and revises you've stuck into it, to make it the kind of Leipzig Conservatory stuff you'd write if you could write anything at all. I've heard it and it's just so much Zopf!"

"Giles, Giles, nothing went into your score that was mine. You approved every change and every cut; many of the revisions were in your own hand. Now let's be reasonable—"

"Revisions I made with a pistol at my head! I never wanted to revise; I damned well knew when the opera was finished. You were the one who wanted to tinker."

"All right, let's forget that for the moment. But really, my dear man, if you peel off sometimes as many as seven revisions from a score you must expect trouble. The concert-master tells me that the conductor's room was knee-deep in gummed paper—"

"I knew he'd be clearing himself to you! They all run to you! Did he tell you he said he understood the revisions?"

"He told me he argued with you, and finally said they'd do their best. Be sensible, Giles. He doesn't speak English particularly well and I expect you bullied him. The orchestra are first-rate men, but they can't do miracles; you should have realized that when you'd pulled off all the revisions there were bound to be difficulties, because quite a few of them weren't gummed to the parts—they were written in by hand. Still, it's done now, and we'd better say no more about it at present. It's not the end of the world."

Giles would no doubt have retorted that it was the end of the world, simply from necessity to dissent from Domdaniel, but it was at this moment that Signor Petri, the manager, came in. A huge man, of immense dignity, and at this moment deeply solemn.

"Mr. Revelstoke, this was very, very wrong of you," he said.

"I don't see that. If your orchestra can't follow a score, why is it my fault?"

"Mr. Revelstoke, I have been with Gnecchi, and he showed me the orchestra parts and they were incomprehensible in many places. There is a place in Act Three, in the ballet, where there are discrepancies of as much as six bars in some of the parts. Signora Render is very distressed and who wonders? The theatre doctor is with her now. You made her look a fool. You should not have—what is the word I seek—monkeyed with that score.

"I did not monkey with the score. I restored it to what I wrote, and it was as clear as day."

"To you, perhaps. To no one else."

"Damn it, Petri, my score had been revised and patted and pulled and buggered about and I wanted it to be played as I wrote it. Has a composer no rights in this theatre?"

"Every right, Mr. Revelstoke. Every respect. La Fenice has presented new scores by Verdi, do not forget it, and by many very great men. But not even Verdi has a right to insult my audience, and make my artists appear to be analphabets in public, and that is what you have done. Now hear what I have to say—"

"Jesus Christ, Petri, come off it; and stop talking at me like a musical Mussolini, you fat—"

"Now Giles, now Giles," said Domdaniel, "let's not have a scene."

"No, no, no; by no means; no, no, no," said Signor Petri with the calm of a thunderstorm restraining itself.

Giles howled with laughter. "It only needed that!" he cried; "the ultimate touch of farce! No, no, let's not have a scene. The Jew is cool as a cucumber; the Wop is a monument of marble calm. Only the Englishman has lost his phlegm. Why not have a scene? Give me one good reason. I'm the one who's been wronged, and I'd bloody well like to have a bloody great scene."

Signor Petri lifted the hand of a Roman consul. "You forget, Mr. Revelstoke, the presence of the Signora Gowl," said he. "Now listen to me: you will not conduct this opera again in this theatre, and by tomorrow night the orchestra parts must be restored to their proper condition, or my men will refuse to play. Perhaps you do not realize it, but tonight's reception would have been disastrous if we had not been pulled through by our efficient claque. That is all I have to say. An apology to the company, to Gnecchi on behalf of the orchestra, to the Signora Render and a generous recognition to the leader of the claque—these things I leave to your own discretion. Signora. Sir Benedict." With a splendid mingling of courtesy, and scorn for Giles, Signor Petri made his departure.

Giles was laughing again. His laughter seemed a little forced, but it did not stop until Sir Benedict spoke very firmly to him.

"Cut out that nonsense," said he, "and stop playing the fool. Face the fact, Giles, you've made a mess of this business. The best thing you can do is take Petri's advice and go around now and make your peace with everybody. Then we can all forget this fiasco and get ready for the job of putting those parts right tomorrow. It'll take several hours, but if we all get down to it early, it can be done in plenty of time."

"I've no intention of being the goat for you and Petri. Everybody seems to think themselves wronged in this matter. What's the trouble with you? Surely you've gained face? The great Sir Benny can pull the company through anything; you don't catch him messing about with scores. He's even independent of the claque. Hurray for Benny!"

"I've lost face with Petri because I begged him to let you conduct. I personally guaranteed you. But that's no matter. You're perfectly right. You are the one who matters. And that's why you had better start on a round of the dressing-rooms right now, smoothing things over."

"Is that an order, Sir Benedict? Because if so you can relish the unusual experience of having one of your orders disobeyed. I'll do no apologising and no smoothing. Not even with the Signora Gowl. So you can get into your street clothes just as fast as you like, Monica, because I discern that the Big Boss is going to take you out for another of those charming little suppers at the Danieli, and you can both have a lovely time telling one another what a naughty boy I've been."

"Now Giles, no use taking it out on Monica."

"Oh no, let's leave Monica out of it, of course. I've written an opera, and you've put the finishing touches on it. And I've made a singer, and you are in the process of putting the finishing touches on her. She's been my mistress for nearly two years, but you always work best on somebody else's material."

"Giles, don't talk like that," said Monica.

"Why not? Why are we all so mealy-mouthed this evening? Go with Brum Benny if that's what you want. He can do a great deal for you. Much more than I."

"You're being unreasonable and silly, and saying things you don't mean," said Monica. "I'm not going anywhere with anybody; I'm here for you. But I'm not here to encourage you to make a fool of yourself. Sir Benedict is right; this isn't the end of the world. All you have to do is admit you tried something that didn't work, and it'll all be forgotten within a week."

"Nobody is going to hold this against you," said Sir Benedict; "not even Aspinwall."

"What about Aspinwall?"

"He was here tonight. I didn't mean to tell you. He had of course heard about the revisions—I mean the big re-writes, not the trivial things that you dispensed with tonight—and came to hear the work in its new form. A pity he came tonight. But I was talking with him, and he's coming tomorrow night, so—"

"So he'll hear *The Golden Asse* as it ought to be heard, under the baton of the great conductor and with all his personal ideas worked into it! This was all that was needed! You've been canoodling with Aspinwall!"

And Giles broke into a flow of obscene abuse against the critic which was remarkable even for him. His face, so white before, became blotched with red, and there were moments when it seemed that he must choke.

"Christ, this is the end," he said, at last. "This has been a great night for me. You've grabbed my opera, you've grabbed my girl, and now you've been apologizing for me to the man I hate and despise most in the world. All right: take the lot!"

He made for the door, but Monica caught him before he could go.

"Wait just a minute," she said. "I'll come with you."

"I don't want you with me."

"But I want to be with you."

"Oh, you think I need you? The conceit of women! When a

man is angry or down on his luck, he must need one of them.
Get away from me. You've been insufferable ever since you came
back from Canada with that potty little bit of money. Do you
think I haven't seen you playing the suffering saint all over the
place, sacrificing yourself right and left, and thinking you were
getting immortality in return? Because you gouged a tuppenny-
halfpenny Canadian trust, you crooked little bitch? Not a penny
of it came out of your hide. Because you used your money to buy
a good part in my opera, do you think I'm eternally sold to you?
Oh, really, Monica, you're even stupider than I'd supposed! Of
course it was your money that got you into *The Golden Asse;*
what else? Not your talent, I can assure you. Not your slate-
pencil squeal on a high D. Get out of my sight; your vapid mug
makes me spewl I've made a passable singer of you, and taught
you the elements of your other principal use. And I'm heartily
sick of you."

This time he went.

(4)

NEXT MORNING AT half-past nine (which is bright and early for
people who have finished their previous working day at mid-
night) Sir Benedict and Monica were hard at it in Petri's office,
restoring the orchestral parts to their original form; Domdaniel
dictated, Monica transcribed (those who have taken music from
dictation know what fidgetty work it is) and Gnecchi gummed
the freshly-written slips into their proper places on the music.
By half-past four the job was done, and that evening the opera
was performed, after a few early moments of nerves, better than
ever before. It was not until Monica was back at her hotel that
she had the time and the calm of mind to consider the scene of
the night before.

Giles had disappeared. He had left no forwarding address, but
had gone very early in the morning, presumably to catch a train.

But what train no one could say, for at Padua he could have gone southward, or from Milan he could have made his way back to England. Sir Benedict had taken this news calmly.

"He'll cool in the same skin he got hot in," said he.

"You don't think I ought to try to find him?"

"It will be easier for all of us, if we don't meet for a few weeks. Do you particularly want to see him soon?"

"Yes; I'm worried about him."

"What a forgiving nature you have."

"No; he didn't mean what he said. You know how terribly he exaggerates everything."

"And so you're willing to hunt him up, and let him make a doormat of you."

"No, no; but I'd like to be sure that he's all right."

"Well, I never give advice in love affairs, but I've been in love myself, and it's always useful to preserve your self-respect."

"I'm sure you're right, Sir Benedict."

Of course he was right. She knew that Giles' hard words about her buying herself into his opera were just the froth of his anger. Still, when all the anger had been discounted, might there not be some drop of truth left? Was that the way he really thought about her? Had he really endured her simply because she could bring him the money—little enough, in terms of the sums involved in staging even so modest a production as *The Golden Asse*—that he needed? No, that was unthinkable. If money was all he wanted, he need not have slept with her, and though he had never told her that he loved her, he had never concealed his pleasure in their physical union. Much more than a physical union it had become, and well she knew it; not only could Giles not conceal his need for her and his dependence on her tenderness and unquestioning adoration (for that was what it was, and she could not pretend otherwise) but the spite of Persis was strong corroborative evidence. Nevertheless, Monica had not the self-confidence or the detachment to trust her judgement in this matter. Who has, that is deeply in love? The love which is strong as steel under one assault, may crumble like ash under the breath of another. Giles had touched Monica on her weakest point, which was her belief in her own worth as a woman, a lover; she was deeply convinced that she was, like Fotis in the opera, only a clumsy pretence-enchantress.

She pondered for another day on the subject, turning it over and over, until at last self-doubt, masquerading as self-respect, made her write a letter.

Dearest Giles,

After thinking for a long time about what you said on Thursday night, I am sure we had better break off, and not see each other again—at least not for a long time. Of course I didn't take what you said at its face value, because I knew how angry and hurt you were. But you hurt me very much. Just the fact that you knew so well how to hurt me makes me think that you had been turning some of those things over in your mind, and when you were angry, they came out.

What I have felt about you has been plain, I think. I could have said some of it, if you had wanted that, but I tried to show it in other ways. You once told me that when you loved me you would say so, and as you have never said it I know that you don't, and Thursday night—even with all the anger left out, makes me fear that you could very easily despise me. So I won't come for any more lessons, and perhaps after a while when I don't feel about you as I do now, we will be able to meet again, quite ordinarily.

Please understand what I am trying to say. I could give everything for you, even self-respect and wanting to be a really good singer and all that, if you wanted me to. But you don't, and I won't go on forcing it on you. But as I can't stay with you and be a doormat, I have decided to leave you and do the best I can on my own. I love you, and I always shall, but you don't want love. So God bless you (though I know how you hate people to say that) and I will ask Bun to pick up my things from Tite Street.

MONICA

It was not in the least like any of the letters she wanted to write—the splendidly haughty one, the moving unaffected one, the poetic one fit for an anthology of great love-letters—but she had neither the heart nor the talent for literary flights. She sent it off to the Tite Street flat, and concluded her engagement in Venice in deep distress of mind. Even the great reception which *The Golden Asse* was given at its last performance, and the good notices she had from all the critics, and the flowers from some unknown music-lover, and the eloquent farewell of Signor Petri, had no power to ease her inward hurt. She changed her plans for a holiday in Italy, and a visit to Amy Neilson, and returned to London as fast as the airways could take her.

(5)

MONICA HAD NOT long been in her flat in Courtfield Gardens before Mrs. Merry appeared.

"I've brought you a few letters which came during the past two or three days," said she. They were dull; one with a Canadian stamp, addressed in George Medwall's careful hand, was on top.

"There were no messages," said Mrs. Merry. "Mr. Revelstoke telephoned yesterday to know when you would be home, and as I had had your telegram I said you'd be back this evening."

Was Giles anxious to see her, then? He had been too sure of her devotion to show any concern about her goings and comings before. Did he feel that he should unsay the cruel things he had said in Venice? But cruel things cannot be unsaid; they may be forgiven, and Monica was ready to forgive, but she was certain that she would not forget. She unpacked because it gave her something to do—something which would keep her in her flat. But all the time she wanted to go to Tite Street. She must not do so, for her letter had been plain; she had broken with Giles. Apparently he had received her letter, and he wanted her; otherwise why that unaccustomed enquiry? Did he think he knew

her so well that he could be sure she would run to him as soon
as she came back to London? Then he did not know her at all.
Desperately as she loved him, she had some pride; she must
preserve her self-respect, as Sir Benedict said.

But suppose he were lonely and hurt? The bad performance
of *The Golden Asse* had ravaged him as only she knew. It was
all very well for Sir Benedict and Petri to say that it had not been
disastrously bad; they meant only that the audience had not
hissed—or had only hissed once. To Giles anything below the
high mark of achievement which he set for himself was disaster.
What had Ripon called him, in mockery? A Satanic genius?
True, for he was proud as Lucifer. But he had not Lucifer's self-
sufficiency. She knew that, better than anyone else in the world.
For although he would not tell her how much he needed her
tenderness and understanding, she could feel it. And feeling his
need, could she withhold herself from him? Was she not, in this
realm, more knowledgeable than he? Was she not one of the
Eros-men, and had not Domdaniel called her a fellow-artist?
Should she not have a spirit above personal hurts? Should she
not be ashamed to withhold her presence and her comfort from
Giles as a means of revenge?

Yes, what she was doing was revenge—a tortured, unworthy
passion which fouled her love. What she was doing was all
those things he hated, and rightly. It was provincial. It was
common. It was probably colonial and Saltertonian and Non-
conformist and typically American and lower-middle-class and
non-U and all the other things he taunted her with being, in
his impatient desire that she should be, like himself, a true
artist who looked at the world with level and open eyes.

It had been a little after nine o'clock when she reached Courtfield Gardens from the air terminal. It was half-past eleven when
she climbed the stairs in Tite Street.

(6)

THE HOUSE HAD A Sunday night stillness, and the tiny globes
which Mrs. Klein used to light the stairs exaggerated the chapel-
like gloom of its Ruskin Gothic. On the second flight, which led
to Giles' top floor, the cat Pyewacket was sitting; he miaouled
when Monica stooped to stroke him, and ran upward ahead of
her. The door at the top of the stair was closed.

She remembered that earlier time when she had returned from
a journey to find Giles in bed with Persis; the door had not been
closed then. Did this show some greater degree of caution? But
suppose Persis were again with him? Did it really make any
difference to the consuming fact that she loved him, and could
not live apart from him, and must therefore endure anything
from him? If Persis were there, she would have to accept it,
and drudge for Persis as she drudged for Giles. The abjection of
her love was complete.

The door was locked. She had a key—the only key other than
Giles' own, and he had given it to her not in order that she might
have free access to the flat, but because he was always losing his
own key, and wanted another in safe keeping in case he should
at some time find himself locked out. She unlocked the door
and pushed it open. It moved heavily, for a blanket lay on the
floor against it.

She had meant to call "Giles"— but the gas stifled the name
in her throat and she retreated down the stairs, choking and gasping. Pyewacket, who had rushed through the door ahead of her,
dashed out of the flat and down the stairs, spitting and snarling.

Get help? No; go in. She crumpled her scarf over her mouth
and nose, and ran through the living room to the windows, which
were closed but not fastened, and opened easily. Was it safe to
turn on a light? She knew nothing of gas. Would it ignite? Would
there be an explosion? Where was Giles?

Giles lay on the floor, in pyjamas and dressing-gown. In a score of films which Monica had seen, the discoverer of someone in such a position ran to them at once, felt the pulse, listened to the heart, stared into the face. But she was so frightened that she shrank against the windows, to get air and to be as far as possible from him. It was some time before she found courage to creep forward (why? did she fear to waken him?) and look at his face in the very little light which came through the windows. His skin was dark; it seemed to her that it was black. His lips were parted, and he did not breathe. She should take his pulse. But she dared not touch him. He was dead, and she was afraid of his body.

It did not occur to her until this minute to turn off the gas-fire which hissed a foot or two from his head. Now she did so, walking around the body in a wide circle because she dared not reach across it to the gas-tap. And as she knelt by the grate she saw that in each of his hands was a piece of paper. In one of these she recognized her letter.

Was it her first thought that she had driven him to take his life? It was not. Her first thought was that if that letter were found, she would be accused of having done so.

Danger dispersed her panic. She must behave sensibly now, or God knew what would happen to her. She retreated to the window again, and made her plan.

Thank Heaven she was wearing gloves! Monica was not a great reader of detective fiction, but she knew that dreadful retributive magic could be worked with fingerprints. With luck, nobody need know that she had ever been in the flat. Less fearful than before (but still fearing that he might wake and blast her with some sarcasm, as he had done at times when he woke from sleep to find her looking into his beloved face) she went to the body, and gently drew the letter from the right hand fingers. It was not difficult. With it safely in the pocket of her coat, she looked quickly through the flat. A few of Persis' undergarments were, as usual, hanging wetly above the bath. Leave them? Yes.

Let Perse look out for herself. Then she crept back into the living-room and closed the windows as they had been before.

The other paper? Without a light she could not tell what it was, but it was a long clipping from a newspaper. Well, there could be no harm to her in that. Without a farewell glance at the black face Monica turned on the gas once again, tip-toed to the door, closed and locked it, and went as quietly as she could down the stairs. The blanket could not be pulled back into place, but that could not be helped. Pyewacket was at the street door, and she and the cat went out together into Tite Street. The squalling of babies in the hospital over the way was audible almost until she reached the Embankment. It was now twenty-five minutes to twelve.

She did not stay there long. Mist was rising from the river, and the Embankment was cold and inhospitable. Nevertheless, there were people there: lovers soddenly embracing, hands groping beneath their mackintoshes; a man and woman in middle age, talking passionately in some unknown language; one of London's inassimilable poor, filthily bearded and rustling from the newspapers which were stuffed in the legs of his trousers. Monica walked slowly, trying to think, but repeating: Giles is dead; he wanted them to think I drove him to it; he wanted to get me into trouble; he loved me; he didn't love me; he wanted to spite me; he did it from despair; he did it for revenge; he hated me. It led nowhere.

A policeman passed and re-passed her. "Anything wrong, miss?" said he.

"No; nothing thanks."

"Waiting for anyone?"

"No."

"Well, if I may suggest it, miss, if you've seen all you want to see of the river, it might be a good idea to go home. Would you like me to get you a cab?"

"Thank you; that would be very kind."

Why a cab? She was well-dressed, and wearing gloves. Amy

always said that a lady should never appear on the street without
gloves. How providential it was, sometimes, to know the ropes
of ladyhood.

(7)

THE CORONER WAS that fortunate creature, a man really happy in
his work. He delivered his summing-up to the jury with a professional flourish and a sense of style which, without being in any
way unseemly, showed a degree of satisfaction.

They had heard the evidence, said the Coroner, and he hoped
that they had heeded his two or three adjurations to mark it
well, for it was of a complexity not common in such investiga-
tions. The body of Giles Adrian Revelstoke had been identified
by Mr. Griffith Hopkin-Griffiths of Neuadd Goch, Llanavon, his
step-father; who had also testified that his stepson was thirty-
four years old and so far as he knew had been in good health.
The body had been discovered at half-past nine on the morning
of September 29 by his landlady, Mrs. Maria Augusta Klein, and
his pupil, Miss Monica Gall. Miss Gall, who acted as a secretary
and amanuensis to Mr. Revelstoke, had arrived to do some work
on the magazine *Lantern*, of which Mr. Revelstoke was one of
the editors, and had found the door of his flat locked—an unusual circumstance. She had called Mrs. Klein, who assured her
that Mr. Revelstoke was at home, and accompanied her to the
door of his flat. After repeated loud knocking, Miss Gall had
opened the door at Mrs. Klein's suggestion, using a key which,
as a member of the *Lantern* staff, she had with her. They found
Mr. Revelstoke dead on the floor, with some evidences of a
paroxysm, and had called the police.

The evidence of the police was that there was a strong smell
of coal gas in the room, that the windows were closed, and that
a blanket had apparently been used to block the crack under the
main doorway. The police pathologist had testified, however, that

death was not caused by gas, but by suffocation. Although the
tap of the gas-fire was turned on when the police arrived, no
gas was coming through and examination of the meter—one of
the familiar shilling-in-the-slot meters—showed that it had run
out at a time which could not be determined. It appeared, therefore, that Mr. Revelstoke had been overcome with gas, and that
when the gas in the room began to disperse—for the windows did
not give a tight seal to the room—he had partly recovered.
Nausea from the gas had caused him to regurgitate a considerable
quantity of vomitus into his mouth and in his partly-conscious
state he had been unable to free himself from it; the heavy,
snoring breathing characteristic of certain stages of gas poison-
ing had caused him to draw a quantity of vomitus into his lungs,
which had brought about death by suffocation. The opinion of
the pathologist was that this had happened six or seven hours
before he was discovered, which was to say at some time between two and three in the morning.

A verdict of suicide would certainly occur to the jury, but
they must weigh the following considerations very heavily
against it. The evidence of Miss Persis Kinwellmarshe (present
in the court with her father, Rear-Admiral Sir Percy Kinwellmarshe) and another associate in the *Lantern* work was that she
had seen the dead man after his return from Venice, and that
he had appeared to be in his usual spirits, sardonic but cheerful.
She had prepared a picnic supper which they had shared on the
night of Sunday, September 28. Mr. Revelstoke had spoken then
in his usual amusingly unrestrained fashion of a critique of his
opera *The Golden Asse*, written by Stanhope Aspinwall of the
Sunday *Argus*, which she had brought to him. This was the newspaper clipping which had been found in the dead man's hand;
she had received it from Mr. Phanuel Tuke, a co-editor of
Lantern, who had thought that Mr. Revelstoke would like to
have it. The dead man had laughed at Mr. Aspinwall's critical
pretensions.

Mr. Stanhope Aspinwall, the respected music critic, had given
evidence that he had never known Mr. Revelstoke personally,

though he had once sat in front of him at a concert, and had received two or three very abusively-worded letters from him. Therefore there could be no question of enmity between these men. The critique found with the body referred to the revised version of the composer's opera which Mr. Aspinwall had travelled to Venice to see within the past fortnight; he had seen it twice, and some part of his review had been devoted to a comparison between the opera as conducted by the composer, and by Sir Benedict Domdaniel. He had said that Mr. Revelstoke was a thoroughly incompetent conductor, and in that capacity was the worst enemy of his own genius as a composer. The intention of the review was favourable, and certainly it must be considered so by an unprejudiced reader.

There was the evidence, however, of John Macarthur Eccles, the other friend who had visited him on Sunday night, that Mr. Revelstoke was extremely sensitive to criticism, although he pretended to hardihood respecting it. There was the evidence, also, of Sir Benedict Domdaniel, the dead man's musical and literary executor, that Mr. Revelstoke had been under unusual strain during the revision of *The Golden Asse*, which had brought on exaggerated alternations of melancholy and defiant high spirits, and that Mr. Revelstoke had left Venice abruptly after being told by Sir Benedict and the manager of the Fenice opera house that he could not conduct his opera there again.

There was the evidence also of Mr. Phanuel Tuke that the magazine *Lantern* was in financial straits.

Taken with a romantic predisposition this added up to a story of a gifted young man who felt that the world had scorned him and who had taken his own life in a period of depression. But on the other hand, there had been equally strong evidence that Giles Revelstoke had loyal friends, that his latest and most ambitious work had been received with acclaim on the continent, and by Britain's foremost musical journalist had been mentioned as "of the same great family as Mozart's *Magic Flute*, one of the serenely wise creations which form the crown of beauty in music". A conductor of world fame—Sir Benedict Domdaniel again—had said that Giles Revelstoke was a composer of unquestionable genius who was just beginning to come into his mature productive period. Therefore, before they blotted the close of such a life with the stain of a suicide verdict, let the jury reflect that while it may have been possible, and indeed seemed probable, that Giles Revelstoke meant to take his life, he had not in fact done so; the gas supply had failed, and had it not been for the unlucky fact that he had suffocated before fully waking he would not have died. Under the circumstances the Coroner recommended a verdict of death by misadventure.

The jury were not of a romantic turn of mind. They were, with two or three exceptions, elderly, poor men who hung about in Horseferry Road with the hope of being called for duty on coroner's juries, counting the few shillings they received as a pleasant windfall to add to their pensions. After a brief drag at their pipes in the retiring-room they shuffled back into court, and gave the Coroner the verdict for which he had asked.

And so it was pronounced. The Coroner, who did not get a distinguished audience every day, and who liked to give a cultured twist to his duties when he could, had passed the time while the jury were conferring, scraping in the ashes of his mind for a live coal. And, from some long-ago popular article about Schubert, he produced one which flamed quite brightly for the moment.

"By the death of Giles Adrian Revelstoke," said he, "music loses a rich treasure, but even fairer hopes."

Good, kindly man, he almost wished that he had not said it, for so many of his hearers wept.

(8)

IDEALLY, IMPORTANT THINGS should happen late, as the climax of the day, but the inquest took place in the morning, and from its close until bedtime all was slow, torturing diminution for Monica.

There was luncheon with Stanhope Aspinwall, who sought her out when the court adjourned, asked the favour of her company and bore her off to the ladies' annex of his distinguished club. He was a short, bald man, one of the dwindling army of pince-nez wearers, precise in speech, and clearly burdened with guilt.

"If I had for one instant supposed," he said as they took coffee, "that my comments on his conducting—fully justified, I firmly insist—might have put such a dreadful thought in his head nothing could have induced me to publish them in that form. For there was asperity; I admit to asperity. He had pestered me with letters—such letters as nothing would induce me to show to anyone, though I have kept them—and my personal feeling toward him was cool, though certainly not hostile. But for his talent—let us be honest, and say genius—I had nothing but admiration. I say this to you because you have become associated with his work in the mind of the public, and I expect that you will be even more so in future. Of course it is foolish for me to link myself even in my own mind with this tragedy, but I do so. How can I do otherwise, foolish or not? Those letters—who would not have resented them? I admit to you freely that this will be a dreadful lesson to me. Asperity: asperity is the bosom-sin of the critic."

The afternoon papers had not, all things considered, much to say about the inquest. The worst comment was headed—

ADMIRAL'S DAUGHTER IN LOVE-NEST
"My Knickers": Lush Model

Another one dug up the fact that Giles had been a regular visitor to the prison where Odingsels was serving his time, and spoke sternly of highbrow filth and *Lantern*. But Revelstoke was not likely to be known to most of their readers and they had rottener fish to fry.

Mrs. Merry insisted on a long heart-to-heart with Monica, wearing an exaggerated version of her usual expression of anguished distinction. "Her haemorrhoidal rictus", Giles had called it, and the phrase recurred to Monica again and again, spoken in Giles' voice, as the landlady talked.

"I shall never forget the night that he and Sir Benedict played for me," said Mrs. Merry; "a moment to be cherished in memory, now alas, in sorrow. It was his kindness which won one." 'She talked for a satisfactory hour, revising her memory of the past in the light of the present.

Monica found that she had to give Bun Eccles a scratch dinner in her flat. He clung to her, and he would talk of nothing but Giles. He had brought a bottle of whisky, of which he drank all but one tot, and it was only by showing great firmness that she kept him from passing out.

"What stonkers me, Monny, is that it was gas." This was the burden of his cry. "Poor old Giles, to go by the gas route. Because I'd hocussed his meter, you see, Monny. Made it give more than it wanted to for a bob. And if I hadn't done that, there mightn't have been enough to do for him, see? Maybe if it had conked as little as five minutes sooner—Jesus God, drowning in his own puke like that, poor old chap! I killed him, Monny. No, it's no use saying I didn't. Maybe I didn't in law, but I did in fact, and I'll always have to live with that. God knows what it'll do to me. It's not so tough for you, Monny—no, no, I don't mean you're not hurt like us all, and worse than anybody. But you've nothing to reproach yourself with. You were always wonderful to him. Yes, yes, you were the only one. Old Perse was bellowing like a heifer in court today, because her old Dad had been giving her the gears. She gave Giles that piece of old Aspinwall's; shouldn't have done it, of course, but who was to know? Now she's saying she killed the only man she loved, or who really loved her. Aw, but—Perse was just a recreation to Giles; he knew what she was. Anybody could butter Perse's bun, and he knew it. But you were true to him, so you haven't anything to regret. And you're game, Monny. Game as Ned Kelly, and you'll get on your feet again. Wish I thought I'd do the same. You brought him life, Monny, and me, with my meddling, I greased the skids for him. How am I going to face that, every morning of my life? Poor old Giles. The best of chaps."

At last she got rid of Bun, and when he was gone she wished him back. For what was she to do now? She had not opened her letters for several days, and she turned to them to avoid the horror of thought.

Only three were other than bills and circulars. The McCorkills, in the kindest terms, offered her the refuge of Beaver Lodge, if she wanted it; if she wanted to be alone, said Meg McCorkill, that was how it would be; they hadn't seen anything of her for a long time, but if she needed them, she had only to say the word.

The second letter was from Humphrey Cobbler. Had anybody troubled to tell her, he asked, that Veronica Bridgetower was pregnant? The child was expected late in December or early in January. He was sure she did not know, and it was none of his business, but if the Bridgetower Trust did not see fit to warn her that, in a few months, she might be displaced as beneficiary of that money, he thought it pretty shabby. And where could he get copies of some of Giles Revelstoke's songs? Was there a chance that he could get his hands on a score of *The Discoverie of Witchcraft?* He had been asked, out of the blue, to do something for a special program of the Canadian Broadcasting Corporation, and he wanted to make their eyes pop. Or ears pop. Or whatever popped when you got a musical suprise. Any use writing direct to Revelstoke himself? He wished her well in Venice and was hers with love.

The third letter was the one from George Medwall which had been waiting for her when she returned from Venice. It read:

Dear Monica;
    This is not an easy letter to write, because I am not sure there was ever anything definite between us. Still and all, I had definite ideas that I wanted to marry you, and maybe you got some idea of that kind from something I said. But we have not had a chance to talk for a long time what with your mother's death when you were last home and being very busy with the concert.

The fact is if there was ever anything like an engagement between us or even a firm understanding I am asking you now to release me from it as if you do I am going to ask another girl as I am in a position to do so now. You know her. She is Teresa Rook whom you will remember as Mr. Holterman's secretary and a cracker-jack in her job. It is plain now and has been for quite a while that our paths have seperated, but there is no reason why we can not be friends. I am not saying a word to Tessie till I hear from you which I hope will be as soon as convenient.

Your sincere friend
GEORGE MEDWALL

Her first feeling was one of surprise that George should ever have thought it possible that she might marry him. This gave way at once to shame at such snobbery, and a recollection that she had once had fuzzy, but real, designs on George. But it did seem queer now, and there was no use pretending. Had not George said to her many times, during the period of their intimacy, "Get wise to yourself, Monny; you have to get wise to yourself, or you're everybody's stooge." Since those days she had been trying to get wise to herself.

Of course she remembered Tessie Rook; she was just made for George; together they would go far, and George would probably end up as president of the C.A.A., a towering figure in the allied worlds of sandpaper and glue. She sat down to write a generous reply at once, and tears which she had not been able to weep in the coroner's court poured out now, pretending to be tears of happiness, as she thought of good old George and that sweet Tessie.

But in the end this diversion was at an end, and Monica was left with no course but to face the fact that Giles Revelstoke had not been dead when she took her letter from his hand, and that if she had thought more of him and less of herself he need not have died at all. By her selfishness and littleness of spirit she had killed him.

(9)

IN DESCRIBING DOMDANIEL as Giles Revelstoke's musical and
literary executor the Coroner was premature; but it was Sir
Benedict's desire to act in that capacity, and he lost no time in
showing his fitness for it. Giles left no will. When Griffith Hopkin-
Griffiths arrived at the Tite Street flat, late on the day that the
body was discovered, it was to find Sir Benedict virtually in
charge; with great tact he undertook to have Giles' belongings
packed and sent to Wales; from that it was no great step to secure
permission to take care of his manuscripts until their fate was
decided. It was not many days until a great music publishing
house showed interest in acquiring at least some of them.

In the period immediately following Giles' death it might have
appeared that Sir Benedict used Monica without proper regard
for her feelings. He insisted that she pack all the dead man's
clothing and books and arrange for their removal; she found
that she had to sell the furniture, which was of small value, to a
dealer in the King's Road; she had to arrange for the removal of
all the rubbish which comprised the files and business apparatus
of *Lantern*. Mrs. Klein needed her flat, and it had to be cleared.
Tuke and Tooley had nowhere to house the wreckage of the
magazine; Raikes Brothers certainly did not want it. As Monica
could not bring herself to get rid of it, she put it in storage, in
her own name.

Thus she was in and out of the flat a dozen times a day, arranging for the sale of things which had grown dear to her, including the very bed in which she had so often lain with him.
But nothing was worse than the making of a rough catalogue of
his music, which she prepared under Domdaniel's direction.
Thin, pale and silent, she did as she was bidden.

When the great house of Bachofen began to show interest in
the music, it took Mrs. Hopkins-Griffiths surprisingly little time

to arrange for Sir Benedict to have full power to deal with them. The daily papers had taken small interest in Giles' death, but the important Sunday papers carried long articles and many letters about him, and within three weeks England was given to understand that she had lost a man of consequence. The first person to see the possibility of this situation was Phanuel Tuke, who arranged with a publisher to bring out a collection of Giles' *Lantern* articles, prefaced with an appreciative essay by himself; for this purpose he wanted the *Lantern* files, and was greatly vexed with Monica because they were already in storage, and Miss Tooley was put to the trouble of doing her master's drudgery in the British Museum.

It was a shrewd move on the part of the music publishers to put themselves behind the promotion of a Commemorative Concert of Giles' work; it would serve as a test of his possible popularity. Sir Benedict was holding out against their offer to buy some of the publication rights; he wanted them to buy all. They were willing to bide their time. Meanwhile they were ready to spend something to see how much Giles was potentially worth.

The announcement of the concert, to take place in late November, was productive of more interest than the publishers had thought possible in their most sanguine dreams. Among musical people there was a sudden vogue for Giles Revelstoke, much of it attributable to Stanhope Aspinwall, whose two commemorative articles, published on successive Sundays in the *Argus*, set off the enthusiasm of lesser men. Not that Aspinwall was wholly commendatory; the faults which he had found in Giles' work while he was alive were still censured—but his virtues were praised much more generously. The change in emphasis, though carefully engineered, was noteworthy and effective.

"Believe me, Monny, if you want to attract real, serious attention to your work, you can't beat being dead," said Bun Eccles. He had several sketches of Giles and reproduction rights were selling well. "I've half a mind to try it myself, one of these days. Let 'em think they drove me to it by neglect. Trouble is, how are you going to cash in when you're dead?"

Sir Benedict was organizing the concert, and the first artist he secured for it was Monica. Speaking for the publishers, he was able to propose the highest fee she had ever been offered in her brief career.

"But am I the right person?" she asked. "My name won't draw anybody into the hall. Why not Evelyn Burnaby?"

"She'll be there, as well," said Domdaniel. "A good deal of Giles' latest and best stuff was written for you, and that's very good publicity, discreetly used."

Monica did not like that suggestion, and said so.

"We'll have lots of time for fine feelings afterward," said he. "Our job right now is to get the best and showiest hearing possible for Giles' work. He taught you some of the things you'll sing; they're built into your voice, precisely as he wanted them. Don't fuss."

"I hate to have my personal relationship with him exploited."

"It's your artistic relationship with him that's being exploited— if that's what you want to call it. Years after Trafalgar, Lady Hamilton used to go to concerts where Braham was billed to sing *The Death of Nelson*, and at a telling moment in the song she would faint noisily and have to be carried out. I'm not asking you to do anything like that. I'm asking you to make known the authentic voice of Giles Revelstoke—because that's what you are —and to begin the establishment of an unquestioned tradition about the performance of some of his best work. You ought to be damned thankful you're in a position to do it. The fact that you were his mistress is trivial. If that's what's troubling you, for God's sake go back to Pumpkin Centre or wherever it is you came from, and set up shop as a teacher. Now, make up your mind, and don't waste my time."

Monica had never known Sir Benedict in this mood, and it did not take her long to decide that she would do as she was told. Amy Neilson had been right; she was not a big person; she must be obedient to her betters.

Still, the idea was hateful to her, and when she told Sir Benedict of her decision he knew it, and softened a little.

"There's a necessary element of showmanship in every performing artist, however great or however sensitive," said he, "and without it they're not worth a damn. As long as you have it under control, it's quite all right. Don't fuss; I'll see you through."

Don't fuss. But it wasn't fussing; it was terror barely kept under control. Terror that, while cataloguing Giles' music, she might throw herself on the floor and howl like a dog. Terror that, when she haggled with a secondhand dealer about Giles' bed-clothes, she might wrap the counterpane about her and rush shrieking into the King's Road, like widowed Hecuba. Terror that, when she saw a policeman, she might cry, "I killed him," and put out her wrists for the handcuffs.

She knew very well that she would not do any of these things. They were not things she *would* do but rather things which, from time to time she *wanted* to do. She was astonished at her own capacity to suffer inwardly, to give way to excesses of grief and panic, and at the same time to present a stoical front to the world. Three times she dreamed that Giles came to her, his eyes ablaze, his mouth distorted with rage, and menaced her with a bloody knife. But although this dream paralyzed her with terror, its after-effect was life-enhancing, and she woke moist, panting and stirred to the depths of her being. Her mirror told her the strange news that such dreams were becoming. "Get wise to yourself, Monny," said George Medwall; she felt that she had never been farther from self-knowledge in her life, though self-possession never deserted her.

Nevertheless, her nervous exhaustion could not be wholly concealed. Molloy was well aware of it, for she worked with him every day, in preparation for the concert, and he was unsparing. Since the incident of the Vic-Wells ball his attitude toward her had changed; he was less eager to impress, he was more diffident and yet more intimate; he demanded more and hectored less. She had quite lost her fear of him, and they were good friends.

"You're riding for a fall," said he, one October day after a particularly rigorous hour. "You want a vacation the worst way. Mind, you'll be all right for the concert; I guarantee't. But after that, I wouldn't want to be answerable. Get away t'hell out o' this for a while. Go back to Canada, why don't you? Then come back and start afresh. You're on the quicks of your nerves now, and that can't last. Sit down for a while and I'll get Norah to give us all some tea."

A few days later it was Sir Benedict who suggested a holiday. "I'd thought about Canada for Christmas," she said. "Some friends of mine are having a crisis in their lives, and I'd like to be there." And then, greatly to his astonishment, she told him about Solly and Veronica Bridgetower, and the curious condition which governed the existence of the Bridgetower Trust. "So you see how it is," she concluded; "if they have a son—and I truly hope they will—it will be the end of all this for me. My good luck has depended on their bad luck, and ever since I found out about it, I've felt like the most horrible kind of gold-digger. If it hadn't been for *The Golden Asse* I couldn't have gone on. I'm glad I did, but that's all over now, and I want to behave decently, if there's any way of doing so."

Thus it was that, with Sir Benedict's permission, and some arrangements with Boykin, she found herself in Cockspur Street a few days later, booking a steamship passage for the last week in November. As she filled out applications, her gaze travelled upward to a poster which urged settlers to come to Canada at once. Radiating health and goodwill like a red-hot stove, a young man in shirt-sleeves stood in a field of wheat, his bronzed face split with a dazzling grin. I suppose he represents my country, thought Monica, though I've never met anybody like that in my life. Odd that he should be so young, and that I feel so old.

Before the week of the concert, there was a duty which could not be shirked; she must go to Neuadd Goch, and present an account of what she had been doing to Giles' mother. She longed to get out of it. She would have done anything to avoid it. But Domdaniel could not go, and there was no one else. So, in a dreary wet week she went, and found herself once again in the familiar house though not, she thanked Heaven, in the bedroom she had occupied before.

Mrs. Hopkin-Griffiths was more business-like than Monica had expected. She understood everything; she accepted the few pounds which had been realized by the sale of Giles' odds and ends without shame; she signed the papers which needed signing. It took about an hour.

"Thank you, my dear," she said when it was all done. "I'm sure you know how grateful Griff and I are for all of this. I'm sure it must have been hateful—all the selling and arranging and ridding-out. I couldn't have faced it, and Griff hates London so much. You and Sir Benedict have been perfectly wonderful. Funny—I've always been the kind of person that people do things for. I wonder why? I wish there were something we could do for you. Of course, it was always so extraordinary about you being Giles' pupil; he never had any others, you know; and turning up like that at Christmas. It seemed a sort of fated thing—but I suppose that's silly, really."

"You will be coming to London for the concert, won't you?"

"Dear, will you think me utterly dreadful if I say that I won't be? I honestly don't think I could face it. No, I shall stay right here. The funeral was too awful. I don't know how I got through it."

"Certainly for those who knew him, a concert of his music, at this time, may be very moving."

"Do you think so? Perhaps. I couldn't say. You see, I don't really know anything about Giles' music. I really knew nothing of that side of him. Was his opera really terribly good?"

"Stanhope Aspinwall keeps relating it to *The Magic Flute.*"

"Really? Is that very good? Griff and I never saw it, you know. Is it likely to be done again, ever? When it was on in London Griff was seedy and we simply didn't feel up to the journey at that time. And then when it was done in Venice, we had already been to Baden, where we've gone for years—really I don't think

I could face the winter without it—and what with the extra expense, and the time it was done, and everything, we simply didn't make it. Of course I reproach myself now. But what's done's done, eh?—Would you like to see his grave?"

Monica had determined that she would not go back to London without visiting Giles' grave, but she did not want to do so with Dolly Hopkin-Griffiths. But there was nothing for it but to do as she was asked, and so they set off on foot.

The churchyard at Llanavon was a pretty one in summer, but in the early days of November it was dank and cold, and the dripping yews were at their gloomiest. The mound beneath which Giles lay had been sodded, but had not subsided to the level of the ground and as yet there was no marker; but he lay in the influence, so to speak, of a large Celtic cross which was dedicated to the memory of the Hopkin-Griffiths family. It was an early Victorian cross, ugly but strong, and the sight of it raised Monica's spirits; it was so solid, it must surely last forever. She was glad that Giles lay there among all those red-faced Welsh squires, with open countryside beyond the churchyard walls; it stilled a deep feeling which had troubled her that he was somewhere, agonized, confined and alone. This was, she well knew, a pagan concept of death, but she had not until this time been able to subdue it.

Mrs. Hopkin-Griffiths prayed briefly, and wept a little, but she had no power to remain silent for long. "I come every day, unless the weather is simply dreadful," said she. "Guilt, I suppose. You see, my dear, I have a terrible feeling that I failed Giles. Can it have been about marrying Griff? But Griff was as good to Giles as Giles would let him be—and I felt I had a right to happiness, you know. But children judge so harshly. I loved him very much, and he surely knew that. But I've always been such a selfish woman, and silly, too—yes, don't deny it, dear, out of politeness. I don't know why it all went wrong. I've argued with myself about it so much, and Griff has been quite wonderful about reassuring me. But all the same, I come back to the

feeling that if I hadn't failed him—whenever or however it was
—Giles wouldn't be here now. Griff won't let me say it, but I'll
say it to you, dear: I sometimes feel I killed Giles."

Monica, who was utterly convinced that she had killed Giles
herself, did what she could to dispel his mother's unhappiness.

"You're very kind, dear," said Dolly; "although we haven't
really known you long, Griff and I both think of you as a very
special friend. Indeed—I said we wanted to do something for
you, and I don't see why everything has to be so secret—you
know those musical manuscripts of Giles'? Would you like one
of them? Sir Benedict suggested it, really. He said that one of
them was dedicated to you. Perhaps you'd like to have it. I don't
know whether it's a proper gift or simply a piece of scrap. But
I'm sure Giles must have been fond of you. I wish he'd been
fonder of you, or somebody like you. We had hoped it would be
Ceinwen, but she's been engaged for months to a dentist in
Rhyll; Griff likes him, because he's descended from Brochwell
Yscythrog, but I do wish he were a proper doctor, and not a
dentist; but there it is; you can't have everything. It would have
made me very happy to see him settled, with somebody to look
after him."

That night, when they were going to bed, Dolly brought up
the matter of the manuscript of *Kubla Khan* again. "I'll write to
Sir Benedict, and say you're to have it," said she. "And my dear,
perhaps you'd like to have this as well." She pressed something
into Monica's hand; when she reached her bedroom she looked,
dreading that it might not, after all, be the thing she hoped it
was. But she need not have feared. It was Giles' ring.

In the mid-eighteenth century James Tassie made a great
many beautiful copies of Greek gems; Giles' ring was one of
these—a green stone in which was engraved a figure of Orpheus
bearing his lyre. The naked god was incised, and could be transferred to wax, as a seal. Giles had always worn it on the little
finger of his left hand, but Monica slipped it on her fourth.

She left for London the following day, and although she de-

sired it passionately, she could not arrange to make another visit
to the churchyard without revealing the purpose of her walk to
Dolly, and thereby getting her unwanted company. However,
the train passed within sight of the church and the yews around
it, and as it did so Monica was at the window of her carriage,
the ring at her lips.

(10)

THE NIGHT OF the Commemorative Concert found Monica more
nervous than ever before. She had been wretched all day, and
Molloy, coming into the artists' room very early himself, found
her there before him, white and tense.

"Now see here, it's time you learned proper concert behaviour,
because you won't always have me around to nursemaid you,"
said he. "B'God you look like a picture o' 'Found Drowned'.
You've been worse than cryin'—you've been holdin' in! We're
goin' to do some work right this minute, m'lady."

After ten minutes of bullying and cajolery he had restored her
poise.

"Now you can breathe," said he. "You'd breath enough before,
but not usable; you were all puffed up with grief—chest locked,
throat tight, all blown out like a frog. What's got into you? Is it
Giles?"

Of course she did not say that it was Giles; it took Molloy a
few minutes to persuade her to admit it.

"Well, you can just forget about Giles till tonight's work's over.
Yes, I said forget about him. It's his memorial—I know that as
well as yourself. If you're going to do him proud you must think
about yourself, not about him. Yes, yes; a public performer's
first duty is to himself, and unless he remembers that he can't do
his duty to the public. You must understand it rightly: cherish
the art in yourself, not yourself in art, as the Russian fella says.
That's the pitfall; so many singers just have a lifelong love-affair

with Number One, and they've no rivals, I can tell you! Cherishing the art in yourself is a very different class of thing."

"But I'm so anxious to do well tonight, for Giles' memory, I've let myself get into a state. I couldn't help it. I'm sure you understand really, Murtagh. You're only pretending to be cross."

"Listen, girl, I know what you mean, and don't think I'm not sympathetic. But I'll tell you something about Giles; he was always an amachoor, as far as public performance went. Oh, a fine composer, I grant you. Some o' that stuff'll live, you mark my words. But as a performer, he was an amachoor, and I don't just mean inexperienced; I mean he was the prey of all kinds o' silly ideas; he couldn't concentrate on the job—not in the right way. Genius—yes: discipline—not an idea of it. Now you're a professional. You've got standards he didn't know about and I've given you training he never had. So keep hold of yourself; you and the music are the important things for the next couple of hours."

Thus enjoined, Monica comported herself very creditably. She sang *Kubla Khan;* she sang the soprano part in *The Discoverie of Witchcraft;* she sang with Amyas Palfreyman in the Potion and Metamorphosis Scenes from *The Golden Asse*. And, at the close of the concert, she joined Evelyn Burnaby and Palfreyman in Giles' three-voice setting of the Dirge from *Cymbeline*. So great was the professional calm of concentration with which Molloy had pervaded her that she never faltered, and afterward, at the party in Domdaniel's house she was praised by everybody. Molloy did not praise her, but when their eyes met, he winked a wink that was like the slamming of a door and that, so far as Monica was concerned, was praise indeed.

When the last guests were going, Domdaniel asked her to stay for a moment. "I'll take you home," said he, "but there are one or two things I want to talk about first. You're away to Canada tomorrow night, aren't you?"

It proved to be a long moment. When all but Monica had said goodnight, he kicked off his pumps, removed his evening coat and lay down on a sofa; she began to collect glasses and plates to take them to the kitchen.

"Leave that alone," said Domdaniel; "Fred'll take care of it in the morning."

"I'll empty these ash-trays; if they're left, they'll make the room smell."

"Let is smell. Sit down. Or would you like to lie down? Take your shoes off."

Monica was conscious now that she was very tired. So she did take her shoes off, and as she walked toward a couch across the room from him, Domdaniel laughed.

"Dance Micawber," said he. "The first time I saw you I told you to take your shoes off, and you played Dance Micawber for me."

Monica blushed; it was not pleasant to be reminded of her earlier simplicity.

"Rather a Dance Micawber we've been through tonight," he continued. "Thank God it's out of the way; we've all done our duty for a while, and it's a relief."

"Did you think it went well?"

"Very well."

"Were the people from Bachofen's pleased? Will they go ahead with publication now?"

"Yes. They've known what they were going to do for a couple of weeks; the ticket-sale for tonight convinced them. They'll bring out the whole of Giles' stuff, taking eighteen months or a couple of years, probably, but making a good job of it."

"Mrs. Hopkin-Griffiths will be pleased. Do the royalties go to her?"

"Oh, certainly. For a woman who professes to know nothing of business or music, she's remarkably astute. Well, good luck to her."

"I suppose the royalties will amount to quite a big thing?"

"Impossible to say. We've done everything possible—filled Wigmore Hall for a concert of contemporary music, by a young composer, recently dead under circumstances which some people think romantic. That's only six hundred people, but an important six hundred. It'll keep the music from sinking out of sight and having to be painfully revived."

"But the music itself—Mr. Aspinwall has called the opera great. Do you think so?"

"I suspect Aspinwall of having a bad conscience about Giles. I don't like to talk of greatness, because I'm never entirely sure what it means; Giles' music is individual, melodious and I admire it very much. Haven't I shown that?"

"Yes; I didn't mean to be prying. It's just that Mr. Aspinwall has been so lavish with his praise—for him. He even says Giles' libretto for *The Golden Asse* is marvellous, and he was always complaining about Giles being literary at the expense of music. But he says now that it's philosophical."

"Yes, very funny, that, because nobody was less philosophical than Giles. Extraordinary how people sometimes create so much better than they live. The metamorphosis of physical man into spiritual man: a great theme. But though he could do it in art he couldn't do it in life. Ah, well; the future of his music lies now with Bachofen and the gods. I've done my part for the present and I'm glad it's over."

"You've been marvellous about it all. I know Giles would be terribly grateful."

"It would be for the first time, then."

Monica said nothing.

"Have I shocked you? *De mortuis nil nisi bunkum*—is that the line? Well, I'm sorry. I don't want to be bitter, but I knew Giles, and gratitude wasn't one of his characteristics."

"I knew him, too."

"Yes. You loved him. And tonight I'm in just a sufficiently nasty mood to ask you this: did he ever show any understanding or appreciation of your love?"

Again Monica said nothing.

"You slaved over his music. Did he ever say anything about that? Did he ever thank you for the way you sang his stuff?"

"Why should he? I was lucky to have the chance. And I must say, Sir Benedict, that I haven't been trained to expect thanks or praise for the way I sing. Neither you nor Mr. Molloy has ever told me I sing well. Not directly, anyhow. There have been times when a good word would have been very helpful, but I learned not to look for it. I assumed it was the custom between teacher and pupil. If I have any opinion of my own voice, or the way I sing, I've learned it from the critics, not from my teachers. Giles was like you and Murtagh in that."

"Twaddle! We were demanding, as was entirely proper; but I've seen him treat you like dirt. Perhaps humiliating you in public was his way of showing affection. Maybe you're the kind of woman who gets her satisfaction from being kicked. I never saw Giles treat you other than badly."

I should never have spoken to him like that, thought Monica. No wonder he's cross with me. And didn't he call me a fellow-artist? How could I be so forgetful, so ungrateful? And Murtagh was so good to me tonight. Am I becoming one of those people who never get enough praise?

Apparently Domdaniel regretted what he had said, for he continued: "Don't suppose I wasn't fond of Giles myself. I was. Too fond of him, I've often thought. I did all that I could to bring him forward. I never grudged anything that I could do to advance him, or help him. I even sent you to him for teaching when I knew he was desperately hard up. I've regretted that often enough, if you want to know. I'm a perfect fool about people; I thought somebody like you might humanize Giles; that's why I went through all that cloak-and-dagger business to get you to his family for Christmas, a couple of years ago. I meddled in Giles' affairs, and in yours. And don't suppose I don't realize now that I meddled disastrously."

Monica spoke now. "No, I don't think that. Not disastrously."

"Yes, disastrously. I committed one of the great follies. I tried to mould somebody else's fate. And you've seen how it ended. Don't think I don't know that I killed Giles."

Sir Benedict had expected this to produce an effect, and he

was ready for incredulity, for tears, for hysteria, for anger. But when Monica burst into peals of laughter he sat bolt upright on his sofa, glaring.

"What's the trouble? Are you all right? Would you like a drink? Some water? For God's sake stop that laughing! What ails you?"

"It's just that you are the fourth person who has insisted to me that he killed Giles Revelstoke." And she told him about Bun Eccles, about Stanhope Aspinwall, about Mrs. Hopkin-Griffiths.

"But that's rubbish," said Sir Benedict, angrily. "Fiddling with a gas-meter: half London does it. Aspinwall's article—he flatters himself; ever since somebody suggested that cruel criticism killed John Keats every lint-picker hopes to get his man. I simply don't believe it about his mother; the world is full of perfectly healthy men who had silly, selfish mothers. I'm talking about something quite different—something serious. Giles was jealous of me, of my reputation, in spite of the twenty years between us. Incredibly stupid of him, because he was something I wasn't— a composer, and I cherished and loved that part of him. But I was a conductor, very much in the limelight, and he wanted to be that, as well as what he was. Utterly senseless. But it was an obsession. This suicide—I can only think that it was a way of getting back at me. When I made it plain at La Fenice—and got Petri to back it up—that he was no conductor and probably never would be, it killed him. But this is the terrible thing: I was so angry with him, so resentful of his nonsense, that I genuinely wanted to do him down. I got a mean pleasure from it. Of course he committed suicide, but that's by the way; he died of mortification and thwarted ambition, and I suppose I'm responsible. Morally, I killed him."

Should she speak? Yes—whatever might come of it—yes!

"Morally, you may have had something to do with it. But in cold fact I killed him; first I broke his heart, and then I deserted him when he was dying." And Monica told him her story at length.

For some time Sir Benedict said nothing. Then he rose and

prepared himself a large brandy-and-soda. Returning to his sofa he sat, in shirt-sleeves and stocking feet, leaning forward toward her.

"You're convinced you killed him?"

"Yes, I am."

"Feel dreadful about it?"

"Every morning I wonder how I'll live till night without telling somebody. And now I've done it."

"You mustn't tell anyone else. Understand? I'm not talking idly. What you did would probably be considered—not murder, most certainly not that—but manslaughter, or criminal neglect, or something of that order. Because, after all, you did turn the gas back on. Nothing can change that. And it's vital that you should clarify your thought on this matter. Whatever deception you may have to practise on other people, you must not, under any circumstances, deceive yourself. Now swear to me that you will never tell anyone. Come along. This is very serious."

"What should I say?"

"Oh—let's not bother with operatic oaths. But I command you never to tell anyone. Will you obey?"

"Yes. I promise."

"Right. I'm your sin-eater. Now, quite apart from legal nonsense, let's consider this matter. You found him, and thought he was dead."

"Yes, and my first thought was to save my own skin."

"Because he held your letter in his hand—your letter in one hand and Aspinwall's hard words about his conducting in the other."

"Yes."

"He laid himself down to die with those two papers, in order to make it plain to the world what had killed him."

"I suppose so."

"He knew you were coming back to London that night. Do you think he counted on you going to the flat?"

"He may have done."

"He knew you. He was much cleverer than you. He knew

there was a good chance that you would find him. Indeed, you had the only key."

"I've thought of all that."

"Well, what shall we call it? A self-pitying act, or the act of a scoundrel? Or was he out of his mind?"

"Considering the way I behaved myself, I have no right to make a judgement."

"Not on him. You are perfectly right. But you must—you absolutely must—make a judgement on your own behaviour. Suppose that letter had been found? Do you think anyone would have seriously believed that you drove him to suicide? Nobody thought Aspinwall had done so—except himself, and it may teach him to mind his Ps and Qs in future—because his notice was about ten lines of blame, and nearly a column of high praise. This letter of yours was a love-letter, wasn't it?"

"I told you. It was breaking off with him forever. It was a cruel letter, and—" She could not finish.

"Have you it still? Could I see it?"

She had it with her always, for she could not destroy it, and yet she dared not leave it where it might be found. She gave it to him from her evening bag.

Sir Benedict read and re-read it. "That's what you call breaking off forever, it is?" said he. But Monica, who was weeping as she had not wept since Giles' death, said nothing. He threw the letter into the fire, and in an instant it had gone forever.

"I believe that makes me what is called an accessory," he said.

(11)

SEA-SICKNESS HAS NEVER been recommended for its tonic effect on the spirits, yet as Monica made her return voyage across the North Atlantic her distress of body was parallelled by a marked improvement in her state of mind. She could not account for it, and it was not like her to try. Confession to Domdaniel had been very helpful. She had wanted to tell someone of her guilt, and the only other possible person was Eccles, who would never have done. Not only was he convinced that he had killed Giles himself—though with the best of intentions—but he had gone on the booze, and could not be trusted to keep her secret. Still, he was a dear friend. He had given her the best of his sketches of Giles. It was the one which had appeared on the cover of the program at the Commemorative-Concert; Tuke had wanted it for his book, but Bun was determined that Tuke should not get it. This, and the fact that Aspinwall rather than himself had been asked to write the appreciation of Giles which appeared in that same program, had made Tuke very waspish, and he had threat-ened to sue Monica for seizing the physical assets (a cardboard box of subscribers' cards, five muddled files of dog-eared cor-respondence, a complete run of the magazine, and three cartons of assorted trash) of *Lantern*. But nothing would come of that. Nobody cared about *Lantern* any longer, save Raikes Brothers, who were trying to collect their bill from Mrs. Hopkin-Griffiths. All that was behind her. And, to her surprise and shame, Giles seemed to be behind her, too. She grieved for him, but her guilt was retreating from her; he no longer appeared in her dreams. The numbness of her spirit was vanishing, and to her astonish-ment it left regret and bereavement, but little pain, behind it. When she stepped off the boat in Canada it was with the sensa-tions of a widow, but not of a murderess. She was still sure that she had killed Giles, and that it was through grievous faults in her character that she had done so. But, somehow, she had ac-cepted the fact. To that extent, at least, she had clarified her thinking.

Salterton, this first few days of December, was looking its grey worst. And her home, now that Ma was gone, was unwel-coming—not because of anything that was said or done, but because it was empty of spirit. Of course, there was the physical difficulty about beds. There were only two bedrooms; Dad had one, and Aunt Ellen the other. Monica declined the offer of a

place in her aunt's bed; sleeping alone or with a man had un-
fitted her for a tucking up with an elderly maiden lady who had
two regular, resounding coughing-fits every night. Neither Dad
nor Aunt Ellen was at home between half-past eight and half-
past five, and what was Monica to do? She visited Alice once or
twice, but that did not serve her turn, for when she was with
her elder sister all London, all Paris, all self-possession and hard-
won self-knowledge seemed to slip from her, and they quarreled
as bitterly as when they had shared the tiny bedroom at home.
As bitterly? Far worse, now, for both had gained substance of
personality. Alice was aggrieved that Monica had money; that it
was money which had "fallen into her lap"; that her own ambition
scorched mercilessly upon the need for a new and bigger house,
whereas Monica had no such vital problem; that Monica had
acquired high and mighty ways which (Ah, shade of Ma Gall!)
could not possibly be real because she had not been born to
them, and was therefore guilty of "sticking it on". It was incon-
ceivable to Alice that what had been learned, and thoroughly
digested, could become more truly one's nature than the attitudes and customs of the family into which one had been born.
She was herself in flight from her family, but the ball and chain
was always on her leg. She grudged Monica her freedom from
this servitude, and believed that it had been easily won. A couple
of visits to Alice were quite enough.

One obligatory evening, spent at the movies with George Medwall and Teresa Rook, and a silent friend of George's, exhausted
that source of companionship. She liked Kevin and Alex still,
but could not conceal from herself the fact that they were a little
afraid of her.

So there she was, sleeping on the sofa in the living-room of her
father's house, without even a place where she could stand her
picture of Giles. She had to keep it in her music-case, and get
it out like a miser his treasure, when nobody was at home.

It was foolish, and she knew it was foolish, but Monica caught
herself thinking that it was somehow inconsiderate of everyone

she knew to be working when she herself was on holiday: she was so much a Londoner now in her own estimation that she supposed that people in smaller places must necessarily be less busy than herself. What a fool I am, she thought, when she surprised herself in this mood; I need a metamorphosis, like Lucius in Giles' opera. I'm in great danger of a love-affair with Number One.

But if the welcome of her family was feeble, that of the Bridgetowers was unexpectedly warm. Diffidently, Monica had telephoned to Veronica to enquire after her health, and had at once been asked to dinner. So friendly was the atmosphere that she was able to say how much she hoped that the child Veronica was carrying would be a boy, and so plain was her sincerity that Solly and Veronica believed this, at first appearance, improbable statement.

"It's extremely good of you," said Solly. "Of course, we have hopes. You know that things haven't been easy. But we aren't pinning everything on it. If it's a boy—wonderful! If it isn't, it's not the end of the world. I think one of the secrets of life is that one must give up caring too much about anything. I know that sounds terrible, but for a lot of people it's the only possible philosophy. You blunt the edge of fate by being stoical. My Mother cared too much about having her own way; result—a remarkable artist gets her start—well, that's what they say about you, Monica, so don't protest—an extraordinary opera gets its first production. Neither of them things Mother would have foreseen or desired, to be truthful. She just wanted to let us feel the weight of her hand. Well, let's not talk about it any more, or I shall be saying things like 'It makes you think, don't it'."

Not only from the Bridgetowers, but from the Cobblers, Monica received a flattering and heart-warming welcome. And though she had not meant to do any work for a time, she began to do some daily practice with Cobbler, to get her out of the unfriendly little box that she called her home. There was no piano there, for Aunt Ellen had been compelled to part with hers; her new home had no room for it.

It was Cobbler who persuaded Monica to sing on the occasion of the fourth Bridgetower Memorial Sermon. "Come on," he said; "you sang at the old girl's funeral. Since then you've become the great interpreter of Revelstoke's songs, among other things. This may be the last of these memorial capers—I'm betting on a boy—and we want to do it up right. The choir is going to do *Lo, Star-Led Chiefs*—top-notch Christmas rouser—because the Dean wants to preach about the Wise Men of the East. Now, why don't you sing Cornelius' *Three Kings* from his *Weihnacht-slieder* and top the thing off in style? We'll shove it up a couple of tones, and show what you can do. Come on, be a sport! This may be your last year on the Bridgetower gravy-train; why not show you've no hard feelings."

But Monica would not consent, until one day Dean Knapp telephoned and asked her so pleasantly to assist at the service that she could not refuse without seeming churlish. She still resented the Dean, because of Auntie Puss Pottinger's rebuke, when she had spoken of him as "Reverend Knapp". Well, it was high time to get over such nonsense.

High time indeed. On the morning of December the sixth, which is St. Nicholas' Day, and the day also of the Bridgetower Sermon, she went to Cobbler's to rehearse, and found Humphrey and Molly in a great state of triumph and excitement.

"I was right," shouted Cobbler, dancing in the middle of his chaotic living-room. "It's a boy!"

"What's a boy?"

"Baby Bridgetower! Who else? Here safe and sound, everything screwed on tight, fingers and toes complete—even hair, I'm told by those in the know. You see what a prophet I am; I'm going to go into the business. Slip happy couples my card at weddings—'Five Months hence, Consult Cobbler; Put your Sexpectations on a Scientific Basis; Strictest Confidence Observed'. There's a fortune in it!"

"But I thought it wasn't due for another month or more?"

"Sit down, and have some coffee," said Molly Cobbler. "And shut up, Humphrey, you're being silly. As a matter of fact, it was a rather nasty business. Veronica has been awfully well during her pregnancy, you know. Not a bit like last time. So they weren't worrying about a thing. But last night, somewhere around three in the morning, Veronica woke up and thought she heard a storm window rattling in another room. Now shut up, Humphrey—I'm telling this and I want to tell it my own way. The room in which she heard the sound was old Mrs. Bridgetower's room, which was queer, because nobody ever opens the windows in there; it's kept just as the old lady left it, and Puss Pottinger sees that nothing is moved. But Veronica must have been confused by sleep—Humphrey, shut up!—and went in there. Solly woke when he heard a terrible scream, missed Veronica, and started to look for her. But he didn't think of looking in his mother's room until he had searched in several other places, and when he finally found her, she was on the floor in a terrible way—very badly frightened, a bit irrational and quite a way on in labour. Anyhow, they got the doctor, and he popped her right into old Mrs. Bridgetower's bed, and that's where young Solomon was born at half-past five this morning."

"And serve Ma Bridgetower damn well right," said Humphrey. "She got the first child, but Veronica was too many for her this time. Now Molly, nobody's going to convince me that Veronica didn't have some kind of wrestle with that old woman in the middle of the night, so shut up! That's love. That's devotion, and I call your attention to it," said he, shaking his head at his wife like a solemn golliwog. "Why don't we whip over there right now and drink a toast to the infant trust-breaker? Better take our own bottle; the Bridgetowers aren't always prepared for toasts. But there's a better day coming on, if I may say so without giving Monny the fiscal creeps."

So it was that about a quarter of an hour later Monica was in what must still be called Mrs. Bridgetower's drawing-room (for it never lost that character) drinking a toast to Mrs. Bridgetower's grandson. In spite of Cobbler's efforts the feeling in the room was restrained, and Monica knew very well why it was so: the Bridgetowers, for all their goodwill and kind words, felt that they were taking from her money upon which she counted for another year, and were wondering how much she resented it.

Well, thought Monica, it's up to me. I'm the one who has been trained to communicate emotion readily, and gracefully, and with an artist's control. Unless this gathering is to be a wretched frost, I must supply the warmth. We've all got to grow up some time, so here goes.

"Is there any chance that I could see Veronica and the baby, just for a moment?" she said to Solly.

"As far as I'm concerned, certainly," he replied. "The doctor did a lot of fussing earlier—apparently it's unsanitary, or illegal, or inconvenient for the profession, or something, for a baby to be born at home; he insists on referring to the child as 'a preem'; I think I've persuaded him that the worst is over and Veronica can stay here. Come on up."

Old Mrs. Bridgetower's bedroom was not a pretty room, but it had much frowsty comfort about it, and old Ethel had made a fire in the grate; it was not needed, but it was very cheerful and a touch of childbed luxury. Already there were flowers from the Knapps and—marvellous in the telling—some from Miss Puss. Veronica was lying back on a heap of pillows, eating bacon and eggs.

"I know it's unromantic for a gasping, new-delivered mother to be so hungry," she said, "but I've had a long sleep, and I'm famished. Look at him. Isn't he a pet?"

The pet lay in a small clothes-basket on a low table by the bed. Monica, who had never seen so new a baby, found it rather repulsive. But that was not what she had come to say.

"He's adorable, and I wish him long life and every happiness," said she, breathing a fairy-godmother muhd and bending over the basket. *After all* said a voice, startlingly loud and familiar in her head, *you're giving this goblin upwards of a million dollars—not that it was ever yours.* She started slightly, for it was the voice of Giles Revelstoke. Was he, like Ma, going to be

one of the voices which complicated her life, and at the same
time kept her romanticism from running away with her?

These thoughts did not interrupt her as she turned from the
basket to the bed. She leaned over it and kissed Veronica gently;
but Veronica was chewing at her late breakfast, and as she did
not halt in time, Monica kissed an undulant, chewing cheek.
They both began to laugh: Veronica because she was happier
than she had been in her life; Monica because the inner critic
had made her prima donna-like performance seem ridiculous.
Stop behaving like Ludwiga Kressel, said Giles' voice. And as
they laughed, Solly and the Cobblers began to laugh, though
they could not have said why, and Mrs. Bridgetower's bedroom
rang with happy laughter. The embarrassment had quite gone,
and Monica knew that nobody there was wary of her any longer.

"Let's have another nip," said Cobbler; "Veronica too. But we
mustn't get stewed. There's the Memorial Sermon at four-thirty."

"You must all come back here afterward," said Solly. "We'll
have a party—small but select. But—oh, hell, I suppose we must
ask The Trust. Well, it'll be for the last time. Tea for them,
Ronny, from Old Puss's Rockingham service."

(12)

AT TWENTY-FIVE MINUTES past four that afternoon Monica was
sitting on a small chair beside the organ console in St. Nicholas'
cathedral; it was a position of vantage, for she could see all of
the nave by peeping between two large pillars, but she was not
likely to be seen. She felt silly in a purple cassock and a ruff,
and she did not think that the veil on her head was becoming;
still, it was what Cobbler wanted her to wear, and she would
not be a complainer, as Anglicans seemed to attach so much importance to ritual dress. But if she had to wear costume, she
wished it could have been a better fit, and did not smell so
pungently of choir-boy. She was not to walk with the choir in
procession: no women—apparently it was another Anglican ca-

price. "You're to be clearly heard but not clearly seen," Cobbler had said, and she was well enough content to slip into her place unnoticed.

Cobbler himself now joined her. "Let's have a look," said he, leaning over her shoulder to peep between the pillars. "Quite a good house; nearly a hundred; not bad for a weekday and a business day; old Nicholas, Bishop and Confessor, ought to be pleased; the late Louisa Hansen Bridgetower would have expected a bigger crowd for her memorial sermon, but she had no humility. There's Solly . . . old Snelgrove . . . Auntie Puss; the Bridgetower Trust in force. You know, the cathedral will soon have its Bridgetower bequest? Wonder if I could get any of it to rebuild the organ? Well, here goes." He played a brief flourish and then was silent, as the choir was heard in the distance, beginning the processional hymn.

The Dean read the lesson for the day, and Monica paid little attention after the words . . . *thy voice shall be, as one that hath a familiar spirit* . . . reached her ears. Like me, she thought; only I have two; Ma speaks to me sometimes, in her very own voice, so that I'm sure I'm not talking to myself, and today Giles has spoken to me twice, as though he were right behind me. Yet I don't think I'm out of my head, and I'm certainly not a spiritualist. Will it always be so? Will I acquire other voices as I go through life? It isn't frightening—not a bit—but it's certainly odd. Is it perhaps my substitute for thinking—orders and hints and even jokes from deep down, through the voice and personality of someone I've loved—yes, and feared? I ought to make up my mind. Certainly before I decide what I've got to decide. But I've never been much good at making up my mind, and I'm rotten at deciding things, especially since I went away to study and got into such deep water.

Musing thus, she heard nothing of the Dean's prayer in which he petitioned that God might make all assembled there mindful of the goodness and example of St. Nicholas, bishop and confessor and (extraordinary juxtaposition, which the Dean deeply relished) of Louisa Hansen Bridgetower, and all others our benefactors. But she came out of her musing when Cobbler and the choir burst into the "top-notch Christmas rouser" in which Dr. William Crotch of Oxford so melodiously bodied forth the eighteenth century piety, the formal fervour, of Bishop Reginald Heber—

> *Lo! star-led chiefs Assyrian odours bring,*
> *And bending Magi seek their infant King!*

Here was splendour which glorified the dank December twilight and made the modest cathedral, for its duration, a true dwelling-place of one of the many circumscribed, but not therefore ignoble, concepts of God.

Solly, too, heard nothing of the prayer after the mention of his Mother's name. If ever there were a time to make peace with his Mother's troubled spirit, it was now—now that the son was born who would deliver him from the hard humiliating conditions of her will. Yet—did that spirit desire a reconciliation? What had called Veronica from sleep so early this morning? With what had Veronica struggled in Mrs. Bridgetower's bedroom, so that he had found her unconscious amid overturned tables and chairs? He was neither mad nor fanciful: he had no doubt who, or what it was that had sought to prevent the live birth of his son. He knew what it was, also, that was at last defeated.

It was a time for forgiveness. Against the strict prohibition of his faith, Solly prayed for his Mother's soul.

The anthem over, the lights were dimmed and, somewhat carelessly marshalled by the verger, the Dean went into the pulpit, turned to the East, and said: "In the name of the Father, and of the Son, and of the Holy Ghost, Amen.

> *Dearly Beloved: We have gathered here as part of the celebration of the festal day of our patron, St. Nicholas of Smyrna, but particularly in obedience to the wish of the latest of our benefactors, Louisa Hansen Bridgetower, who desired that*

for a fixed period a sermon should be given on this day, relating to the subject of education.

Monica was scarcely conscious of withdrawing her attention. As a child she had never listened to sermons, and now that she was a grown woman she had never re-considered her position; she was one of the many who feel that it is quite enough to be present while a sermon is being preached. If the Dean had been conscious of her state of mind, he would have recognized it sadly and without condemnation. He had never concurred in the opinion held by many of his brother clergy that learning and eloquence are forms of worldly indulgence to be eschewed; he tried to preach as well as he could. But he had not risen to a deanery without knowing how many people resent being asked to use their heads in church.

What should I tell him, thought Monica? He'll let me have all the time I want, I know, but it isn't fair to him to dawdle, as though I were the only person concerned. She began to run over Domdaniel's letter in her head; it had come three days ago, and she had read and re-read it until she had it by heart:

> I can't think of any way of putting this gradually (it had begun) so I'll say it at once, and not make two bites of the cherry: will you marry me?
>
> Your immediate decision, I am certain, will be to say no. I understand how you felt about Giles, and I am not such a fool as to think that I would ever command love of that sort from you or anyone. Certainly this is the wrong time to write to you in this vein, but I have been quite unable to help it. Because I love you.

He wouldn't say that unless he really meant it, thought Monica. He's always terribly direct. The people who call him Brum Benny only see his formal, courteous manner, and they mistake it for palaver. But he's never said a thing to me he didn't mean. If he says he loves me, he does.

As she pondered this unaccustomed sensation of being loved, the Dean was getting into his sermon.—

Education is learning; and learning is apprehension—in the old sense of sympathetic perception. We cannot all perceive the facts of our experience in the same way. As we draw near to the sacred season of Christmas we may fitly turn our attention to the ways in which the birth of Our Lord was perceived by those who first knew of it. Much has been made of the splendour of the vision of the shepherds, as told by St. Luke. But so far as I know, little has been said of the fact that it needed an angel and a multitude of the heavenly host to call it to the attention of these good men that something out of the ordinary had happened. Nothing short of a convulsion of nature (if I may so call it without irreverence) could impress them, and the Gospel tells us that they praised God 'for all the things that they had heard and seen'. There are many now, as then and always, who learn—who apprehend— only by what they can hear and see, and the range of what they can hear and see is not extensive. And, alas, instructive interruptions of the natural order are as few today as they were two thousand years ago . . .

Nevertheless, no girl thinks very much about marrying a man seriously older than herself, and one whom she has respected as a being far above her, and a figure of world renown in his particular form of art. How had he written of that?—

I am old enough to be your father; nevertheless you must take my word for it that I am still young enough to be a lover. But I will not deceive you; at my age love is not, and never can be, the whole significance of life. I have known enough of love in my own experience, and seen enough of it in the lives of other people, to have some fear of it, as well as the awe and delight which it inspires. I cannot say, I will be young for you, because that would be folly; let me say that I will be the best that is in me for you. I do not ask you to love me as you might a young man, but to love me, if you can, for what I am.

If you say that this cannot be, I shall understand very well why; but do not suppose that I shall not be downcast. It would be dishonest to say, as a younger man might have every excuse for doing, that my love for you is the whole of my life. At my age, my work is bound to be the mainspring of my existence. But if you were with me, my work would have a sweeter savour. Because it is your work, too, I know that you will understand this, and not think that I am being either cool or pompous. You are the custodian of an important musical tradition—you know how Giles wanted his songs to be sung. I do not seek to intrude on that, but I think I could be helpful with it.

Your work, too! like being called a fellow-artist! Still, he was fifty-four—or was it fifty-five, now? And there was Giles' voice, hatefully bawdy, as she had last heard it on the train to Venice—

I lay with an old man all the night—

How dare Giles! But what would people say? That she had done it to be Lady Domdaniel. What would Alice make of that? Oh, Alice! Family always knew where to dig the knife in! But Giles, Giles was not someone who could be put aside. Particularly not when she had failed him so disastrously.

But could she not admit, now, that when she found him seemingly dead on the floor, beneath her revulsion from his blackened face, her stunning loss, her self-accusation, there had been —perceptible for an instant and then banished as a blasphemy against her love—a pang of relief, of release? Should she not clarify her thought? No! Let others talk of clarity. It is a cautery too terrible to be applied to one's own most secret wounds. Perhaps, working for a worthy perpetuation of his work, there might be atonement. And, after atonement, a recognition of what she had felt in that instant of naked truth.

Meanwhile the Dean was continuing with his sermon:

If the shepherds needed a prodigy to stir them, the Wise Men needed no more than a hint, a new star amid the host of heaven. In art, and especially the Christmas card art which will so soon

be with us, that star is usually represented as a monstrous illumin-
ation which a mole might see. That is so that the shepherds
among us may understand without a painful sense of insufficiency
the legend of the Kings. For legend it is; the Gospel tells us but
little of these men, but legend has set their number at three, and
has given them melodious names. The legend calls them Kings,
and Kings they were indeed in the realm of apprehension, of
perception, for they were able to read a great message in a small
portent. We dismiss great legends at our peril, for they are the
riddling voices by means of which great truths buried deep in the
spirit of man offer themselves to the world. Gaspar, Melchior
and Balthazar stand as models of those—few, but powerful at
any time—who have prepared themselves by learning and dedi-
cation to know great mysteries when the time is ripe for them
to be apprehended by man . . .

Of course a girl really wanted a lover who was hers alone,
who had never loved anyone else—or at least not seriously—and
who promised to give everything to love. That was what all the
magazines which were dismissed as "cheap" said, and the cheap
magazines were right; that was why cheap magazines sold in
hundreds of thousands, instead of in tens, like *Lantern*. But even
at twenty-four, one could see that sometimes these knights, when
they appeared, had a way of dwindling into something like
Chuck Proby, who was probably living for love if you gave him
the benefit of every doubt, but who never mentioned it, and
seemed to be making a hard struggle of it. Or a sobersides like
George Medwall, who was so proud of the fact that Teresa
would not have to work after their marriage, but who saw life in
terms of accretion—get some money, get a wife, get a house, get
some children, get a bigger house, get more money—all for love,
but the world hopelessly lost somewhere along the line. Domdaniel made no pretence:

Kind friends have probably told you that I have been married
before. (They hadn't, and this had surprised her.) It is true that
when I was a young man I married and if you have ever been

curious enough to look me up in *Who's Who* the 'mar. dis.' there will tell you what happened. She was a singer, like you—though in the cold light of recollection I can say that she was never as good a singer as you—and it didn't work. Nobody's fault entirely. Now I know that marriage between artists of any kind needs a little more understanding than matches where there is no relentless, fascinating rival perpetually working to seduce both parties. I wanted you to know this.

I want to go on, but I have said everything that is to the point, and I know that pleading and begging and entreaties, though they might work on your gentle heart, aren't fair in a case like this. I would cut a ridiculous figure as a whimpering suitor. So I shall say only that I love you, and if you are ready, even in the most tentative fashion, to consider marrying me, will you let me have some word?

BENEDICT DOMDANIEL

One must be logical. If Giles had never been, or if she had never known him, what would she say to this? But what was the good of thinking like that? Giles couldn't be wished away. And she would never be free of him. By his suicide he had put his mark on her forever. Moving the green Orpheus slowly back and forth on her finger, Monica gave herself to tender thoughts of Giles.

The Dean, having dealt with the Magi to his satisfaction, had moved on.—

A third figure, who perceived Our Lord in his own fashion, is particularly sympathetic, and presents in one of the most touching stories of the childhood of Christ another sort of apprehension, and that the rarest. He is the aged Simeon, who knew Our Lord intuitively (as we should say now) when He was brought to the Temple on the eighth day for His Circumcision. Not the forcible instruction of a band of angels, nor the hard-won knowledge of the scholars, but the readiness of one who was open to the promptings of the Holy Ghost was the grace which made Simeon peculiarly blessed. We see him still as one of those rare beings, not so much acting as acted upon, not so much living

life as being lived by it, outwardly passive but inwardly illumined
by active grace, through whom much that is noblest and of most
worth has been vouchsafed to the world. . . . Oh, trusting, patient
Simeon, the first to know, of his own knowledge, the Holy Face
of God!

It's a muddle, thought Monica. A muddle and I can't get it straight. I wish I knew what I should do. I wish I even knew what I want to do. I want to wipe out the terrible thing I did to Giles. I want to go on in the life that has somehow or other found me and claimed me. And I want so terribly to be happy. Oh God, don't let me slip under the surface of all the heavy-hearted dullness that seems to claim so many people, even when they struggle and strive to keep their heads above the waves! Help me! Help me!

"Psst! He's winding up. You next." It was Cobbler's voice.

Monica sang, giving her full attention to what she was doing; sang well and happily, all her perplexities banished as she balanced the delicate vocal meditation above the great chorale in *Three Kings from Persian lands.* And when she was finished, she found that her mind was cleared, and she knew what she should do.

Benediction, and a rustle as the congregation rose from its knees. "Wait for me in the vestry," said Cobbler, "and we'll get back to Bridgetower's for the party. But meantime, I simply can't resist this. Keep your eye peeled to see if any of the Bridgetower Trust get the Joe Miller of it." And triumphally he burst into *For unto us a child is born, Unto us a son is given* on the great organ.

But Monica did not wait. Before the party she must go to the cable office to send Benedict his answer.

FOR THE BEST IN PAPERBACKS, LOOK FOR THE 🐧

In every corner of the world, on every subject under the sun, Penguin represents quality and variety—the very best in publishing today.

For complete information about books available from Penguin—including Pelicans, Puffins, Peregrines, and Penguin Classics—and how to order them, write to us at the appropriate address below. Please note that for copyright reasons the selection of books varies from country to country.

In the United Kingdom: For a complete list of books available from Penguin in the U.K., please write to *Dept E.P., Penguin Books Ltd, Harmondsworth, Middlesex, UB7 0DA.*

In the United States: For a complete list of books available from Penguin in the U.S., please write to *Consumer Sales, Penguin USA, P.O. Box 999— Dept. 17109, Bergenfield, New Jersey 07621-0120.* VISA and MasterCard holders call 1-800-253-6476 to order all Penguin titles.

In Canada: For a complete list of books available from Penguin in Canada, please write to *Penguin Books Canada Ltd, 10 Alcorn Avenue, Suite 300, Toronto, Ontario, Canada M4V 3B2.*

In Australia: For a complete list of books available from Penguin in Australia, please write to the *Marketing Department, Penguin Books Ltd, P.O. Box 257, Ringwood, Victoria 3134.*

In New Zealand: For a complete list of books available from Penguin in New Zealand, please write to the *Marketing Department, Penguin Books (NZ) Ltd, Private Bag, Takapuna, Auckland 9.*

In India: For a complete list of books available from Penguin, please write to *Penguin Overseas Ltd, 706 Eros Apartments, 56 Nehru Place, New Delhi, 110019.*

In Holland: For a complete list of books available from Penguin in Holland, please write to *Penguin Books Nederland B.V., Postbus 195, NL-1380AD Weesp, Netherlands.*

In Germany: For a complete list of books available from Penguin, please write to *Penguin Books Ltd, Friedrichstrasse 10-12, D-6000 Frankfurt Main I, Federal Republic of Germany.*

In Spain: For a complete list of books available from Penguin in Spain, please write to *Longman, Penguin España, Calle San Nicolas 15, E-28013 Madrid, Spain.*

In Japan: For a complete list of books available from Penguin in Japan, please write to *Longman Penguin Japan Co Ltd, Yamaguchi Building, 2-12-9 Kanda Jimbocho, Chiyoda-Ku, Tokyo 101, Japan.*